THE FAMILY AT FAIRLYDEN

Also by Gwen Kirkwood

Fairlyden
Mistress of Fairlyden

The Family at Fairlyden
Fairlyden at War.

THE FAMILY AT FAIRLYDEN

Gwen Kirkwood

With Best Wishes

Gwen Kirkwood

HEADLINE

First published in 1992
by HEADLINE BOOK PUBLISHING PLC

10 9 8 7 6 5 4 3 2 1

British Library Cataloguing in Publication Data

Kirkwood, Gwen
Family at Fairlyden
I. Title
823.914 [F]

ISBN 0–7472–0504–3

Typeset by
Letterpart Limited, Reigate, Surrey

Printed and bound in Great Britain by
Clays Ltd, St Ives PLC

HEADLINE BOOK PUBLISHING PLC
Headline House
79 Great Titchfield Street
London W1P 7FN

AULD LANG SYNE
by Robert Burns

Should auld acquaintance be forgot,
And never brought to min'?
Should auld acquaintance be forgot,
And days o' lang syne?
   For auld lang syne, my dear,
   For auld lang syne,
   We'll tak' a cup o' kindness yet,
   For auld lang syne!

We twa hae run about the braes,
And pu'd the gowans fine;
But we've wandered many a weary foot,
Sin auld lang syne.

We twae hae paidl't i' the burn,
Frae mornin' sun till dine;
But seas between us braid hae roared,
Sin auld lang syne!

And here's a hand, my trusty fiere,
And gie's a hand o' thine;
And we'll tak' a right guid willie-waught,
For auld lang syne!

And surely ye'll be your pint-stoup,
And surely I'll be mine;
And we'll tak' a cup o' kindness yet,
For auld land syne.
   For auld lang syne, my dear . . .

One

'Mercy me! Whatever's a frightening the hens in the middle o' a bricht summer afternoon?' Agnes Jamieson muttered to herself as she hurried into the field behind the Fairlyden rickyard. She almost ran down the slope towards the burn and three wooden huts. She was dismayed to find feathers flying; the new Leghorn pullets were squawking hysterically, while the older Rhode Island Reds fussed and clucked and angrily spread their wings.

'Surely it canna be a fox in broad daylight!' she panted. At fifty-three Agnes was long past the first flush of youth and she was red and flustered by the time she reached the door of the first hut. Before she had even grasped the handle, the door was flung open and a boy of about eight emerged clutching a protesting piglet in his arms.

'Agnes!' Logan Fairly's mouth formed a startled 'O' at the sight of his mother's irate maid. His grey eyes widened anxiously. 'Ye willna tell Mama that Peggotty got in amongst the hens again, will ye?' he pleaded urgently.

'Mistress Fairly'll no' be needing me tae tell her, young Logan, not when she sees all these feathers scattered o'er the grass. I reckon there'll be nae eggs in the boxes either when she comes tae collect them. The puir hens hae had such a fright they'll all be feared tae gang back in, much less settle themselves doon tae lay eggs!' Logan's arms tightened instinctively around the ugly little pig snuffling into his tweed waistcoat.

'It wasna Logan's fault, or Peggotty's, Aunt Agnes . . .' At the sound of the soft, beguiling voice Agnes Jamieson peered past the boy into the dim interior of the little wooden henhouse.

'Beth!' she muttered sternly, but both the children knew her gruff tone hid a wealth of love for her motherless young niece.

'Papa put wire along the bottom o' the gate,' the little girl went on earnestly. 'He said it would keep Peggotty awa' frae the hens. Somebody left the latch undone. She must have squeezed through.' Agnes shook her grey head and sighed. There was only

1

one person at Fairlyden who would leave the gate unsnecked deliberately, knowing how the wee pig liked to investigate. She pursed her lips. The damage was done now but Mistress Sarah would be far from pleased. She needed all the eggs she could get to sell at the market.

'I should hae kenned ye wad be here with Master Logan, Beth. Now ye'll both be in trouble. I darena think what the Mistress'll say! She'll have that wee demon o' a pig shut up in a pen for sure this time!'

'Oh no, Aunt Agnes!'

'Oh, Agnes! No!'

The two young voices echoed as one and Agnes sighed again as she looked down at them. Logan Fairly had celebrated his eighth birthday in March. Beth was nearly three months younger and the two had been friends since Beth learned to toddle from her father's cottage up to the farmhouse, aye and even before that, Agnes recalled. Mistress Sarah Fairly had a kind heart and she had welcomed Beth into the Fairlyden household from the week she was born, for all she was a widow with five bairns of her own. Sometimes Beth's close association with the Fairlys of Fairlyden worried Agnes. Already she loved the farm, the land, the animals – and Logan. But there would be no secure place at Fairlyden for a labourer's bairn – not if Miss Sadie Fairly had her way. She would never let anyone forget that her grandfather had been an Earl, for all the family fortunes had been scattered to the four winds by that evil uncle of hers.

Logan was the youngest of the Fairly family by ten years. He had been a puny wee thing, slipping into the world the day his mother had received news of the Master's death on board a ship in the middle of the ocean. Agnes shivered. She would never forget that cold day on the first of March, eighteen hundred and ninety-eight. There had been a lot of changes in the eight years since then – both at Fairlyden and in the world outside. What with the queen dying and the king having an operation for appendicitis, and the coronation having to be postponed.

Agnes's eyes had a dreamy look as she gazed over the green fields. It was twenty-eight years since she had come to work at the little Scottish farm and her room above Fairlyden's cosy kitchen had become the only home she knew. Miss Sarah had been just nineteen when she hired her, Agnes reflected. And she doesna look a day older than thirty even now, in spite o' bearing six bairns and being widowed. Except for a wee bit thickening around the middle she's still as slim and leish as a lassie, and there's scarce a wisp o' grey in her thick brown hair either! Agnes pressed her hands against her own ample girth, then twitched her cap into place to cover her steel grey hair.

'There's nothing skinny about ye now, Master Logan!' she spoke her thoughts aloud as she looked at the boy's sturdy frame. He was more broadly built than his two brothers and his eyes were grey instead of brown, but he had his mother's lively, enquiring mind and her kindly nature. Agnes liked the way he cared for any sick animal or injured bird; he never seemed to mind Beth tagging along, for all she was a girl, and such a dainty bairn.

'Eeh, ye're a queer-like pair,' she muttered, shaking her head as she looked from one to the other. She found it hard to sustain her anger with them. Logan looked up at her with his earnest gaze. She could see the golden flecks lightening the grey irises, but his brows were dark and well shaped like his mother's and his eyelashes were thick black crescents against his rosy cheeks. Agnes could never see anything of her late master in the youngest Fairly – and secretly she was glad, though William Fairly had never done her any harm.

'Please, Agnes? Promise ye willna blame Peggotty?' Logan pleaded and his freckled nose wrinkled in an appealing grin.

'We'll no' let Peggotty near the hens again, Aunt Agnes! We promise, don't we, Logie?' Beth added her own brand of gentle persuasion and Agnes had to struggle to maintain her stern expression as she looked at the long, honey-brown curls and wide blue eyes which seemed to swamp her niece's pixie face.

'Och! I dinna ken why ye canna both be content wi' a wee kitten or one o' the collie dogs for a pet!' she exclaimed.

'But we saved Peggotty's life!' Logan protested. 'She's oor very ain – Beth's an' mine!'

'And we love her!' Beth added, scratching the little pig's back until she stretched contentedly in Logan's arms, almost asking for more. Loving was very important to Beth, especially since her mother's death. 'We do love ye, Peggotty, even if ye are the littlest pig Papa has ever seen.'

'She's such an ugly wee thing wi' her turned-up snout and short spindly legs,' Agnes remarked. 'I dinna ken how she moves sae fast, or gets intae sae much trouble.'

3

'But listen tae her happy grunts, Agnes,' Logan coaxed with his irresistible smile. 'Peggotty likes me and Beth.'

'She does, Aunt Agnes! That's why she didna want tae go tae the angels,' Beth added her support, 'not like Mama . . .'

'Och, ma bairnie . . .' Agnes murmured gruffly, and stroked her niece's shining head with a gentle work-roughened hand. 'Your Mama didna exactly *want* tae go . . .'

'I ken,' Beth nodded soberly. 'That's what Papa said, but God said it was time . . .' She smiled wistfully. It was nearly a year since Sally's death. Agnes knew her sister-in-law had adored Nick, and their only child. Still, Beth was luckier than most bairns in her situation; Mistress Sarah had taken her to her heart since the day she was born; her father was respected and he had a secure position. Miss Sadie Fairly was the only one who refused to acknowledge that his skills and management were essential to Fairlyden. She treated him and his motherless bairn like dirt under her feet because they lived in a cottage. Agnes's mouth tightened. She was sure Sadie Fairly had unsnecked the gate. She could never bear to see other folks happy, especially Logan and Beth. She was evil – and sly with it . . .

'Aye. Well. Come on wi' me then.' Agnes squared her shoulders and ushered the two children out of the field and into the farmyard. 'We'll search for some nests in the sheds.' Her tone was suddenly brisk, hiding the secret ache in her own heart. She knew her brother appreciated her help with the washing and cleaning, but he did not want her to live with him and Beth in the Fairlyden cottage. Agnes shared the Jamieson pride and she still felt a mite rejected, although Mistress Fairly had helped to smooth things out.

'Nick wouldn't want you to give up your independence to keep house for him; besides he knows we need you too. Ask him if he and Beth would like to have their meals with us, here at Fairlyden,' she had suggested. 'Except maybe on the Sabbath. I'm sure he'll appreciate you making his Sunday dinner at the cottage.'

Gradually they had all adapted to the changes which Sally Jamieson's death had wrought in Fairlyden's little circle of men and maids, of Mistress and children.

Nick Jamieson had thrown himself into his tasks with a grim determination. The cycle of work had been completed – ploughing and harrowing, sowing, hoeing and harvesting as the

4

seasons demanded. Hedges had been laid, thistles chopped, ditches cleaned, carts painted, buildings emptied of manure and washed with lime. Billy, the second of the three Fairly sons, complained amicably.

'There's never a minute's peace around here these days.'

'Naw, Nick hasna stopped since Sally died,' Thomas Whiteley agreed. 'Still, I dinna suppose hard work will kill either o' us, Master Billy,' he added cheerfully.

Logan and Beth ran jubilantly into the Fairlyden kitchen, each clutching a couple of eggs. Agnes followed more slowly, holding her apron in a pouch with the rest of the eggs they had wrested from a reluctant hen who had intended brooding her hoard in secret.

'We found a new hen's nest behind the meal kist in the stable, Mama!' Logan greeted his mother with sparkling eyes, while Beth smiled her singularly sweet smile and held out the precious eggs.

'Why, that's splendid!' Sarah exclaimed to their delight. 'Maybe I shall spare an egg for each of you for tea now . . .' Logan's eyes fell and he bit his lip, wandering whether to confess about the havoc Peggotty had caused amongst the other hens. Child though he was, he knew how thrifty his mother had to be, how hard she worked and saved to keep them all fed and clothed and to pay wages to Nick and Agnes and Thomas. Sarah's brown eyes were shrewd as she studied her youngest son. Her gaze moved to Beth's anxious young face. Something was bothering them, but no doubt she would hear all about it eventually.

'How many eggs did you find then, Beth? I thought some o' the hens must be laying away frae their huts.'

'Eleven!' Beth announced proudly. 'Aunt Agnes is bringing the rest in her pinny.'

'That's fine then,' Sarah smiled. 'O-oh!' she exclaimed and her smile faded as her eye fell on Peggotty now searching for her two young companions, her pink snout snuffling along the kitchen floor. 'That wee pig! She thinks this is her home too! I suppose she's hunting for the pair o' you? Just look at the mess her four little trotters make on my clean flagged floor!'

'Shoo, Peggotty!' Logan called, suppressing a giggle as the little pig went snuffling under the table.

'I'll take the eggs! You two get that animal out of here and

5

dinna let me catch her following you into my kitchen again!'

'Yes, Mama, I mean no . . .' Logan chuckled softly and darted under the table after the piglet while Beth ran round to the other side to prevent Peggotty's escape. It was a game they all loved to play – but not in Mistress Fairly's kitchen. Agnes almost tripped over Logan's protruding feet as she came in with her apron full of eggs.

'Ach, what are ye doing underneath the table, laddie? Surely that wee demon o' a pig isna in the kitchen next!'

'It is!' Sarah sighed and shook her head in mild exasperation, but she could not suppress a faint smile at the antics and squeals of the pig and the two children. 'The bairns are just taking her outside. I don't know who decided that pigs have no brains. I'm sure Peggotty understands every trick there is!'

'Tricks! That animal is a wicked monster!' Beneath the table Logan's heart sank as he recognised the sharp tones of his sister Sadie. 'It should have been knocked on the head when it was born! I dinna ken why ye ever allowed Logan tae keep it, Mother! Ye wad never have let me have a pet like that!' Logan seized Peggotty, holding her defensively against his chest, willing the little pig to keep quiet. Beth, still crouching on her haunches, peered anxiously under the table to make sure their four-legged friend was safe; she knew Sadie Fairly never hesitated to give the little pig a hard kick with her pointed boot. Both children had good reason to be wary of her uncertain temper, with or without Peggotty. They had painful memories of her chasing them, and their pet, with the broom and wielding it none too lightly. Logan edged cautiously towards Beth, hoping to make his escape with the pig unnoticed.

Agnes recognised the spiteful gleam in Sadie Fairly's pale eyes. She had been in a nasty mood ever since she knew her sister, Ellen, had been invited to take tea at the Manse to meet the young minister's aunt. Jealous she was and she didn't care who suffered, the maid thought grimly as she tried to divert Sadie's attention.

'We've found a grand nest o' eggs in the stable. I'll just put them in the pantry tae keep them separate frae the rest, shall I, Mistress Sarah?'

'Ye'll need more than that tae make up for the damage that pig'll have done!' Sadie hissed triumphantly as Agnes squeezed past her.

6

'What did you say, Sadie?' Sarah looked sharply at her eighteen-year-old daughter and her heart sank at the malevolent gleam in her eyes. She had tried hard to love all her children equally but Sadie had always been different – even as a baby, later as a schoolgirl . . .

'You never wanted a pet to love . . .' she spoke her thoughts aloud.

'And I was right! Katie loved her silly little dog more than she loved me!'

A look of pain passed fleetingly over Sarah's face at the memory of the adorable child who had been Sadie's twin.

'That's all in the past!' Her voice was unusually brittle. Sadie's remarks conjured up painful memories.

Sensing that his mother's and sister's attention had been temporarily distracted, Logan shuffled from beneath the table still clutching Peggotty. Beth followed on tiptoe as he made for the nearest door, intent on escaping from the kitchen as quickly as possible. Unfortunately the nearest door led into the scullery. They would have to go through it, and then through the dairy to get outside, and the dairy was forbidden territory. Peggotty was certainly not allowed near it under any circumstances!

Sadie saw them out of the corner of her eye; she waited until Logan was creeping towards the dairy with the pig in his arms.

'Where d'ye think ye're going!' she demanded, deliberately drawing her mother's attention back to her younger brother.

'Logan! Beth! Come back in here at once. You know you're not to use the scullery and the dairy as a shortcut to the yard! You know how hard I try to keep it clean.'

'Sorry, Mama.'

'We're sorry, Mama Fairly,' Beth apologised simultaneously.

'They meant tae take that beast in there tae!'

Sarah nodded. Why did Sadie resent Logan so much, she wondered, as she always did when her daughter was so spiteful. Was it because he had taken her own place as the youngest member of the family? Yet she had been ten years old when Logan was born, no longer a baby; or was it possible that Sadie had some sixth sense which told her that Logan was a cuckoo in the Fairly nest? She drew in her breath sharply. Sadie was the last person she would want to guess her secret! She turned her steady gaze on her youngest son.

'Peggotty never forgets anything you two teach her. I canna have her getting into the dairy.'

Logan nodded guiltily, and began to cross the big kitchen to the other door which led to the stone-flagged passage and out into the farmyard. He had to pass close to Sadie, the very thing he had been trying to avoid. His arms tightened protectively around the little pig and Beth walked close beside him as though to add her support.

'Phew! That animal smells!' Sadie exclaimed as they sidled by. 'Dinna expect me tae wash your clothes!' She grabbed Logan by the shoulder before he could make his escape.

'Ouch, ye're hurting, Sadie!' he exclaimed. 'Your fingers are like needles!' He wriggled, trying to free himself without releasing his hold on the pig.

'Don't tease him, Sadie.' Sarah's voice was sharp.

'That pig isna worth all the stuff it eats, but at least it should be shut up in a sty!'

'Oh no, Sadie! Peggotty likes tae be free . . .' Beth was driven to protest. She touched the little pink snout with a gentle finger and received a soft grunt in response. 'Listen! She says so!'

'Dinna blether! It's time ye grew up! Mama Fairly this, and Mama Fairly that! Ye ken fine she isna your mother! If ye stayed in your ain house, where ye belong, there wadna be half sae much trouble . . .'

'That's enough, Sadie! Beth's place is here with Agnes when Nick is working. You know he is scything the edges o' the meadow ready for Billy to start with the mowing machine, and that's certainly no place for a bairn to be!'

Despite her swift intervention Sarah saw the shadows of uncertainty in the little girl's wide blue eyes. Had Sadie tried to make her feel unwanted at Fairlyden before? She reached out instinctively and drew Beth to her side. It was nearly forty years since she had been Beth Jamieson's age but she could still remember how it felt to be young and motherless – so vulnerable. Besides, Beth was like one of her own family, and she had promised Sally she would make sure her bairn had a home.

Sadie's narrow face paled with angry resentment at her mother's affectionate gesture; her fingers clenched on Logan's shoulder.

'Let me go!'

'Tell Mother what your precious pig has done then! Go on, tell her the damage ye've caused between ye!'

It did not seem strange to Beth that she should recall this scene from her childhood with such clarity. Sadie's malice had never ceased, and it extended to anyone and anything which spelled happiness for Logan and herself.

'But how could I have been so gullible now! Why, oh why did I trust Sadie tonight?' Beth choked back a sob of frustration and mounting fear. The intense darkness of the hayloft seemed to be closing in on her. She fought down her hysteria and crouched on the rough boards of the floor once more, her fingers scrabbling in vain for the edge of the trapdoor. She could see nothing, not even her own hands. She had always hated the dark, ever since Sadie had shut her in the cupboard under the stairs at Fairlyden a few days after they had taken away her mother in a coffin. She had been terrified that no one would find her, that she too would be shut up for ever, buried in the earth. How clearly she remembered Sadie's taunts! The same terror gripped her now. 'Why, oh why was I so stupid! But I couldna have left the horses all night without their hay ... Sadie knew I would never neglect them . . .' In truth Beth had been too weary to think clearly; far too exhausted to argue with Logan's sister . . . So exhausted she hadn't even remembered Aunt Agnes's warning until she found herself a prisoner . . .

'However could I have forgotten?' She shuddered and bit back another sob, seeing again the fear and anxiety which had filled Aunt Agnes's eyes . . . Even her words seemed to echo and re-echo round the dusty rafters of the half-empty loft.

'Dinna trust Sadie Fairly! Never trust her!' Beth knew the voice was in her own head; it had been hammering in her brain ever since the trapdoor had slammed shut imprisoning her in the inky blackness, with only the mice for company. She had heard Sadie moving the ladder, but even then she had not really believed that Logan's sister intended to leave her – not all alone – not all night – not in her present condition! Or was that the real reason? Had Sadie planned this? Did she really want her to die? Certainly no one would think of searching for her in the hay loft on a night like this.

Mama Fairly will think I've gone to rest in my room, she thought despondently. Every evening for the past two weeks she

9

had crawled wearily to bed as soon as she had eaten her supper. The work was always hard in winter, even without the dreadful war which had taken away so many young men – even without the burden which seemed to be weighing her down . . .

How could I have been so stupid as to climb into the loft myself? To leave Sadie with the lamp, and the ladder! I should have guessed she was up to another o' her sly tricks! Beth shivered violently. The January day had been bitterly cold, the sky a sullen grey; as darkness fell there had been a flicker of snow.

'It's going tae be a bitter night,' Thomas Whiteley had muttered as he hurried across the yard to the dairy with the last pail of milk. But it was more than the outward chill that made Beth's teeth chatter.

'Sadie really wants me tae die!' she whispered aloud. 'Me and Logan's bairn! How can it be a sin tae love anyone as I love Logie? Our love is a beautiful thing . . .' Her whispers seemed loud in the echoing darkness. A mouse scuttered across the floor, its claws scratching over the bare boards. I dinna care about a wee moose . . . but what if it was a rat? Thomas had seen a rat slinking across the stable floor three mornings ago! Dinna think about rats! she scolded, but she clenched her small fist and hammered frantically on the floor.

'Sadie! Let me out! Bring the ladder back! Sadie!' Her voice rose almost to a scream. There was no reply. Beth sank back, exhausted.

Sadie wants me tae die, she thought again. She fancies herself as Mistress o' Fairlyden! She's ambitious, greedy! Yet she hates the work! She doesna love the farm! She thinks she should be a lady, with servants tae dae her bidding – just because her grandfather was the Earl of Strathtod. She thinks everyone else is beneath her, even her own mother! I ken that now. Beth's thoughts hurried on. She did not want to think of her own predicament. In her heart she knew that the weariness which was dragging at every muscle and sinew in her young body was more than the natural tiredness from a hard day's work, though she had been up since dawn. Mother nearly died having me . . . I could be dead before morning if . . . if . . . Dinna think o' such things! Take a grip on yourself! Where's the courage that Logan aye admired?

In the stable below, one of the Fairlyden Clydesdales moved

10

restlessly, the iron-shod hooves ringing on the granite cobbles of the floor. She had come up to the loft to get hay for the horses because Sadie had forgotten to get it earlier . . .

'The hay. The hay is warm . . . Must keep warm . . .' she muttered and began to grope her way over the uneven floor towards the back of the loft. A cobweb dangling from the rafters brushed her cheek and she brushed it away with a shudder. Normally Beth would scarcely have noticed such a thing, but fear and loneliness emphasised the slightest sound, the faintest touch. She almost fell into the pile of hay at the back of the loft, but at least it was soft and springy and she longed to lie down and stretch out her weary body. She thought of the mice again, the rats . . . Dinna think! Just keep warm. She made herself comfortable, pulling the hay over her. She longed for a cup of hot tea . . .

'Nae harm will come tae ye if ye think o' pleasant things, ma bairn. Ye'll soon be asleep . . .' Beth could scarcely remember her mother, yet she seemed to hear her gentle, soothing voice calming her childish fears. The hay was from one of the meadows, the only good hay they had made last summer. It smelled of clover; it reminded her of other summers, the sunshine . . . We had such happy times when we were bairns – Logan and me . . . Sadie always made trouble though . . .

'Troubles can be overcome, lassie, if ye've strength and courage . . .' Her father's voice, warm and reassuring. A little smile lifted the corners of Beth's soft mouth and a thousand memories filled her head, driving away the insidious fears as she burrowed deeper into the sweet-scented hay. Down below in the stable one of the horses snorted gently. It was a comforting sound . . .

'I will think o' pleasant things . . .' she whispered. 'I must! For the sake o' my ain bairn, Logan's bairn . . .'

Two

It was inevitable that Beth's thoughts of childhood and her happiest memories should centre round Logan, her constant companion – and Fairlyden, their little world of adventure, their secure haven. Even so it was impossible to dismiss those who had lived and worked on the little Scottish farm. Mistress Fairly had played a large part in their lives with her wisdom and kindness, as had Sadie with the malice she had inflicted on everyone around her – even the harmless little pig.

Poor Peggotty had been confined to a pen in the orchard after her rampage amongst the pullets, Beth recalled as she settled herself more comfortably amidst the warmth of the sweet-smelling hay. She had always suspected that Sadie had left the gate open deliberately knowing the little pig would be sure to explore the hens' houses, knowing, and possibly relishing, the dire consequences to Logan and herself as well as their pet.

An even worse fate had befallen them on the hot summer's afternoon when they had been allowed to take the men's tea to the hayfield while Mistress Fairly and Ellen visited the Manse at the invitation of the Reverend Morrison's aunt. They had been too young to realise that Sadie was jealous of her elder sister's invitation, even though Ellen's ambition was not to attract the young minister, but to seek his aunt's help and advice on becoming a nurse.

'We didna ken Sadie would vent her evil spleen on puir Peggotty when we set off sae happily tae the field with the basket and the can o' tea . . .' Beth murmured to herself. 'She must have spied on us that day . . .'

Sadie had indeed watched Logan and Beth from the obscurity of a gnarled old apple tree. She knew Agnes would be enjoying a cup of tea before it was time to start the milking because the maid had been picking berries in the garden all afternoon and she had looked hot and tired.

13

Peggotty had been on the receiving end of Sadie's ill temper more than once and she cowered warily at the far side of her pen while Sadie untied the gate and pulled it open, just enough for a young pig to squeeze through. After a little coaxing however Peggotty could not resist the prospect of freedom. She followed Sadie through the orchard grunting and snuffling softly; past the closet and the garden wall they went, round the back of the cart sheds and a few yards down the track to the open gate of the Long Meadow. Several hundred yards away Beth and Logan paused to change their burdens from one hand to the other; it was some distance to the far end of the field where the men were working.

Peggotty heard their happy laughter and trotted towards them, snuffling, and rooting experimentally in the hedgerow as she went. Sadie stood close to the hedge and watched for a moment, her thin lips twisted in a travesty of a smile, then she turned and retraced her steps, leaving the pig to wander at will.

There was no sign of Billy and the horses when Logan and Beth reached the lower half of Long Meadow but there were several swaths of hay lying where they had fallen. Logan shielded his eyes with one hand and stared down the sloping field.

'There's a hollow in the bottom. I expect we'll see the horses appearing in a minute. Let's go nearer tae the hay that's still tae cut.'

Beth agreed readily. 'I love tae hear the whispering grasses. Maybe I'll be able tae pick some moonpenny daisies and some buttercups for Aunt Agnes.'

They wandered in a diagonal path towards the uncut hay. Further up the field Peggotty saw them heading towards the middle of the meadow. She trotted happily on her short legs towards the waving grasses. She could not resist exploring. Soon she was lost to sight. She enjoyed the feel of the dried grasses brushing gently against her skin and she wandered further and further into the uncut hay.

The sides of the Long Meadow were far from parallel. They went in towards the middle and broadened out again at the bottom. Consequently there was now only a narrow strip of uncut hay in the middle. After another round or two the mower would cut it down leaving two separate, elongated triangular sections still to mow.

14

Peggotty was lost. She could see nothing but waving grasses, but she was happy; she knew the children were around somewhere.

'There's Billy and the horses now!' Logan shouted in excitement. 'Can ye see the horses' heads just coming oe'r the rise?' He waved eagerly. Beth waved too, but Billy was concentrating on guiding the horses and keeping a sharp eye on the crop so that the mower cut an even swath, neither too much to obstruct the mower bed, nor too narrow to waste the horses' energy in making extra rounds.

'They're coming towards us, up this side,' Logan announced. 'Billy's seen us! See, he's waving back. I think he wants us tae move nearer the hedge.' He tugged Beth's arm.

'There's Papa and Thomas!' she cried excitedly. 'There, on the other side o' the field with their forks. They're coming tae join us. Let's find a nice shady patch tae sit.' Neither of them noticed the strange movements as Peggotty snuffled her way through the long grasses.

Beth and Logan set down the basket and the can of tea in the shade of the hedge and settled to wait for the men to join them. Logan picked a stem of grass and began to suck the sweetness out of the end as he had seen Thomas doing.

'What's that, Logan?' Beth clutched his arm suddenly. She was staring at the swaying grasses.

'It must be a rabbit . . .'

'Or a hare? It's bigger'n a rabbit.'

'It's going nearer tae the mower instead o' awa' frae it!' Logan scrambled to his feet. 'Move awa! Go the other way you silly rabbit!' He hated to see anything get hurt, even the rabbits and there were plenty of them.

'Logan! It's Peggotty!'

'It canna be . . .'

'It was pink! It's a pig! There! Look!' Beth began to run. Billy and his mower would soon be on a level with them. Logan shuddered and ran to pull Beth back to safety. She was more important even than Peggotty, more important to him than anything! The horses were still moving at a good pace. Billy had explained once that the faster the horses went the faster the pointed knives moved backwards and forwards; it was important to keep an even rhythm. All Billy's attention was fixed on the mower and the horse nearest the edge of the standing crop.

15

Beth glimpsed a flash of pink skin and broke free of Logan's restraining grip, running as fast as she could. The mower had almost reached Peggotty! Beth screamed. The startled horses jerked out of control, cutting an unexpected swath into the middle of the field. The mower jammed instantly. There was an ominous grinding noise. Billy thought he heard something squeal but he was too busy trying to control the horses with one hand, while he struggled to raise the bed of the mower with the other. Suddenly the swath divider reared upright like a giant bird. A small pink shape flew through the air to land with a sickening thud on the newly cut swath. Billy stared in startled horror at the motionless body of a young pig.

'Peggotty!' he whispered hoarsely. Then, 'Logan!' Shock, and a subconscious relief, caused Billy to bellow angrily. 'Why did ye bring that animal tae the field? Have ye no sense?' He paused as Beth burst into tears. He watched her run to Peggotty's limp little body, oblivious to the blood which immediately stained her white pinafore as she crouched over the young pig. His dark eyes flashed to Logan again. 'Surely ye kenned better than . . .'

'Whisht, Billy!' Nick Jamieson gulped for breath as he reached them. His face was white. His eyes darted to Beth. 'I heard the scream. Thank God it wasna either o' the bairns!' he breathed fervently.

'But it was sich a stupid thing! Tae bring the wee pig with them!' Billy struggled for control. His first thought had been for Logan, then for Beth. His mother would never have forgiven him . . . He shuddered.

'We didna bring Peggotty . . .' Logan whispered hoarsely. His young face was pale and strained as he stepped past his angry brother, struggling to hold back his own tears as he joined Beth and Thomas Whiteley beside the inert body of the pet pig they had reared with such patience and loving care.

Three

At the Manse Miss Morrison's features relaxed in a brief smile. 'Please take a seat, Mistress Fairly, Miss Fairly.' She waited until her guests were comfortable and then seated herself economically, feet together, hands neatly clasped. 'I am pleased you found time to come this afternoon. My nephew tells me it is most inconsiderate of me to take you away from the farm during the haymaking . . .' Her voice ended on a slight, questioning rise which invited Sarah to deny that her hostess had ever been inconsiderate in her forty-nine years, but Sarah's brown eyes met and held the blue-grey gaze steadily.

'Haymaking is indeed a busy time,' she acknowledged gravely. 'I am pleased the Reverend Morrison understands the demands of the countryside; but I understand your own visit to Muircumwell is short and I am pleased to have this opportunity of meeting you, Miss Morrison.'

Maud Morrison regarded Sarah with some surprise, and with a glimmer of reluctant respect. Here was no ordinary country bumpkin about to fall on her knees with gratitude because a helping hand had been extended to her daughter. Her nephew's report of Mistress Fairly had not been exaggerated then. He had voiced his opinion that she was an intelligent woman, capable, and of impeccable character; he had also suggested she was blessed with an inner strength which even a minister might envy.

His aunt had almost dismissed his opinion, believing him to be prejudiced in favour of the Fairly family. She had seen the way he watched Ellen Fairly on her last visit. He had escorted the girl to the door himself, taking longer than necessary about it too, and then returned with an unmistakably bemused expression.

Miss Morrison had given the matter some serious thought. It was time dear Mark had a wife; every manse should have a mistress, preferably a calm, capable, kindly person – exactly the type of young woman she judged Ellen Fairly to be. The girl

17

would have made an excellent nurse, she was sure of it, but she had made a private bargain with her conscience. If the girl's family, especially her mother, met with her approval, that is if she felt they were suitable connections for her dear nephew, and his life at the Manse, she would withdraw her support for Ellen Fairly's proposed hospital training. If the girl remained at Fairlyden Mark would have ample opportunity to visit her and to win her hand in marriage.

She glanced at Ellen's serene face and soft dark eyes, her hands and feet held neatly together, yet relaxed. How soothing she would be to the elderly patients, how calming to the children . . . Miss Morrison frowned. She would have to give some reason for changing her mind. She was not in the habit of going back on her word. Maybe the girl would faint at the thought of blood? Operations were carried out regularly these days and assisting the surgeons was becoming an essential part of every nurse's training.

Yes, she would say that on reflection she had decided Ellen Fairly was too gentle for hospital life; her life had been too sheltered; her talents would be better employed visiting the sick in her local parish. Yes, that would be the perfect solution. Surely it was her duty to assist her nephew on the path to holy matrimony? She would withdraw her support for Ellen Fairly as a nurse, but she would give her every encouragement to become a minister's wife. And yet . . . She sighed.

Sarah had been regarding Miss Morrison with equal candour but for the first time in her life she was at a loss to assess the woman's character. It was almost as though a war was waging within that small neat skull. The grey-blue eyes alternated between determined flashes and regretful shadows.

Half an hour earlier the Reverend Morrison had left the Manse reluctantly when Aunt Maud Morrison insisted he should attend to the needs of his parishioners, rather than wander aimlessly while she entertained Miss Fairly and her mama.

It was far too soon for him to return indoors so he walked the long way round, skirting the high wall which separated the Manse grounds from the village. At length he came to the track leading to Strathtod burn, the bridge, and ultimately to Fairlyden. He was just about to enter the tall gates which would take him through a corner of his own glebe land and up the drive to the Manse when he saw the figure of a child stumbling down the track from Fairlyden. Even from a distance he could see she was in some distress, gasping for breath between her sobs, holding her side as though cramped from running. He strode to meet her.

'Why, it's young Beth Jamieson!' he exclaimed, and almost in the same breath, 'so much blood! Has there been an accident? What . . .?'

'P-please, S-sir,' Beth caught her breath on a trembling sob. 'I want Ellen. I-I . . .' Beth had run, or stumbled, nearly all of the three and a half miles from Fairlyden to the outskirts of Muircumwell and suddenly her knees buckled. Mark Morrison seized her just in time and, oblivious to her grubby, blood-stained pinafore he lifted her in his arms and began to stride effortlessly towards the Manse. He frowned as he looked down into the delicate heart-shaped face. There were tear stains on her cheeks, her eyes were closed and twin crescents of curling, gold-tipped lashes rested against her soft skin; her thin chest was still pumping labouringly as she strove to regain her breath. Instead of wasting time going round to the back door of the Manse, Mark Morrison mounted the sandstone steps and entered the front hall. Beth's eyes opened in alarm as she smelled the beeswax polish and felt the change of air.

'Put me down,' she muttered urgently and began to struggle. 'Please! Oh . . . oh . . .' Her small face crumpled and her blue eyes were wide with anxiety. 'Mama Fairly may be c-cross . . . Must wait outside . . . Ellen . . .'

'Hush, child. Ellen is here.' He pushed open another door to the right of the hall and the conversation in the room halted abruptly. Three pairs of startled eyes turned towards the incongruous sight of the young Minister and his bloody burden.

'Beth!' Sarah's face turned pale, but it was Ellen who started to her feet and took Beth's trembling body from his strong arms and set her on her feet on the hearth rug, going down on her knees so that her face was on a level with the child's.

'Tell me what has happened . . .?'

''s Peggotty!' Beth sobbed, raising drowned blue eyes to Ellen's. 'I-I ken ye'll make her better. I-I had tae c-come . . .' Ellen expelled a long breath and heard her mother do the same. She drew Beth close in a comforting hug. Even as she murmured soothing words Miss Morrison noted that she was deftly untying the tapes at the back of the child's neck, removing the little

19

blood-stained apron, folding it inside out and rolling it into a neat parcel.

'There now,' Ellen sat back on her heels and gave an encouraging smile. 'Tell me slowly, Beth. What has happened tae Peggotty tae bring ye all this way, and in such a state?'

'Thomas said she was alive. He tore a strip frae the tail o' his shirt. B-but he couldna stop Peggotty bleeding, not properly. Oh, Ellen!' Beth gave a gulping sob. 'Ye've got tae save P-Peggotty!' She looked up, her blue eyes pleading. Over Ellen's shoulder she saw Miss Morrisson watching her in a bemused way. Her anxious gaze moved to Sarah. 'Th-they dinna ken I've come. I-I ken I shouldna . . .'

'It's all right, Beth. I understand you needed Ellen. Where is Peggotty now?' Sarah asked, already on her feet and preparing to take her leave.

'Who or what,' demanded Miss Morrison, 'is Peggotty?'

'A pig. But she's a very special pig to Beth and Logan, my youngest son. I'm sorry, Miss Morrison, but we canna wait for tea. We must hope Ellen can get back in time to help . . .'

'The child obviously believes Ellen can save the pig. You have stitched animals before?'

'Only once,' Ellen conceded, already clasping Beth's hand and on her way to the door.

'I will accompany you,' Miss Morrison announced unexpectedly. 'Mark, summon Symons to bring Mistress Fairly's trap,' she added imperiously.

''Tis already at the door!' the ancient Symons wheezed from the hallway. 'I saw the bairn i' the Minister's arms, and the blood on her . . .?' Sarah saw the question in his eyes and recalled that he had been in service at the Manse with the Reverend Mace, and even before that with the Reverend Mackenzie. There was scarcely a babe in the village, or even in the whole of the straggling parish, that Symons did not know. Sarah satisfied his curiosity.

'One thing is clear,' Miss Morrison said as her nephew helped her into the trap. 'Miss Fairly will make a fine nurse. It would be a waste of the talents the Lord has bestowed upon her if we were to wish her any other fate than to heal the sick.' She held her nephew's gaze steadily.

Peggotty was still a very sick little pig three days later. They had

20

almost given up hope of her recovering, until the morning Beth and Logan ran excitedly into the kitchen as Sarah was setting out the bowls of porridge.

'Peggotty's standing up! All by herself!'

'She's awfy wobbly because she's only standing on three legs!'

'Ach, she'll get better now then!' Thomas chuckled.

'Aye, she'll soon learn to put her leg down when the wound heals,' Nick grinned, patently relieved that Beth's misery was reaching some sort of conclusion.

'Indeed she'll be running all over the yard again before long, no doubt!' Sarah agreed, but her smile echoed Nick's relief. 'It's thanks to Ellen.'

'And the bottle o' whisky we used tae stop the tape and the needle infecting Peggotty's wound!' Ellen smiled.

The atmosphere was one of celebration round the Fairlyden breakfast table on that bright July morning.

'For guidness' sake, I dinna ken what all the fuss is about! It's only a pig!' Sadie exclaimed sourly. 'And a useless wee runt at that!'

'Aye, but it means a lot tae the bairns,' Billy declared, fixing his dark eyes thoughtfully on his sister's sullen face.

When breakfast was finished Nick and Thomas went out to work but Billy did not accompany them as he usually did. He waited until his mother and Agnes had gone to the dairy.

'Logan said he and Beth didna let Peggotty out o' the orchard that day.' His tone was deceptively mild, almost conversational, but his black eyebrows were drawn together in a frown, making him look older than his twenty-one years. 'I believe them!' His voice hardened. 'There was only Agnes here – and you, Sadie. You must have opened the gate o' Peggotty's pen.'

Sadie's face paled and then flushed angrily. 'Why would I want tae be bothered with that evil-smelling animal!' she sneered. 'I'd work tae dae. Mother and Ellen were away enjoying themselves at the Manse!'

'Aah . . . So that's it!' Billy's dark eyes glittered with contempt. 'Ye were jealous because the Reverend Morrison didna invite ye tae the Manse! Ye canna bear tae see anybody else happy. It might hae been Logan or Beth that got hurt with the mower if they'd seen Peggotty any sooner . . .' He shuddered. 'Ye're evil, Sadie Fairly, even if ye are ma ain sister.'

'I am not! I'm always the one tae be left at home tae dae the work! There's Ellen!' she glared sullenly at her sister. 'Going away tae be a nurse, expecting me tae dae her work! As for him!' She glared at Logan. 'Everybody spoils him – just because he's the youngest!'

'That's not true, Sadie!' Ellen protested. 'Logan helps whenever he can! Beth tae . . .'

'Yes I dae!' Logan was indignant.

'And we can both milk now . . .' Beth added staunchly, but her face was pale. Sadie Fairly looked so ugly in her anger. Almost like a witch. Beth shivered.

'Of course you both help,' Billy agreed in a gentler tone, 'but I think ye should both go and see if Peggotty's still standing up, eh . . .?' Billy watched them hurry outside. 'They both help willingly. Ye've never done anything willingly in your life, Sadie. Nae wonder the Minister doesna fancy ye!'

'I hate you, Billy Fairly!' Sadie's voice was shrill. She pushed back her chair and jumped to her feet but before she could run to her room Billy darted round the table and grasped her wrist.

'I dinna care whether ye hate me or not, but dinna let me catch ye up tae any more o' your nasty little tricks. Leave Logan alone – and Beth Jamieson.'

'Beth Jamieson!' Sadie spat the words angrily. 'She almost lives here! She should learn her place . . .'

'Her place is here. She's as much part o' Fairlyden as you or I. She was born here and . . .'

'She was born in the cottage and that's where she should stay!'

Billy's eyes expressed his contempt. 'There'll never be peace while ye're here, Sadie. Ellen is wise tae get awa' frae Fairlyden! I'll be thankful when it's my turn tae leave tae!' He turned towards the door into the long passage which opened on to the yard. Ellen moved swiftly, detaining him with a gentle hand on his arm.

'Billy . . .?' Her dark eyes scanned his face. 'I'm not running away frae Fairlyden! I dinna want tae leave. But I want tae be a nurse, I really do . . .'

'I ken, Ellen,' Billy summoned a smile, 'And ye'll be a fine nurse.'

'Surely ye dinna plan tae leave Fairlyden? What would Mother dae without both o' us?' Ellen's brown eyes were anxious.

'Well I dinna plan tae stay here for ever. I never wanted tae be a farmer. Logan will make a far better job o' it. He loves

Fairlyden already, and the horses, and the cows, as well as Peggotty!' He smiled ruefully, then pinched Ellen's cheek. 'But dinna worry, little sister, I wouldna leave Mother in the lurch.' He raised his head and his dark eyes met Sadie's narrow-eyed stare. 'And dinna go telling your tales tae Mother and worrying her with your nasty little tongue! I'll tell her my plans when the time's right for me tae leave.'

'Is that why ye've never tried tae take over frae Nick, Billy?' Ellen asked.

'Nick kens what I want. He's pleased enough tae leave the machines, and the working o' them, tae me. I leave the rest tae him. We'll all get along fine as we are for a few more years – until Logan leaves the school anyway. Maybe he'll marry Beth when they're old enough!'

'I do believe ye're a romantic fellow at heart, Billy Fairly!' Ellen relaxed with a grin. 'But ye canna plan Logan's life . . .'

'Oh, I'm not planning anybody's life! Still, I reckon Mother thinks o' Beth as a daughter already.'

'Well, Beth loves Fairlyden, and she has a mind o' her own, although she's still a bairn . . .'

'Aye, she has a funny kind o' dignity already,' Billy mused with a smile. 'Maybe she'll make as good a Mistress here as Mother one day.'

'She's a labourer's brat!' Sadie hissed suddenly. 'She'll never be Mistress here! Never!'

Four

Sarah had arranged a small family gathering for the Sunday before Ellen was due to start life as a nurse. As usual on Sundays Thomas Whiteley was spending an hour or two with his mother and his two younger sisters in their rooms over Jardine's Store and Agnes was cooking the Sunday dinner at the cottage for Nick and Beth. Upstairs Ellen and Sadie were changing their dresses and pinning up their hair.

Just for a little while Sarah found the house unusually quiet. A large leg of lamb was roasting in the shining blackleaded oven; the fire was drawing well; a pan of new potatoes bubbled gently on the ribs beside a large pot of cock-a-leekie soup. Ellen had shelled a big bowl of peas from the garden ready to boil and Sadie had chopped the mint for the sauce. On the stone bench in the pantry a trifle and a rhubarb pie stood in readiness beside a jug of fresh cream. Sarah glanced around the tidy kitchen. A bowl of bright summer flowers added a touch of gaiety and a new rag rug covered the stone flags in front of the fire, its multifarious colours still untrammelled by feet. On the wall the brass pendulum of the clock slowly ticked away the minutes.

A smile of satisfaction gave her mouth an upward curve and she walked lightly along the passage and out to the yard. The freshness of the summer morning caressed her warm skin and she lifted her face pleasurably. Her dark eyes scanned the track which led to Muircumwell, watching for the first sight of the Mains' trap. Her smile broadened. Her father was almost seventy but she had no doubt he would be holding the reins himself. Sandy Logan had lost none of the independent spirit he had had when he first came to Fairlyden as a young man.

I'm glad Beatrice has agreed to take a rest from housekeeping at the Mains for once, Sarah decided happily. She was looking forward to exchanging family news and a little harmless gossip with her oldest and dearest friend. It had brought her added joy to know that Beatrice was more than a friend, that they shared

25

the same father; they were half-sisters, although few people knew their secret.

Beatrice had been grateful for a home at the Mains for herself and her children after her husband's death. Poor Dick, he had worked so hard on the little farm they had rented in Yorkshire, and he had loved his wife dearly. Sarah frowned. Had he ever guessed what a burden his pretty, vacant-minded daughter would prove to be . . .?

'Why are ye looking so pensive, Mama?' Ellen asked, coming out to perch on the big stone slab outside Fairlyden's back door.

'Was I?' Sarah smiled ruefully. 'You're too observant, lassie, but I suppose that's a good quality for a nurse. As a matter of fact I was thinking of Beatrice. I'm glad she agreed to come today.'

'Mmm, so am I. Indeed I think I'm honoured. Aunt Beattie doesna go out much these days, does she? I suppose it's difficult for her with Meg though . . .?'

'Mmm, Meg's dreamy ways were bad enough when she was eight, but they're worse at eighteen! She's so lovely too. It's such a waste . . . Alex has always shown a remarkable tenderness towards her. He seems to think they're kindred spirits, though for the life o' me, I canna imagine why . . .'

'Is Richard coming with them?'

'Aah, I don't know. Richard has a mind of his own and no mistake! He's another heartache for Beattie! I don't know how she and Dick could have produced a son as moody as young Richard. I knew his grandmother and his grandfather; you couldna have wished for gentler, more kindly folks than the O'Connors . . . Aah, look, there's the trap! I do believe Brad Leishman is with them too . . .'

Ellen's cheeks coloured rosily. 'He must have managed tae catch the train frae Edinburgh after all,' she murmured a trifle breathlessly.

'I'm glad he could come, lassie.' Sarah's voice was warm. 'He's a fine young man.' She had good reason to be grateful to the young American doctor herself. He had assisted at Logan's birth on his very first evening at Fairlyden, after bringing her news of her husband's death.

Ellen wanted to pick up her skirts and run to meet their guests, but she stood beside her mother and waited decorously. Yet nothing could hide the glow in her dark eyes. Alex and Richard O'Connor were astride their ponies, riding side by side behind the trap. Brad's head was twisted round as he chatted to Alex and she heard their laughter carrying clearly on the summer air. Her spirits soared. One day, when she had completed her training and become a real nurse, she hoped Brad would be proud of her; further than that she would not think. He never mentioned other young ladies in any of his letters, for all they were so long and full of the daily trivia which made up his life as a doctor, but Ellen knew he was almost twenty-nine; surely no man as attractive as Brad could be expected to lead the life of a monk? she thought with a realism completely at variance with her own innocence. She had little experience of life in the wider world beyond Muircumwell.

She hugged her grandfather warmly as he stepped from the trap, for Sandy Logan held a very special place in Ellen's heart and she knew the feeling was reciprocated.

'My, lassie, ye grow more like your grandmother every day! Ye're bonnier than ever!' Sandy's blue eyes twinkled beneath his bushy brows, which were still a sandy-brown colour despite the snowy whiteness of his hair. Ellen kissed Beatrice and Meg dutifully on the cheek, and then at last she turned to Brad, her dark lashes lowered shyly, the delicate colour rising on her high cheekbones. She had forgotten just how he towered over her. Grandfather Logan was tall, and still erect, but Brad was taller. She found herself looking up into his smiling face, but it was the look in his grey eyes which made her catch her breath.

'Ellen . . .' He murmured her name softly, smiling, then he bent his head and kissed the back of each hand in turn. Her dark brows arched in surprise, her colour deepened.

'I'd much rather kiss you properly,' he murmured amidst the excitement of exchanged greetings.

Billy appeared from one of the cart sheds with Logan and Beth skipping along beside him. They led away the pony and trap as Sadie flounced out of the house, her thin face flushed with the thrill gleaned from the magazine she had been reading in her bedroom. She longed for a young man like the ones in the stories she read, but none of those in her life measured up to her dream heroes.

Meanwhile Alex was greeting Ellen with an affectionate grin, his dark eyes alight with curiosity as they moved from her to Brad and back again. She had forgotten how observant her eldest brother was. It was the secret of his success as a farmer,

27

and even more so as a breeder of fine horses; his sharp eyes and intuition more than made up for his crippled feet, though she knew he would not agree. She loved Alex dearly and she sensed that he was secretly ashamed of his thick boots with their specially made soles which made him look so clumsy. 'No last minute regrets about leaving Fairlyden?' Alex asked, eyeing her shrewdly.

'Fairlyden's home,' Ellen said simply, honestly. 'I hate the thought o' being away frae it.' She paused, gazing around the little farm steading with its neat stone sheds. Her smile was wistful. Beyond the steading the fields were sprouting freshly green where the hay had been cut and gathered, already the field of oats was changing to palest gold, and beyond the fields and meadows the purple-green hills rose and fell, stretching across the skyline. 'Ye were only a laddie when ye moved tae Mains of Muir, Alex, but ye've managed well enough . . .' There was a faint question in Ellen's tone and her brown eyes watched him closely. Alex sensed the anxiety and nervousness which she was striving to hide.

'Aye, but I missed ye all when I first went tae the Mains,' he admitted ruefully, 'even though I had Grandfather Logan.' He and Ellen had never been less than truthful with each other. Suddenly he wished he could confide in her now; share his own bewildering discovery that Aunt Beatrice really was their aunt. But this was Ellen's day of celebration; he must not trouble her.

Brad Leishman had seen the faint shadows of uncertainty in Ellen's lovely eyes.

'I guess it would be a strange thing if you did not miss your own home, Ellen, my dear. Fairlyden is such a warm and happy place. You have a delightful and loving family too, but none of them need you as the sick people in hospital will need you. They will all look upon you as their own special angel from heaven.' He smiled, and his craggy features were transformed. 'Indeed I almost envy those who will be in your care, but at this precise moment I have to confess that I am ravenously hungry!'

'Oh! How thoughtless of me to keep ye standing here!' Ellen exclaimed, her own doubts and fears instantly cast aside, as Brad had intended. She took his arm and almost dragged him into the house. Already the rest of the family were gathering around the big table in the kitchen.

'Where's Mr Bradshaw, Mother? Is he no' coming after all?' Billy asked.

'Mrs Bunnerby said he intended coming to see Ellen before she goes away.'

'Mrs Bunnerby!' Brad Leishman echoed with a smile. 'That's a comforting, homely sort of name, to be sure!'

'Yes, Mrs Bunnerby is the housekeeper at Fairlyside, the new house which Mr Bradshaw has built just below Nick's cottage,' Sarah replied with a smile. 'She is just as comforting as her name suggests. Logan and Beth can tell you that! The pair o' them rarely come home frae school without calling on her, and I'm sure they never leave without a biscuit or a bun to eat! Isn't that so, Logan?'

'Aye,' Logan grinned sheepishly, then he brightened. 'Mrs Bunnerby said Uncle Crispin would be coming. He's bought a box with a kind o' trumpet thing that plays music. He's going tae wind it up for Beth and me tae hear.'

'Ye mean a gramophone,' Billy informed his young brother. 'But will he be here for dinner?'

'Mrs Bunnerby said he wadna miss Mama's roast potatoes or her trifle for anything!'

Sandy laid aside the carving knife.

'Maybe we should wait a wee while longer for Crispin then, Sarah?'

'No, I'm sure Brad must be dying of hunger . . .'

'We doctors are always starving,' Brad grinned, 'and I guess Mrs Fairly has the measure of my appetite, but I would not wish to be the cause of offending your landlord . . .'

'Mr Bradshaw willna mind,' Ellen assured him. 'Maybe he does own some o' Fairlyden land, but he's Mother's friend as well. He's one o' the most understanding men I ken . . .'

'Did I hear somebody taking my name in vain?' a cheerful voice boomed from the open door.

'Crispin!' Sarah hastily set the dishes of soup on the table and turned to greet him, her smile warm and welcoming. 'You are just in time!'

'I'm sorry if I'm holding up the meal, Sarah.' Crispin Bradshaw's gaze flickered over her face, noting the faint blush, before encompassing everyone round the table. He smiled, showing two square front teeth with a slight gap between them; it made him look almost boyish despite his greying sideburns. The lines seemed to fade from his lean face and his grey eyes sparkled with flecks of green and gold. Now that Logan's got his new front teeth, his smile is just like Crispin's, Sarah realised with a start, surprised that she had not noticed the increasing resemblance before. Not for the first time she wondered if her father had ever noticed the likeness. Certainly he knew Crispin Bradshaw was no ordinary landlord, but even he did not know the full extent of Crispin's involvement in her life – or his generosity.

She finished dishing up the soup before allowing her eyes to move slowly over the little assembly gathered around her table. Meg and Sadie, the one so beautiful, the other so plain, made an unlikely pair; Meg's pretty blue eyes looked no further than the surface and her ears detected none of Sadie's spiteful innuendoes.

Billy was already regaling Alex with his latest ideas for a machine which he was convinced would sow the seeds more evenly than sowing by hand. Alex seemed unusually preoccupied, Sarah decided and wondered why.

Her gaze moved to Beatrice's only son, listening avidly to Billy's one-sided conversation. She viewed the boy's set young face, wondering at his grim expression. She had no way of knowing that Richard O'Connor was secretly determined to become a more prosperous farmer than any who sat at her table on that summer Sunday. Many times he made the same silent vow. Even his mother knew little of the taunts he had suffered at school, and still suffered, because his father had once served a prison sentence. She would have been dismayed to know that Richard considered every crust he ate at Mains of Muir as charity, charity which he resented bitterly. Neither did she realise how ashamed he was of his pretty sister with her dim wits and childish fantasies.

Sarah's eyes roved round the table to Crispin and her father, already discussing the world of trade and the growing problem of unemployed men.

Beatrice sat quiet, but when she was not eating her hands were clenched tightly in her lap, and Sarah sensed something was troubling her. Logan fidgeted, ever anxious to finish his meals and get on with his youthful ploys, while Ellen was completely absorbed in conversation with Brad Leishman.

When the meal was finished Sadie was the first to rise.

'Meg wants tae see some pictures in one o' my magazines, don't ye?'

'Pictures,' Meg echoed blankly in her high childish voice.

'Aye, pictures! Come on!' Sadie almost dragged Meg from the table in her impatience to escape from the kitchen. Sarah's mouth tightened. She knew Sadie was using Meg as an excuse to avoid washing the dishes. Meg could neither read nor write and she had little interest in pictures, or anything else for long. Her mind was like a butterfly, flitting constantly.

'There's work to be done before you go to your chamber, Sadie.' Her tone was firm and Sadie glowered sullenly.

'There's Ellen . . .'

'I will help with the dishes,' Beatrice offered quickly. She saw Ellen glance reproachfully at her younger sister's retreating back and her smile was warm. 'It's all right, lassie, I'm looking forward tae a wee chat with your mother, and I'm sure Doctor Leishman would benefit frae a breath o' fresh air after being in his stuffy hospital . . .' Her blue eyes sparked with a flash of her old humour. 'And nae doubt your company will be a tonic tae him.'

'Indeed, Mistress O'Connor, you are correct. The company of a beautiful young lady is just what a wise doctor would order for a jaded creature like myself.' Brad grinned at Ellen's pink cheeks and, taking her arm, he led her outside without delay, determined to make the most of his short visit.

'Ye'll take a walk round the fields, Alex?' Billy prompted, eager as always to show his elder brother around their old haunts. 'You coming too, young Richard?' Billy seemed unaware of Alex's hesitation, and of Richard's displeasure at the reference to his youth.

'I'd like tae talk with ye, Mother . . .' Alex began. 'Later,' he added swiftly as his grandfather and Crispin rose from the table and came towards them, still in earnest discussion about the Liberals' landslide victory in the general election earlier in the year and the remarkable success of the Labour party under the leadership of the Scotsman, Keir Hardie.

'Maybe parliament would be better if they did listen to the women and give them the vote . . .' he murmured, raising his eyes to Sarah with a smile.

'Now that thorny question might take all afternoon to discuss, and even then I dinna think we would all agree!' she declared wryly. 'Find yourselves a comfortable seat in the front parlour. Beatrice and I will join you both when we've washed the dishes

31

and had a wee chat of our own. What about you, Logan? Don't you want to go with Billy and Alex?'

'Aye. Can I see if Beth wants tae come? We'll soon catch up with them.'

'Oh, all right.' Her brown eyes were tender as she watched Logan run off happily. When she looked up she caught Crispin's eyes on her. He smiled.

'Those two are inseparable, it seems. Mrs Bunnerby enjoys their visits and regales me with all their latest activities. I've brought a gramophone and some records to Fairlyside. Maybe you will join us when I play them for the children . . .?'

'Thank you, Crispin, I'd like that, especially if you've brought some hymns? Beth has a lovely young voice and she remembers all the words so well. The Reverend Morrison thinks she should have piano lessons and the new teacher, Miss Bell, offered to teach her. I said she could use the piano in the parlour to practise. The Reverend Mackenzie left it to me when he died but no one here can play it.'

'Does Beth want to learn to play the piano?'

'Nick wouldna consent to the lessons. He canna afford to pay for them, and he doesn't want charity. He can be very proud and independent!' she added ruefully. Crispin frowned.

'It seems a waste of talent though, if Beth is musical,' he said slowly. 'Maybe I shall think of a solution . . .'

Sarah smiled mischievously. 'Right now you'd better join my father or he may fall asleep before you have finished your political discussion.'

'Ach! I heard that, young Sarah!' Sandy called from the parlour. 'I'm not that ancient yet, at least not when I get the chance o' a bit o' stimulating conversation!'

Five

'What's wrong, Beattie?' Sarah had almost finished washing the dishes and she had a growing conviction that Beatrice was troubled about something.

'Och, it's Meg . . . well, partly Meg. Last week one o' the carters frae Annan was in at the Mains delivering cattle cake . . . Meg was in the barn. I expect she smiled at him – ye ken, Sarah, the way she does . . .'

'Ye-es . . .' Sarah frowned. 'Meg's always blithe anyway . . .?'

'The man reckoned she was . . . encouraging him. He wadna ken the way o' things wi' Meg. He frightened her. Alex came on them. He said she was whimpering and upset. He was furious with the man . . .'

'I should think so!' Sarah exclaimed.

'Aye, but she looks like a woman grown!'

'But the man had no right to touch her!'

'Alex thinks there's only one way tae protect her.'

Suddenly Sarah stopped washing the dishes. Her hands clenched on the side of the enamel bowl and she stared at Beatrice. Her heart began to thump. 'What did he mean . . .?'

Beatrice bit her lip. She could not meet Sarah's eyes.

'He-he thinks she should have a wedding ring on her finger . . .' Beatrice's voice sank to a whisper. 'His . . .'

'No!' Sarah's exclamation was instant, and vehement.

Beatrice O'Connor lowered her head and stared at the flagged floor. 'I-I'm sorry, Beattie,' Sarah muttered, 'it's not that I've anything against your bairn b-but . . .'

'I understand how ye feel, Sarah. I ken Meg will never be a proper wife tae any man, and Alex deserves tae be happy. Besides he'll need a capable woman at the Mains some day, especially if his success with the horses continues.' She had a mental picture of Emma Braidwood sorting eggs in the pantry. She was bound to have heard Alex telling her he wanted to marry Meg. Emma had been a maid at Mains of Muir since she

33

was thirteen, soon after Beatrice had returned from Yorkshire. Her family had a small farm near Lockerbie but Mr Braidwood had not had enough work for all his sons, let alone his daughters. Emma was a neat, tidy girl, and intelligent too. Recently she had begun to help Alex in the evenings with his stallion notices and accounts for service fees. She knew many of the farmers and she was interested. At first Alex had seemed at ease with her, happy in her company, even eager to set about the tasks he had previously considered irksome.

Beatrice sighed and her voice was weary. 'I couldna sleep for thinking about it all. In the end I-I told your father – our father . . . He talked to Alex. Told him we're s-sisters, that Meg is his cousin. He said she would have enough protection so long as Alex gave us a home . . .'

'Was Alex upset, when he knew about us?'

'He didna believe it – even frae his grandfather's ain lips – not at first.'

'I see . . . I expect that's why he wants to speak to me. Dinna worry about it, Beattie. Alex would have learned the truth eventually. Father planned to leave him a letter so that he would understand why you and your bairns must always have a home at the Mains . . . when he's dead and gone himself.'

'Oh, Sarah! I hate tae think . . .'

'Father made provision for you as soon as he realised that he could be your real father, Beattie, and he was right to do so. I'll speak to Alex before he leaves.'

'Aye . . . Alex can be stubborn though, more like his father than I thought . . . Oh Sarah, he canna marry Meg! She canna cook, or even scrub the floor clean! She canna milk a cow . . . She understands nothing about shopping or mending . . .' Beatrice's voice broke. 'I ken she's ma ain bairn, but sometimes I think it wad have been better if she had died when she was born . . .'

'Oh Beattie, you don't mean that!'

'No. I was so grateful when the doctor said she was alive. Nothing else mattered then . . . and Dick was sae very proud.'

'I know,' Sarah said gently. 'I'll speak to Alex, dinna worry.' She continued washing the dishes automatically, but her mind was in a turmoil. Alex had always had a tender feeling for Meg, ever since he had seen her as a baby. Now she was a very beautiful girl . . .

34

'Alex said he only intended to give Meg his name tae protect her. He – he wadna want her tae bear him any children . . . or anything.'

'You mean he intends to live like a monk! That's not in the breeding o' him!' Sarah's cheeks flushed. 'I-I mean . . .'

'I ken what ye mean, Sarah, and it's the natural way o' things for a man tae want a mate, and . . .' Beattie's own cheeks flushed a bright pink, 'and a woman tae if she's normal. At least if she's lucky enough tae get a guid man,' she added softly. Sarah knew she was thinking of the unexpected bliss she had found with Dick O'Connor; he was the only man she had ever loved.

'Since I've lived at the Mains, I've loved Alex like ma ain son.' She thought of his crippled feet, how sensitive he was! Beatrice understood how inferior he felt. She had felt less than perfect herself once – unable to believe that any man could love her. How wrong she had been, and how wonderful her years with Dick. Did Alex feel that Emma could accept him as an employer and even as a friend, perhaps – but not as a prospective husband? Did he want Meg as a shield for himself, in some quixotic way? Pride, was that the real reason he wanted a pretty, empty-headed wife – for his own protection as well as Meg's . . .? Beatrice sighed. 'I want him tae be happy.'

'I know that, Beattie,' Sarah said warmly. 'Sometimes I was almost jealous! Especially when Alex was younger.'

'Aye, I expect ye missed him at first. He has such a kindly nature. Even now he's a young man he's more considerate tae me than Richard is!' Beatrice was silent for a moment or two and when she spoke again Sarah thought she had changed the subject.

'We had a visit frae Miss Morrison. She came tae see if Emma would accept the post as housekeeper at the Manse for the Reverend Morrison.'

'Emma! Is she looking for a new post then?'

'No. Someone in the village had recommended her tae the Minister's aunt. She would have been mistress o' her ain kitchen there, and she's a grand wee cook – brings lots o' recipes for me frae her mother. But she turned it down. Said she didna want tae leave the Mains.'

'I'm glad. You would miss her, Beattie.' She sighed softly, unaware of Beatrice's suspicions regarding her eldest son's sensitive heart. 'I'm glad we've had a chance to talk. My bairns are growing up and I didna even notice.'

'Well, ye dinna look old enough tae have two grown sons and a lassie going tae be a nurse. I expect Logan keeps ye young, Sarah, and Nick Jamieson's wee lassie. They're great company for each other, and such a happy pair for all the troubles they've had in their young lives.'

'Yes.' Sarah smiled wryly. 'I expect he and Beth are paddling in the burn, for all it's the Sabbath! They're like shadows the way they follow each other around.'

'I've been telling Crispin that ye've signed a contract tae sell most o' your milk to a Cooperative, Sarah,' Sandy declared, as Sarah and Beatrice joined them in the front parlour. 'He says some of the cooperatives have gone bankrupt in Yorkshire. The farmers didna get anything for their milk . . .'

'Only two that I know of,' Crispin intervened hastily. 'And I'm sure you would not sign any agreement without checking up on the firm, Sarah, at least as far as possible. I did not intend any criticism . . .'

'I know. You're like your father underneath that gentlemanly exterior, Crispin.' Sarah smiled. 'He always called a spade a spade. I expect you'll tell me face to face if you think I'm making a mistake. The trouble is, it's impossible to be sure.' She knew her father was concerned about the changes she was making. He would be even more anxious if he knew Crispin had already helped her out of an earlier crisis and that she no longer owned any part of Fairlyden. 'Billy went with me to meet the local managers of two cooperatives. We did ask a lot of questions but it's difficult to judge. We signed up with the man who seemed to be offering the fairest terms. We're to be paid at the end o' every month. I think it will be easier than skimming and churning and trying to sell all the butter at the local markets every week. If I'd lived nearer the village I could have sold some of the milk myself.'

'I wish you lived near enough to supply my workers with good clean milk!'

'Are things all right with the woollen trade?' Sandy enquired.

'The trade comes and goes,' Crispin answered dryly. 'The problem is with Fanny, my sister – or rather with her husband Eric, and my nephew. They want to spend all the profits. They cannot see the need to invest in new looms to maintain our

36

position in the market and the Bradshaw reputation for quality and prompt deliveries.'

'Does that mean you're short of money, Crispin . . .?' Sarah asked tensely. He guessed at once that she was thinking of the money he had tied up in Fairlyden. He smiled, unaware of the sudden tenderness in his gaze.

'No. It means I'm very glad I did not put all my own money into the mills after all. Sometimes I'm sorely tempted to hand over the whole lot to my nephew and end the Trust which my father set up.'

'It wad surprise your father tae hear ye talk like that,' Sandy exclaimed in surprise. 'He aye said ye lived for the mills, laddie. His only regret was that ye didna have a son o' your ain tae follow in your footsteps. He didna seem tae have much of an opinion o' his son-in-law, or the way his grandson was shaping, if ye ask me.'

'The mills have been my whole life, or at least they were . . .' Crispin's grey eyes flickered over Sarah's face involuntarily. 'I still care about them, and the workers I have known all my life. But when I see Robert turning out to be as worthless as his father, it sickens me. Neither of them have any thought for the men and women toiling in the mills to make profits for them. They grudge every halfpenny I spend on improving the factory or repairing the houses, yet they have a house in London and another by the sea. Now they are pestering for money to buy a villa abroad.

'My father realised how it would be with them: spend, spend, spend, whilst doing as little work as possible. That's why he made a condition that the Trust could be broken if ever I did marry and have a son to carry on . . .' This time his brooding eyes were drawn to Sarah as though by a magnet. He saw her sink her teeth into her lower lip; her brown eyes were anxious. Surely she knew he would never go back on his word! He would never hurt her, or their son, and it was plain already that the boy loved Fairlyden as much as Sarah did herself.

'How's the bairns' pet pig getting on these days?' Sandy enquired. 'Peggotty is it they call her?'

'Peggotty's getting on fine. Ellen made a fine job of stitching her up and she doesna drag her leg at all now. She's as quiet as a lamb with Logan and Beth. Nick thinks she would make a good mother. I've no doubt Logan and Beth will be only too eager to

37

take you to see her before you go back to the Mains, Father.'

'You sound as enthusiastic as the bairns!' Sandy chuckled. 'Ach and here's Billy and Alex back frae their walk.' He sighed. 'It's time we were getting on the road again, eh, Beatrice? Have you had a good chat with Sarah over the dishes, lassie?'

'Indeed we did,' Beatrice smiled up at him affectionately. She had grown very fond of Sandy Logan and she was proud to know he was her natural father, even though she would never acknowledge the fact publicly.

'I'd like you to look at one o' the horses, Alex.' Sarah caught her eldest son's eye. 'Maybe we should go now while your grandfather has a cup of tea to put him right for the drive back to Muircumwell.' Alex nodded readily.

Crispin Bradshaw watched Sarah and Alex walk companionably across the farm yard. He saw them lean over the gate of a field where the horses were grazing and guessed there was some private matter Sarah wished to discuss. Alex seemed more lame than usual. Crispin guessed he was tired. No doubt Billy had trailed him round all the crops he wanted to show off. He never seemed to realise that his elder brother required twice as much energy as himself to make his twisted feet carry him where he wanted to go.

Alex leaned his forearms on the top bar of the gate but Sarah saw how tightly clenched his hands were and that there was a muscle twitching in his lean jaw as he turned his head and looked at her. His eyes, dark as her own, were narrowed. 'So you and Aunt Beattie had a talk . . .? Aunt Beattie!' he mocked, but softly. 'Ye're half-sisters. I never dreamed she was really our aunt!'

'We were close friends, Alex. Always. Long before I knew anything o' the tangle that binds us.'

'Humph . . .' The grunt, a mixture of bitterness, disbelief, maybe even disillusionment, was totally alien to her eldest son and Sarah looked at him anxiously. Alex had always seemed so happy and serene, despite his handicap.

'Your grandfather is a good man, Alex,' she insisted quietly. 'Dinna hold the past against him, please. Ever since he's known Beatrice is his daughter he has tried to make amends . . .' Alex remained silent, staring moodily into space. 'Anyway it's all in the past. It's not my story to tell; it's not my business – or yours. You canna blame him, Alex . . .' There was a note of desperation

38

in Sarah's tone. She felt she was speaking to a block of wood instead of Alex, the most sensitive of all her children. 'He's given you a wonderful opportunity to farm; he knew it was what you wanted more than anything else in the world; he took a great risk for you – with his savings . . . giving up his job as factor at Strathtod . . .'

'Och, I dinna blame Grandfather!' Alex grimaced moodily, reminding her of Billy, and of their father, when William had been so unsettled. 'I am grateful tae him. Don't ever think I'm not, Mother!' He scowled. 'Maybe I envy him! Aye, that's it. I envy Grandfather Logan! He was a normal man. Who can blame him if he had two women, and maybe more . . .'

'Alex!'

'I'm sorry, Mother.' His broad shoulders drooped disconsolately for a moment. Then he straightened, raising his head proudly, reminding Sarah that he was almost a foot taller than she was. 'I am going tae marry Meg. Now I ken the truth it makes more sense than ever . . .'

'Sense! How can it make sense? Meg's . . .'

'She and Richard have as much right tae Grandfather's money – aye and tae the Mains – as I have. I've given Richard a chance to work and earn his share – though nothing seems tae please him! But it's my duty tae provide for Meg and her mother now I ken . . .'

'They have no claim to the Mains. Even Captain Fothergill considers you are responsible for bringing it back to prosperity – and he's your landlord! As for the horses, they're entirely your own success. You can provide a home for Meg without marrying her!'

'She needs the protection of a husband. Anyway I shall be proud to have her as my wife. She's very beautiful. Lots o' men would envy me.' How could he tell his own mother his real reason for deciding to marry Meg? He cringed inwardly at the thought of Emma Braidwood guessing how he felt about her – him a cripple! Once he had a wife Emma would know she was quite safe when he asked her to join him, when he sought her company on the pretext of assisting with his accounts for the horses. 'Nobody but Meg would want a cripple for a husband!' he muttered aloud.

'Oh, Alex! I'm sure you're wrong. One day you'll find a woman who would love you, give you bairns – sons to follow in your footsteps . . .'

'Footsteps!' Alex muttered bitterly. 'Crooked, twisted footsteps! No normal woman would marry a cripple! Only a simple, innocent lassie like Meg wad marry me!'

'No, Alex! No!' Sarah grasped his arm fiercely. 'You're wrong! You canna throw your life away on Meg! Look after her, feed her, clothe her, but dinna . . . I beg you, dinna marry the lassie. She depends on you too much already.'

'She trusts me. Mother . . . I've aye been grateful to you, dinna think I haven't, especially when ye were prepared to disagree with Father to give me my chance at the Mains. I was determined to prove you were right but . . .'

'And you have! I'm proud o' you, and so is your grandfather . . .'

'Maybe, but *he* understands there's things I canna dae, things I'll never be able to dae, but you refuse to see anything wrong wi' me at all . . .'

'Och, I know you canna run or walk all day behind the plough, or even with your beloved stallions – but you can teach other men to do such things for you, and you can pay them for it – and most o' them are grateful for the chance to work!'

Alex shook his head. 'There's no many women like you, Mother, even Mr Bradshaw says that, and he's a confirmed bachelor . . .'

Sarah's colour rushed to her cheeks and she turned sharply so that Alex would not see. There were many things Alex did not know about his fellow men. In many ways he's as innocent as Meg, she thought. But Alex was her son. She was fighting for his happiness.

'I always thought you had a brain! I believed I could rely on you to use it! If you marry Meg I shall know you canna see further than your nose end! You'll be just as vain and shallow as any senseless schoolboy!'

'Mother!' But Sarah turned away, unwilling to let him see how much it hurt her to say such things to him. She had done her best, even if it meant being cruel. Now she could only pray he would think carefully, but he was young and impulsive and he had far too much sense of duty where Meg was concerned. He was so clear-sighted about his business, yet he seemed so blind when it came to his own attributes.

Six

Unlike Alex, Billy had no thoughts of marriage, despite his popularity with the local girls. He was alternately filled with a sense of exhilaration at the changes which were taking place in the world at large, and swamped with frustration because he felt tied to Fairlyden and its unceasing demands. There was talk of constructing a tunnel underneath the English Channel, the Wright brothers had succeeded in flying their new airship, and even in the countryside change was coming in the form of a machine which could plough a field without ever seeing a horse.

'I believe we shall even have a machine to milk the cows one day,' he remarked one morning after breakfast.

Logan and Beth gaped at him across the table, caught each other's eye and burst into laughter.

'What's wrong with you two?'

'Oh, Billy, how could ye have a machine tae milk the cows?' Beth chortled.

'Ye'd need tae have a horse in the byre!' Logan gasped amidst his mirth, 'tae drive the machine.'

'Ach ye can laugh, the pair o' ye, but just wait and see!' Billy's dark eyes flashed indignantly. 'I dinna ken how a milking machine would work, but I'll find out some day! I dae ken there's a man at Castle Douglas who has made one and he uses four horns tae put on the cows' teats . . .'

'But how would horns squeeze the milk out?' Beth asked earnestly.

'Something sucks it out – like a calf I suppose . . .'

'Even if there are such things they would only add to the long list o' men and women who canna get work already!' Sarah interrupted. 'There'll be no such changes while I'm at Fairlyden.'

'Ye'll not be approving o' Mr Bradshaw buying a motor car then, Mother . . .?' Billy's tone was bland. He knew Crispin Bradshaw could do little wrong in his mother's eyes.

'Crispin? He's going to buy one o' those noisy machines . . .? I

41

dinna believe it!' Billy grinned triumphantly, his earlier irritation dispelled.

'He said a motor car would be more convenient for some o' his business. I hope he drives it up here, tae Scotland, when he comes back next week. He says there's ambulances driven by motors all over London town now, aye and some o' the streets are lit up by electricity . . . They say we'll soon be able to sit in a chair by our own fireside and listen tae a man in London reading a book. Ye wouldna disapprove o' that, would ye, Mother?'

'That's different. Crispin says we shall soon be able to hear the news on the very day it happens, without waiting for a newspaper. There is one change I'd like to see. I do believe it would be a good thing if women had the vote, and if the men who governed the country would listen to their ideas – at least on family life and health . . .'

'Aah, but not all women are as intelligent as you, Mama!' Billy's dark eyes glinted, reminding Sarah of his father.

She sighed. 'Ellen agrees with me, but I hope she never joins the suffragettes. I really do miss her. I'm looking forward to her next visit, but she works very long hours . . .'

'We miss Ellen too, Mama Fairly, don't we, Logie?' Beth's tone was unconsciously wistful. Ellen had often protected her from Sadie Fairly's spite.

'Aye. I wish she'd never gone tae be a nurse,' Logan agreed.

'She's doing what she wants tae dae with her ain life!' Billy's mouth had a bitter twist. Sarah glanced at him in concern. She sensed an increasing restlessness in him and it worried her.

'Maybe you would be more content if you had the love o' a good wife, Billy,' she said thoughtfully. 'And perhaps a son to work for, plan for . . .'

'I've nae intention o' marrying, Mother! Certainly I wadna bring any girl tae Fairlyden tae bide 'neath the same roof as Sadie!'

'Billy! This is Sadie's home – unless she marries. She's your own sister!'

'Aye, and there's times I'm so ashamed o' her I wish she wasna any kin tae me at all!' He snorted angrily. 'Her spiteful tongue wad never be silent with another woman in the house. She's bad enough with you, isn't she, young Beth?'

Beth didn't answer. She had seen how troubled Mama Fairly looked and she was far too sensitive to add to her worries with tales of Sadie's wickedness. Billy saw that his mother had lost some of her colour too. He knew how much she hated quarrels and Sadie certainly caused plenty.

'I'm sorry,' he said contritely. 'It isna just because o' Sadie that I dinna want a wife.' He grinned. 'I just havena seen any woman as good as ma ain mother!'

'Och, away with you!' Sarah retorted, but her eyes lightened and Billy was relieved to see the pink glow returning to her cheeks.

'I'm going home now, Logan,' Beth announced suddenly. 'Mrs Bunnerby showed me how tae make Yorkshire curd tarts and I've left the curds dripping frae a muslin. Are ye coming tae see if they're ready yet?'

Sarah watched with a smile as the two made their way along the passage to the yard, still chattering amiably.

'Beth's very capable for her age. Lassies seem to grow up quicker than laddies, and Beth's eager to learn so that she can look after her father. Nick thinks the world o' her . . .'

'Aye, but she and Logan are scarcely apart once they've finished their tasks and Sadie is jealous.'

'Their pleasures are harmless enough. If they're not fishing in the burn, they're paddling in it, or looking for birds' nests, or scratching themselves to bits pulling brambles! Aye, they're good company for each other. Sadie canna spoil that.'

'Weel, she tries hard enough! She's been worse since Beth got that music scholarship and started practising on our piano. I heard Sadie raging at her tae stop that noise when I passed the window the other day. How can she play a piano without making a noise!'

'I didna know . . .' Sarah said slowly. 'Maybe I was at the byre . . . I like to hear Beth playing myself. Since Crispin brought us the gramophone Beth has learned to play the tunes, and she can play most o' the hymns we sing at the kirk.'

'I like tae hear her play the piano, especially when she sings tae,' Billy agreed. 'She's quick tae learn. Did ye ever hear who gave the money for the scholarship, Mother?'

'Er, no.' Sarah flushed slightly. It was true she had not actually heard who had financed the music scholarship, but she had a shrewd idea it was Crispin.

A fortnight later Sarah was alone in the dairy when Jim Braid put his head round the door and handed her two letters. One of them was a statement of the milk they had sold, telling her how much money she could expect to collect when she called at the agent's office. Normally she would have opened it eagerly – even anxiously – but she was surprised to recognise Ellen's firm neat handwriting on the other envelope for she was expecting her home the day after tomorrow.

The expectant light died from Sarah's face as she scanned the first few lines, but her own disappointment quickly turned to sympathy, and then to apprehension as she read on.

'Brad says his parents have lost all their life's savings on account of the misfortunes which have affected the American Stock market. The shock has caused Mr Leishman to suffer a heart attack and Brad fears he may not recover. He has managed to book a passage to America and he sails in four days' time. Dear Mama, please forgive me for spoiling our arrangements, but I have to see Brad, just once more, before he leaves our shores. I know my conduct would be frowned upon if anyone were to know I have travelled to Edinburgh just to be with him, but I could not lie to you. I love Brad, and I know now that he loves me. He has been saving money for some time, hoping that we might be married when I have finished my training. Now most of his savings are needed to pay for his passage back to America, but he must be with his parents at this time. No one knows what other troubles they may have to face if all their money has indeed been lost. Please trust me, Mama . . .'

'Oh, lassie, I trust you, I'd trust you with my life,' Sarah muttered, 'but you know so little of life's temptations, of being alone with the man you love, especially at such a time of stress.' Sarah clenched her fists unconsciously. 'It will be hard to part from each other . . . Oh God, please guide them.' Sarah whispered. 'They're human, and young and in love . . . Dinna let Ellen fall prey to the sins o' the flesh, dear Lord . . .'

Sarah uttered the prayer from the bottom of her heart for she understood the temptations that would lie before Ellen and Brad on the eve of parting, not knowing when they would meet again. Would Ellen think of her own father? William had never returned from his voyage across the ocean . . .

Suddenly another thought struck Sarah and her heart turned cold. She put her fist to her mouth and bit her knuckles. Supposing Brad wanted Ellen to go to America with him? Would

44

he have enough money for both of them? She hoped not, and then felt guilty for her selfishness.

Sarah read Ellen's letter once more, then screwed it into a tight ball and shoved it into her apron pocket. Later she would burn it in the kitchen fire. It was better that no one should know Ellen had gone to Brad.

As Sarah had expected, Logan and Beth were as disappointed as herself that Ellen was not coming home as they had expected. They had looked forward to showing off their secret haunts and sharing their childish treasures, and above all watching her marvel at the way Peggotty had grown. She'll be a fine mother when she's blessed with bairns of her own, Sarah thought, then hurriedly, but not yet, dear God! Dinna bless her with a bairn until she has a legal wedded husband to love and cherish her!

Later that evening she put on a clean white pinafore and seated herself at the desk which her mother had used, and which had once belonged to the first Sarah Munro of Fairlyden, her own namesake.

'What are ye writing at this time of an evening, Mother?' Sadie asked with more truculence than interest.

'I'm writing a letter to the Mains. Ellen willna be home after all and your grandfather will be disappointed. He was looking forward to seeing her again. He'd intended to be here in time for dinner and . . .'

'Umph! Grandfather doesna come specially tae see me!' Sadie muttered petulantly. 'It's just like the prodigal son in the bible when Ellen comes home!' Sarah blinked.

'Do you want your grandfather to visit you then?'

'I dinna care,' Sadie shrugged. 'But I canna see why he makes such a fuss about Ellen coming home.'

'Your grandfather doesn't make a fuss! He just enjoys her company. You show little enough interest when he visits, running up to your room – using Meg as an excuse to leave your tasks. Even when Meg's not here you escape before the dishes are cleared frae the table if you get a chance! Dinna think I haven't noticed you running to the hayloft to read your novelettes! You're nineteen now; it's time you read the news sheets and knew what was going on in the world!'

'Why should I be interested in the world? It doesna matter tae me if the King wants tae visit his nephew in Germany or if they do away with the House o' Lords! As for the suffragettes that

Ellen admires sae much – I think they're crazy!'

'That's because you've no interest in anything except yourself!' Sarah retorted irritably. 'Maybe you'd have some conversation that would interest your grandfather if you broadened your outlook!' Sarah paused for breath, her chest heaving. Tension had been building up in her all day, ever since she received Ellen's letter. She knew she should not have lost her temper, but sometimes Sadie provoked her almost beyond endurance. She took a deep breath. 'Shall I tell your grandfather you want him to come then? Will you talk to him, and make him feel welcome in his old home?'

Sadie's pale eyes narrowed angrily. She hated family gatherings; they always made extra work.

'Dinna ask him tae come for me. I'm just a maid!' She tossed her head and snatched up a couple of soiled cloths and the folded apron Sarah had just discarded, whisking them away to the washtub with an air of martyrdom. Sarah gave an exasperated sigh, dipped her quill into the inkwell, and continued the letter to her father at Mains of Muir.

It was not until the following day when Sarah saw her apron flapping in the wind beside the rest of the washing that she remembered how she had screwed up Ellen's letter and put it in her pocket.

'Did you find a wee ball o' paper in my pinny pocket, Agnes?' she asked with a frown.

'No, I didna. Was it important?' Agnes asked curiously.

'No,' Sarah summoned a smile. 'Just a scrap I'd meant tae burn in case the ink ran and stained the rest o' the wash.' Agnes nodded, satisfied, but Sarah went across the grass in case the letter had fallen out. There was no sign of it. 'I must have burned it without thinking,' she decided.

Sadie had felt the ball of paper when she clenched her mother's soiled apron in her fists the previous evening. She had emptied the pocket automatically, tossing the twist of paper towards the fire, already set beneath the copper boiler in readiness for the morning's labours. It bounced off the drawing tin. Later Sadie picked it up as she passed but instead of putting it into the fire hole she smoothed it out. As she glanced down she recognised her sister's writing and began to read. Her eyes widened in amazement.

'So!' she whistled through her teeth. 'Our saintly Ellen's gone off to Edinburgh! Staying with Brad Leishman tae! Just like a bawd . . .' She read the rest of the letter carefully, hoarding its contents in her memory, to be recalled when it suited her purpose. 'No wonder dear Mama didna tell us the reason Ellen wasna coming home! I'll bet she didna write that in her letter to Grandfather!' she muttered, her pale eyes narrowing.

Seven

The day after she received Ellen's letter Sarah drove down to the village and pulled up outside the Muircumwell Store. Dinky was a quiet, patient animal and Sarah rarely bothered to hitch her to the tethering ring set in the wall, but today she hoped Janet might have time for a chat. She was afraid the pony might become restless, especially with the disturbance next door. The bangs and oaths might affect even Dinky's placid nature. Two men were emptying the house which had belonged to old Miss Millicent.

The earthy smell of vegetables mingled with paraffin as Sarah moved between sacks of potatoes and a box of carrots and a newly filled oil can waiting to be collected by a customer. The sturdy oak counter stretched nearly across the width of the shop and behind it small oak drawers with gleaming brass handles rose in a battery almost to the ceiling. Sarah knew they contained everything from buttons and threads, nails and screws, to herbs and spices. Her nose wrinkled with pleasure at the mingled scents of yeast and cheese, apples, bacon, biscuits and a thousand and one other odds and ends from candles and calico to sugar and flour, leather and knitting wools. Best of all was the smell of newly baked bread wafting through from the back premises.

'Good afternoon, Mistress Fairly.' Sarah turned at the sound of Anna Whiteley's cheerful voice as she emerged through the door behind the counter. Sarah had known all the Whiteleys since the day they were born in the cottage at Fairlyden. Anna was the youngest of the four and at twenty-seven she was a comely young woman with her warm smile and fresh clear skin; the thick, shining coil of her brown hair was pinned neatly beneath a white frilly cap and her snowy apron emphasised her slim waist.

'Hello, Anna!' Sarah's tone echoed her surprise and Anna Whiteley's smile widened.

'Ye'll be wondering what I'm doing in the shop at this time o'

49

day I suppose. I'm collecting some loaves for Mistress Lyle. She says she canna make bread as guid as Mother's so there's no point in wasting her time trying.' Anna grinned conspiratorially. 'Mind you, Master Lyle doesna ken his wife buys the bread!' Sarah returned Anna's infectious smile as the girl squeezed through the narrow flap at the side of the counter, carrying a basket containing four crusty loaves.

'It's a good thing ye've inherited your mother's trim figure!' she remarked.

'Aye, Mister Jardine doesna like anything tae be wasted, not even an inch or two o' space!' she agreed ruefully. Sarah grimaced. Ray Jardine was a couple of years older than herself and even as a boy he had been well known for his miserly nature. 'I'll just tell Mother ye're here, then I'll need tae hurry back tae the Hall.'

'Maybe I'd better not disturb your mother if she's still busy with the baking . . .'

'Och, it's Lizzie who's at the baking today. She's been at it a lot recently. Didn't Thomas pass on the news then? Mister Jardine has taken over Miss Millicent's next door. He's going tae knock a door through the wall so that Lizzie can make it intae a baker's shop with cakes and scones and pies, as well as Mother's bread. It was her ain idea, but Mister Jardine must think it'll make him some money or he wadna have agreed!'

'Mmm, well I hope he appreciates his good fortune. The shop is far better run than it used to be before your mother took over. I expect there'll be more trade when they build the new cottages next to the glebe, especially if we get more people like the Lyles.'

'Folks who earn their living in the town ye mean, and can afford tae spend money in the village? That's what Mother's hoping for . . . In fact she was intending tae call on ye at Fairlyden for a bit o' advice. She says ye understand all about business matters, Mistress Fairly.'

'I'm not so sure about that, Anna,' Sarah smiled, 'but it's a while since your mother and I had a chat.'

'Aye, Mother says Sadie usually brings the butter and collects the groceries these days. She'll be really pleased ye've come yourself. She's just finishing clearing up frae the midday meal. I'll give Lizzie your grocery list and ask her tae mind the counter, if ye'd care tae join Mother upstairs in our ain quarters? Mister Jardine's out delivering the orders and it's usually quiet for an hour or so in the early afternoon.'

'That would suit me fine, Anna,' Sarah smiled. 'Dinna let me delay you. I know my way.'

Ray Jardine had grudgingly allocated two small upstairs rooms to Janet and her two daughters when she had moved from Fairlyden cottage to the shop. Twenty years ago she had been a young widow in sore need of work and a roof. She had scrubbed and cleaned and turned the poky store rooms into a real home. Sarah never ceased to admire the atmosphere of cosy warmth and loving care, the gleaming blackleaded grate and the cheery fire, the mantel shelf with its clean cover and its photographs of Thomas, Maggie, Lizzie and Anna, as well as Janet and Louis on their wedding day. Now Maggie's two boys had been added to the picture gallery.

All traces of the recent midday meal had been cleared away and a green plush cloth covered the polished oak table in the centre of the room. Sarah remembered most of the pieces from the days when Janet and Louis Whiteley had first set up house together in the cottage her father had built specially for them at Fairlyden. Sarah had been just eight years old at the time but she clearly recalled how proudly Janet had cleaned and polished her little home, how neat she had been herself, how hard she had struggled with the unfamiliar work in the dairy.

More than that though, Janet had proved herself a loyal friend to the frightened insecure child Sarah had been at that particularly low point in her young life. Later, as Mistress of Fairlyden, she had done her best to repay Janet's friendship when her own plight had seemed so desperate. Fourteen-year-old Maggie was already engaged at Fairlyden as a nursemaid to Alex and Billy when Louis died from appendicitis. Although there were plenty of empty rooms above the shop, and despite Ray Jardine's need of a capable woman to care for himself and his ailing father, he had adamantly refused to take in a thirteen-year-old boy. Poor Thomas had been distraught, considering himself a terrible burden to his widowed mother and two young sisters, instead of their supporter. He was small for his age but Sarah had persuaded William to make a place for him at Fairlyden; it had remained his home ever since and he had proved himself more than worthy of his hire. Janet and her two remaining children had been free to take up Ray Jardine's grudging offer.

It had not taken him long to appreciate Janet's qualities, both

51

as a nurse to his elderly father and in his home and shop. Although she was a few years older than Jardine she was still an attractive woman and she had been widowed barely a year when he asked her to marry him in an effort to bind her to him permanently. As his wife he would have had no need to pay her wages for her work. Wisely, or so Sarah felt, Janet had refused his proposal and kept her freedom and self-respect, along with her meagre earnings. She had proved herself indispensable and Jardine had accepted her independence.

Occasionally Sarah and Janet still exchanged a smile over Ray Jardine's indignation at being rejected. Shared troubles had bridged the gulf between child and woman, as it had between maid and mistress. Now they were both mothers and widows with all the attendant responsibilities, and each had learned to value the friendship and frank opinions of the other.

'Och, it's grand tae see ye, Mistress Sarah!' Janet exclaimed with pleasure. 'I'll just shove the kettle on tae boil and we'll have a nice cup o' tea and a wee chat, if ye've time that is?'

'Of course I've time,' Sarah smiled. 'Indeed that's why I came, but dinna make tea specially for me.'

'Och I can drink a cup o' tea any time, especially when I'm needing a wee bit cheering up! I'm glad ye've called today . . .' Janet's smile faded and a worried frown creased her brow. She looked suddenly older than her fifty-eight years despite her trim figure. Her hair was snowy white now and there were lines around her eyes as though she screwed them up often, as indeed she did when pouring over Jardine's account books, trying to decipher his spidery figures. Sarah waited, setting aside her own anxiety over Ellen. It had been her intention to confide in Janet, who had known Ellen since she was born. Now she sensed Janet had worries of her own.

'Are you needing cheering then? Anna said you wanted to see me?'

'Aye, weel I did want some advice for Lizzie tae . . .' Janet frowned. 'Ray Jardine has bought Miss Millicent's wee place next door. Lizzie thinks we could open a baker's shop and maybe keep more o' our customers frae shopping in the town on market days. But I've had another idea tae. I wondered, dae ye think anybody would come, Mistress Sarah, if we opened a wee tearoom?' she asked diffidently.

'A tearoom!' Sarah echoed in astonishment. 'A tearoom in

Muircumwell . . .' She digested the idea with some excitement. 'Why, Janet, I think that would be a splendid idea!' Sarah's anxiety for Ellen was temporarily forgotten in her enthusiasm for Janet's plan. 'I canna think why no one thought o' that before!'

'Ye really think some folk would use it then?' Janet asked, her cheeks pink with pleasure.

'Well, I certainly would for one!' Sarah declared firmly.

'You, Mistress Sarah!'

'It would be an ideal place to meet Beatrice and have a chat and a cup o' tea if we arranged to come for our shopping on the same day. We only see each other on special occasions now and you know how much we used to talk! It's an eight-mile drive between the Mains and Fairlyden, but it would only be half that for each of us if we could meet in your tearoom. I'm sure there must be other folks would do the same. Indeed I'm sure some auld bodies would be glad to rest and have a cup o' tea when they walk in for their shopping frae some o' the farm cottages, if they can afford it that is . . .'

'Oh, we'll try tae keep the prices as low as we can. I'd have tae convince Mr Jardine o' that!' Janet added darkly. 'Lizzie's a good baker. We thought we would have gingerbread and treacle scones, and drop scones. Of course there'd be tattie scones and oatcakes, as well as bread and butter and jam. Maybe we could bake apple pies and rhubarb pies when the fruits are in season . . .? We'd need good clean milk that didna sour in the summer. D'ye think Thomas could bring us a wee can in the trap each morning when he comes down tae the station with the rest o' the Fairlyden milk? Thomas showed me the new cooler last time I was up at Fairlyden.' She gave a sudden mischievous smile. 'D'ye mind the trouble we had afore I learned about scalding the straining cloths and things, when I first went tae Fairlyden frae the Manse? Och, I was no more than a lassie, for all I'd married Louis . . . The milk went sour and the butter went bad and old Mister Jardine refused tae take it!'

'You look years younger when you smile like that, Janet! Anna's just like you!'

'Aah . . . Anna!' Sarah was dismayed to see the reminiscent smile die from Janet's face. It was replaced by an expression of such deep sadness that Sarah felt distressed by the change.

'What's the matter, Janet? Surely there's nothing wrong with Anna? Why, she looked positively blooming when I saw her earlier – so happy, and pretty . . .'

'Aye.' Janet sighed. 'She is happy. She's in love. She – she wants tae get married.'

'Well, surely that pleases you!' Sarah exclaimed. 'You've always loved bairns and you keep lamenting that Maggie is the only one who has given you any grandchildren. Wouldn't it be nice to have babies in the family again, now that Maggie and Ewan's two boys are growing up? My father says it was the best thing Alex ever did – hiring Ewan and Maggie to work at the Mains when they got married. He says the boys are real wee horsemen already for all they're only eight and six . . .' Sarah knew she was chattering, trying to banish Janet's sombre expression, but the prospect of more grandchildren seemed to make her more tense than ever. Her face crumpled as though she might burst into tears.

'Janet! What is it? What's wrong?' Sarah set her empty cup down and clasped Janet's trembling fingers. Suddenly she knew that it was some problem connected with Anna that Janet had really wanted to discuss. The tearoom had just been a topic of conversation, at least in part. 'Who does Anna want to marry?' she asked softly.

'Jamie MacFarlane.'

'Ja . . .' Sarah's mouth formed a silent 'O'. Too late she realised that Janet's eyes had been fixed watchfully on her face.

'Aye,' she said heavily. 'I can see ye've heard . . . No, no . . .' she held up a hand. 'Dinna deny it, Mistress Sarah. We've aye been honest with each other, and that's what I need now – an honest opinion.'

'Does Anna know . . .? I mean does she realise . . .?'

'There's none sae blind as a woman in love. I've tried tae tell Anna how it will be for her if she marries Jamie, but it'll be an even worse heartbreak if he leaves her with bairns tae bring up. The laddie works sae hard, but he has a struggle tae make ends meet on that wee farm o' his. It's a hard, bleak place . . .' Janet shuddered. 'But I canna bring myself tae put her against Jamie. He's such a lovely laddie ye see. I could fair take him tae my heart . . . It's a wicked shame!'

'Aye . . .' Sarah looked troubled. 'Tuberculosis seems to strike without rhyme or reason for all that German scientist says it's

54

caused by a germ,' she murmured awkwardly, unable to offer any real comfort.

'I havena heard Jamie cough much mind you – except last winter when he was really bad. But he nursed his mother himself and she died o' the coughing disease. I read in the paper that some doctors think it comes frae drinking milk. Did ye ever hear anything sae daft! The MacFarlanes have aye had their ain cow; they drink their milk while it's fresh! They're not like the folks in the towns! Then there's all this talk about getting fresh air tae cure the disease! Ye canna get it any fresher than the top o' yon hill.' Janet sighed heavily.

'It must be hard for Jamie, working the farm on his own and nobody to keep house even . . .' Sarah ventured uncertainly.

'Aye, that's what Anna says. She thinks Jamie will be all right once they're married and she's there tae make him good hot meals after his day's work, and see that he changes intae dry clothes when he's been out on the hill after his sheep. But I wish that was all he needed tae make him well! Jamie's such a kind laddie!' she added brokenly. 'Ye couldna wish for a better. But he has that delicate look about him . . . I never think it's a good sign when a man has patches o' bright colour on his cheekbones, not when ye can almost see through the rest o' his skin . . . D'ye ken what I mean, Mistress Sarah . . .?'

'Yes . . .' Sarah nodded unhappily.

'There's another problem tae . . . with Jardine . . .'

'What sort of problem?'

'He says if Anna keeps on seeing Jamie she canna bide here . . .'

'But that's ridiculous! Ray Jardine isna Anna's father! It's a good job you never married him, Janet.'

'He'd have treated me like a door mat if I'd had his ring on ma finger. But this is his house . . . He's afraid Anna might bring the coughing disease here. He's feart he might get it himself.'

'Aah, I see.'

'He's made Anna more determined tae marry Jamie now that she canna invite him here for a good meal once in a while. Jardine's furious! "Ye needna come back here whining when ye're a widow!" he told her. "And ye'll get no help frae me if he leaves ye with brats tae keep. These sickly men can aye get brats!" '

'What did Anna say?'

'Och, she just gave him that calm bright smile o' hers. Then she said, ever so softly, not nasty ye ken . . . "I love him, Mr Jardine, but that's not something ye can understand I fear." '

'No,' Sarah grimaced. 'Anna's right there. Even so, I'm afraid he could be right for once . . . I don't know what to say, Janet, or how to help you.'

'Ye canna help really, Mistress Sarah,' Janet smiled wanly, 'but I kenned ye'd understand, and I just needed tae talk tae ye about it. She keeps quoting that man Tennyson who wrote poems and things.

> ' ""Tis better to have loved and lost
> Than never to have loved at all."

'Ye'll ken the words maybe?'

'Yes, I know the lines, and maybe there's some truth in them . . .'

'Aye, none o' us ken what's round the corner – even if we marry strong healthy men like my Louis was . . . In my heart I ken Anna will do all she can for Jamie, and take her ain chance o' happiness. I suppose I shall have tae accept it.'

'I'm truly sorry I canna help . . .' Sarah murmured. 'We can only pray that Jamie's health will improve with Anna's love and care . . .'

Eight

Janet and Lizzie had worked hard to get the new bakery shop and tearoom ready, hoping that Mr Jardine would relent and allow them to hold a small wedding party for Anna, but he had remained adamant.

'Everybody kens Mistress MacFarlane died o' the coughing disease,' he hissed at Janet. 'I'll no' have folks saying there's disease in my premises. I've said it afore, and I say it again, that son o' hers has it tae. Dinna bring him near my house!'

'It'll have tae be just one or two o' our closest friends then, in our ain rooms . . .'

'No!' Jardine exclaimed fanatically. 'I'll no' have Jamie MacFarlane in my house!'

Sarah was indignant when she heard.

'After all you've done for him!' she muttered, 'And I can guess he pays you as little as possible for doing it! I know Anna has worked many an hour for nothing too, when she's not working for the Lyles up at the Hall.'

'It isna just money this time though,' Janet explained in a low voice. 'Ye'd think puir Jamie had the plague and that he'd leave it behind in every room! Mister Jardine has refused tae let him and Anna visit me once they're married. He says he doesna want them near his premises.'

'But he canna do that! Half the customers who come into the shop could have tuberculosis for all he knows!'

'Weel, there's nought I can dae tae make Anna a real, happy wedding day, but I've made it plain that if they canna visit me, then I shall go up tae Highmuir tae visit them every Sunday,' Janet declared, compressing her lips to stop them trembling. 'He's no' very pleased about it, but he'll not get any other body tae dae the work Lizzie and me dae, not for the money he pays!'

Sarah nodded, but her brown eyes had narrowed thoughtfully.

'Well, I think we can manage without Ray Jardine,' she declared, thrusting out a defiant chin. 'I'll help you, Janet, and

57

we'll give Anna and Jamie a day they'll remember for ever! What would you say to having a wedding meal up at Fairlyden after they've been to the Kirk . . .?'

'Och, Mistress Sarah!' Janet's voice was gruff, and her eyes were suspiciously bright. 'D'ye really mean that?'

'Of course I mean it. I'll bring down the pony and trap, and maybe we could borrow another trap too . . . We could hire a bicycle or two . . . Och, we'll get everybody up to Fairlyden, just you wait and see. The Reverend Morrison will come to bless the meal and I'm sure he'd drive his own trap and bring a few passengers. We'll have a real celebration and we'll show Ray Jardine that he's a mean, fussy old hypocrite!'

'My, Mistress Sarah, ye're a bonnie woman still, when ye get in a temper! Your eyes fair sparkle!' Janet announced with relish. 'But ye're far too generous.'

'No, I'm not. Anna and Jamie deserve a happy wedding day at least,' she declared huskily. 'Anyway, Anna was born at Fairlyden so there's no reason why she shouldna celebrate her wedding there too. D'you mind if I invite my father? He was very fond o' Louis, and all your bairns, Janet.'

'Mind! I'd be proud if Master Logan came, and so would Anna. He was aye very good tae Louis and me . . . Maybe Mistress O'Connor would like tae come tae? And Alex and Meg?'

'I'll ask them!' Sarah smiled merrily. 'You know, I'm almost glad Ray Jardine wadna have the wedding at his own house.'

Ray Jardine was exceedingly disgruntled when he saw all the wedding gifts, and he was even more put out when he heard the plans for the wedding meal.

'Of course ye'll not be wanting tae come,' Janet said dryly, 'in case ye catch any disease.'

People were wondering why the wedding reception was not to be held in the new tearoom and Ray Jardine realised too late that he had missed an ideal opportunity to show off his new premises. Consequently he vented his anger on Sarah the next time she came to the village to order new hats and gloves for herself and Sadie at Miss Harrison's, the local milliner.

'Ye'll regret this, Mistress Fairly!' he boomed, bustling across the street to waylay her.

'What are you havering about, Ray Jardine?' Sarah demanded, irritated by his manner.

'Ye'll regret encouraging that lassie tae marry a dying man!

There's nought but misery ahead for her, you mark my words!'

'I didna encourage Anna to marry anyone,' Sarah said quietly, gritting her teeth in an effort not to lose her temper with the pompous little man. 'And you shouldna say such things about Jamie. We are all in God's hands. He might decide to take you first if He considers you're growing too fond o' hoarding your money!'

Ray Jardine paled visibly. 'I – You – I'll . . .' he stuttered incoherently.

'Och, for goodness'sake! You were aye a squeamish coward when we were at the school!' Sarah snapped impatiently. 'Mean with it, too! If you'd give a bit more attention to making other folks happy you wadna have so much time to worry about your own ailments!' Sarah knew this to be true. She had not worried half so much about Ellen going to Edinburgh to see Brad since she had been so busy thinking of Anna's wedding.

'Ye're making a big mistake!' Jardine growled angrily.

'I'm trying to give a courageous young woman and a hard working young man the happy wedding day they deserve!' Sarah corrected frostily. 'And if you'd had any human kindness in your miserly heart, you'd have been pleased to provide everything for them yourself, now that they've made up their minds to wed and take what little happiness life might offer them. If we were all as cautious as you the world would come to an end! Anna has lived under your roof for twenty years and I know she's done many a day's work for you, even knowing there'd be nothing for her at the end of it!' Ray Jardine flushed angrily, but he could not deny Sarah's accusation and she was enjoying his discomfiture.

'The whole parish will likely know what a mean, ungrateful wretch you are! At least they will unless you buy a better wedding present than anybody else,' she added suddenly enjoying the encounter. 'Iain McKie has a fine wee cart in his carpenter's shop, just ready for painting. That, and the Frasers' pony, would just suit Anna and Jamie fine.'

Ray Jardine choked and blustered until Sarah cut him short impatiently. 'I've a lot to do so I'll bid you good day!' She flounced away but as soon as Ray Jardine was out of hearing she chuckled aloud. She had longed to give him a piece of her mind for some time; the meeting had given her a great deal of satisfaction, but most of all she hoped he would be shamed into buying the pretty little cart instead of the miserly gift he would almost certainly have offered if he had been left to his own devices.

Anna and Jamie were married in the Muircumwell Kirk. It was a quiet ceremony for Jamie had no close relatives of his own, but half the parish seemed to be waiting to wish them well.

Far more people accompanied them to Fairlyden than either Sarah or Janet had anticipated but so many brought gifts of food as well as presents for the young couple that there was almost an excess. The Reverend Morrison clearly thought so too as he offered thanks to God for His bounty.

'This happy day reminds me of the parable of the five barley loaves and two small fishes,' he remarked afterwards to Sarah and Janet. 'If we had had five thousand to feed I am sure the good people of Muircumwell would have provided a feast for them all!'

Even the weather obliged with a beautiful day and the younger guests spread themselves around the garden under the apple trees in the orchard, and generally made themselves at home, leaving the formality of Sarah's front parlour to the older guests. It was here that Sandy Logan seated himself comfortably and filled his pipe and reflected on the scenes Fairlyden had witnessed.

Thomas, who had been delegated to give away his youngest sister during the marriage ceremony, looked stiff and uncomfortably nervous in his best Sunday suit and his high starched collar, but when Meg entertained everyone with an impromptu dance on the strip of grass in the small front garden he relaxed with everyone else. After that Beth sang a new song called 'If those lips could only speak', which she had learned from Crispin Bradshaw's latest gramophone record.

'Isn't Anna beautiful, Mama Fairly,' Beth sighed ecstatically at the sight of the bride, in her flowing dress of oyster satin. Sarah nodded but the lump in her throat kept her silent, and there were unashamed tears in Janet's eyes. Anna had never been a startlingly beautiful girl but the love shining in her grey eyes seemed to add an inner radiance and there was an expression of such tranquil happiness on her face that it seemed impossible that anything could shatter it. As for Jamie MacFarlane, his whole manner was one of pride and tenderness towards the girl who had consented to be his bride. There was a sensitivity in his thin face which would have made it difficult for all but the hardest heart to resist.

60

'You must have worked very hard, Sarah, but you have given them a memory they will cherish forever, if I am not mistaken.' Sarah turned at the sound of Crispin Bradshaw's voice. It seemed unusually deep and husky and she guessed he was as moved by the happiness of the young couple as she was herself. She had been watching them circulating amongst their guests, spreading their own serenity and joy wherever they paused to speak. Now she looked up at Crispin.

'I didna think you would manage to come.'

'I promised, and I always keep my word. Besides I would not have missed this for the world. They look so happy. They will remember this day for the rest of their lives, thanks to you, Sarah. Will you come with me? I would like you to see the wedding gift I have brought, before I let Anna and Jamie see it.' He frowned uncertainly. 'I thought it was an excellent idea at the time, but now I'm wondering if it will be suitable . . .'

'Oh, Crispin, I'm sure Anna will be grateful, whatever you have brought.'

'Mmm, well we'll see. You had better prepare yourself for another surprise too, Sarah. According to Billy, you'll certainly disapprove of it!' There was a glint of humour which made his grey eyes sparkle with green and gold flecks, exactly like Logan's. He took her elbow in a firm clasp and guided her away from the house, round the corner and into the farm yard.

'Oh, my goodness me!' Sarah stopped short. 'A motor car! Crispin, whatever made you buy one o' those noisy machines?' She moved closer to him, almost afraid that the four-wheeled shining monster might explode, or run over her.

'It is not so very noisy,' Crispin grinned almost boyishly. 'I hope I can persuade you to take a drive with me. Indeed I shall need your guidance to help me find Jamie's farm so that I may deliver my gift.'

'Whatever is it? And what is that great hump in the back of your machine, under that blanket?'

'That is my gift. Come closer and have a look. It is called a chicken brooder. It can rear thrice as many chickens as a broody hen . . .'

'Oh my! I've never seen one, but I've heard o' such things.' Sarah cautiously edged closer to the car and its bulky load. 'Indeed I'm thinking of taking Sadie with me to learn more about the new ways of keeping poultry when the travelling instructress comes round to the villages next winter. She's frae the agricultural college. She knows everything about poultry, so they say. I'd like to see this new brooder so that I'll know what she's talking about.'

'Do you think Anna will use it?' he asked anxiously as he lifted a corner of the blanket which he had draped over the metal pyramid in the back of his car. Sarah cocked her head on one side, and then the other, trying to decide how the strange contraption could possibly sit on three dozen fluffy chicks without squashing them. Where would they feed? How would they keep warm? She frowned.

'I'll lift it on to the ground,' Crispin volunteered, 'and if you consider it unsuitable for Anna and Jamie I will buy them another gift, so I want your honest opinion, Sarah . . .'

'When did I ever give you anything else?'

Crispin paused and his eyes held hers steadily. 'Just once, I think . . .'

'But I always . . .' Sarah broke off, remembering the one time she had been unable to give Crispin a truly honest answer. The ready colour rushed to her cheeks. 'Oh Crispin . . .' she muttered huskily. 'You promised . . .'

'I know. It was just seeing Anna and Jamie so happily married you know . . .' Sarah felt as though he had tugged at her heart strings. 'Don't look so troubled, Sarah my dear. At least I know you do not love any other man enough to marry him. I have reached the conclusion that Fairlyden is your first love. Am I right?'

'You've been so good to me, Crispin, to all of us . . . Sometimes . . . sometimes, like now, I regret that I didna marry you . . . No, no, hear me out,' she added hastily as Crispin opened his mouth. 'I know what you were going to say and maybe we could marry, but it's just the occasion, and the purity of the love between Anna and Jamie, that is making both of us emotional. Soon you'll be going back to Yorkshire. I canna leave Fairlyden, Crispin . . . It's the only home I know. I belong here. Logan loves it too,' she added softly, willing him to understand.

'Yes, I know. And I suppose I can scarcely ask you to give up your own way of life, and your home, when I am unwilling to change my own.'

'The suffragettes would love you for your views.' Sarah gave him a warm smile and squeezed his arm affectionately.

'It is not the suffragettes I want to love me, as you well know!'

He quirked a quizzical eyebrow at her, but he patted the back of her hand reassuringly. 'At least we have remained good friends. Now . . . to business . . .' He began to demonstrate the metal pyramid. 'The oil lamp sits in the middle there and the chickens gather round it for warmth, instead of under the hen. I suppose the light attracts them to it . . .' Sarah bent and examined the brooder curiously.

'It has little curtains all the way round!'

'They keep the heat in. When the chickens get bigger they can have a small wire run round about the brooder and they go out for their food and water, but they can get through the curtains back to the warmth and light when they want to rest . . .'

'Just like gathering under the hen . . .' Sarah mused.

'You buy chickens from farms with flocks which have been tested for their good health – instead of hatching them with broody hens.'

'I've read about them!' Sarah exclaimed. ' "Accredited" they call them?'

'That's right.' Crispin looked relieved. 'So is it a suitable gift . . .?'

Sarah's expression sobered. 'Aren't they very expensive to buy, these chickens from tested hens? I mean . . .' she frowned uncertainly. 'The truth is I dinna think Anna and Jamie will have any money to spare to buy chickens. Highmuir is such a bleak wee place for making a living for all Jamie works so hard . . .'

'Aah, but I have ordered three dozen chickens to be delivered once I know you approve of the brooder. Is it a good idea, or should I exchange it for a butter churn?'

'Oh no, dinna change it! Anna and Jamie will be thrilled, I'm certain, especially when the chicks arrive as well! You're very generous, Crispin.'

'Then I shall deliver the brooder to Highmuir as soon as you have time to show me the way.'

'In – in that monster!'

'It's quite harmless, I assure you, but you will need to tie a veil around your hat to prevent it from blowing away!'

'I think you'd better ask Billy to show you the way to Highmuir . . .' Sarah declared doubtfully.

'Billy can have a ride – even drive the car himself, but I want you to be my very first passenger, Sarah.' He smiled and Sarah

63

knew she had to overcome her fear. In her heart she knew Crispin would never let her come to any harm. She felt almost as young and happy as Anna.

'I will come with you tomorrow afternoon,' she promised gaily and was rewarded by a grin which was a replica of her youngest son's.

Nine

Sarah clung to the leather seat in terror the first time Crispin swung the handle to start the engine of his car. She was convinced it would run away with her before he had time to climb aboard. Beth looked on with concern, but Billy and Logan were grinning widely at their mother's fearful expression. Once they had driven down the track and over the bridge, however, Sarah began to get the feel of the motor car and she felt like a queen when the village folk came running out of their doors to wave. Crispin gave a distinctive toot-toot on the hooter as they approached Jardine's Store, bringing Janet and Lizzie and their three customers rushing to the door.

It seemed no time at all before they were chugging up the hill to Jamie MacFarlane's little farm, but Sarah grew alarmed when she saw the cloud of black smoke belching out behind as the road got steeper. She tugged Crispin's arm and pointed behind.

'It's on fire!' she yelled in his ear. Crispin peered round and almost drove the front wheels into the hedge. Sarah squealed in alarm and clung to his arm, unwittingly adding to his difficulty in correcting the car's course. When they were in the middle of the road again he grinned at her like a schoolboy.

'We're not on fire. It's just the hill that makes it smoke.' He looked down at Sarah's arm still locked around his own and his grin widened. 'But I like the effect it has on you, Mistress Fairly,' he shouted above the noise of the engine and Sarah followed his glance to their linked arms and blushed furiously. For the rest of the drive she sat in her seat and folded her hands demurely in her lap, but her eyes were bright with happiness.

Anna came running out to greet them as soon as she heard the noise and a few minutes later Jamie came from one of the sheds where he had been loading manure on to a cart. He had to hold the horse's head to calm it until Crispin drew the car to a halt and stopped the noisy engine.

'Ye'll take a cup o' tea, Mistress Fairly, Mr Bradshaw?' Anna asked shyly. 'Ye're our very first guests and we've sae many lovely things that I'm dying for somebody tae see them all.'

Sarah smiled at her pink cheeks and the way her eyes were drawn to Jamie's face. 'Have you a minute tae join us, Jamie?' she asked. He hesitated, glancing back at the half-filled cart. Anna gave him a pleading glance. He smiled then and nodded.

'Just give me time tae wash at the pump. I daresay I'll work better after sampling one o' Anna's scones. The smell o' them has been tantalising me for the last hour.' He smiled at his bride of less than twenty-four hours and Sarah found herself uttering a fervent prayer that God would be merciful and grant him good health to enjoy his life with Anna, and strength to manage all the work a small farm like Highmuir demanded of its tenant.

Sarah was surprised when Crispin steered the car into the left fork away from Muircumwell, at the bottom of the hill after they left Highmuir.

'This is not the way home,' she shouted over the chug-chug of the engine.

'I know. We're taking a detour. I have brought a picnic hamper. Mrs Bunnerby made it specially so we shall have to eat some of it.' He grinned boyishly and the years seemed to fall away from him. Sarah felt herself responding to his infectious gaiety. Crispin would be fifty-four soon, six years older than herself, but recently he had looked older and she suspected his nephew and brother-in-law were at the root of his troubles. Occasionally he told her something of his problems when his relatives insisted on demanding money to spend on excessive pleasures, especially when the woollen trade was in a slump.

Today they were both away from their responsibilities and Sarah felt ridiculously light-hearted and free. It was a long time since she had had a whole afternoon with nothing to do but enjoy herself. She glanced at Crispin's profile but before she could study him he turned his head towards her and smiled. It was as though a ray of sunshine had reached out, enveloping them both in its warmth.

When they passed through a hamlet the women and children came out to see the motor car and waved excitedly as they passed. Even the men in the fields paused in their rhythmic hoeing of the turnips or scything the first swaths of the hay. Sarah had to admit she was enjoying herself.

Presently Crispin found a sheltered spot in the lee of a small wood and drew the car to a halt. He helped Sarah down and handed her a rug to spread on the soft turf while he lifted a large wicker hamper from the back of the car.

'My word!' Sarah exclaimed. 'Mrs Bunnerby has certainly packed plenty of food. We shall never eat all this after feasting on Anna's scones.'

'I know,' Crispin smiled, 'but it would have been churlish to refuse Anna's hospitality.'

'Yes, she seemed so pleased to entertain us for a little while and to show us some of her new wedding gifts. She's very like her mother . . . Come on now and load your plate, Crispin. Mrs Bunnerby is a wonderful cook and I think she has excelled herself today, but I shall be as fat as the pigs in the sty if I eat much more!' Crispin eyed her still trim figure, bringing extra colour to her flushed cheeks.

'I don't think you'll ever get fat, lass.' His eyes twinkled as he assumed his native broad Yorkshire accent. He bit into a chicken pasty with relish. 'My father certainly knew what he was about when he persuaded Mother Bunnerby to be his housekeeper. Not that she can cook any better than you . . .' he added quickly and Sarah gave a splutter of laughter.

'I wouldna be offended if you compared me a wee bit unfavourably with Mrs Bunnerby, Crispin. She really is a wonderful cook. I think I must ask her for her recipe for meat pasties . . . Beth and Logan sample them frequently on their way home frae school and they never fail to tell me how good they are. This veal galantine is delicious. Will you try a wee bit?'

'Yes please.' Crispin held out his plate. 'I sometimes wonder how much longer Mrs Bunnerby will manage to keep house for me at Fairlyside. Her age is a well-guarded secret, but she must be in her sixties . . .'

'I suppose so, but she is as spry as ever and she never grumbles.'

'Speaking of being ageless, Sarah . . .' Crispin looked at her thoughtfully over his glass of rhubarb wine. 'I often thought that description fitted both yourself and Agnes Jamieson, but Agnes did not seem quite herself at the wedding yesterday . . .?'

'No-o,' Sarah said slowly. 'She hasna been herself recently. She seems to get quite exhausted. I tried to persuade her to see Doctor Kerr, or at least ask him for a tonic, but she wouldna hear tell o' that. She's a wee bit wary about doctors, even though she's never needed one herself, as far as I know.'

'Yes . . . I suppose Agnes is shy . . .' he suggested with the sensitivity which never failed to surprise Sarah.

'Yes, she is and she has no one of her own to confide in. She would never admit she couldna do her work. She's always been too conscientious. Nick's the only relation she has left now – and Beth of course. I intended to mention some of her complaints to Ellen but . . .'

'But Ellen has her own problems just now,' Crispin suggested gently.

'Mmm,' Sarah admitted reluctantly, 'but how did you know?'

'It's only natural that Ellen should be upset when Doctor Leishman has gone half-way across the world. After all, they've corresponded with each other a long time – since Ellen was eleven. They must have explored each other's minds and hearts pretty well, even before they began to meet again.'

'Imagine you remembering how long they have corresponded with each other!'

'I'm not likely to forget Brad first came to Fairlyden when Logan was born. I shall always be grateful to him. For that reason, if no other, I wish him well in his own life and it does not take a magician with a crystal ball to see that he loves Ellen. They are so ideally matched too, the same strength of character and sincerity, as well as their mutual interest in caring for the sick. You did say he had arrived safely?'

'Oh yes. He wrote to Ellen as soon as he could. Poor Brad. His father died only days before his ship docked. It was delayed almost two days on account of fog, otherwise he might have been in time. Now there's no telling when he will be able to return. He canna leave his mother. His parents lost almost all their savings. In her last letter Ellen said it has taken their remaining money to pay the physician. Mrs Leishman needs Brad so badly. He's her only son. Anyway he will have to save up enough money for his return passage – if he does return . . .' Sarah added almost under her breath.

'I'm sure Ellen will understand his predicament, but I'm convinced Brad will find a way for them to be together, eventually.'

'Eventually . . .' Sarah repeated dully.

'I'm sure Ellen will wait, however long it takes. At least she has her nursing . . . or is there something else troubling you, Sarah?' Crispin lifted her hand, stilling her restlessly curling fingers. 'Remember – a trouble shared is a trouble halved. You can trust me, surely . . .?'

'Oh, Crispin, you're a good friend – and more . . .' Sarah whispered huskily. 'I don't know what I'd have done without you over the years . . . You've always been there when I most needed you. I am worried about Ellen though. You see . . . she went to Edinburgh to say goodbye to Brad. She spent two whole days with him before he sailed.'

'I see. And you are concerned for her reputation? Times are changing, Sarah. Many young ladies have great adventures alone these days. Think of the suffragettes. Many of them are gentlewomen, yet several have spent time in prison!'

'Maybe,' Sarah agreed, 'but most folks around here scarcely know what suffragettes are. The modern world hasna reached Muircumwell yet and there'd be plenty ready to brand Ellen as a – a wicked woman if they knew she had gone all the way to Edinburgh to stay with Brad . . .'

'Do you know she actually stayed with Brad?'

'She hasn't been home again since and she didn't say much about her visit to Edinburgh in her letters.'

'Surely you are pleased they saw each other before Brad left? Time is so precious when they are to be separated for many months, maybe years, and by miles of ocean . . .' Crispin's eyes held a faraway look for a moment and Sarah sensed that he was not thinking only of Ellen and Brad. His next words confirmed her thoughts. 'You will never know how hard it was for me to leave you, Sarah, and sail away to Australia. If I had known you were expecting my child no power on earth would have made me go, even though you were still the wife of William Fairly . . .'

'Oh, Crispin, hush!' Sarah's cheeks flamed and then swiftly paled. 'We did not resist temptation. That is why I understand how hard it would be for Ellen and Brad.'

'We must not judge them. Our circumstances were very different. You almost died that night!' He shuddered, remembering. 'Instead you were alive – and beautiful and in my home! All my iron control vanished at the sight of you. May God forgive me!'

'Don't say that, and dinna blame yourself alone, Crispin,' Sarah murmured.

'Brad Leishman is a true Christian, as well as a doctor. I'm sure he would consider Ellen above everything.'

'I'm glad I told you. Whatever happens now, I feel better,' Sarah declared firmly. She began to scramble to her feet, but Crispin was still holding her hand in both of his and he did not release it.

'I'm glad y'confided in me, lass, but y' should know by now that t'Bradshaws allus take their reward!' He was speaking deliberately in his broadest Yorkshire dialect, his eyes twinkling. Sarah knew he was going to steal a kiss. She blushed as rosily as a schoolgirl, but she offered no resistance. Indeed in her heart she admitted that she enjoyed the strength of a man's arms around her again, and the sensations that his lips aroused as they touched her own, gently at first, then with an irresistible ardour. Sarah found her heart beating a wild tattoo by the time Crispin raised his head and she could do nothing to hide the passion in her bright brown eyes.

'Aah, Sarah, my love!' Crispin breathed the words softly against her cheek. 'If I'd any sense I should forget the Bradshaw Trust – and my father's wishes, and marry you right now . . .'

'Wh-what do you mean?'

'My father's last request was that I should oversee his beloved mill, keep it going, protect his workers from Fanny's grasping husband . . .'

'Oh, Crispin, you could never give up the mill to settle up here . . .?'

'Couldn't I?' The expression in his grey-green eyes sent a thrill of excitement through Sarah, but she had always admired Crispin's strong sense of duty, his responsibility towards those less fortunate than himself.

'The mill, and its people, have been your life's work as much as your father's. He told me so. You couldna live with yourself, Crispin, if you knew they were being neglected. You would never forgive me for keeping you from them . . . Anyway we're too old for this sort of thing,' she added unconvincingly.

'We're never too old for love,' Crispin declared emphatically. He sighed and brushed his lips lightly across her own before he drew away. 'But you are right, as always, my dear. It would break my father's heart to think all his efforts had been in vain. I had expected the time would come when Robert would take care of his inheritance, but unfortunately my nephew seems little better than his father.' Sarah detected an unfamiliar bitterness in Crispin's tone and her heart went out to him. This time it was her turn to comfort and she took his hand and clasped it to her breast.

'I've enjoyed our afternoon together, Crispin, even the ride in that monster of a machine.' She smiled. 'Now that you have it, maybe we shall be able to have other outings together – just the two of us . . .' Her colour rose as she uttered the last few words and she lowered her thick, dark lashes until they swept her cheeks and hid her eyes. Even now that she was a mature woman Sarah was still modest; she hated to be considered forward. Crispin understood exactly how she felt and he put a gentle finger under her chin and raised her face to his.

'I love you, Sarah Fairly.' His voice was deep and husky. 'Don't you ever forget that. As to another drive in my motor car, how about a visit to Mains of Muir tomorrow? After that I'm afraid you are right, I must attend to the mill and its problems, but I shall take the memory of these precious hours with me . . .'

Ten

It was not until the early summer of nineteen hundred and eight that Agnes Jamieson finally admitted to being ill. Beth, ever sensitive to suffering, was deeply troubled. She loved her aunt and she tried to help her in every way she could, but as the months passed she felt a cold creeping fear. Young though she was she knew her beloved aunt was going to die. Sarah also watched helplessly and with a troubled heart. It hurt her to see Agnes dragging one foot after the other in her determination not to give in, or neglect the tasks she considered hers.

'Doctor Kerr would give you something to ease the pain, Agnes,' she ventured persuasively; they were alone for a brief spell in the kitchen. Sadie was collecting the eggs, Logan and Beth had not yet returned from school and the men were finishing the last of the turnip hoeing. Agnes sat in the wooden chair beside the fire, her arms wrapped around her body as though she was cold. She barely seemed aware that she was rocking back and forth. 'I'll pay the doctor's fees if that's what's worrying you.' Sarah's voice was gentle.

'No, Mistress Sarah,' Agnes shook her grey head slowly. 'I thank ye kindly, but there's nought anybody can dae for me now, not on this earth anyway . . .' Even her voice sounded weak and weary.

'Oh, Agnes,' Sarah's voice was husky. She had known Agnes since the day she started school. There was seven years between them and Agnes had shown her where to dry her coat and boots one very wet morning. Sarah had never forgotten that, nor the other small kindnesses the three young Jamiesons had shown her in those days of lonely misery.

'It's just that I've had a bad day,' Agnes sighed. Sarah knew it must be the understatement of the year, but she would go along with it if it made Agnes happy.

'Aye, maybe you'll feel a lot better tomorrow.'

'Aye.' Agnes hesitated, then she went on in a rush. 'I'm not worried about money ye ken, Mistress Sarah. I've enough tae pay the doctor if I really need him. I've enough put by for ma funeral, ye ken. It's in a wee wooden box under ma bed . . .'

'Och, Agnes,' Sarah swallowed the lump in her throat with an effort. 'There's no need tae worry about such things. Anyway,' she made an effort to sound cheerful and brisk and bright, 'now that we've got a new Prime Minister the government intends tae provide for everybody in their old age.'

'Aye,' Agnes said dryly, but her eyes were closed and she continued her constant rocking to and fro as though it eased her pain. 'Mr Asquith has some wonderful ideas, aye and that Mr Lloyd George, but I dinna suppose they'll carry 'em oot.'

'They intend to introduce a pension of five shillings a week for everybody over seventy, seven and six for married couples . . .'

Her voice trailed to a halt. Agnes would never see seventy, nor even sixty, and they both knew it, so what was the use of pretending. Agnes was silent for several minutes as though gathering strength, or perhaps choosing her words. Her eyes remained closed. Sarah lifted the last of the scones from the girdle and covered them with a cloth. She swung the swey away from the fire. At length Agnes spoke in a low voice, 'Ye'll tell Nick I'd like tae be buried next tae ma mother and father, Mistress Sarah . . .'

'Yes, dinna fret.' She moved to the chair and took Agnes's wasted hands in her own, holding them as though she would transfer her own strength along the knotted blue veins which stood out so prominently since the flesh had fallen away from the maid's broad, once sturdy frame. Agnes stirred restlessly. 'Is there – is there anything else you would like me to do for you, Agnes?'

'Ye've aye been good tae Beth. I ken ye'll keep an eye on her . . .?'

'Of course I shall. We all love Beth . . .'

'Weel, most folks dae,' Agnes agreed. 'But there's aye some tae take a spite. Life can be hard, ye ken, and she's nae mother o' her ain . . . There's many a thing a man wadna think o'. If there should be a shilling or twae left in ma wee box after – weel after I'm gone, ye'll see that Beth gets it?'

'I shall do exactly as you say, Agnes.' Sarah squeezed the thin hands gently and straightened up. 'Now we'll have a nice cup o' tea and a scone before the bairns come home. It'll be time to bring the cows in for milking in half an hour.'

Agnes's condition seemed improved during the next few days, much to Sarah's surprise and relief. Maybe their brief talk had set her mind at rest. But when Agnes asked if she could have the wooden armchair from the kitchen placed in her bedroom Sarah knew Agnes's new brightness was only a temporary veneer.

Two mornings later Agnes did not appear for the morning milking and Sarah crept up the wooden stairs which led directly from the kitchen to the maid's room above. She found Agnes slumped in her chair in her flannel nightgown with a blanket draped around her thin shoulders. Her mouth was open and she was snoring gently but her lined face was ravaged with pain and Sarah knew she must have spent a long pain-wracked night before she fell into an exhausted sleep sitting upright in the chair. She desperately needed the peace which only sleep, or death, could bring.

Ten minutes later the fire was burning brightly in the kitchen and the kettle was beginning to sing but there was still no sign of Sadie. Sarah ran briskly up to her daughter's room.

'This is the second time I've called you, Sadie! Agnes will not be at the milking. We'll both have extra cows to milk and Thomas must get to the station in time for the milk train!'

Sadie grunted and turned over.

'For goodness' sake, lassie! Dinna be lazy!' Sarah snapped impatiently. The next moment, to Sadie's astonished fury, she pulled the blankets from the bed. 'Dinna be more than five minutes before you're down the stairs and into the byre! I hear Logan stirring already. Maybe he'll milk a couple of Agnes's cows as well as his own two before he goes to school.'

Sadie glared mutinously at her mother, but she made no effort to uncurl her slim body in its voluminous flannel nightgown. Sarah strove to control her anger. 'We shall have to do a bit extra — all of us, so there's no good lying there sulking. You know you should have been dressed at least a quarter of an hour ago. Agnes canna go on any longer. Surely you can see that!'

'See what?' Sadie muttered lazily.

'See that Agnes is dying.' Sarah wanted to shock her daughter into feeling something for the loyal maid who had helped to care for her since the day she was born. She felt tense enough without Sadie's provocation; she prayed fervently for the strength and calm she needed to help Agnes over this last great hurdle in her life.

'Why should I care? She's only a maid . . .' Sadie uncurled her slim body and stretched languidly, her pale eyes mocking.

Sarah's anger flared and boiled over. She grasped Sadie's shoulders and shook her until her teeth rattled. 'I said hurry, and that's exactly what I meant!' She turned and shut the door sharply behind her.

Back in the kitchen Sarah glanced longingly at the teapot waiting on the hob; normally she and Agnes had time for a quick cup before they started the milking but she felt she had wasted too much time already this morning. She hurried to the dairy to collect her piggin and milking stool before making her way swiftly to the byre.

Billy and Thomas were tying the cows by the neck chains into their respective wooden stalls. They had more cows than the number of stalls available but Sarah calculated it was more profitable to keep extra cows now they had a contract to sell the milk. Time was always short in the mornings. It was a four-mile drive to the railway station and the horse's speed was limited when the cart was full.

Sadie understood all this, and she knew how important it was not to rush the milking. The manager of the cooperative had expressed his satisfaction with the Fairlyden consignments and he had agreed to take more milk than the original contract had stated, but he would not, or could not, offer any more money per gallon, even though the milk was well above the new standards which the government had drawn up, and Fairlyden milk did not sour as quickly as that from some of the other producers either, despite the foul-smelling milk cans which the town dairies returned unrinsed each day.

Back at the house Sadie seethed with shock and anger at her mother's unexpected treatment.

'Pulling the clothes frae the bed as though I'm a wayward bairn!' she stormed silently. Revenge was the only thought in her head as she clattered down the stairs to the kitchen. The brown teapot was still on the hob, untouched. Sadie took time to pour herself a cup of tea. She hated milking and the longer she delayed the fewer cows she would milk. She set her empty cup down with a thump and glanced at the short flight of wooden steps to the maid's room.

'Why should I milk extra cows while she's sleeping up there?' she muttered resentfully. Seconds later she was at the top of the stairs, pushing open the door of Agnes's small sanctuary. Sadie's pale eyes narrowed as she stared disdainfully at the older woman's slack jaw and haggard face, at the sleeping cap perched askew over straggling wisps of long grey hair. She grasped Agnes's shoulder and shook her roughly, without a vestige of pity. Agnes's brief release from pain ended instantly. She whimpered in protest as consciousness returned; her heavy eyelids opened with an effort and she struggled to raise herself. Sadie's hard thin fingers tightened cruelly on the arm which had once been firmly plump. Now it was no more than a wrinkled pouch of skin covering the bones.

'What's wrong?' Agnes mumbled dully. 'Is't bedtime?'

'It's morning, ye auld fool!' Sadie hissed scornfully. 'Ye're late for the milking! Mother's raging in case Thomas misses the milk train.'

'Late!' Agnes Jamieson had never been late in her life. Her eyes widened fearfully. 'I-I'll be at the byre soon as I'm dressed . . .' she gasped breathlessly, but even as she moved pain deepened the creases which etched her face.

'Dinna be long!' Sadie commanded pitilessly. 'I'm not milking your cows while ye lie around up here pretending ye're dying!' Agnes's eyes focused slowly on Sadie's narrow features.

'Dying . . .' she whispered hoarsely.

When Agnes stumbled into the byre carrying her stool and piggin, Sarah gasped in surprise. 'Och, Agnes!' Her face was filled with tender compassion. 'I hoped you'd manage to sleep a wee while longer. You shouldna have come out this morning.' Agnes did not answer, but her eyes flickered strangely, fixed on some object over Sarah's shoulder. Sadie was milking her own cows further down the byre so she could not hear, but she gave a smirk of satisfaction.

When Thomas brings the milk churns frae the station I'll leave the wretched auld woman to wash them as well, she vowed silently, while Mother's away drinking tea with Aunt Beattie! Sadie resented Sarah and Beatrice's fortnightly meetings which had become a pleasant interlude for both of them since Lizzie Whiteley's tearoom opened.

'I think you should go back to bed and rest . . .' Sarah declared anxiously as Agnes tottered towards one of the cows she usually milked. 'I've already milked Buttercup and Silky and . . .'

'I'll manage.' Agnes set her mouth. 'Dinna ye fret, Mistress . . .' Sarah watched helplessly as she settled herself uneasily between two other cows further up the byre. It seemed Agnes would cling to her independence until it killed her, she thought sadly, but if she was determined to work at all perhaps it was better that she should be at the milking. Sarah had always found it a restful and satisfying task, and it could be oddly soothing. Agnes had always enjoyed milking too, when she was in good health, but then the early rising had never been a trouble to either of them as it was to Sadie.

'Mama, I've finished milking ma ain cows,' Logan came up the byre to where Sarah was standing. 'Shall I milk the last one o' Agnes's?'

'Aye, do that, laddie.' Sarah smiled down into his earnest grey eyes. 'Thank goodness you dinna grumble about the milking,' she added fervently.

'Och, I like milking, Mama. So does Beth. We'll both help ye until Agnes gets better again . . .'

'Oh, Logie . . .' Sarah muttered gruffly. How could she tell him that Agnes would never get better? 'Beth has enough to do while her Aunt Agnes is ill. She cleans her father's house and does the washing and ironing all by herself. She's a grand wee worker already, for all she's only ten years old . . . Now you help Agnes and I'll go and put on the porridge and set the breakfast out or everybody will be late this morning.'

After breakfast Agnes carried the dishes through to the scullery and began to wash them. Sarah brought in the potatoes and vegetables she intended to prepare for the evening meal. She liked to get everything organised early in the day.

'I'll be going into Muircumwell soon, Agnes. I would have sent Sadie instead but Beatrice will be waiting for me at Lizzie's tearoom. You rest in your room while I'm away. I'm sure you cannot have had much sleep last night.'

'Maybe I will,' Agnes agreed wearily. Her ready compliance told Sarah more plainly than words that the pain was really bad.

Some weeks ago she had mentioned her concern to Doctor Kerr and he had promised to give her something to bring a little relief when the time came. She resolved to call at his house without further delay. Her meetings with Beatrice at the tea-room would have to cease. Agnes needed her now.

Eleven

The moment Sarah set out for the village Sadie went to find Agnes and ordered her to scrub and scald the milk cans which Thomas had brought back from the station. Agnes gaped at her.

'I doot I'm past that, Miss Sadie,' she said wearily. 'Ye'll need tae dae your ain work today . . .'

'If I say it's your work, it is yours! And ye'll dae it!' Sadie's pale eyes gleamed like ice.

'My time's a' but o'er. There's nought ye can dae tae hurt me noo, lassie. I'm awa' tae ma . . .'

'Ye'll awa' tae the dairy and scrub the cans when I tell ye!' Sadie paused, her eyes narrowed. 'Or it'll be the worse for your brat o' a niece!' Sadie had aimed unerringly at Agnes's most vulnerable point. She went on with a sneer. 'Dinna forget she'll expect tae bide at Fairlyden a while, depending on oor charity! Or dae ye want tae take her tae the poorhoose wi' ye!'

Agnes's face blanched as she saw the malice in Sadie's sharp features. She was a disgrace to Fairlyden and to the good mother who had born her. 'Ye're as different frae your ain twin as night frae day,' Agnes muttered under her breath.

'What are ye mumbling about now, you stupid auld woman?' Sadie demanded angrily. 'Ye needna think ye'll tell Mother. I'm telling ye Beth Jamieson will be the one tae suffer if ye dae!'

'Nae wonder Katie was taken frae ye! Sae young she was, and pure as an angel. The devil aye looks after his ain and he spawned ye withoot a doot! But the guid Lord'll see ye pay some day . . .' Agnes's tone was defiant. 'Aye, He'll have His revenge . . .' she muttered as she tottered off into the dairy. Once inside her flash of strength ebbed and she had to lean against the wall for support.

Gradually Agnes summoned all her energy. She had no doubt Sadie would vent her evil spleen on the bairn unless she attempted to do the work. But the ten-gallon milk cans were heavy even when they were empty. It exhausted her just prising off the lids. The sour smell made her feel sick. Agnes knew she had not the strength to scrub the cans, or to lift the buckets of hot water from the boiler to scald them. Slowly, with many pauses, she rinsed each one with cold water from the tap, then she set them to drain, each paired with its own lid.

Sadie was not in the kitchen when Agnes went back into the house and for that small mercy she offered a silent prayer. She looked longingly at the kettle on the swey. She would have loved a cup of tea but she hadn't the strength left to make it. She turned to the short wooden steps which led to her room and crawled up them and on to her bed.

She was still there, dazed with pain and exhaustion, when Sarah returned. Gently she helped Agnes to undress and pulled the blankets over her, then she brought her the cup of tea she had craved for the last few hours.

'Take one o' these pills, Agnes, they'll help the pain.' Agnes Jamieson was too ill to question the source of the pills. She swallowed them meekly. In her heart she knew she would never descend to the Fairlyden kitchen again – not on her own two feet.

Two mornings later Thomas returned from the station, his face pale and anxious. He came straight to the kitchen door holding his cap in his hand, twisting it nervously.

'Whatever is wrong with you, Thomas?' Sarah looked up, her rolling pin poised in mid air.

'It's the milk, Mistress. Yesterday's churns have all been returned. Still full! Every one rejected!'

'Returned? Still full?' Sarah stared at Thomas as though he had gone crazy.

'The station master said the milk must have been sour by the time it arrived at the creamery,' Thomas mumbled unhappily. 'He says that's what the creamery managers dae tae other farmers when the milk isna good enough. I told him it never happens tae Fairlyden milk.'

'Indeed it does not!' Sarah declared indignantly. 'There must be some mistake!'

'I looked in all the cans afore I brought them back. They're set solid. Sour as can be . . .'

'Well, I suppose the milk is bound to be turning by now . . . but surely it can't be solid?'

"Tis, Mistress. Just like cheese.'

'I canna believe it!' Sarah's face was pale now. They could not afford to lose the payment for a whole day's milk, but neither could the creamery, she thought fairly. 'If all the milk was bad, both frae the morning and evening milkings, the churns must be at fault . . .' she said slowly.

'Aye,' Thomas mumbled and stared at the flagged floor. He looked more unhappy and uncomfortable than ever and Sarah regarded him shrewdly.

'Sadie,' she murmured to herself. 'I was away at the village longer than usual the day before yesterday . . . I had to call on Doctor Kerr . . . Sadie must have skimped the dairy work! Maybe she didna scald the cans . . . Yet there was plenty o' hot water. I filled and lit the boiler myself.' Aloud she concluded, 'It must have been Sadie's fault . . .'

'No, Mistress,' Thomas spoke reluctantly. He had no love for the sharp-tongued Sadie but he was a fair man and he could not stand aside and let her take the blame for a loss such as this. 'I dinna think it was Miss Sadie . . . She aye sets the cans upright, and leaves the lids piled on the stone table, all together. Agnes sets them tae drain and she puts each lid with its ain can, ready for the next milking. They were like that when I went tae set up the sieve and put the first can beneath the cooler . . .' Sarah looked at Thomas sharply, her thoughts running backwards.

'Agnes wasna well. I told her to rest in her room . . . She was still there when I came home frae meeting Mistress O'Connor . . . She was exhausted . . . barely conscious in fact . . .' She frowned in concentration. Her face grew grim. Thomas quailed in his boots. Mistress Fairly didn't often get angry . . . but she was fearsome when she did.

'I'm sure Agnes wouldna mean tae cause sae much bother . . .' he began tentatively.

'Och, Thomas . . .' Sarah's voice was almost a groan of anguish. 'This was not Agnes's fault . . .' She pursed her lips, biting back bitter condemnation of her own daughter.

'Empty the sour milk to the pigs please, Thomas, then set the cans in the dairy. Sadie will wash them.'

'Miss Sadie?' Thomas's eyes widened. 'They've a terrible smell . . .'

'I've no doubt they have,' Sarah said grimly. 'She will need to

83

kindle up the copper fire and refill the boiler.'

When Thomas had gone Sarah went in search of Sadie, her mouth tight with anger. Sadie was not cleaning the bedrooms, neither was she tidying Thomas's bothy. In fact it soon became apparent that Sadie was nowhere in the house, despite the amount of cleaning she still had to do. Sarah frowned and marched down the garden to the closet. The door was firmly shut and Sarah pushed it open without warning. Sadie was perched in a corner of the white scrubbed bench, her knees drawn up to her chin, totally engrossed in a novelette.

'Mother!' Her thin face coloured with guilt and anger. 'This is a private place! Ye've nae business . . .' In answer Sarah marched forward, grabbed the paper novel and tore it in two. Her mouth was clamped tight with suppressed anger.

'Ye've ruined it!' Sadie screamed indignantly. 'Ye've . . .'

'No! I've ruined *you*!' Without another word she grabbed Sadie's shoulder and hauled her to her feet and out of the little whitewashed building. 'I can scarcely believe one of my own flesh and blood would treat a dying woman as harshly as you must have treated Agnes Jamieson in my absence!' Sarah's voice was icy with contempt and anger. The words of denial died on Sadie's thin lips when she recognised the scorn in her mother's dark flashing eyes.

Sarah's fingers curled more tightly as she swung Sadie's face close to her own. 'Now listen to me, and listen well. You will buy no more magazines frae the Store until I give you permission, and no more ribbons either! We've lost the money for a whole day's milk on account of your laziness. From now on you will do your work thoroughly, and you will need to help me with Agnes's work as well. I . . .'

'Agnes's work!' Sadie interrupted indignantly.

'In the little time she has left to her, I mean to see she has whatever comforts she needs – be it night or day! So you . . .'

'Ye're going tae nurse her? Here?' Sadie's mouth set mutinously. 'I willna dae the work while ye run after a maid! She's Nick Jamieson's sister. Let him and that brat o' his look after her, if she canna go tae the workhouse!'

Sarah's face went white with anger and before she could help herself she slapped her younger daughter across her pale, spiteful face. 'I'm ashamed that I ever gave you life! May God forgive me!' Sadie clasped her hand to her burning cheek and looked back at her mother uncertainly, but it was beyond her to control her tongue.

'Why should I care? Agnes Jamieson means nothing tae me and . . .'

'Well she means a lot to me! She is under my roof and that is where she will stay!'

As the days went by Agnes's condition deteriorated and Sarah grew more strained and tired. As soon as she came home from school Beth ran to see her aunt, ever fearful that she might find the little room empty. Sometimes Agnes was too tired even to greet her, but Beth always returned again after she and Logan had helped with the milking. But Beth was troubled.

'Sadie says she's my aunt so I ought tae look after her,' she confided anxiously to Logan as they hurried home from school. 'I would look after her, if I could, but Papa says I canna miss the school. I baked her some o' her favourite biscuits yesterday, but she couldna eat them . . .'

'Dinna worry, Beth, Mama will look after Agnes. She willna let them take her away like Sadie said.'

Despite Logan's innocent reassurances Beth knew that his mama was very tired and much too busy.

'Papa's worried tae. He says your mama has too much work tae dae without nursing Aunt Agnes. He sits beside her every night after tea . . . I think dying is awful!'

Felicity Bell, the assistant teacher, had noticed Beth's subdued manner and unusual pallor and she knew something was seriously wrong when Beth had not done her piano practice two weeks in a row.

'Tell me what's troubling you, Beth? Maybe I can help . . .?' Her voice was kind and gentle and suddenly Beth burst into tears, but at length she told Miss Bell of her anxiety.

'Then we must say a prayer for your aunt, and for Mistress Fairly. God will find a way, my dear child.'

'D'ye really think He will? I say my prayers every night . . .'

'Then perhaps I should ask the Reverend Morrison to say a special prayer for you and your family. Would that comfort you?'

Beth nodded and dried her eyes. 'Th-thank-you, Miss Bell, and I will learn my piano pieces, I promise . . .'

Felicity Bell was genuinely concerned for her young pupil. She knew Beth was a practical, sensible child and not given to exaggeration. After some serious thought she made up her mind to call at the Manse. Nothing would have persuaded her to call upon the young Minister for herself, but Beth was one of her star pupils and she was deeply distressed.

Mark Morrison not only gave the matter of Agnes Jamieson a great deal of thought, he promised to find a solution. More than that, he insisted on escorting Felicity back to her lodgings before going on to have a word with Doctor Kerr. Having satisfied himself that Agnes Jamieson was indeed nearing the end of her life he paid a visit to Fairlyden the following morning.

'I'm sorry Beth has been so worried.' Sarah apologised wearily. 'She's a good bairn . . . does all she can to help. Mistress O'Connor, frae the Mains, would have come to help me with the nursing, but she is extra busy herself since Emma Braidwood was called away to nurse her own mother.'

Half an hour later the Minister was riding to the railway station. He caught the train to Dumfries by the skin of his teeth and arrived at the hospital, but he was forced to wait until his aunt, Miss Morrison, could be brought to him. When she came at last she was quite put out by his request that Nurse Ellen Fairly should be given leave to help her mother nurse a maidservant, however loyal. She shook her head indignantly so that her cap fluttered like a giant butterfly.

'But Mistress Fairly needs her daughter's help . . .'

'If I allow Nurse Fairly to go home at a moment's notice, all the nurses will be inventing ailing relatives whenever they want to visit someone. I cannot allow my patients to be neglected, not even for you, dear boy.'

'And I cannot allow one of my parishioners to work herself to death when the very person who could help her is here. I must see Ellen. The choice must be hers . . .'

Maud Morrison looked at her nephew with a glint of approval – not that she liked the idea of Ellen Fairly going home, but she did like the air of maturity which Mark had developed, and in her heart she knew he was right. Ellen Fairly was an excellent nurse already, but she was also a devoted daughter and she would never forgive anyone who forced her to neglect her own mother. She remembered the child too, Beth Jamieson, who had run to the Manse, her faith in Ellen implicit.

'We-ell, I suppose it could be arranged. Nurse Fairly has done several extra duties recently. Indeed she has been immersed in her work – almost as though she is using it to drown some private sorrow . . . Perhaps a short break would be good for her after all, but I must have time to rearrange my staff,' Miss Morrison declared stiffly.

Twelve

Sarah was amazed to see Ellen the following morning.

'Aah, lassie, ye're an answer to my prayers!' she declared fervently. Then to her dismay she felt tears spring to her eyes; she brushed them away hastily.

'Oh, Mama . . .!' Ellen's voice was husky with emotion. She flung her arms round Sarah as though she was still a little girl. She was deeply disturbed by her mother's white strained face and the dark shadows under her eyes. She was thinner too. Ellen was filled with remorse. She should have come home sooner. Instead she had taken on extra duties, willing herself to forget her parting with Brad, tiring herself with work in an effort to swamp her regrets. 'You have been doing too much, Mama! Ye look exhausted . . .'

'Och, it's just that Agnes had such a bad night last night, and Sadie . . .' Sarah grimaced. 'Even Beth does her best to help and she's only ten years old.'

'I know.' Ellen patted her mother's shoulder as though she was one of her young patients. 'It's hard enough to see folks suffer when they're strangers, but Brad agrees it is worse when ye've known someone most o' your life.'

'Brad? Is his mother well . . .?'

'Mrs Leishman is not in good health – though she ails mentally more than physically. Brad is working in a hospital near the new house he has managed to rent for them. But enough of my affairs.' She swung off her cape and smoothed the long blue dress. 'I will go up to see Agnes.'

When Beth arrived home after school that afternoon she was as delighted to see Ellen as Sarah had been. She flung herself into her arms.

'I ken God sent ye!'

'God?' Ellen was bemused by Beth's welcome and the relief in her wide blue eyes.

'Miss Bell kenned Papa and I couldna look after Aunt Agnes. I

89

told her Mama Fairly has too many things to do already and how tired she is. Miss Bell said I must pray and she would ask the Reverend Morrison tae say a special prayer as weel – and now ye're here and I ken everything will be all right.' She paused for breath.

'I see . . .' Ellen offered a silent prayer of her own. However things had come about she knew her mother needed her very badly indeed – and Agnes too if she was to die in the peace she deserved.

Often Agnes had not even enough strength to open her eyes, much less to talk, so Beth was surprised the day after Ellen's arrival when her aunt opened her eyes and smiled, almost as she used to do. She seemed more alert, and even pulled herself up a little on her pillows. Beth brightened.

'Bring that wee stool, lassie, and sit beside the bed a wee while, eh?'

'Yes, Aunt Agnes.' She complied eagerly and when Agnes stretched out her withered palm on the patchwork quilt Beth put her small hand into it at once and felt the feeble pressure of her aunt's fingers. Once they had been rough with work, now the skin was flaccid and wrinkled, the bones as brittle as a bird's.

'I've wanted tae talk tae ye for a while, lassie, but I've been that tired. I feel better today . . .'

'I'm glad, Aunty. Logan an' me . . . we kenned Ellen would help ye.'

'Aah, Logan . . .' Agnes nodded slowly. 'He's a good laddie. Kind eyes he has. 'Minds me o' Mr Bradshaw . . . same eyes . . . same smile . . .' She paused dreamily. 'But the pair o' ye willna be bairns much longer . . .' The creases in her papery brow deepened. 'There's things ye ought tae ken, Beth . . . and nae mother tae teach ye . . .' Agnes sighed heavily and her eyelids drooped.

Beth waited patiently, her blue eyes faintly puzzled. Presently Agnes continued, but it seemed a great effort for her tired mind.

'Mistress Fairly'll aye be a friend tae ye, lassie, if ye dae what's right like the Guid Book says. Ye must aye remember your place, but ye've nae cause tae be ashamed o' your roots, whatever Miss Sadie says . . .' She paused again. 'Did ye ken your Grandfather Jamieson and Mr Logan were good friends when they were young men? He's a fine man, Mr Logan . . . worked at the Mill then – a working man tae, same as ma father . . . He deserves his good fortune. He was a kind friend tae us when ma father was killed, and him sae young . . .' Beth listened with interest to her aunt's ramblings. She knew little about her ancestors, save that Grandfather Jamieson had been killed before her father was born. 'If ever ye're in trouble, Beth, promise ye'll go tae Mistress Fairly?'

Beth's eyes widened, there was a new urgency in Aunt Agnes's croaky voice now. 'Ye can trust her tae dae what's right, even though she is the Mistress o' Fairlyden and ye're a wee maid . . . Ye'll need a friend, I ken ye will!'

'Logan is my friend, Aunt Agnes . . .' Beth said in her clear soft voice. Her young face was puzzled.

'Aye . . . I reckon he may be more than a friend tae ye – sae long as the flower o' love doesna get eaten i' the bud . . .' Agnes muttered anxiously. She looked up, over Beth's shoulder. Suddenly her eyes filled with fear. Beth glanced behind, thinking someone must have entered the room without her hearing, but there was nothing except the sloping ceiling and the square of blue sky through the window which sprouted out of the roof. She looked again at her aunt's wrinkled face. Her eyes were fixed as though seeing some fearful apparition. 'Never trust her, Beth! Never! Never!'

'Hush, Auntie, dinna be feart! There's naebody there.' Beth murmured soothingly. Agnes's gaze came back to her niece's slight figure crouched on the low stool beside the bed; to the earnest young face framed by the honey-gold curls which danced like summer sunbeams when she ran; her blue eyes were wide and innocent, her nose so small and the rosy lips so wide, so generous, meant for laughter; yet Agnes trembled.

'Never trust Sadie Fairly!' Her voice was harsher, stronger. 'The strangers'll dae ye nae harm. She's the evil one! I beg ye . . .' She slumped back exhausted against the pillows, her eyes closed. Beth sat on, her hand still resting in her aunt's on the quilt, uncertain whether she should go or stay.

Presently Ellen came in and smiled at her, her dark eyes kind.

'I think ye should go out into the sunshine now, Beth. Logan's waiting to show ye a hedgehog he's found, and your father'll soon be finished his work.' Beth nodded and stood up. She bent and touched her soft lips to Agnes's papery cheek. The old woman opened her eyes and smiled at her.

'Goodbye, ma bairn.'

"Bye, Aunt Agnes. I'll see ye tomorrow . . .'

91

Beth turned to Ellen as soon as they had descended the short stairs from her aunt's room into the kitchen. Her blue eyes were grave and wise beyond her ten years.

'I'm glad ye're here, Ellen. Logan thinks ye'll make Aunt Agnes better, but I ken ye canna dae that . . .'

'No . . . I'm afraid ye're right, Beth.'

'But ye'll help her.' It was a simple statement. 'Sadie said she'd burn in the devil's fires, but I'm sure she'll go tae Heaven . . .' Ellen thought she detected just the faintest question in Beth's earnest tone and she felt a surge of anger at her insensitive sister.

'I know she will go to Heaven, Beth. Your Aunt Agnes has been a good woman all her life. She told me she was not at all afraid to meet her Maker, so you mustna be afraid for her either. Of course she doesna want tae leave you and your father . . .'

'Oh, I forgot tae tell her Mrs Bunnerby is teaching me tae make the Sunday dinners. I can make Yorkshire puddings now. I'll tell Aunt Agnes tomorrow, then she willna worry.'

There was no tomorrow for Agnes Jamieson. Early the following morning Sarah wrote a brief note and gave it to Thomas Whiteley as he was setting off for the station with the milk cart.

'Be sure to give this to the Mains' carter, Thomas, please? I've written to tell my father and Mistress O'Connor that Agnes has found peace at last. I will let them know about the funeral arrangements when Nick has seen the Reverend Morrison.'

Sarah was surprised to see Alex riding up the track before midday.

'We got your note, Mother.' He smiled gently, but his dark eyes were studying her face and she knew they missed nothing.

'I shall soon be myself again,' she said briskly, almost brusquely. 'I shall miss Agnes, but I canna grieve for her passing; her pain was terrible.'

'I understand, Mother. I just came to see how ye are, and if there's anything I can do?'

Sarah smiled. 'You can share a pot o' tea with me. Suddenly I feel as though I could drink the whole pot dry! We'll take it into the parlour. Nick said the Reverend Morrison would be visiting shortly to confirm the arrangements. I expect Ellen will join us in a wee while.'

'I didna ken ye were expecting Ellen!'

92

'I wasna expecting her . . .' she said slowly, 'but I was more relieved to see her than I can tell you. Yet we've had so little time to talk, and Ellen is so thin . . . Her cheeks seem quite hollow . . .' She could not voice her secret fears. She longed to talk, really talk to Ellen about her visit to Edinburgh.

'I suppose she's missing Brad. Is there any word of him returning?'

'None. He couldna leave his mother when she's newly widowed – and penniless too. Brad is all she has in the world . . .' He might never return, a small voice nagged insistently. A few minutes later Sadie ushered the Reverend Morrison in and brought a fresh pot of tea with cups and saucers for herself and the Minister.

'Where is Ellen?' Alex asked.

'She's packing her bag.'

'Packing . . .?' Sarah looked up startled.

'The Reverend Morrison says he is taking her to the station!' Sadie sniffed with disapproval.

'Actually that is why I am here, Mrs Fairly.' The young Minister threw Sarah an apologetic glance. 'I promised my aunt that your daughter would return to her work at the hospital as soon as she felt able to leave you. Miss Ellen sent a note with Nick Jamieson when he came to the Manse earlier this morning.'

'But surely she'll stay for the funeral . . .?' Sarah broke off. 'I never did ask Ellen how she came to be here, just when I needed her so badly . . . It seems a strange coincidence when I think of it. I fear my mind has been a little dull. Did you get special leave for Ellen then . . .?' She looked enquiringly at the young Minister. 'And how did you know I needed her so badly?'

'Beth Jamieson was very concerned because you had so much to do. It troubled her that she could not help you more when Miss Jamieson was so ill. Miss Bell told me and I was pleased to be able to help . . .'

'Then I thank you . . .' Sarah looked up to see Ellen standing beside her chair, carrying the long cloak which was part of her nurse's uniform.

'Ye'll have tae wait until the Reverend Morrison has drunk the tea I brought him!' Sadie objected.

'I'm sorry if I've put you to any trouble, Miss Fairly. Your sister has a train to catch . . .'

'Thomas could take her! There's nae need for ye tae rush

away . . .' Sadie suggested eagerly.

'I'm sure Thomas must be busy, especially with Nick Jamieson away at the registrar's and dealing with the joiner . . . Anyway Miss Ellen and I have an arrangement . . .'

'Ye have an arrangement!' Sadie's sharp features flushed. She felt the young Minister was rejecting her in favour of her sister – again! She glared at Ellen, still standing patiently by her mother's chair. 'How dare ye arrange engagements with the Minister as soon as your fine Doctor Leishman is out o' the way! I'll wager ye didna tell the Reverend Morrison ye rushed away tae Edinburgh tae keep an assignment with him tae!' Ellen stiffened. 'Did ye tell him ye spent two whole nights with your fine doctor afore he sailed awa'?'

Ellen gasped at the venom in Sadie's tone, but as she turned to look into her mother's face, her dark eyes filled with surprise and reproach. Sarah sat stunned, staring at Sadie, shaking her head in bewilderment. Mark Morrison wondered at the sudden tension.

'I didna ken ye'd managed tae see Brad before he sailed, Ellen,' Alex remarked with interest. 'That would give him a wee bit comfort then.'

'I'm sure it did, and it would have been churlish to refuse Sir Quentin and Lady Mossman's hospitality.' The Reverend Morrison looked puzzled by Sadie's attitude. 'Clearly they must have held Doctor Leishman in high regard to invite your sister to stay with them so that she might share his last days on Scottish soil.'

Ellen watched Sadie's narrow jaw fall.

'Sir Quentin and Lady Mossman!' she was exclaiming incredulously. 'There wasna any mention o' them in the letter . . .' She broke off and bit her lip. She saw her mother's eyes darken with contempt as she stared across the room.

'Ellen, there is some clean washing I forgot to give you . . .' Sarah rose abruptly. Ellen followed her from the room, but she knew there was no washing. They faced each other as soon as they were out of the others' hearing.

'I didna betray your confidence to Sadie, Ellen . . .'

'No. I think I can guess what happened . . . Oh, Mama, I should have come home for a proper visit before this. I know that now . . . but I was so miserable I couldna bear to think of my visit tae Edinburgh. But I should have told you how kind Lady Mossman was to me . . . I was dreadfully nervous when Brad

94

met me at the railway station and told me he had arranged for me to stay with Sir Quentin Mossman. He is one of the chief surgeons at the hospital where Brad worked. They have two adorable little daughters . . .' Ellen looked up and caught her mother's dazed stare. 'What's wrong, Mama . . .?'

'I er . . . I, nothing, at least, that is . . . I thought you were to stay at Brad's lodgings . . .'

'But he lodged at the hospital – in the rooms for single doctors. I thought ye knew that . . .?'

'No,' Sarah said faintly. 'Er . . . this Sir . . . was he . . .?'

'They were all wonderfully understanding and sympathetic, even the children. Lady Mossman was a nurse too. She has friends who are suffragettes . . .' Ellen's colour rose. 'She speaks her mind plainly. Brad – he wanted me to marry him . . .' Her voice choked.

'Och, lassie, I didna want to upset you, and you have to catch your train . . . but – but did you refuse him, Ellen? Is that why you have been so miserable?

'I didna refuse. He couldna book a passage for me. Lady Mossman reminded him that I should be left behind without a husband, and neither would I be able to continue my work as a nurse if I were married. I miss Brad, Mama . . . I miss him dreadfully . . .' Her cheeks coloured faintly; she could not confess to her own mother just how much her body ached for him, or how she regretted their restraint now that he had gone. 'But at least I have my work, and many of my patients do appreciate my efforts. I could not give it up now – except to be with Brad. Do you understand, Mama . . .? I love Fairlyden, and all of you here, but . . .'

'I understand, Ellen.' Sarah was smiling now. She felt as though a great weight had been lifted from her mind. 'And I'm grateful to this Lady Mossman for her guidance. It's easy to be impulsive when you're young and in love.'

'Aye, I suppose so.' Ellen sighed softly. 'But Brad seems so very far away now, and he has no idea when he will be able to return. He needs to earn money . . .'

They heard the parlour door open.

'We must be on our way if we are to be in time for the train . . .' the Minister called.

'How did the Reverend Morrison know about the Mossmans?' Sarah whispered hurriedly.

'I told him when he met me at the station, to bring me here . . .' Ellen whispered back. She had regretted confiding her troubles to the young Minister afterwards, but he had proved a sympathetic listener. He had remarked on her pallor and her loss of weight, and threatened to take his aunt to task for working her too hard. Now she was glad she had told him the real cause of her changed appearance, and of her visit to Edinburgh, otherwise Sadie would have given him entirely the wrong impression. 'I'm glad I came, Mama, even if ye hadna needed me tae help nurse Agnes. I feel happier now. I'm lucky tae have ye, and Fairlyden. I shall come again soon, I promise.'

Thirteen

Sarah knew it was silly to be sentimental but she had been unable to accept the idea of a strange maid taking over Agnes's room. She had put an advertisement in the paper for a local maid and settled for a girl named Moll Black who would cycle over to Fairlyden each morning from Strathtod village in time to help with the milking. Sadie was not at all pleased with this arrangement since it meant the girl would not be at their beck and call from dawn to dusk as Agnes had so often been.

'You didna appreciate Agnes when she was alive, so maybe now you will realise how fortunate we were to have her,' Sarah had declared.

'Fortunate! There wadna be half sae much work if we did less for Nick Jamieson and his brat!'

'We have been over that before. There will be no changes!'

So the weeks had passed into months and the arrangements with Nick and Beth had remained unchanged, at least on the surface. Only Beth was aware of Sadie's constant hints and jibes and she did her utmost to be as independent as her time and youthful abilities allowed. Mrs Bunnerby became an ever-ready adviser with her wealth of household knowledge and Beth was quick to learn.

'We're tae have a General Election in the New Year,' Billy announced one evening towards the end of nineteen hundred and nine. 'At least that should be the end o' all the wrangling over the "People" Budget.'

'Mmm, Mr Lloyd George will be disappointed that the House of Lords rejected it, I suppose, but it will not make much difference to anyone at Fairlyden. Anyway I've better news than that. Ellen hopes to be home for New Year's Day. I think I shall arrange a family gathering if the weather is reasonable. It would be a fine start tae another year.'

Sarah had resumed her fortnightly meetings with Beatrice in

the Muircumwell Tearooms and she discussed the arrangements for the New Year gathering the next time they met.

'I'm sure nothing will keep any of us away!' Beattie smiled.

'Will Richard be home?' Sarah asked and saw the shadows which temporarily darkened Beatrice's blue eyes.

'No. He rarely writes now that he is settled into a job in England, but he seems happy enough to be making his ain way in the world.'

Sarah nodded and tactfully changed the subject. Richard O'Connor had brought little comfort to his mother's life and she felt the Mains must be a happier place without his moody presence.

'I've asked Nick and Beth to join us for the New Year dinner but I expect Nick will go home for a wee nap afterwards. He works far too hard. Sometimes he looks very tired.'

'Mmm. I expect he misses Agnes, for all she didna live at the cottage. He seems to live for his work at Fairlyden – and Beth of course. Are Beth and Logan still as good company for each other?'

'Yes. Nick asked me to bring that new book called *Wind in the Willows*. He is giving it to Beth for Christmas. I expect Logan will read it too.'

'Och, they're a fine pair . . .' Beattie smiled. 'Aah, Janet! Come and join us for a cup of tea while the shop is quiet?'

Sarah looked up as Janet Whiteley approached their table but her own smile of welcome changed to a frown. 'You look tired, Janet – worried too . . . Is anything wrong?'

'Och, Mistress Sarah, ye were aye too observant! I was just coming to join ye both for a wee chat, and enquire for everybody's guid health.'

'Sarah's right though, Janet, ye do look tired . . .'

'We-ell, it's Anna . . .' Janet admitted reluctantly.

'Sit down and tell us,' Sarah said, drawing out a chair and pouring tea into a clean cup from the adjoining table. 'Is Anna ill?'

'No, she's well enough but she's expecting another bairn and the wee lassie hasna been sae grand. Maybe it's just teeth again but she's a delicate wee thing at the best o' times. Jamie hasna been in guid health either. He caught a chill working with the sheep . . .' Janet trailed off unhappily.

'That wouldna help his condition,' Sarah agreed with concern.

'Has Ray Jardine relented at all? Does he allow Anna and wee Daisy to visit you here?'

Janet shook her head. 'Sometimes I'm tempted just tae leave him tae his shop and go tae help Anna when she needs me sae badly but there's Lizzie tae consider tae. She enjoys baking and she's made this wee tearoom a real success, especially in the summer – not that Jardine gives her much praise, mind ye, but he's more generous tae her than he's ever been with Anna and me and I have tae think o' the future . . .' Janet broke off frowning. She swallowed hard. 'I-I mean what wad we dae, Mistress Sarah, if – if anything happens tae Jamie?'

Sarah bit her lip, at a loss for words. Jamie had seemed so much stronger and healthier after his marriage to Anna Whiteley, but the improvement had not lasted. 'Anna would be left wi' two bairns and there's not much money tae be made frae that wee farm o' theirs,' Janet went on anxiously. 'It's a hard place, thin soil, bleak tae; I'd need my ain work and the money Jardine pays . . .'

'Indeed ye would!' Beatrice agreed gently. 'Dinna dae anything hasty, Janet.'

Sarah nodded agreement. 'Maybe Thomas could spend New Year's Day with Anna now he's got a bicycle, if you're sure you and Lizzie canna go . . .? It wouldna please Ray Jardine if you left him on his own, I suppose?'

'No it wouldna!' Janet declared shortly, 'though it's what he deserves!' She sighed heavily. 'I expect we'd better stay and humour the auld scrooge, but I'm sure Anna and Jamie wad be pleased if Thomas could spend Ne'er Day with them. They were aye close, Thomas and Anna . . .'

Crispin Bradshaw wrote to say he would be spending New Year in Scotland. Sarah was secretly delighted; she chided herself for feeling like a love-sick young girl, but she lost no time in calling on Mrs Bunnerby.

'We would like you and Mr Bradshaw to spend the day with us, Mrs Bunnerby,' Sarah assured Crispin's homely little housekeeper.

'Well, I don't want t'be a bother t'you, Mrs Fairly, but I must say, it'd be grand t' spend t'day with a real family like yours, especially if Beth and Logan'll be there. They're a luvely pair.'

Sarah smiled. 'So that's settled then.'

'Ee, I'll really look for'ard t'it. You'll not mind if I make some uv me marzipan fruits and a little sugar mouse or two for't youngsters, will you, Mrs Fairly . . .?

'We should be very grateful, Mrs Bunnerby. I've heard Beth and Logan talking about the treats you make for them. I think you spoil those two!'

'On'y young once they are, and they're growing up fast!' Mrs Bunnerby nodded and her eyes twinkled happily. 'I'll allus be grateful t'you, Mrs Fairly, for persuading Mr Crispin t' build this 'ere 'ouse and 'im letting me stay up 'ere, 'stead uv sending me back t' Yorkshire. I know 'e likes t'come up and get awa frum t' factory for a bit. Does 'im good it does, this fresh air. I tell 'im 'e works too 'ard, but 'e don't listen t'me. Thinks t'world o' your little Logan, 'e does, and young Beth. She's coming on a treat with t'music lessons, 'e says. Mebbe she'll play some songs for us all?'

'I will ask her,' Sarah promised. 'I like to hear her play too. We'll see you both on Saturday then.'

'Ee aye. I'll look for'ard t' seeing nineteen 'undred an' ten after all. I was feeling a bit low, sitting 'ere thinking I'm gettin an old woman, but I've a lot t' be thankful for wi' such luvely neighbours as you an' your family, Mrs Fairly.'

That New Year's Day at Fairlyden proved a happy one. Later that evening Ellen looked with pride and affection at her mother's face, still flushed with pleasure.

'I expect ye're tired, Mother, though ye dinna look it!' She smiled as they sat in front of the fire for a companionable chat before lighting their candles to go up to bed.

'Tired?' Sarah sighed happily. 'Well, a wee bit, but I did enjoy having everybody gathered around my own table. But it's grand to have time for a proper talk with you, lassie, now the old house is at peace again. I'm glad you dinna need to leave until the morning train.'

Logan was already asleep and Sadie had gone to her room with one of the oil lamps instead of her usual candle.

'I expect Sadie is eager to read the magazine you brought for her. She's sparing with her thanks, I know, but she appreciates your thoughtfulness, especially since I refused to buy any more after the way she treated Agnes. I suppose I've punished her long enough. She certainly derives a lot of pleasure frae reading, but I think some of the stories warp her judgment of real life. She has no interest in any of the young men in the village . . .'

'Except the Reverend Morrison perhaps . . .?' Ellen smiled.

'Well . . . maybe, but she seems to want a golden Adonis – all blond curls and blue eyes and sweet smiles.'

'And blind tae all her faults, I suppose?' Ellen sighed softly. 'Life isna like that. Poor Sadie . . .'

'Mmm, well maybe she would give Beth more peace to practise on the piano if she had something to occupy her own leisure.'

Ellen nodded. 'Logan must have been extra tired when he went tae bed without being told.'

'He and Beth worked hard, helping to do everything that could be done before the New Year, and again this morning. Billy wasna so fit for work after spending Hogmanay first footing in the village and round about so he was glad of their help too. They're a grand pair.'

'Aye, I heard Alex remarking how well they had done. His praise brought a real glow tae their faces.'

'Mmm. Billy seemed eager to ride part of the way back with Alex after supper,' Sarah murmured with a glance at the clock on the wall. She was momentarily hyptonised by the brass pendulum swinging to and fro. She brought her gaze back to Ellen. 'I thought he would have been home by now. He must have found company in the village for I'm sure Alex wouldna linger on such a cold night.'

'Maybe Billy has gone intae the Crown and Thistle to drink to the adventures he hopes another year will bring. Or maybe,' she smiled merrily, 'he's drinking tae the health of the new serving maid . . .?'

'I wish he would marry a nice lassie and settle down as Master of Fairlyden. He and Rab Brydon's lassie were very friendly for a while, but Billy is so restless! He even gets impatient with Logan these days when the laddie doesna share his enthusiasm for his machines. Logan canna wait to leave school, but he wants to spend his time with the cows, and breeding horses and working with Nick and Thomas . . .'

'He'll be twelve this year. He's so strong and sturdy for all he isna very tall yet! It's funny really . . . Logan's not at all like Billy or Alex to look at, and yet . . .'

'Och, we'll not waste precious time talking about your brothers!'

Sarah said hastily. 'Tell me your own news, lassie? How's your work at the hospital?'

Ellen's pretty face always seemed serene, but Sarah glimpsed a pensive look in her soft brown eyes as she stared into the glowing heart of the fire. Her next words confirmed Sarah's intuition; it was not her work as a nurse which was uppermost in her mind as the new year stretched ahead.

'Sometimes I wonder if Brad will ever be free tae return tae Scotland,' she murmured almost under her breath.

'Is he . . .?' Sarah hesitated, reluctant to pry, yet sensing Ellen's desire to talk about the man who held her heart. 'Do you still love him, lassie, for all he's so far away?'

'I'll never love another man as I love Brad,' she said with conviction. 'I ken he loves me too, but he canna leave his mother. I wouldna love him so much if he was the kind o' man to neglect her in her time o' need. He thought he had persuaded her to come with him to Scotland as soon as he had saved enough for both their passages, but in his last letter she had changed her mind again. Still,' she summoned a smile, 'at least I have my work. I shall miss the bairnies terribly when Brad does come back to marry me.'

'Och, you'll have bairnies of your own to love and care for then!' Sarah smiled encouragingly. 'You're a good lassie, Ellen. I'm sure the Lord will bless you and Brad one day. I'd love to have a grandbairn or two . . .' She stared into the rosy embers behind the iron ribs. 'Alex would have made a fine husband and father . . . but he's so sensitive about his twisted feet, for all he's made such a success of his life in other ways.' All her mother's instinct told Sarah that Alex was not happy but she was powerless to help him. Ellen had always been close to Alex and she shared her mother's concern for his happiness but she changed the subject gently.

'How is Anna, and is Jamie MacFarlane keeping better?'

'No, he's not well at all. Poor Janet is so worried about them, though she dotes on wee Daisy. Anna is having another bairn come the summer. Despite their troubles Jamie and Anna are so happy it cheers a body just to see the pair of them together, at least it cheers everybody except Jardine; he's as miserly as ever. He refuses to have them in his house in case he catches some ailment. That's why Thomas went up to Highmuir. It's a wonder he isna back yet!'

'Mmm, Thomas never stayed out late, I remember. It's a long way for him to cycle frae Highmuir in the dark though. Some o' the hills are steep and I expect he'll be tired. If I ken Thomas he's sure tae have been working – helping Jamie with his sheep, no doubt.'

'He has had a sore throat again these past few days. Doctor Kerr once said he should have had his tonsils out as a boy, but Janet wouldna hear of it. I don't think he would have gone to Highmuir today if he hadna promised Anna. I suppose I just worry about him like I worry about Logan and Beth . . .'

'And Billy, and everyone else except yourself,' Ellen teased affectionately. 'What was Alex saying about building extra stalls in the byre? It would be easier for ye now that ye've more cows to milk than the byre can hold.'

'Och, Alex is young and full of bright ideas . . .'

'Alex thinks the world o' ye, Mother,' Ellen said softly. 'He only wants to make things easier, and he does have some good ideas. Grandfather says Captain Fothergill told him Alex uses his head and it more than makes up for his feet . . .'

'Aye, well he's certainly making a success with the horse breeding.' Sarah could not keep the pride out of her voice. 'That will have brought in extra money, I suppose . . . Alex is like you, Ellen, he's never been selfish; but I refuse to borrow money frae my own son. He has enough responsibilities . . .'

'Mr Bradshaw seemed tae think it was an excellent idea to extend the byre now that ye have a contract for the milk. He even offered to arrange it . . .' Ellen broke off at the sight of her mother's flushed face. She could not make up her mind whether it was a guilty flush or an embarrassed blush but unlike Sadie she was too tactful to pursue the matter. 'We all want whatever is easiest for ye,' she said gently. 'I'm sure ye must still miss Agnes.'

'Yes, I do, but everybody has to lend a hand in the byre now that we have more cows.'

'What about Moll Black? Is she a good riser in the mornings?'

'She's a good timekeeper – both ends o' the day!' Sarah grimaced wryly. 'She's a clean enough milker, but she's slow and she spends half of her time making sheep's eyes at Nick and smiling foolishly whenever he walks past to empty his pail . . .'

'Nick! Surely he's old enough tae be her father!'

'Aye, he is. He gets very irritated with her adoration at times.

103

If Moll doesna mend her ways I shall have to have a word with her. Even Logan and Beth have noticed. The other evening she was so busy watching Nick she was milking on to the floor instead of into the luggie!'

'Oh dear!' Ellen murmured but she could not suppress a chuckle.

'Nick doesna think it's funny! He must be all of fifty-four, I think . . .' Even so Sarah's own mouth quirked with humour at the sight of Ellen's merry brown eyes.

'The suffragettes say convicts and lunatics dinna have the vote and politicians link we women with them! Maybe they're right after all, at least in cases like Moll Black.'

Sarah stifled a yawn. 'Well, I haven't read so much about the suffragettes lately.' She stretched wearily and yawned again. 'We canna wait up any longer for Thomas to come home. It will be morning before we know where we are, and you've to catch the early train, Ellen my dear.'

'Och, I'll be up. Thomas will give me a lift in the milk cart when he goes to the station I suppose.'

'Aye, he'll be pleased to have your company. I'd meant to make him a hot drink to warm him up when he gets back, but he'll have to make do with the drink o' buttermilk I put out for him earlier.'

'It's certainly a cold night, but I expect the cycling will have kept him warm,' Ellen said practically, 'and it would only trouble Thomas if he thought he had kept ye frae your bed.'

'I expect you're right, lassie. I'll bring our candles frae the scullery. It's been a long day . . .'

Thomas Whiteley was in the byre, already holding his milking stool and piggin, when Sarah entered early the following morning, but he was leaning against one of the stalls and his back was turned towards her.

'Aah, good morning to you, Thomas. I'm relieved to see you're safely back. I thought . . .' Sarah's cheerful greeting trailed to a halt as Thomas slowly straightened and turned to face her. His face looked white and haggard and there were dark rings under his eyes as though he had not slept. 'You look awful, Thomas!'

'Ach, I'll be fine . . .' Thomas's voice was no more than a wheezy croak.

'Ye dinna look fine,' Billy remarked, coming to join them. He grinned. 'Indeed ye look more like ninety-six than thirty-six! Ye must have had a fine celebration tae welcome the new year!' Sarah frowned but Billy avoided her eye and went on in his jocular tone, 'Ye must have been late back last night, Thomas? Your bicycle wasna in the shed when I stabled Boyo.'

Thomas did not answer. He seemed to drag one foot after the other as he went to milk the first of his cows. Sarah watched him, then she turned to Billy and her voice was sharp with anxiety.

'He isna well but it wouldn't be drink that's responsible, I'm sure o' that!' Billy shrugged and turned away, unconvinced. He had spent a merry evening at the Crown and Thistle himself; he still felt elated and it was as much from the conversation as from the drink he had consumed. There had been several arguments about the growing strength of the German army and navy. He had been surprised by the views expressed so frankly by men whose tongues had been loosened with a drink or two. He wondered if it was true that the British army was short of horses because so many had been exported.

At breakfast time Thomas refused to eat anything; he seemed to have difficulty swallowing even a cup of tea. Ellen insisted on peering down his throat, despite his embarrassed protests.

'Your throat is infected and your tonsils are almost blocking it. It's a wonder ye can swallow at all, Thomas.' He responded to her kindly smile as all her patients did.

'It isna ma throat that's worrying me, Miss Ellen, but I hae the mother and father o' sore lugs!' He touched his left ear gingerly. 'I couldna sleep at all for it when I got tae bed. I suppose it didna help being out in yon cauld wind either!' He grimaced. 'I was helping Jamie bring his sheep doon frae the high ground and we got caught in a sleety shower.' He shivered at the memory. 'It's a cauld bleak place on yon high ground at Highmuir. Then tae make matters worse I took a wrong turn on the way hame in the dark and I ended up half-way tae Dumfries instead o' in Muircumwell.'

'Well, that certainly wouldna help,' Ellen agreed, but Sarah saw the concern in her daughter's dark eyes and she guessed that Thomas would probably feel even worse before he recovered. Typically his main concern was not for himself.

'I hope I havena left any troubles wi' Anna and Jamie.' He looked up at Ellen with a troubled frown. 'Jamie canna walk two paces up yon hill without stopping tae cough, and the wee lassie is a bit delicate tae . . .'

'Well, the main thing is to get you well again, Thomas,' Sarah said firmly. 'Billy will have to take the milk to the station this morning; you'll need to be quick too, lassie, if you are to catch the early train.'

'I'm almost ready,' Ellen announced. 'Miss Morrison would never forgive me if I missed the train.'

It was the first time in his life that Thomas had been forced to stay in bed and miss his work, but for several days he was too ill and in too much pain to realise where he was. Despite visits from Doctor Kerr, and the medicine he prescribed, Thomas could get no relief. Eventually his infected eardrum burst. Although it brought relief from the intense pain the poison pervaded his system, making him weak and listless, and he shivered as though he had an ague one minute and was burning hot the next.

As his strength returned, Thomas began to worry.

'Ye've aye been guid tae me, and to all ma family, Mistress Fairly. It vexes me sair tae be lying here idle and you running after me. There's Billy and Nick tae – doing all my work! All the turnips tae be chopped for the beasts and . . .'

'Dinna worry about the work, Thomas.' Sarah spoke loudly into his good ear. 'Doctor Kerr says you can take a walk in the fresh air each day if you wear your cap and keep warm. Beth will be pleased if you wear the muffler and gloves she knitted for you.'

Thomas's eyes softened. He was very fond of children for all he seemed to have no inclination to take a wife and start a family of his own.

'Have ye had any word o' Anna and Jamie and wee Daisy?' he asked anxiously on his third day out. He was finding it difficult to get used to being deaf and Sarah had noticed that it was making him irritable and moody. Everyone tried to speak more clearly but it was easy to forget; Sadie was particularly aggravating and Sarah suspected she mumbled deliberately.

'I've heard no news since Sadie collected the groceries frae your mother last week, Thomas.'

'No, ye canna hae had time, what wi' looking after me and extra kye tae milk . . .'

'The main thing is that you're almost better,' Sarah reassured him with a smile, but it was a forced smile. Earlier in the week she had written to Beatrice cancelling their usual meeting at the Muircumwell Tearoom until Thomas recovered. Beatrice had replied immediately to say she was also extra busy herself. Thomas's eldest sister, Maggie, had begged permission to go to Highmuir. Anna and Daisy were extremely ill but Ray Jardine had again threatened to put Janet and Lizzie out of his house if either of them went to Highmuir. He had become obsessive in his desire to avoid illness.

'I'm sure your mother will be relieved to see you when you feel up to visiting her, Thomas,' Sarah said now. In truth she was anxious for news. The little family at Highmuir had been much on her mind since she received Beatrice's news. If Thomas could be so ill, what would such an illness do to Jamie?

Thomas set off for the Muircumwell Store on his bicycle the following morning.

'I'll no' stay more than half an hour,' he announced, adding grimly, 'auld Jardine will see tae that! If he's at hame he'll no let me o'er the step! I'll be fit for the milking tonight if I can bike tae Muircumwell and back.'

'Well, dinna exhaust yourself, Thomas,' Sarah warned. 'You're scarcely ready for much exertion.'

It was a cold, bright January day with a gusting wind but Thomas was well wrapped up and looking forward to testing his strength, for he was anxious to get back to work again. Besides it gave him real pleasure to see the white clouds scudding across the sky and the grey hills rising in the distance. He had half believed he was already in hell when his illness was at its peak, when the fever had burned his body and the pain from his ear had hammered like a steel mallet until he wanted to scream. He grasped the high handlebars firmly and his back was straight as he pedalled steadily along the track to Muircumwell. He viewed even the commonest sights with new appreciation that winter's morning, though he welcomed the intermittent shelter of the sturdy trunks of the beech trees when the wind whistled through the leafless hedges.

Thomas had not returned by the time the light began to fade and the January day grew cold and sullen.

'I canna think why he's stayed away so long,' Sarah said

anxiously as Billy and Nick and Sadie gathered in the dairy to collect their pails for the milking.

'If he's fit enough tae gang gallivanting tae Muircumwell he should be here tae help with the milking,' Sadie muttered sulkily.

'Maybe he isna fit!' Sarah insisted. 'Maybe I shouldna have put the idea into his head, but I was worried about Jamie McFarlane – and Anna and the bairn of course. Janet would be pleased to see Thomas too . . .'

'Dinna worry, Mother. Thomas would have turned back if he wasna weel,' Billy declared reassuringly. 'Aah, here come Beth and Logan, galloping up the track like a pair o' young Arabian stallions!'

'Did you see . . .?'

'Here's a note for ye, Mama . . .' Logan panted breathlessly.

'Mistress Whiteley sent it,' Beth gasped. 'She said to hurry . . .' Beth stared at Sarah with wide anxious eyes and Sarah's heart sank. Beth was sensitive and intelligent. She had seen Janet; she would sense any trouble . . .

She broke the seal with trembling fingers as everyone gathered round her expectantly.

'Oh dear God, how could he . . .?' Sarah gasped aloud and the blood drained from her face. Billy put a comforting arm around her shoulders and began to read the brief missive himself.

Fourteen

Billy read the note a second time before he looked up. He saw the little circle of anxious faces.

'It's the bairn – Thomas's wee niece, Daisy. She – she died last night. Janet says Thomas blames himself because he went to Highmuir when he wasna weel . . .'

Sarah took the note from him and read Janet's words aloud.

'He is shaking like an aspen leaf. It must be the shock. I know I should get him into a warm bed but . . .' Sarah's tone grew bitter, ' . . . but Jardine refuses to let him bide under his roof. Please, can you help, Mistress Fairly? I am sorry to ask after all you have done . . .' Sarah broke off.

'Ray Jardine is a sinner and a hypocrite!' Her mouth was tight. She looked up. 'Billy, will you saddle the pony and trap and bring Thomas back to Fairlyden . . .?'

'But, Mother!' Sadie protested explosively. 'It isna our . . .'

Sarah quelled her daughter with a single glance which made even Sadie shrink. 'Fairlyden is Thomas's home – always has been, always will be!' she retorted. 'Billy, take a blanket. I expect Janet's right, and we dinna want Thomas to catch pneumonia. The sooner he's in bed the better.'

Billy nodded and set his milking pail aside. Sadie's pale eyes glittered resentfully. Nick bit his lip.

'Puir Thomas,' he murmured softly. 'Blaming himself for the bairn's death . . . I ken how he feels . . .'

'Wee Daisy has never been strong,' Sarah reminded him quietly. 'Now we'd better get to the milking. Sadie, tell Moll to leave the kitchen work and come to the byre now or she will be heading home across the glen before half the cows are milked.'

'I'll milk some o' Billy's cows,' Logan offered promptly.

'I'll help tae,' Beth offered simultaneously.

'You're good bairns.' Sarah summoned a smile. 'We'll be glad o' extra hands tonight.'

'Indeed we shall,' Nick agreed, glancing fondly down at Beth.

Thank God she has been spared, he thought fervently, remembering her long, difficult birth. Yet he often blamed himself for Sally's death. It had been her dearest wish to give him a child and she had paid a high price for it in the end.

Everyone was astonished when Thomas presented himself at the byre early the following morning. He looked haggard and ill but he collected his stool and piggin with grim determination.

'Are you sure you're well enough to be out, Thomas?' Sarah asked in consternation, staring at his pale drawn face and sunken eyes. She had to repeat the question close to his ear to avoid shouting and frightening the cows.

'I'm all right, thank ye,' he answered morosely. He scarcely spoke even when they all trooped in for breakfast. Billy insisted on taking the milk to the station, at least for a few more mornings, and Sarah saw the flash of gratitude in Thomas's grey eyes. She guessed it was more than grief which made him want to hide from the world. He was clearly uneasy in company on account of the deafness.

Until now Sarah had always thought of Thomas as scarcely more than the boy he had been when he first started work at Fairlyden; he had always looked young for his age, slim and sprightly.

Suddenly it struck her that he was already well on the way to being a middle-aged bachelor, spending the rest of his life in the bothy. She made a silent vow to bring a little more comfort to his solitary existence.

The kirkyard showed evidence of many infant deaths. This fact did not lessen the grief of little Daisy MacFarlane's relatives, but Janet accepted it with remarkable stoicism. Her chief concern was for the living – Thomas, her only son; Anna white-faced and stricken. But Anna and Jamie shared their loss and Anna's young body was quickening with another life. At the very least this would blunt the sharp edge of their sorrow. Thomas on the other hand stood alone and withdrawn.

Sarah shared Janet's concern at the change in him. He had lost weight during his illness and he seemed shrunken inside his best Sunday suit. He had grown a beard too and Sarah felt he wanted to hide away from the world behind it.

Even Janet found it difficult to offer words of comfort and

110

consolation when she had to raise her voice to make him hear. She was relieved when the Reverend Morrison took Thomas aside for a quiet word as the rest of the mourners were dispersing.

A week later Sarah went to the Muircumwell Store to collect the Fairlyden groceries. As she had hoped, the shop was quiet and she and Janet had an opportunity to talk.

'I'm pleased to see you are managing to accept Daisy's death so well, Janet,' she said gently.

'Aye, weel . . . There's nought else I can do and I ken the bairn would never have been strong . . .' Janet sighed heavily. 'She was such a bonnie wee thing though . . .'

'Sometimes it's hard to understand the will o' the Almighty,' Sarah remarked quietly.

'When the Reverend Morrison came I thought he was too young tae be a minister o' the kirk wi' a parish o' his ain,' Janet confessed. 'I dinna ken what he said tae Thomas, but he seemed tae bring my laddie some comfort. Of course there'll never be another minister like the Reverend Mackenzie,' she declared loyally. 'I never forget the days I spent at the Manse when I first went there as a young maid. I'm awfy pleased they're going to build a village hall in his memory.'

'Yes.' Sarah accepted the change to a more cheerful topic. 'The idea would have pleased Mr Mackenzie greatly. I knew he had left a small legacy to be used for the good of the community, but it was the Reverend Morrison's idea to use it to build a hall, I believe? He and Miss Bell, the school teacher, must have worked very hard to raise the extra money required.'

'Aye, she's a nice young lady, Miss Bell. She'll make a fine wife for the Manse tae if the rumours are true.'

'Aah, I see . . .' Sarah murmured. Now she knew why Sadie disliked the young school teacher; but Sadie was far too intolerant and impatient to be a minister's wife, she admitted honestly, even if the Reverend Morrison had shown any interest in her. Poor Sadie, would she ever find a husband to love her? Real men were never like the heroes in the novelettes she read. 'Beth thinks Miss Bell is wonderful,' she said aloud, 'and she has taught her to play the piano beautifully.'

'When the hall is built there's tae be a dedication ceremony,' Janet announced. 'It's tae be called the Mackenzie Memorial

Hall – or so Jardine says and he's on the kirk session.'

'Mmm, it sounds very appropriate – The Mackenzie Memorial Hall.' Sarah nodded approval as she picked up her basket of groceries but as she turned to leave she realised that Janet's brightness had taken a supreme effort.

Now her mouth trembled and she said gruffly, 'Thank ye, Mistress Sarah . . . for being sae guid tae Thomas and – and everything. Ye'll let me ken how he's faring.'

'Of course I will, Janet. Try not to worry.'

Thomas was a son of the soil and as the days lengthened, however slightly, new hope rose within him; he felt the first stirrings of spring as surely as the crows in the tops of the chestnut trees: he glimpsed the first slender points of snowdrops beneath the apple tree and saw the snow disappear from the ley which he had ploughed with such care before Christmas. Now the stiff resistance of the furrows was breaking down, with the soil expanding and contracting as the weather changed from frost to rain and back again; now only lacy white lines edged the furrows to remind him of winter snows. The clouds moved swiftly, high and free in a sky changed from sullen grey to silver, with just the faintest promise of blue to assure the world that spring was on the way. Thomas sighed softly. Anna's bairn would never see the beauty of the earth but, as the Minister had reminded him, she would never know its pain either.

'Suffer the little children to come unto me,' he quoted as the Minister had done, and the sadness in his heart eased a little.

Of course there were many days of winter still to be endured, days of keening winds and endless chopping of turnips hauled from the frozen pit, days of thrashing corn when the great black steam-engine trundled its ponderous way up the track from Muircumwell or from Strathtod, depending on the situation of its last farm. The great iron monster with its gleaming brass bands would belch out steam as it climbed the last of the slope to Fairlyden, pulling the green wooden thrashing mill behind it. Days before Nick had sent a horse and cart to bring supplies of coal from the station, while indoors the women baked and cooked from dawn to dusk in readiness to feed the mill men.

There were neighbours who came to help too. Such help had to be reciprocated; Thomas or Billy, and sometimes Nick also, had to make up a thrashing team for another farm.

So Thomas had little time to brood as the short days came and went. The winter passed and gradually the days grew longer and milder. One Sunday morning found Billy and Nick leaning over a field gate discussing the sowing of the spring oats. They stood side by side, chins resting on brawny arms folded along the topmost bar. Even Billy was nodding amiably, less impatient than of late, when Thomas joined them. Billy had not the slightest desire to usurp Nick's authority and take over the running of Fairlyden, but there were times when he was irritable with the older man's acceptance of traditional methods. He always deferred to Nick when discussing the right time to sow, the condition of the soil, or the tilth of the seedbed, yet when it came to the use of even the simplest machine it was Nick who sought Billy's advice.

'Ye made a fine job o' ploughing that pasture, Thomas,' Nick declared now as Thomas copied their stance. Nick always took care to speak into Thomas's good ear, knowing how irritated the younger man became if he did not hear correctly.

'Aye,' Billy agreed. 'Ye buried every blade o' grass, Thomas, and the furrows are laid as straight and regular as a man could wish. It shouldna take much working wi' the harrows before we're ready to sow. Don't ye agree, Nick?' Nick nodded and Thomas glowed with pride.

'Aye, but the new plough shares ye had made at the smiddy helped, Master Billy, especially ploughing pastureland,' Thomas admitted modestly.

'Grandfather Logan aye says your father was one o' the best ploughmen in this area,' Billy remarked. 'Ye must hae inherited his skill.'

Thomas shrugged. 'I dinna ken. I watched him often enough as a laddie, but he died afore I was auld enough tae seek his guidance.'

At the beginning of April the oats were sown and the lambs were frisking in the meadow once more. Bullock sheds were cleaned and whitewashed. As the days lengthened and the nights grew warmer the milking cows were turned out of the byres too. After their long winter confinement they were more than happy to be free. Even the oldest matrons dashed madly round the field, kicking up their legs and swinging their udders until they finally exhausted themselves and settled down to graze. Thomas watched this spectacle in the first few days of

113

May with Logan and Beth at his side. They grinned in delight at the wild bovine dance, rejoicing with the cows; the byre cleaning was a relatively easy chore once the cows could stay out night and day.

'It will be another year before Beth and I can leave school and help ye limewash the byre and sow the crops and hoe the turnips,' Logan declared with a note of impatience. 'Unless Mama permits us to go as half-timers . . . We could, now that we're twelve.' It did not occur to Logan that Beth would want to do anything different to himself; he could not imagine Fairlyden without her; he assumed she would work in the house and in the dairy, even help him in the fields when she could be spared. Beth would have agreed. Fairlyden was her world, with her father and Logan at the centre of it.

'Ach, dinna wish away your schooldays,' Thomas frowned at them. He frowned more often these days, Logan thought, though often it was in concentration, as though he was listening with his whole head, especially his eyes.

'You were younger than us when you left the school,' Logan reminded him almost accusingly.

'I didna have any choice. Ma father died.'

'Is that why your mama left Fairlyden and went to live at the Muircumwell Store with Mr Jardine?' Beth asked.

'Aye.' Thomas chewed thoughtfully on a piece of grass for a second or so. 'Lately I've wished I'd had more schooling . . . Is the new hall nearly finished in Muircumwell?' He looked at Beth, but it was Logan who answered.

'Aye, it's tae be blessed by the Reverend Morrison at the end o' June. The Dominie says we're all to be present.'

'It's historical, Miss Bell says,' Beth informed him.

'She's a fine young woman, Miss Bell,' Thomas agreed. 'When the hall is ready she's going tae arrange for boxes o' books tae be brought once a month frae the library at Dumfries, at least that's what the Minister says. I'm going tae join maself.'

'Mother said ye'd taken tae reading since ye were ill, Thomas.' Logan looked up curiously. 'She says ye read the Scottish Farmer Magazine almost as soon as she brings it hame.'

'Aye, it's surprising what ye can learn about other farmers and their ways, young Logan, but I expect your mother has told ye that already?'

'Aye,' Logan sighed. 'I like the farming books fine, but we have

114

a lot o' books frae the school tae read tae. Haven't we a lot, Beth?'

Beth nodded. 'I like reading though,' she told Thomas. 'Maybe I'll be able to go tae the new hall and join the library and borrow books when I leave school?'

'Likely ye will, lassie.'

'Logan likes arithmetic, don't ye, Logan? He can add up a long line o' figures faster than anybody i' the school,' she added proudly.

'I like learning poems as well though,' Logan reminded her.

'Och, I never liked learning things by heart,' Thomas recalled suddenly. 'Maybe it's not sae bad leaving school after all. I can please maself what I read now. Mistress Fairly says I can have a loan o' her books tae read when the winter comes again.'

'I want tae learn all about breeding cows and horses, aye and pigs, when I leave school. Billy says that's old-fashioned, but I'm not interested in his machines. Neither is Alex, and Grandfather Logan says he's a good farmer so I'm going tae be like him and breed good Clydesdales, aye and good cows.'

'Ye'll be a wonderful farmer, Logie,' Beth assured him fervently. 'I'll bet nobody ever has a pig as good as our Pegotty either, but your mama willna let ye leave the school before ye're thirteen. I heard Mr Bradshaw telling her that ye ought to go to the Academy at Dumfries because the Dominie recommended ye. That would be longer still!'

'The Dominie thinks ye should go tae,' Logan reminded her, 'and he hardly ever recommends lassies. Anyway, Mama kens I wouldna want to leave Fairlyden.'

'Aye,' Beth nodded sagely. 'She told Mr Bradshaw that. He sighed as though he was a bit sad. Then he agreed and said it was plain tae see your mind was set on farming Fairlyden.'

Thomas was silent. He had heard Billy arguing with his younger brother because the boy did not understand how to set the plough. They argued more now that Logan was old enough to express opinions of his own. But the laddie's shrewd, Thomas decided. He'd seen him and the Mistress discussing the price o' seeds and linseed cake and some of the other things that had to be carted from the railway station; the laddie seemed tae keep as keen an eye on the figures as his mother. Thomas bit his lip and frowned. He hoped the peace of Fairlyden would not be shattered by the arguments of the two Fairly brothers when Logan left the school. They're not a bit alike, even to look at, he thought.

A few days later, on the sixth of May, there was news which rocked most loyal subjects of the British Empire.

'The King is dead!' Sarah announced.

'I wonder if the Kaiser will come to the funeral?' Billy's dark eyes held a gleam which Sarah found vaguely disturbing.

'Of course the Kaiser will come! The King is – was – his uncle, and he is the German Emperor. Of course he'll come.'

'Aye, I suppose he'll need tae be there,' Billy conceded. 'So now we'll have King George V and Queen Mary tae rule the British Empire. I wonder if the new King will be able tae pacify the government, or deal any better with all the Irish troubles . . .'

'Only time will tell,' Sarah murmured. 'There's a lot o' poverty and unemployment – and women still have no right to vote. Surely the country couldna be any worse with the influence of women.' She sighed. 'I suppose we're lucky here at Fairlyden – even if we do work hard for our living.'

Billy did not reply. His mind was many miles away from Fairlyden.

More than a month later the Reverend Morrison rode up the track to Fairlyden bringing the good news that Anna MacFarlane had given birth to a fine baby boy on the last day of June.

'Mistress Whiteley told me when I called at the Store,' he said to Sarah, 'so I've taken it upon myself to bring you the good news. I'm sure Thomas will be pleased to know his sister is well and the baby too.'

'Indeed he will!' Sarah exclaimed, smiling broadly. 'We all are. Janet will be so relieved! It was good of you to come, Reverend Morrison. You'll stay and take a cup of tea and a fresh scone?' The young Minister hesitated but Sarah swept aside any protest. 'We always have a cup before we start the milking and Thomas will be in frae the hay with Billy and Nick when they see Moll Black bringing the cows frae the field. You can give him the good news yourself.'

Thomas looked anxious when Sarah informed him that the Minister had called to see him but his apprehension swiftly turned to joy.

'Your sister and her husband have decided to call their son James Thomas MacFarlane.'

'James Thomas,' he repeated. 'Thomas . . .' His smile spread across his lean face almost from ear to ear. Mark Morrison was glad he had obeyed his impulse and ridden to Fairlyden with the news. He wanted everybody to be happy because he was feeling so full of joy himself.

He had half feared that Felicity was wedded to her career as a school teacher, indeed he respected her for her commitment to her young pupils, but he had been elated when she shyly accepted his proposal. Felicity Bell had even fewer family connections than he had himself, so the wedding would be a simple, quiet ceremony in their own church. They had agreed to wait until after the dedication ceremony of the new village hall but he would not have long to wait now.

Fifteen

The people of Muircumwell parish, especially the women, were disappointed when news filtered out that the young Minister's wedding to Miss Felicity Bell was to be a quiet affair. They decided to demonstrate their affection and respect for the young couple who had brought so much to the community.

So Muircumwell's celebration of the year was planned with generosity and enthusiasm and the Minister's wedding grew and grew until the whole parish seemed to be involved in one way or another.

The Dominie was determined to add his own contribution to the happy occasion. His young assistant had proved herself an excellent teacher of the younger children as well as a great asset to his school with her musical talents. He knew she had taken a great interest and pride in Beth Jamieson, the pretty, modest child from the Fairlyden cottage. It was to Beth he turned his attention. He would give Miss Bell a surprise, as well as demonstrating to the parish her achievements as a music teacher.

Beth was proud but nervous when the Dominie outlined his plan and swore her to secrecy. She was also worried. She would need a new dress for she would hate her beloved Miss Bell to be ashamed of her clothes. How could her father afford the sort of dress her young heart craved for this wonderful occasion?

'We'll take advice frae Mistress Fairly,' Nick declared promptly when Beth diffidently told him she was to sing, all alone, at the very front of the church, especially for Miss Bell and the Minister.

'But it's tae be a secret! I canna even tell Logan!'

'Mistress Fairly'll keep your secret, lassie.'

'There's an even bigger surprise for later . . .' Beth lowered her voice to a hushed whisper, although there was no one else in the cottage.

'And what might that be, lassie?' Nick asked, his blue eyes

filled with quiet pride, though his mind was swiftly reviewing his meagre savings.

'Captain Fothergill is buying a piano. It's tae stay in the Mackenzie Hall. It's a gift tae the . . . the community. That's what the Dominie said. He says the Captain is a very generous beni . . . benefactor . . .'

'He is indeed!'

'I'm tae be the very first person tae play it. I've tae choose three o' Miss Bell's favourite tunes frae the ones she's taught me. Then the Dominie is going tae ask Miss Bell . . . only she'll be Mistress Morrison by then . . . to play for everybody. Ye will come and listen, Papa?' Nick looked down into her wide blue eyes; she reminded him painfully of his beloved Sally; he did not enjoy public gatherings these days.

'Aye, lassie, I'll be there tae hear ye.'

The following morning Nick asked Sarah if she could advise him about Beth's new dress.

'I hae money tae buy the material,' he announced firmly, 'and Beth says she can sew it herself . . . But . . . well I'd like ma lassie tae be suitably clad . . .'

'But that's wonderful news, Nick! It will be worth all the hours Beth has practised to have such a moment of glory. She'll remember it all her life. I'd be more than willing to make her dress for her . . .' Sarah looked Nick in the eye and smiled. 'But I know she has the same proud independence as her father . . .'

'Aye . . . er weel . . .' Nick frowned uncertainly. 'A man ought tae be able tae manage his ain affairs, but there's some things . . .'

'I know, Nick. Some things are women's work. Sally would have been so proud,' she added softly. 'Beth has inherited all her skill with the needle too, so she'll make a fine job of her dress if we get the right material and one o' the paper patterns from Miss Harrison's.'

'Thank ye, Mistress,' Nick said simply, but his voice was gruff with emotion. Sarah knew how much he missed his wife. How tired he looks, she thought with a pang of concern.

'I hope you're not working too hard, Nick? We have only just finished the hay and now the harvest seems to be upon us.' She frowned. She had never known Nick to have a day's sickness. 'I don't know what we would do without you . . .' she added frankly.

'Och, I'll be fine,' Nick shrugged, but his usual reassuring smile was absent and there was a weariness in his eyes which troubled Sarah. Surely he could not be worrying on Beth's account. She sang as naturally as she talked, in a clear sweet treble which would charm the stoniest heart.

Sarah resolved to see that Nick's daughter had a dress they would both be proud of. She had a private word with Miss Harrison before she took Beth to choose the material.

The little spinster guessed the dress was for an extra-special occasion but she was always discreet, just as Sarah had known she would be. She showed Beth bolts of sprigged muslin, flowered cotton, crepe de chine, and silk. Then she placed a smaller roll of blue satin beside the rest. She watched the young girl's eyes light up. Beth stroked the shining material almost reverently, then she sighed and turned her gaze back to the muslin, aware of the few precious coins in the small purse her father had given her just before Mistress Fairly called for her.

'If ye'll take an old woman's advice,' Miss Harrison said softly, catching Sarah's eye, 'ye'll choose the blue satin. It's a real bargain because there's not enough left to make a lady's gown; but ye're such a dainty lassie for all ye'll soon be a young lady . . .' She pretended to size up Beth's slender form. 'Aye, I'm sure there'd be enough tae make a bonnie gown for ye, and it's just the colour o' your een. Of course if ye prefer the muslin I've plenty o' that and some o' it has blue flowers . . .'

'Oh no!' Beth exclaimed breathlessly, her eyes bright with dawning hope. 'I think the satin is beautiful, Miss Harrison, b-but I thought it would c-cost too much . . .'

'Aye, and so it would if there'd been enough tae make a gown for a full-grown woman, but what wad I be doing with a wee bit like that, eh? I've just the kind o' simple pattern to suit ye. Shall I open out the material and make sure there's enough?'

'Oh yes, if ye please!' Beth breathed ecstatically. Sarah watched in silence, a little smile lifting the corners of her mouth. It was worth the small deceit to see the pleasure on Beth's face. Miss Harrison apparently thought so too as her nimble fingers unrolled the shiny satin. Carefully she placed the paper pattern pieces. Naturally they fitted. There was scarcely an inch to spare and Beth expelled a sigh of relief.

'Mmm, there's just enough,' Miss Harrison murmured, and no one would have guessed she had carefully measured out the piece of satin two hours earlier and rolled it on to a fresh board in readiness for her young customer's visit. 'Wad ye be planning tae sew the dress yourself, lassie? I've heard Miss Bell saying ye're fine and handy with a needle.'

'Aye, I mean yes, Miss Harrison. I'm going tae make the dress myself . . .' Beth gulped.

'Ach well, now that we've got the pieces all laid out we may as well cut them, eh? It would save ye buying the paper pattern for I'll be sure tae use it again for some other body – if ye're sure ye like the long gathered skirt and the high bodice?'

'Oh yes, yes! I do like it, and it would be very kind o' ye, if – if . . . that is, unless it costs extra . . .? The cutting of the pieces I mean . . .' Beth gazed anxiously up at Miss Harrison's wrinkled face. The faded eyes behind the steel-rimmed spectacles were kind. Mistress Fairly had promised her a dozen eggs and a pound of butter, as well as paying the extra money for the material, but she would have helped the child anyway. Such a sweet, earnest face she had and she would look lovely in her blue dress with her long honey-coloured curls and her wide blue eyes.

Miss Harrison sighed wistfully. 'I've some blue ribbons for a sash and to trim the neck and sleeves . . .'

'Oh, I couldna buy ribbons!' Beth exclaimed anxiously.

'Och, lassie, ye dinna need tae buy the wee bit ribbon it will take. I'll give ye that and maybe one day ye'll mind o' wearing the dress and spare a thought for me, eh?'

Beth bit her lip uncertainly.

'Maybe you could bake Miss Harrison a cake like the one Mrs Bunnerby was teaching you to make, Beth?' Sarah suggested, afraid the girl might begin to suspect too much generosity, for Beth was extremely intelligent. 'Miss Harrison doesna have much time to bake for minding the shop and making hats, isn't that right, Miss Harrison?'

'Och, I could bake a cake!' Beth agreed readily. 'Would that be enough to pay ye for the ribbons, Miss Harrison?'

'Aye, more than enough, lassie. It would be a real treat for me.'

'I wonder if you could set aside enough of the green silk to make Sadie a new gown?' Sarah asked. 'I will send her down tomorrow to see it for herself, just in case I've chosen the wrong colour.' Nothing seemed to please Sadie these days. Sarah guessed she was jealous of Miss Bell since the Minister had asked her to be his wife. Maybe a new gown would sweeten her acid tongue and make life pleasanter for everyone at Fairlyden.

'Everybody is making new dresses for the Minister's wedding,' Miss Harrison sighed. 'I'm making the brown silk for myself. What are ye fancying, Mistress Fairly? Or is Master Bradshaw bringing ye special material frae his mills?'

'Oh no!' Sarah hastily denied such a possibility, but she felt her colour rising, highlighting her cheekbones as it had done since she was Beth's age, she thought irritably. 'I think I shall manage without a new gown . . .' She saw Miss Harrison's look of disappointment. 'But maybe you could make me a new hat to match the royal blue I had last year.'

Beth was well pleased with her purchases and she could not wait to start the laborious task of sewing the seams, pintucks and hems of her new dress. She longed to confide in Logan; they had shared all their secrets since they learned to talk – all except one and that was a private matter which made Beth's cheeks burn. She did not look forward to the new monthly occurrence. The bleeding had terrified her, until Mistress Fairly had gently explained it was a normal part of growing up, at least for girls. She was almost a grown woman now. She was aware of changes in her body – and in her thoughts too.

Suddenly she had grown taller than Logan. Sometimes she felt older than him too, despite his three months' seniority. But she still loved Logan with all her heart and she revelled in the rare freedom of summer afternoons when they wandered together over the fields and in the woods, paddling in the burn, guddling for trout, or gathering brambles from the thorny thickets on the edge of the wood.

Logan also enjoyed such wanderings in Beth's company, when he was not pestering Nick to allow him to work with the horses or to teach him some new task. Beth's sudden need to stay indoors so often, especially on a particularly fine summer afternoon, puzzled him. He felt mildly resentful of her preoccupation.

'Och well, I'm going tae the auld quarry with Jake Dodds, if ye're no' coming out . . .?'

Beth hesitated. It was a beautiful Saturday afternoon. But time was getting short and she still had such a lot of tiny stitches to make to finish her dress in time for the wedding of her adored teacher. She really wanted Miss Bell to be proud of her, and her father, and Logan and his mama.

'Please, dinna go tae the quarry, Logan . . .' She shivered. 'Your mama says it's dangerous. A woman drowned there once, and two wee bairnies . . .'

'That was before we were born!' Logan protested. 'Anyway it was different then. There were huts beside the quarry. The rain washed her house away.'

Beth watched uneasily as Logan jumped on the bicycle Billy had made for him, and went pedalling furiously down the track to Muircumwell.

'I canna understand where Logan has got to. He's never late for the milking but there's no sign o' him and we're almost finished.' Sarah was growing anxious.

'I expect he's skulking away up the fields until we've done his work!' Sadie muttered sullenly.

'He never shirks. Besides he was so proud when I agreed to let him milk Queenie's heifer in addition to his usual cows. And he has Peggotty to feed too. She's squealing her head off. I expect she's hungry with that big litter of hers tugging at her continually.'

Beth lifted her piggin and stool and carried them back to the dairy. She looked pale and strained, Sarah thought with a frown. She followed her.

'Have you seen Logan this afternoon, Beth?'

'I . . . er, he wanted me tae gang with him tae the wood. I – I couldna, Mistress Fairly. I havena finished sewing my dress . . .'

'So Logan went alone . . .? Maybe he's fallen, hurt himself perhaps . . .' She stopped as Beth shook her head unhappily.

'He said he was going tae the auld quarry at Muircumwell with – with Jake Dodds and his brother . . .'

'With the Dodds boys! To the quarry!' Sarah repeated Beth's words incredulously. The two Dodds brothers were always up to mischief; wicked mischief too on occasion. 'The old quarry is dangerous! Surely you're mistaken, Beth . . .?' But Beth shook her head unhappily and stared at the ground.

'I – I saw him go down the track on his bike . . . I'm sorry, Mistress Fairly.'

'I canna believe it! But it isna your fault, Beth,' Sarah added, sensing the girl's distress.

'It is. He wanted me tae keep him company because Papa wouldna let him help the men stook the corn in the wee field while Billy was still working the binder . . .'

'Aah, here's your father,' Sarah interrupted with relief at the sight of Nick leading home two tired horses. 'Maybe Logan went to the field after all . . .' Again Beth shook her head unhappily but Sarah was already hurrying away.

'I blame masel!' Nick exclaimed in dismay when Sarah explained. 'He was eager tae come wi' me . . .' He broke off. A year ago Nick had been forced to watch helplessly when the binding machine severed the hind legs of his favourite collie as easily as a knife cutting butter. The memory had made him exceedingly wary. Yet he had sensed an unfamiliar restlessness in the laddie; he should have guessed he was missing Beth's company. He could easily have kept an eye on him . . . if only he hadn't felt so tired and irritable . . . Nick insisted on setting out immediately to search for Logan despite his own weariness.

The edges of the quarry were overgrown, sloping downwards in places, but dangerously vertical where the rocky outcrops had crumbled away. Daylight was beginning to fade and Nick breathed a sigh of relief when he heard a wavering voice in answer to his calls and whistles.

Logan was stuck on a ledge little more than six feet from the top of the quarry but he had been well hidden by the scrubby bushes and the overhanging rock. Below him he could see only water and he had heard the sickening plop of the loose stones and scree which plummeted downwards whenever he moved.

'Are ye hurt, laddie?' Nick called anxiously.

'No, but I canna get a hold tae climb past the rock above me,' Logan called.

'How did ye get doon?'

Logan was silent for a moment. Then he said, 'We were playing a game.' His young mouth set. He had been an easy prey to Jake Dodds' trickery. 'I slipped and fell on to a ledge.'

Once the two Doddses realised he had not fallen to his death, they had laughed. Then they had run off home, calling, 'We'll tell wee jammy Jamieson, yer wee shadow, if ye're still hanging on by the morn!'

Logan knew it was only by good fortune that he had landed on the edge of the narrow rocky projection and managed to grasp a sprouting bush. It had held just long enough for him to haul himself to temporary safety. He knew now that the Dodds brothers were not the fearless adventurers they claimed to be; they lied outrageously about their exploits and saw no wrong in their tall tales. Beth had never been impressed by their claims and he felt a wave of shame that he had tried to win her attention in such a foolish way.

'I can see ye now, laddie!' Nick called. 'I'm over to your right – but I canna reach ye. I'll have tae go back to the village for a rope.'

'I canna get any further up.' Logan peered through the scrubby grasses clinging to the crevices in the rocks.

'Dinna even try!' Nick called back urgently. 'I'll be back as soon as I can get help.'

Nick was deadly tired as he scrambled up the slope away from the old quarry and ran across the small field behind the Mill yard. Beth would never forgive him if young Logan fell asleep and rolled off the narrow ledge; neither would Mistress Fairly. Indeed I'd never forgive myself; the laddie's almost like a son tae me, Nick thought as he tried to make his weary legs move faster. He had never known Logan to be foolish in his adventures before. If only he had been more patient with him . . . but he felt permanently tired these days, it made him irritable, less patient. Maybe once the harvest was over . . .

When he reached the yard of the deserted mill and saw Billy and Thomas hurrying towards him he was filled with overwhelming relief. His knees seemed to sag and he sank on to a low stone wall.

'Man, Nick! Ye're awfy white aboot the gills! Is – is the laddie all richt?' Thomas panted before he had even reached Nick's side. It was Billy who put a firm hand on his shoulder, pressing him down when he would have risen.

'Logan?' he asked tensely.

''S not hurt. I canna reach him. We need a rope.'

Billy nodded, taking charge instinctively. 'I'll run tae the smiddy. Wait there.' Billy had noted Nick Jamieson's lethargy recently and his short temper. He pondered the reason. Nick Jamieson had always been one of the most tolerant and patient men he knew.

Sixteen

Sarah scolded Logan roundly, despite her relief that he was uninjured. He knew he had behaved stupidly. Deep down he had been hurt because Beth had refused to keep him company, but how could he explain that to his mother and brother without sounding as soft as a baby. He couldn't say, 'I wanted Beth to be worried about me. I wanted her to care!'

He sensed changes in his childhood companion and he did not care for anything which threatened to spoil their friendship. Beth was his closest confidante; she meant more to him than either of his sisters, more than the boys who were his school friends. They were half forgotten the moment he crossed the bridge to Fairlyden with Beth at his side, running homeward through wind and rain, or wandering in the spring sunshine as they explored a new bird's nest or a rabbit burrow, the first clump of primroses or a squirrel's hoard. Beth could climb the beech tree almost as fast as he could himself; how often they had viewed the world together from their little eyrie. She was as nimble and quick as any of the boys, and far more intelligent. He bowed his head in shame and accepted his mother's scolding in silence, knowing that he deserved it.

Logan's fall from grace was soon forgotten amidst the general excitement of the wedding.

Beth hoped she would be a credit to Miss Bell after all her patient teaching; she was determined to do her best. Consequently, with Sarah's full approval, she practised her chosen piano pieces whenever she had an opportunity. She was completely engrossed in the *Magic Flute* early one morning – so early that the occupants of Fairlyden were still finishing the morning milking in the byre. She did not hear Sadie enter the room until she marched up to the piano and without warning slammed the lid down with all the force she could muster, making the fixed brass candlesticks shudder. Beth jerked her hands from the keys

– but she was not quite quick enough. The heavy lid caught the middle finger of her left hand with such force that the pain brought tears rushing to her eyes. She was scarcely aware that she had let out a piercing yelp.

'Shut up!' Sadie hissed, but Beth had already thrust her throbbing finger into her mouth in an instinctive bid to ease the pain. It brought little relief. She clamped her hand under her arm, rocking backwards and forwards on the screw-top piano stool. The initial shock abated, though not the throbbing. She stared up at her tormentor.

'What did ye dae that for!' It was more an accusation than a question and she blinked her eyes impatiently as the tears still blurred her vision of Sadie's spiteful face. 'Maybe ye've broken ma finger . . .'

'Weel at least it'll stop the racket ye're making! Ye've nae business being in this house, especially when everybody else is at the milking. Who dae ye think ye are? Lady J . . .'

'I was practising my music. Your mama gave permission.'

'Well I'm sick o' hearing it – the same things over and over . . . Why ye even ken that one by heart!' Beth ignored her but she could not ignore the pulsing pain. She drew her hand slowly from under her arm and stared at her finger. Already it looked red and swollen and there was a white dent between the first joint and the knuckle where the edge of the oak lid had caught it. Tentatively she tried to straighten it, wincing unconsciously. Sadie glared at her bowed head with the shining honey-gold curls. She had sensed that Beth was putting her heart and soul into perfecting her piano playing for days now; she was sure her own mother and the Jamieson brat had some sort of secret . . . Anger and jealousy engulfed her. 'Ye werena even using the music! Ye didna need tae play them again. Ye ken the tunes already. Ye're nothing but a cheat and a liar, Beth Jamieson! Ye were skulking in here tae miss the milking!'

'I was not!' Beth's head shot up. 'I got up early. I milked my ain cows before ye even came tae the byre! Ye're the one who hides tae avoid the work!'

Sadie's eyes narrowed. Beth rarely answered her back, but she knew her restraint was for the sake of her father and his position at Fairlyden, rather than because she was afraid. Some devil in Sadie determined to destroy the youthful challenge in those swimming blue eyes, shatter the control of that firm young

128

mouth. 'I suppose ye fancy yourself as a teacher tae, since that stupid woman filled your head wi' nonsense about hidden talents! Well, ye needna think ye're any better than anybody else. She's only teaching ye music tae get extra money. I dinna suppose she's that good herself or . . .' Beth jumped up from the piano stool, her blue eyes blazing, forcing Sadie to step back.

'Miss Bell isna stupid! She's patient and clever and she can play beautiful tunes . . . Ye're jealous o' her, Sadie Fairly! We ken ye're jealous – Logan and me. Ye wanted tae marry the Reverend Morrison yourself! He kenned ye werena nice enough tae be a minister's wife and . . .' Sadie's hand flew out. Beth's head snapped backwards under the blow, her pale cheek reddening instantly. She blinked back the tears of pain with an effort and stared up at Sadie defiantly.

'The Dominie thinks Miss Bell is *excellent*! He said so. He says she's taught me enough for me tae gang tae the Academy in Dumfries – and I *could* learn tae be a teacher if . . .'

'You! Be a teacher! Even if ye were clever enough, your father's just a common labourer! He couldna afford tae let ye gang tae the Academy and bide in the students' hostel . . .' Sadie broke off suddenly, her eyes narrowing. 'So that's why ye're practising sae much! Trying tae impress *my* mother, I suppose! Worming your way round her next! Wanting charity . . .'

'No! No!' Beth's pale face went whiter than ever, except for the red imprint where Sadie had slapped her cheek.

'What're you shouting about, Beth?' Logan popped his head round the door. 'Mother says tae tell ye the porridge is cooling. It's nearly time we were going tae school.'

Sadie rushed past him into the kitchen. Sarah was in the scullery so she did not see her daughter dash up the stairs.

'What's wrong with her?' Logan asked curiously, watching his sister's retreating back. Beth hastily rubbed her eyes with the back of her hand, but her left hand was cradled protectively against her thin chest. She shrugged as Logan turned to her with a questioning glance.

'We'd best eat up quick then.' She hurried past him, to her place at the table. The bowls of steaming porridge were set out, each with its own small bowl of cream. Beth wriggled awkwardly on to her seat, only glancing up as her father came in from the yard. How strained and tired he looked! Her throbbing finger was temporarily forgotten as she stared at the dark circles beneath Nick's eyes and the lines etched from his nose to the corners of his mouth. I wonder what the Dominie wrote in the letter he gave me to bring home from school? she wondered suddenly. Why didn't Papa tell me as he usually does . . .?

'Why are you holding your hand like that, lassie?' Beth scarcely heard Sarah's question as her troubled eyes studied her father's drawn face. 'Beth? Have you hurt your hand?' She looked up then. Over Sarah's shoulder she saw Sadie sauntering into the kitchen; there was a threatening look in her narrowed eyes. Beth cared nothing for that, but she would not add to her father's worries with tales of Sadie Fairly.

'I – I trapped my finger. The piano lid . . . f-fell on it . . .'

'Let me see! Oh, my goodness me, Beth!' Sarah looked down into Beth's pale face in consternation. Surely her cheek was red, and had she been crying . . .? Sarah frowned. 'However did it happen . . .?' Beth did not answer but she drew in her breath sharply as Sarah gently straightened her finger. 'I don't think it's broken, but it's going to be badly bruised, lassie . . .' Her dark eyes were anxiously asking, 'However will you play the piano?'

'See Beth's finger, Nick. Do you think it's broken? Nick . . .?' Nick seemed to gather his thoughts as he came round the table and gently examined his daughter's dainty hand.

'Surely that's more than a piano lid falling, lassie . . .?' He looked up, saw the pleading in Beth's blue eyes. Whatever she had done, he knew she did not want to discuss it. He nodded.

'It's not broken, thank goodness. But it's badly bruised and it'll be too stiff to . . .'

'We'll bathe it!' Sarah said quickly. 'Logan, bring some Epsom salts while I get a bowl of hot water.'

'We shall be late for school . . .'

'The Dominie will understand if you tell him, Beth. I'll bring in some comfrey leaves and wrap them round your finger . . . Oh dear, I do wish I could remember all the cures my mother kept for such things . . .'

At last the great day arrived. Beth ran to the window the moment she hopped out of bed. She saw the white mist in the hollows like a gently swirling sea. Her father always said it was a sign of a good day to follow. Sure enough, before the morning milking was finished and the cows had ambled back to their field, the mist began to lift and spider webs festooned the hedges.

'They look just like fairy garlands,' she said shyly to Sarah as she helped her drive the last lingering cow through the gate on her way to the cottage.

'They certainly do, Beth,' Sarah smiled, 'especially with all the dewdrops shining like crystals in the sunlight. It's going to be a beautiful day! Is your finger quite better?'

'Nearly. I did as ye said and bathed it and kept wrapping it up and wiggling it.'

'I expect you're excited?'

'Aye, a wee bit . . . But I dinna think I feel as bad as Papa. He's worried in case I let Miss Bell down . . .'

'You'll do just fine, lassie.' Sarah smiled affectionately into Beth's anxious face. 'I will make sure your father is home in plenty of time to change into his Sunday clothes. It wouldna do for you to be late. He will be taking you in the pony and trap.'

'Oh, Mistress Fairly! Are ye no coming?' There was no disguising the disappointment in Beth's eyes.

'Of course I shall be there, Beth! I wouldna miss it for the world! Mr Bradshaw will be there too. He arrived last night and he will bring Logan and me in his motor car. And everyone frae Fairlyden will be at the hall later to hear you play the piano and join in the dancing.'

Beth nodded, her smile restored. 'I've starched Papa's collar and ironed it just as ye showed me,' she confided proudly, 'and it's hard and shiny.'

'You're a good bairn,' Sarah murmured softly. She sighed. 'Indeed you're almost a young lady. How proud your mother would have been today.'

'That's what Papa said . . . He's talked a lot about Mama lately . . .' She looked up earnestly at Sarah. 'When Logan sees my new gown, d'ye think he'll understand why I couldna go with him the day he went tae the quarry with Jake Dodds?'

'I'm sure he will, Beth. But Logan must learn he canna demand all your attention. He's still a boy at heart, for all he understands so much about Fairlyden and the animals.' Beth nodded, but she was not quite sure what Mistress Fairly meant, or why she was looking at her so gravely. After all, she and Logan were the same age. She still liked to do all the things they had always done together; but there were always so many other things to do and recently her father seemed to depend on her

131

more and more; she often did tasks he had previously done himself, especially at home.

The afternoon in late August could not have been better. Several people smilingly declared the Minister must have said a special prayer to arrange the weather.

Sarah, waiting patiently, was grateful for the quiet peace in the blessed coolness of the church. She caught her breath at the vision of innocent fragility Felicity Bell presented when she arrived on the arm of the Dominie, but she knew Miss Bell possessed a quiet strength and a great deal of patience. She would be an excellent wife for the Minister.

At last, when the main formalities were over, the Dominie discreetly beckoned Beth from her seat near the front. Sarah saw Nick tense. She could only see his profile but she saw the blood suffuse his weathered cheeks and then ebb swiftly away leaving him unusually pale.

'Why's Beth going up there?' Logan whispered urgently, but Sarah put a finger to her lips. Nick need not have worried, she thought, as Beth's voice rose pure and true to sing the twenty-third psalm.

Sarah felt a lump in her throat as the last notes died away and she knew she was not alone. At her side Crispin turned his head and smiled; her own smile was wobbly and she felt his hard fingers clasp hers briefly. They saw the pleasure Beth's singing had brought to the bride and groom and to all the congregation.

As the evening shadows lengthened, those who had been unable to see the bride and groom in church now congregated at the new village hall ready to join in the dancing and good wishes. The newcomers included Billy, Sadie and Thomas Whiteley from Fairlyden and Alex and Meg with some of the Mains of Muir workers, including Thomas's sister Maggie with her husband Ewan.

'It's lovely to see so many people coming to wish them well,' Sarah murmured as her father came to sit beside her.

'I havena seen sae many kenned faces for a long time,' Sandy declared in a bemused fashion. 'I'll just wait until the bride and groom begin the dancing and then I think I'll ride back to the Mains. I'm getting too old for such excitement.' Sarah and Beatrice, sitting on either side of him, smiled in amusement.

'Och, you're still fitter than most of us, Father!' Sarah teased.

'Ach weel, I canna grumble,' Sandy beamed. 'But it's thanks tae you two that I've lasted so long, and to Alex.' A small frown creased his brow as his blue eyes searched the hall for his eldest grandson. Alex was talking to Billy. Meg was with them, her small foot tapping as though impatient to dance. She smiled at Billy almost coquettishly and clasped his arm, pressing herself to his side like a purring kitten. Meg looked a very desirable young woman, despite her childish mind. Sarah wished Alex had not set himself up as her personal protector. She glanced at Beatrice and saw a troubled expression in her blue eyes, but before she could speak there was a murmur of excitement at the door.

'Och! Here they come . . .' Sandy announced. His eyes travelled around the large room. 'It's a grand building. The Reverend Mackenzie would have been real pleased tae see sae many o' his parishioners gathered together and enjoying themselves.'

Nick was as taut as a fiddle string when the Minister finished thanking them all for their gifts and good wishes to him and his bride; he concluded by inviting Beth to join him on the small dais. Beth rose and walked calmly to the far end of the hall but Nick could feel the uncomfortable thumping of his heart; it was becoming an increasingly familiar sensation lately, even without his anxiety for Beth.

Afterwards he thought how foolish he had been to worry. He should have known Beth would do her best. He was overwhelmed by the pleasure she had given to so many people, and there was no doubt that more than a little of the pleasure came from Beth's sweet smile and modest manner as well as her delight in making music. Tired though he was he could not refuse when Beth pleaded with him to teach her to dance the Scottish reels and jigs as the evening progressed amidst the laughter and the music of the fiddlers who had volunteered to play for the dancing.

After a particularly strenuous jig he was thankful to sink on to one of the nearest benches lining two sides of the hall and wait for his thumping heart to return to its normal rhythm. He found himself next to Sandy Logan.

'Ach, I'm too old for this,' he gasped, but even as he looked up Sarah joined them, laughing breathlessly, her cheeks flushed with exertion and her brown eyes sparkling. Crispin Bradshaw was not the only man in the room to cast her an admiring glance, but Nick's eyes held a look of near despair. Mistress Fairly was only a couple of years younger than himself, yet she was as spry as the young folk when it came to the dancing. Sandy glanced from one to the other but the teasing words he had meant to utter remained unspoken as he caught Nick's expression. His sharp blue eyes held concern.

'I doubt ye must have been working too hard at the harvest, Nick? Sarah was telling me earlier that ye're finished cutting at Fairlyden and just waiting for the stooks to dry out before ye begin carting. We've still two fields waiting for the binder at the Mains.' Sandy talked slowly, giving Nick time to regain his breath. Gradually a more natural colour returned to his weathered cheeks.

'Aye, the fields are all stooked, Mr Logan, and looking well.' Nick summoned a wry smile. 'I havena forgotten your advice . . .' He thought of the neat rows of golden stooks standing like soldiers in Fairlyden's fields. 'But it's tempting tae cart them in a bit quicker when the weather's good.'

'Aye, maybe,' Sandy mused, 'but it's early yet and the oats are better tae ripen i' the stook than sweat i' the stack.' Sandy's bushy brows were white now and as he observed Nick's strained face they drew together in a frown.

'Is something troubling ye, Nick?' he asked gently as Sarah accepted Crispin Bradshaw's invitation to dance again. Nick watched her go. How could he tell Mr Logan that he felt like an old man by midday when the Mistress worked so hard and never seemed to tire? 'What is it, laddie?' Sandy asked kindly and his eyes followed Nick's gaze to Beth. Billy was instructing her in the steps of the dance and the pair were laughing happily, while Logan watched them with a thunderous frown. 'Is it Beth? Ye should be proud o' the lassie. She's such a modest bairn for all she can play the piano sae nicely. Sarah tells me she is good at her lessons tae . . .'

'Aye.' Nick looked more anxious than ever. 'The Dominie and Miss Bell . . . er, Mistress Morrison that is, they think Beth could be a teacher if she had more schooling. The Dominie thinks she should gang tae school in Dumfries. But it wad mean her biding at the hostel through the week. I couldna afford that, Mr Logan . . .'

'I see . . .' Sandy said slowly.

'The Dominie thinks Mr Bradshaw would help with the money and Beth could repay him when she gets tae be a teacher, but I dinna want her tae set out in life wi' a debt tae pay . . . Anyway, a man has his pride, Mr Logan!' Nick turned to fix Sandy with a defiant glint in his eyes.

'Pride's no bad thing, Nick, but . . .'

'But am I depriving ma ain bairn? I keep asking maself that,' he added huskily. 'Am I being selfish, Mr Logan?'

'What does Beth want to do?'

'I havena asked her.' Nick sounded surprised. 'She loves Fairlyden as much as young Logan . . . Maybe that's another thing I should think o'. The two o' them are awfy fond o' one another . . . Maybe they'd be better tae pairt now . . . Yet I can scarce bear the thocht o' pairting wi' her either, an' that's the truth,' Nick muttered hoarsely.

'Well, Nick . . . maybe ye should ask Beth what she wants tae dae with her ain future. Sarah says she's a sensible lassie, and it seems tae me the time's coming when we men'll have tae accept that women have a mind o' their ain . . . You think on't, laddie.' Sandy stifled a yawn. 'It's time I went awa' home, Nick, but come and talk tae me at the Mains if ye think it would help. Your father was a fine man and a good friend tae me. I'd be pleased tae help you, or Beth, if I can.'

'Thanks, Mr Logan,' Nick watched almost enviously as Sandy made his way to the door, stopping many times as people greeted him. I wish I was at home too, he thought, until he saw Beth still enjoying the dancing. She looked as pretty as a picture in her new blue dress, he thought proudly.

His gaze moved on to Alex Fairly standing alone. Nick frowned. Alex was one of the happiest and friendliest young men he knew but now his expression seemed unusually sombre as he leaned against the wall, his eyes fixed on his brother dancing with young Meg – not that Meg was a bairn anymore, Nick reminded himself, for all she still talked like one. She was beautiful . . . and judging by the look on some of the men's faces he was not the only one who thought so either. Billy was certainly enjoying having her for his partner. So Nick's thoughts ran on until Beth appeared at his side. He did not realise she had been watching him sitting alone.

'Shall we go home now, Papa?' Beth asked as the dance finished. 'I heard Alex Fairly saying the Minister and Miss Bell have slipped away to the Manse so everyone will be going home soon. He wanted to go when Mr Logan went but Meg didna want tae go. Poor Alex, it's such a shame he canna dance with his funny feet,' Beth sighed.

'I expect everyone will be leaving soon,' Nick agreed readily. 'What about Logan? Does he want to ride home in the trap with us?'

'No. He's going home in Mr Bradshaw's motor car.'

It was a peaceful evening with scarcely a breath of wind to stir the leaves on the trees as Beth sat beside her father in the Fairlyden trap.

'Isn't the moon beautiful, Papa,' she sighed happily. 'It's just like a golden ball floating above the tree tops.' She leaned her head against her father's broad shoulder; she was tired now. 'It was a lovely day.' Nick smiled down at her sun-bleached curls spread against the dark material of his best jacket. He transferred the reins to his other hand and put his free arm around her slender shoulders, cradling her closer.

'Sleep if ye want, lassie. Ye've had a lot of excitement today.' He smoothed the blue satin of her dress with the tips of his work-roughened fingers. 'Ye were the prettiest wee maid in the hall in your new goon,' he added gruffly. Beth smoothed the shiny material of her skirt lovingly.

'Thank ye for buying me such lovely material, Papa. Mistress Fairly and Mistress O'Connor both admired it.'

'They'd be admiring your ain fine sewing, I've nae doubt.' Nick sighed softly and looked up at the moon and the purple shadows of the night sky. The scent of honeysuckle came wafting from the hedgerow as they trotted by. It awakened so many memories . . . 'Aagh,' he groaned softly, 'your mama wad hae been sae prood o' ye today, Beth, really prood.' Beth smiled sleepily.

'Mistress Fairly likes to hear me sing, and Logan kens now why I couldna gang with him tae the hill that day . . .'

'So ye're the best o' friends again, eh?' Nick smiled faintly. 'You and Master Logan.'

'Mmm, but I dinna think he liked Billy teaching me tae dae the dancing steps because he hasna learned them yet.'

'Och, he'll not be long. And now there's a hall i' the village I expect there'll often be dances. Your mama loved the dancing, aye and the music. Maybe ye take it frae her. Ye sang like a wee linty i' the kirk and my, I was prood o' ye.' Nick's voice was husky.

'But ye were a wee bit worried that I might forget the words, weren't ye?' Beth teased gently.

'Aye, but I should have kenned ye wadna forget . . .' He was silent for a while and Beth was almost lulled to sleep by the movement of the trap before he spoke again. Even so she sensed the tension in his voice and she knew something was troubling him.

'Beth . . .? Would ye like tae be a teacher?' he asked. 'Mistress Morrison thinks ye could manage fine.'

'I'd have tae go away to school . . . to Dumfries!' Beth was wide awake now and she turned her head to look warily at her father. Did he want her to go away?

'The Dominie thinks ye should go . . .' Nick bit his lip. 'That's why he wrote me the letter. He mentioned it again today.'

'I dinna want tae be a teacher. I want to stay here, with you, and Logan and Mistress Fairly. You promised Mama ye'd never send me awa' frae Fairlyden . . .' It had been a long day and Beth was very tired; she could not prevent the tears which sprang to her eyes so unexpectedly.

'Aah, Beth . . .' Nick pulled her back against his shoulder, patting her gently. 'I dinna *want* ye tae leave Fairlyden either, lassie. But I dinna want tae spoil your life . . . making ye a servant tae me – or tae Fairlyden . . .'

'But I love Fairlyden, and you, Papa! I don't ever want tae live anywhere else – not ever!'

Nick smiled in the darkness but he forced himself to go on.

'There's nothing for ye but to be a dairymaid and work in the house if ye dinna take your chance with the schooling, Beth . . .'

'But that's what I want to do . . .'

'Even – even if it means being a maid tae Sadie Fairly?' Nick asked tightly. He knew how Sadie resented Beth's modest talents and her pretty face. For a moment Beth was silent.

'I think Sadie hates me,' she said in a low voice.

'Och, no one could hate ye, lassie! But Miss Sadie . . . well she can be a mite . . . weel nasty . . .'

'Aunt Agnes said I wasna tae trust her,' Beth recalled, stifling a yawn. 'But I dinna care about her so long as I can stay here wi' you and Logan . . .' She snuggled against Nick's shoulder and he said no more. He felt happier than he had felt all day. It had worried him in case he was depriving Beth. But she wanted to stay with him, here at Fairlyden. Now he felt at peace with himself. He looked down at her bowed head and saw she was almost asleep. His gaze moved dreamily to the night sky and the clouds slowly drifting by. 'Ye were aye happy here at Fairlyden, weren't ye, Sally,' he murmured softly. 'We were both happy . . . together.'

Beth barely stirred when Nick lifted her from the trap and carried her into the cottage and through to her own small bedroom.

'I'll just take the harness off the pony, lassie. I'll no' be long. Pull off your new dress, and climb intae bed.' Beth obeyed instinctively but she had no recollection of snuggling into bed and pulling the bedclothes over her head, neither did she hear her father return, his footsteps dragging as he stumbled up the path and sank gratefully into his own armchair.

Seventeen

Logan had looked forward to the thrill of driving back home in Crispin's motor car with all its lamps lit but he was almost too sleepy to appreciate it. He needed no second bidding to go to bed either.

'You'll have a cup of tea before you leave, Crispin?' Sarah automatically stirred the embers of the fire into life, adding dry wood from the box beside the hearth. 'Mrs Bunnerby will have been asleep for some time, I think.' Crispin watched her deft movements with pleasure. They had been in each other's company most of the day, yet it was only now, in the dimly lit peace of Fairlyden's kitchen that he felt they were really together.

'You are very quiet.'

'I find delight in watching you, Sarah. You move with a rare grace at the end of such a tiring day. Indeed I've often thought you must possess the secret of eternal youth.' Sarah smiled but she blushed faintly at Crispin's compliment. She knew he did not possess a sugary tongue, or compliment every woman he saw.

'I enjoyed the wedding,' she confessed. 'It was nice to see so many friends all together, and so happy . . .' But Crispin saw a shadow pass over her expressive face. He knew instinctively she was thinking of Alex. There would always be a special tenderness in her heart for her firstborn son, despite the fact that he had already proved himself a worthy man, and a successful farmer.

'Sit beside me?' Crispin made room on the oak settle beside the fire. 'We're seldom alone together, really alone, with time to talk.'

'It's very late, and there will be cows to milk in the morning . . .' But Sarah's was only a token protest. She reached for her own cup and settled beside Crispin, sharing the feeling of tranquillity as the firelight danced on the walls; the old house creaked softly. For a little while they sat in companionable silence, watching the flames shooting up the wide chimney.

'Sadie and Billy went to the village on their bicycles so I don't suppose they'll get home for a wee while yet,' Sarah murmured contentedly.

'Billy and Meg certainly enjoyed the dancing . . .'

'Mmm, it's almost as though Meg is becoming a woman at last.'

Sarah frowned and Crispin wished he had not spoken his thoughts aloud. 'She hasna a vestige o' common sense yet, though.' There was an unfamiliar edge to Sarah's voice. 'Billy is almost as bad! And as soon as Meg and Alex had gone, that Lisa MacClean was at his side – and he encouraged her too!'

'Well, he's a handsome fellow!' Crispin grinned. 'And he has his mother's charm as well as his father's looks.' He wondered if Sarah knew that her second son had something of a reputation with the ladies. Yet he had heard Billy declare more than once that marriage held no attraction for him. 'I think Billy can look after himself. He's a man now and there's no use you worrying your lovely head about him, Sarah.'

'I suppose you're right. You usually are. It's strange that you should understand so well when you're not a family man yourself . . .' Sarah mused. She smiled up at him. Crispin caught his breath. Her soft brown eyes and sleepy smile still had the power to arouse a storm of emotions in him, and she didn't even guess.

'Whose fault is that?' he growled softly, setting his cup and saucer aside and clasping her fingers firmly.

'F-fault?'

'That I'm not a happily married man with a ready-made family. You know, Sarah, I could still share your troubles if you would marry me . . .'

'Oh, Crispin . . .' Sarah's voice was tremulous. 'You're just letting yourself be affected because there are weddings in the air.'

'It is not the weddings that affect me, and well you know it . . .' Crispin's voice had deepened and his eyes compelled Sarah to look at him. Slowly he bent his head to hers and she had not the strength, nor the will, to draw away. His kiss was long and searching and when he raised his head Sarah was trembling all over.

'Oh, Crispin . . .' she whispered shakily. He put his finger gently over her lips, then replaced it once more with his mouth, drawing a response which Sarah had believed belonged only to the days of her more passionate youth.

'Dear God, I must be mad . . .' she breathed. 'To feel like this at my age . . .'

'You're human and very attractive and age has nothing to do with the way we feel, Sarah. I want you still.'

'It is madness!' Sarah gasped softly. 'We're both crazy . . .'

'Well, if this is being mad I hope I never regain my sanity,' Crispin declared huskily and held her close, kissing her deeply until he felt her body yield against him.

Later, in the lonely darkness of her bedchamber Sarah knew she would have surrendered herself completely to Crispin's loving if they had not heard the rattle of Sadie's bicycle. Her petulant voice, raised in complaint to Billy and Thomas, had shattered the magic, but it had not stopped Crispin repeating urgently, 'When will you marry me, Sarah?'

'When you're ready to settle down at Fairlyside perhaps . . .?' She had felt, rather than seen, the wry twist of Crispin's smile and she had heard his sigh.

'I can't leave all our workers and the mill to the mercy of my mercenary nephew. But somehow I will find a way to carry out my father's plans without ruining both our lives. We have so much . . .' She heard his heartfelt sigh.

'I know, Crispin. I know, my dear, and I understand.' Sarah had meant the words she uttered, but lying alone in her chamber there was an ache of regret in her heart. Yet she could not desert Fairlyden and her family, any more than Crispin could break his father's trust and desert the hundreds of men and women who depended on him for their daily bread.

It was later than usual when Sarah wakened the following morning. She felt tired and unrefreshed; no one else was up either. She shouted to Billy and Sadie impatiently and then went to the bothy to waken Thomas.

'Why does everyone have to depend on me?' she asked Billy sharply when he appeared pulling on his braces and pushing back his mop of unruly black curls.

'Because ye aye waken first,' Billy grinned sleepily. He was tired but he had enjoyed the previous night's revelry. He gulped down the cup of buttermilk Sarah had poured for him. His spirits

141

rose as he felt the cool fresh air of late summer through the open door.

'I do believe even Nick has slept in this morning,' Sarah called. 'There's no sign of him bringing in the cows anyway. You'd better get away to the field for them, Billy, or the milk will never be ready for Thomas to take to the train.'

Billy had brought the cows from the field and they were all tied by the neck in their respective stalls; even Moll Black had arrived, but still there was no sign of Nick.

'Poor Nick, he was under a lot of strain yesterday,' Sarah said sympathetically as she settled on her stool to milk the first cow. 'And he does seem to have been more tired than usual lately. Even so I think you'll have to go to the cottage, Billy. If you don't give him a knock we'll never be finished the milking in time.'

'I'll gang tae waken Nick, Mistress Fairly!' Moll Black almost flung aside her milking stool in her eagerness to go to Nick's cottage. Sarah's mouth tightened.

'Get on with the milking, Moll.' The girl's cheap adoration irritated Nick intensely; he had done everything possible to discourage her, but the maid was too slow-witted to take a hint. 'Hurry up, Billy! Though I daresay Nick will be scrambling into his breeches by now. I've never known him sleep late before. The dancing must have been too much for him.'

Beth heard the loud knock on the cottage door as in a dream. She stretched sleepily and a soft smile curved her young mouth as memories of the previous day came flooding back. She opened her eyes. It was broad daylight! It must be late!

I never even heard Papa going to the milking, she thought. Beth always dressed and lit the fire, then followed Nick to the byre to milk the two cows which stood next to Logan's, although Mistress Fairly said she had enough to do looking after her father and the cottage. But I like the milking and the company, she mused dreamily. Hadn't Papa told her that all the women in his family learned to milk long before they left the school. Beth knew he was proud of her because she was not lazy like Sadie Fairly.

She jumped, startled out of her day-dreaming when the knock came again. It was louder, almost urgent. It had not been a dream. The door opened. Someone was calling. Beth blinked and scrambled out of bed. That was Billy Fairly's voice! What could be wrong? She grabbed her shawl and pulled it round her thin shoulders and over her nightgown and then ran on bare feet, pulling open the door between her little bedchamber and the main room of the cottage. Billy was pushing the outer door wider, his face puzzled. He stepped inside. A teasing grin started to his mouth at the sight of Beth's tousled curls and sleepy blue eyes – but the grin vanished instantly. He gasped and strode to the armchair which had been out of his line of vision before.

Nick was stretched out in it, his hands clasped across his broad chest as though in prayer – but he was still wearing his best Sunday clothes – the clothes he had worn to the Minister's wedding! He had cast aside his necktie and loosened the collar which Beth had starched and ironed with such care. Beth rushed after Billy, coming to a halt beside her father's chair.

'Papa! Papa!' In her anxiety she forgot her shawl – and her childish modesty. She tried to tug her father's arm, but Billy caught her hand.

'Dinna, Beth! Aah, lassie . . .' Billy's own voice was unsteady as he tried to hold Beth away from her father.

'Papa! Oh Papa, wake up! Please, oh please wake up . . .' She gave a sob like a small animal in pain. Billy turned her to him then and held her tightly, helplessly, trying to think what he must do. Beth's head scarcely reached past his waist. He smoothed the tangled curls clumsily. Beth did not cry but Billy could feel the shuddering sobs shaking her slight frame as she strove for control. She knows her father is dead, Billy thought dully. She's too intelligent not to guess; she's seen death often enough . . . Suddenly she raised her head and looked him in the eye.

'My father's dead . . . He is, isn't he, Billy?'

Billy would have given everything he possessed in that moment to be able to tell Beth that Nick was only asleep. But he could do nothing – nothing except hold her.

'Get dressed, Beth.' He knew his voice was gruff. He squeezed Beth's thin shoulders. 'Put your clothes on, lassie, ye're shivering. I-I'll take ye tae ma mother . . .' She'll ken what to do, he thought silently. But would she? What could anybody do? He knew exactly how Beth's world had been shattered. He could remember clearly how he had felt when he learned that his own father was dead, that all their plans and talks together were at an end . . . Deep down he had been bitter about it ever since. But at least I had a family, he thought now. He had not appreciated them then, or since, he realised with a shock. Beth had no one – no one at all. Her mother had been an orphan, brought up by her grandmother. Nick was the last of the Jamiesons . . .

Beth's fingers seemed numb and useless as she fumbled with her buttons and laces. She was shaking violently but her eyes felt hot and dry, her head was spinning.

Sarah was carrying a pail of milk across the yard to the dairy and wondering irritably what was taking Billy so long. Then she saw him coming from Nick's cottage, his arm around Beth's shoulders. Even from a distance she could see that Beth's face was ashen and as they came closer she saw the child's blue eyes seemed to swamp her pointed face. She's never looked more like her mother, Sarah thought irrelevantly, trying to fathom the reason for Beth's shocked expression. She set down the pail of milk and moved towards them with a premonition of impending disaster.

Her eyes met Billy's dark ones. She saw the distress in them, the strain on his white face.

'Nick . . .?' Her own voice was a croaky whisper. 'Is – is he ill?' Beth began to shiver and Billy's arm tightened round her but she broke away from him and ran to Sarah. The tears she had controlled for Billy now spilled down her pale cheeks and she clung to Sarah, sobbing as though her heart would break.

'Papa's dead!' she gasped, 'Oh, Mama Fairly . . . What shall we do . . .?' Sarah's arms tightened instinctively round Beth's slender shaking form. She bent and rested her cheek gently against the fair tousled curls, but her own heart was thumping. Nick dead? It was not possible! She raised her eyes to Billy's face and saw the unmistakable nod of his dark head.

Sadie appeared at the byre door.

'We're waiting for the empty pail, Mother!' she called peremptorily. Then her eyes registered the scene in front of her, her mother taking time to show such affection for the Jamieson brat! And telling everybody else to rush through the milking! 'Surely she had enough attention yesterday without demanding more!' she sneered. 'Have ye no' emptied the pail yet? I'm waiting for it.'

Sarah felt Beth wince at Sadie's sharp tone and her arms tightened protectively. Her mouth hardened with instant resolve. Sadie would resent Beth more than ever now. She would cause more trouble if she could . . . but Fairlyden would be the

144

girl's home for as long as she needed one. It never occurred to Sarah that she might meet with opposition from Crispin Bradshaw, as well as from her own daughter.

Beth was twelve years old and mature for her age, but the shock of her father's death forced her to take the giant leap into the adult world – a world of doctors and ministers, of strange men and stranger formalities – a world full of fear and uncertainty. Sarah, recalling the anxieties of her own childhood, her ordeals with the terrifying O'Leary woman, and the dreadful feeling of isolation, tried hard to reassure her from the moment she heard her pitiful plea.

'What shall we do, Mama Fairly?'

'Fairlyden is your home, lassie,' she said gently. 'You were born here, it's in your blood as much as it is in Logan's – and in mine. There will always be a place for you here, Beth. Always.'

It was because she understood Beth's bewilderment, her feeling of insecurity and loss, that Sarah came nearer to quarrelling with Crispin than she had ever been in their long acquaintance.

Crispin had slept badly after leaving Fairlyden – frustrated by his own, unassuaged desire for Sarah, torn by his longing to think only of himself and make her his wife, spending the rest of his life in Scotland; as always his sense of duty prevailed and he had turned and tossed, only to waken from a troubled sleep to hear the news of Nick Jamieson's death. He had volunteered to ride to Mains of Muir with the sad tidings. Now he confronted Sarah with less than his usual patient tact.

'Boarding at the school would be the ideal solution for Beth if it can still be arranged. I am more than willing to pay for her board and lodging at the hostel if the Dominie can arrange a place for her at the Dumfries Academy. Your father told me this morning how worried Nick Jamieson was, in case he was depriving her of an opportunity to use her talents to the full. You have more influence with Beth than anyone, Sarah. You must persuade her to go . . .'

'No!' Sarah was shocked. 'I could never suggest she should leave Fairlyden and everything that is familiar – especially at a time like this!'

'Perhaps you do not want Beth to have an education which would open so many doors to her in the future? Is that it, Sarah?

145

Maybe you want her to be another slave to Fairlyden? Bound to it for life – as you are!' It was the first time Crispin had spoken harshly to Sarah and the moment he had uttered the words he knew they were totally unjustified. As she stared at him the hurt in her wide brown eyes was plain.

'Such a decision would have to be entirely Beth's,' she insisted stubbornly, and her tone was cold.

Silently Crispin cursed himself for a fool. What he had considered a suitable solution to Beth's immediate future apparently seemed a monstrously callous suggestion to Sarah.

'I know Beth will be too upset and shocked to be confronted with such a proposition right now,' he defended himself. 'But you know I must return to Yorkshire in the morning. I cannot wait for the funeral. I thought you would be able to explain to Beth that I am willing pay for her education at the Academy, and for her training as a teacher, if that is what she decides to do. Believe me, Sarah, I was thinking of you too. I wanted to relieve you of yet another burden, at least during the school terms . . .'

Sarah was slightly mollified but her voice was crisp.

'You are generous with your money, Crispin, but I remember how it feels to be insecure and bewildered . . . to lose a beloved parent . . .'

'I have known such loss too, Sarah, but the . . .'

'I promised Beth she would always have a home at Fairlyden! In my heart I know I am the last person to suggest she should go away to live in a hostel amongst strangers. She would think I do not want her here! No, I will not do it!'

'It is such a waste of fine talent to keep her here!'

'Perhaps you should write a letter to her when she has had a little time to adjust – or perhaps you could ask Mrs Bunnerby to speak to her. She is very fond of Logan and Beth. At least that way Beth will know she has a choice – that you are concerned for her happiness too. I promise I shall help her in any way I can if she decides to go to the Academy, but I believe she needs friends, to be with people who are familiar to her right now. The new school term is almost upon us. Besides . . .' She hesitated, then added, 'Logan and Beth are inseparable. He would miss her dreadfully. As it is he will miss Nick too . . .'

'Yes,' Crispin agreed bleakly. 'He probably regarded Nick as a father since he has never known his own.'

★ ★ ★

146

Beth was as bewildered and uncertain as Sarah had predicted. She was reluctant to leave the cottage. She felt she was deserting her father. But Sarah helped her to pack her few personal belongings and move them to Fairlyden. This necessitated a general rearrangement; Sadie had to vacate the largest bedroom so that Billy and Logan might share a room, leaving Logan's free for Beth. Sadie grumbled at the change, at the work, at the inconvenience. Sarah was disgusted by her selfishness. Surely even Sadie must have some compassion in her stony heart – yet her uncle had had none at all . . .

'Nick's death will affect everyone at Fairlyden. Surely you must realise how much he did for all of us? How much he meant to Beth, her only relative . . .'

'That doesna stop her frae sleeping in the maid's room. She should consider herself lucky to have it. She's an orphan and a pauper . . .'

Sarah was tired and strained and it was the end of a long harrowing day. There were still so many things to organise. 'You are the most selfish, hard-hearted daughter any woman could possess,' she exclaimed in a rare burst of temper.

Sadie considered herself beyond reproach, especially by her own mother. 'Beth Jamieson has always meant more tae you than I have, with her smiles and her warbling! I'm your ain flesh and blood!' she cried resentfully. 'I suppose ye think ye can treat her as one o' the family now!'

'Yes,' Sarah said, straightening wearily from sweeping up the hearth – one of the many tasks Sadie had neglected that day. 'Yes.' She held Sadie's cold, pale stare steadily. 'From now on Beth Jamieson is part of my family, and Fairlyden is her home as much as it is yours.' Sarah's chilling tone would have forbade further argument from anyone else. Sadie stared at her mother incredulously.

'Her father was a labourer! A common labourer! She's not one of us. She never will be . . .' Sadie slammed out of the kitchen and up the stairs in a jealous fury.

At the top she came to an abrupt halt. Beth was standing uncertainly in the doorway of her strange bedroom. She could not sleep and the sound of Sadie's voice raised in anger had troubled her. She knew Sadie Fairly had never liked her, but her pointed face was pale and pinched, her eyes too big; there was no doubt she had heard Sadie's angry words.

'I'm s-sorry, S-Sa . . .'

'Oh, go to bed!' If there was a flicker of compassion in Sadie's heart at the sight of Beth, standing forlornly in her nightgown, she quenched it swiftly, slamming her bedroom door in the troubled young face.

Billy rushed on to the landing, his nightshirt hanging over his breeches, his braces looped around his hips in his haste. He lifted his fist to hammer furiously on Sadie's bedroom door, then he let it fall and shrugged his shoulders as he turned to Beth.

'She's no' worth cryin' o'er, Beth. She doesna mean half o' what she says and she doesna ken why she says it.'

'S-Sadie hates me,' Beth stammered. 'And she's right. This isna my house. I dinna belong here. I should hae stayed at the cot . . .' She stopped. Her huge blue eyes dilated with shocked horror. 'The cottage isna Papa's now! I dinna belong anywhere!'

'You belong here, young Beth. My mother says so and I say so and dinna you forget that.' Billy's tone was firm and kind as he scooped Beth up in his arms and carried her back into the bedroom, leaving the door ajar. He laid her gently on the bed and pulled the blankets up to her chin, then he knelt beside her and pulled a dry but grubby handkerchief from his trouser pocket and wiped away her tears. Gradually Beth grew calmer and Billy began to talk, his deep voice low and soothing, his hand lightly stroking the silky hair from her brow.

As Billy talked he surprised himself as much as Beth. He told her of his boyish dreams, how they had been shattered when his father died. How he had believed his mother needed him at Fairlyden.

'She didna really need me, I ken that now. She had your father. He was a fine man, Beth; a father tae be proud of. I should have left Fairlyden while I had the chance . . .' he murmured almost to himself.

'But why? And where would ye go, Billy?' Beth lay watching him, her blue eyes dull with exhaustion and grief, yet she was amazed by Billy's revelations. She had always thought he was happy at Fairlyden – Billy with the sparkling dark eyes and his big smile. He had already left the school before she was born – fourteen he must have been. She had always thought of him as a man. She had never dreamt he had had fears just like her, or doubts about the future; she couldn't imagine anyone *wanting* to leave Fairlyden. To Beth the very name meant security and happiness, the sunshine that had coloured her childhood – hers and Logan's, growing up together, roaming at will . . . exploring the wood at the top of the hill, lying in the sun listening to the pigeons cooing softly . . . running through the low meadow that reached almost to Muircumwell village . . .

She wondered if Logan knew Billy wanted to leave, had planned to leave when he finished school? 'Where would ye go, Billy?' she repeated softly.

'I thought ye were asleep,' Billy smiled. He began to tell her of his dreams, of the countries he had hoped to see, still hoped to see one day. 'I dinna want tae be married, tied down with a family like other men . . .' He talked of the machines that could plough and sow and cut the corn without ever seeing a horse . . . of big ships and wide prairies . . .

Beth was lulled to sleep that night, the night of her father's death, by Billy's deep voice; when she wakened in the morning his grubby handkerchief was still beside her pillow. She found a peculiar comfort in it as she crumpled it tightly in her small fist. It helped her to know that Mama Fairly and Billy and Logan were missing her father – even if it was not quite in the same way as she would miss him. She made a silent vow to avoid Sadie Fairly whenever possible.

Eighteen

The Fairlyden harvest of nineteen hundred and ten took longer than usual and was not without mishaps. Nick Jamieson had been a thorough and careful organiser, quietly fitting the men and maids at his disposal to the tasks which suited them best. Even Sadie realised this after a second load of corn tipped on to the ground before the cart had even left the field.

'Well, I never had tae build the corn on the carts afore!' she stormed at Billy. 'Anyway it was Moll Black's fault. She didna make the corners square enough . . .'

'It wasna my blame!' Moll flared. 'Ye can dae it all yersel' frae now on!'

'Ye're paid tae dae as ye're told!'

'Weel ye can keep your job! I'm leaving come the November term! There's naught worth staying here for noo ma puir Nick has gone and deid!'

'He was never "your" Nick!' Sadie scorned.

'For goodness' sake stop arguing, you two!' Billy snapped. 'Ye're wasting time. Now we'll need tae right the cart and rebuild the sheaves.' His face was pale and tense. He was missing Nick's unobtrusive management more than he had believed possible.

Logan and Beth had helped as much as they could and they returned to school at the end of the summer with reluctance. Sarah had refused to influence Beth over Crispin's offer to send her to Dumfries Academy, but, to Sadie's chagrin, she adamantly rejected the idea of Beth leaving the village school to earn her living.

'If you still want to work at Fairlyden when you leave school, Beth, there will always be a place for you. I promise you that, lassie, but you must learn all you can frae the Dominie first.' Sarah had softened her words with a smile, adding, 'You know I couldna manage the milking without your help, and Logan's,

151

when everyone else is at the harvest, especially with so many extra cows.'

So Beth promised to do her best at school for another year, knowing that her father would have agreed with Mistress Fairly, despite his pride, but she was quiet and subdued, aware that she was dependent on Mistress Fairly's generosity.

Crispin Bradshaw had written her a kindly letter offering to pay the fees if she cared to attend the Dumfries Academy. Mrs Bunnerby had talked to her about it.

'I dinna want tae go away tae school,' Beth told her, her blue eyes wide and frightened. 'I dinna want tae leave Logan and Fairlyden – not ever.'

'Well, I promised Master Bradshaw that I'd talk t'you about it, lass, an' I 'ave.' The wrinkled face broke into a smile and the kind old eyes peered at Beth's pale strained face. 'I wouldn't go either if I was you, that I wouldn't! Now you forget about it, eh? Nobody ain't going t' make y' go away t'school. You just do your lessons for the school master, and y'can come down t'me and I'll larn you t'bake cakes an' t'cook. I like a bit uv young cump'ny, that I do.'

On one of his visits to the inn at Strathtod, Thomas Whiteley had met a man who was looking for farm work. Abe Porter was a middle-aged bachelor who lived with his widowed mother five miles on the other side of Strathtod Village, but he owned a bicycle and was willing to travel to Fairlyden every day. He had two conditions – he did not work on Sundays and he wanted his money in cash every Saturday night instead of at the term. Sarah and Billy considered this was reasonable; he would not be boarding at Fairlyden so he would need money for food and coal each week for himself and his mother. It soon became clear that it was not his principles which kept Abe from working on the Sabbath so much as the ill effects of his Saturday night visits to the alehouse. However, Billy and Thomas were glad to have his help with the winter work, lifting the turnips and storing them in earth pits against the winter frosts, cleaning out the midden and spreading the manure on the fields in readiness for the ploughing.

As the November mists and damp increased, Jamie MacFarlane's health deteriorated and Thomas approached Sarah and Billy anxiously after breakfast one Saturday morning.

'I wandered if ye might spare me tae help Anna wi' the heavy work at Highmuir on Saturday afternoons, just until Jamie improves a bit . . .?' He stood twisting his cap nervously, clearly torn between his loyalty to Fairlyden and his concern for his youngest sister. Sarah understood his dilemma. She also felt a great deal of sympathy for Anna.

'I'm sure Moll Black will be pleased to work a bit longer on Saturdays and earn an extra shilling or so,' Sarah said. 'Of course you must help Anna if she needs you, Thomas.'

'I forgot tae mention it, Mother! Moll Black said she would be leaving at the term. She had a bit o' a quarrel wi' Sadie at harvest time. She hasna mentioned it since though . . .?'

'Then I must ask her what she intends to do,' Sarah frowned. 'Troubles never seem to come singly!'

'Aye, I'm leaving. I on'y kept comi' tae see Nick,' Moll muttered in her gruff monotone when Sarah questioned her.

Billy and Sarah were discussing this change in the situation round the kitchen table after Logan and Beth had gone to bed one evening. Sadie was crouched under the oil lamp reading her latest fashion magazine.

'I dinna think Abe Porter will stay much longer either,' Billy remarked grimly. 'He seems to flit frae place tae place. He's worked on more farms than I ever heard o'. Maybe we should hire a married man at the term to live in Nick's cottage?'

'Maybe you're right, Billy. A married man might be more reliable. I'll speak to Beth about clearing the cottage,' Sarah said slowly. 'Poor lassie, she's so young to have to deal with such decisions. I will advise her to sell the furniture and put the money in the bank for when she needs it . . .'

'Money in the bank!' Sadie looked up sharply. 'Beth Jamieson should be paying for her keep instead o' . . .'

'That's enough, Sadie!' Sarah's voice was cold. 'The bairn has lost enough. As for earning her keep, I've been more than glad of her help since Nick died, and I've never needed to call her in the mornings.' Sadie flushed. She hated getting out of her cosy bed now the mornings were cold and dark and she always waited until she knew the fire would be blazing up the kitchen chimney.

The new occupants of Fairlyden's little cottage were a Mr and Mrs Hardie. Beth hated the thought of anyone else living in what she thought of as her father's house but George Hardie was a quiet, patient man, if a little slow and lacking in wit. He had no children of his own and he was so insignificant that Beth soon grew used to him living in her old home.

His wife, Ruby, had agreed to work in the dairy and help with the milking and the hens, though like Sadie she abhorred pigs and the smell of them. Most of all she disliked Peggotty, who had never forgotten she had once been a pet, roaming freely wherever and whenever her restless spirit took her; whenever Ruby passed her pen she would rush out with loud grunts and jump up on her hind legs with her front trotters clinging over the door and her snout thrusting into the air with a look of piggy disdain. If by chance Peggotty had escaped from her pen Ruby Hardie invariably screeched, 'Gang awa! Away, ye horrid beast!'

To Sarah it seemed as though the ambling sow took a delight in pestering the thin, fluttering woman with her tinny voice; she seemed to take on a new burst of youth, trotting gaily after Ruby, grunting loudly until the cottage door was banged in her snout. Then she would return calmly to the orchard or to her sty. Sarah, coming upon this spectacle unexpectedly, felt sure the pig was laughing, if pigs were capable of such things. Certainly Logan and Beth almost collapsed with silent mirth the first time they saw their harmless old pet giving chase to Mistress Hardie as she took to her heels and ran back to her house instead of proceeding on her way to the dairy.

On the first day of the new year, nineteen hundred and eleven, Sarah was not at all amused when Ruby flew into an uncontrollable rage in the middle of the milking. There had been nothing to provoke her, except that she was suffering from an over-indulgence of Hogmanay celebrations. Sarah's voice was chillingly cold as she bid her control herself and her language. Beth and Logan stared at her in alarm as she frenziedly beat a defenceless cow with her milking stool, shouting the foulest oaths imaginable, and upsetting the other cows until every one of them lifted their tails, sending a nervous shower up the byre walls, over the pails and everything else in sight. No amount of soothing could calm them for the rest of the milking and some of them could not relax enough to let their milk flow freely; the day's yield was far less than usual.

Ruby's outburst made Sarah wary. The thin, almost scraggy, woman bore no physical resemblance to Maureen O'Leary, the terrifying scourge of her own childhood, yet her violent tantrum reminded her vividly of the terror she had suffered at the hands of the sadistic woman who had come to Fairlyden as a wet nurse. The episode troubled her.

As the spring days lengthened Beth and Logan reverted to their old happy camaraderie, exploring the countryside they loved, catching tadpoles, searching for birds' nests, even getting their shoes and stockings wet trying to reach the biggest kingcup. Although they both had their duties to perform – feeding and cleaning Peggotty and her latest litter, milking their own few cows and helping Sarah search for the nests of those hens and ducks intent on wandering – Beth found she had more time than she had had looking after the cottage while her father was alive. It was true that she still missed her father for he had been a kind and patient parent, but she knew that Logan shared her loss, and even Billy and Mistress Fairly seemed to understand a little of the awful inner loneliness which sometimes threatened.

In June the Coronation of King George V and Queen Mary provided a cause for celebration, but the occasion was overshadowed by the strife and discontent which was rocking the very core of the British people: workers wanting more money; women demanding the right to vote; unemployed men desperate for jobs; children needing shoes on their feet and food in their bellies.

Thousands of women of every class marched through London in a bid to force the government to give them the right to vote.

'I firmly believe women have as much right to vote as men,' Sarah declared sharply when Billy condemned the women as lazy troublemakers. 'Though I would never have had the courage to go all the way to London and stand up for my rights.' She suppressed a shudder. 'Even less could I have gone to prison. I'm very glad Ellen is too busy nursing her sick children to take time to join the marchers.' But I wish Brad Leishman would return and make her a happy wife and mother, she added silently. In spite of her support for the suffragettes, her own earnest wish was to see her daughters happily married, and to hold her first grandchild.

The seamen called for a national strike when their demands for wages of five pounds ten shillings a month were refused.

'I canna believe such things can be happening in Great

Britain!' Sarah said anxiously when Crispin Bradshaw returned to Scotland in August for a brief visit. 'Imagine the troops being called out. Some of the rioters have been shot! Killed!'

'Mmm, Winston Churchill has certainly taken a tough line with the strikers,' Crispin agreed, his expression troubled. 'But almost the whole of our transport system has come to a halt. There is food rotting in the docks while thousands of people go hungry! Manchester is said to be on the verge of famine. The situation is explosive even amongst our own workers. I cannot stay away too long.'

'Well, ye canna wonder at folks being upset when the government has voted to pay Members of Parliament four hundred pounds a year. Keir Hardie incites the strikers, Winston Churchill wants them shot!' Billy's dark eyes sparkled angrily. 'As for the food, nobody cares where it comes frae until they're hungry! According tae some o' the English dealers at Annan market, farmers in the south have been forced tae give up altogether. They and their workers are swelling the queues o' unemployed instead o' growing grain to fill all the hungry bellies.'

Crispin nodded, but his eyes moved to Sarah, noting the wisps of silvery grey which had appeared at her temples since Nick Jamieson's death almost a year ago. 'Are things going all right here, at Fairlyden?'

'Our crops have never been better, in spite o' folks complaining o' the dry weather in the south.' It was Billy who answered and there was a note of pride in his voice now, his swift anger had abated. This was his first harvest without Nick's help. Suddenly he snatched up the basket from the table. 'I'd forgotten about the tea! If I dinna hurry back tae the field George Hardie and Thomas will think their throats are parched for life – or maybe they'll go on strike tae!' He grimaced wryly. 'Anyway it's good tae see ye again, Mr Bradshaw, and I'm sure Mother will be glad o' some sane company.'

Crispin lifted one eyebrow in that quizzical way which Logan was beginning to imitate, only there was something in Crispin's gaze which brought a faint blush to Sarah's cheeks. Their coolness over Beth's education was quite forgotten. Imagine reaching fifty-two and still blushing when a man looks at you, Sarah chastised herself silently. But it was not just any man who could make her blush – only Crispin.

'So,' he said, seating himself comfortably on the wooden settle and stretching out his long legs. 'Are you in need of sane company, Sarah? What did Billy mean?'

Sarah grimaced and proceeded to tell him about Ruby Hardie and her rages.

'To tell the truth it isn't a joke any more . . . I never leave Logan and Beth alone with her now, and I don't like to leave her in the byre with the cows even – though sometimes I have to . . .'

'Have you spoken to her about her moods?' Crispin frowned.

'Oh yes, but she can be quite pleasant when she's normal – almost as though she doesn't believe how awful she has been. I even talked to George about it but he just shrugs and says you get used to her in time . . . . I don't think I'll ever get used to her, Crispin!' Sarah shuddered suddenly.

'Get rid of her.' Crispin's voice was tight. 'I thought you seemed under a strain, Sarah. It's not good for you – nor for anyone else here.'

Sarah nodded. 'I know it's what we ought to do. I do need someone sane to talk to! Billy was right about that! But I don't think he understands how much the problem of Ruby Hardie has been on my mind lately; he rarely has to work with her himself. I suppose he doesn't want to lose her husband; he's a good worker, even if he is a bit slow.'

At the end of October Billy told George Hardie he would have to look for another place at the term.

'Aye,' the man sighed, 'I didna think ye'd want us tae stay much longer. She canna help it – Ruby and her temper, I mean. I'm sorry, Mr Fairly, for I've enjoyed working here.'

'I felt terrible, Mother,' Billy reported later. 'Are ye sure ye canna put up with Ruby a bit longer?'

'I'm quite sure,' Sarah insisted firmly. 'But I shall tell her myself when she comes to the milking.'

Ruby did not wait until milking time. The moment George had broken the news to her at midday she flung herself out of the cottage and came hammering on the door of Fairlyden. Billy had just sat down to eat his own meal. For the first time he understood his mother's apprehension. Ruby had evidently snatched the saucepan from the fire when George broke the news; it still contained the hot mashed potatoes intended for her husband's dinner. Now she hurled it at Billy's head. He ducked just in time and the saucepan hit the kitchen wall with a dreadful clatter and a shower of mashed potato. The scene might have been funny except that Ruby's rage did not end there and Sarah was truly thankful that Billy was strong enough to restrain her from doing further damage until George arrived on the scene and led her, swearing and kicking, back to the cottage.

When Sarah called at Jardine's Store a few days after Ruby had attempted to decorate the kitchen walls with mashed potato, Lizzie asked if she would join her mother for a cup of tea in their upstairs rooms. Sarah readily agreed. She thought she would tell Janet of the episode with Ruby. She would be sure to laugh at the woman's foolish escapade. No doubt Janet would see the whole thing in its proper perspective too . . .

Sarah never did tell Janet about the Hardies, though. As soon as she entered the neat little parlour above Jardine's shop she realised Janet was near to tears, and she was not a tearful woman.

'What's wrong, Janet?' Sarah asked gently as the older woman poured a cup of tea into her own cup and forgot to pour any into Sarah's, although she passed her the milk and sugar and the empty cup. It was a sure sign that Janet had something on her mind for she was always hospitable.

'Och, it's Anna,' Janet muttered. 'Such a silly thing tae dae . . .'

'What has Anna done?' Sarah asked in bewilderment.

'Jamie has taken a turn for the worse this past fortnight . . . I expect she was tired. I ken she's worried. But ye see, Mistress Sarah, she clean forgot tae fill up the brooder lamps with oil . . .'

'But surely she has no young chickens at this time of year?'

'They were a late batch – out o' season. Some sort of an experiment and worth a lot o' money. They werena that wee either, but it was a cold night . . . They must have huddled together when the lamp went out. They smothered – every yin o' them. Such a loss for Anna it is, specially after feeding them sae long . . . They've sae little money coming in with Jamie being ill for sae long . . . I dae what I can . . .' She shrugged helplessly. 'And Jardine watches me like a hawk in case I take her anything frae the shop without paying for it! As if I ever would!'

Sarah did her best to comfort Janet but there was little she could say and indeed her own heart bled for Anna struggling to

158

make a living and look after her sick husband and young child on the small bleak farm.

'Does Ray Jardine still object to her coming here to visit you?' Sarah asked.

'Oh aye. He'll never change his mind about that. He's feart for his ain skin,' Janet said bitterly. 'But as he says, he's given me a home and work all these years . . .'

'But you've earned it, Janet! More than earned it the way you and Lizzie have looked after the shop and opened the bakery and looked after him. You even nursed his father until he died . . .'

'Ach, auld Mr Jardine was no bother . . .' Janet's face softened for a moment at the memory of the old shopkeeper. 'And he was that grateful for everything I did tae make him comfortable. I suppose Ray Jardine's not that bad really,' she mused, trying to be fair, 'not when ye get used tae him, and naebody has many pennies tae spare these days. It's just that he has this queer idea about catching the coughing disease . . . But tae tell ye the truth . . . I wouldna like tae leave the shop now. I've got used tae living i' the village. I'd miss the company and bustle o' it all, and so would Lizzie for all she's sae quiet. It's just Anna I worry about. I ken in my heart that Jamie canna go on much longer, puir soul . . .'

Two weeks later Thomas received a note from his mother to say that his brother-in-law had died during the night.

'Naturally you must go to Anna, Thomas,' Sarah agreed when Thomas stood before her, pale-faced and anxious as he strained to hear. 'She will need you to help with the funeral arrangements and other things.'

Nineteen

A few days after Jamie MacFarlane's funeral, Thomas approached Sarah and Billy looking white-faced and distinctly miserable.

'I hae tae tell ye that I'll need tae be leaving Fairlyden at the November term.'

'Leaving, Thomas! B-but why?' Sarah stared at him in dismay. He gazed back at her mutely. It's almost as though he hopes I'll perform some sort of miracle, she thought – but what?

'I didna think ye'd ever leave Fairlyden!' Billy's tone was hurt and angry. 'And at such short notice. Ye ken we've already asked the Hardies tae look for another place . . .'

Thomas frowned, struggling to catch all Billy's words for he had a habit of speaking quickly when he was upset and Sarah had noticed that Thomas's hearing always seemed worse when he was tense.

'If you want to leave Fairlyden, Thomas, we shall give you our blessing,' she said clearly.

'*Want* tae leave!' He twisted and retwisted his flat cap. 'I've never wanted tae leave Fairlyden . . .' There was a catch in his voice. 'I've never forgotten how ye and the Master took me on afore I was big enough tae reach the side o' the cairt . . .'

'So why are ye leaving, then?' Billy demanded. 'Are ye like Moll Black? Is't because Nick's no here anymore? Is't because o' me . . .?' Sarah was surprised to hear the underlying uncertainty behind Billy's anger.

'No, no, Master Billy! It's Anna! She canna keep on the tenancy o' Highmuir without a man tae help her. The laird reckons the farm's been neglected for the want o' a fit man these past two years. She can scarce afford tae pay the rent; she couldna pay a man tae work . . .' Thomas looked at them helplessly and Sarah's heart went out to him.

'But how will you all live when there's no money coming in? No stock or milk tae sell? It's such a bleak, cold place even for sheep.

161

Highmuir needs far more than a fit man to make it pay in these times!'

'There's nowhere else for Anna tae gang.' Thomas shrugged dejectedly. 'At least she'll have a roof o'er her head.'

'Does your mother know? What does she say, Thomas?' Sarah asked slowly.

'Weel, Jardine wouldna take Anna back, not wi' the babe, that's for sure! Mother isna happy about it. She reckons Highmuir eats money instead o' making any . . .'

'She's probably right at that!'

'Anna would make a grand housekeeper, and she's good with the poultry tae, but who would want her with a young bairn?' Thomas shook his head to and fro despondently. 'I'm sorry, Mistress . . . Master Billy . . .' Sarah could almost have sworn there were tears in his eyes as he turned abruptly and strode away.

'Well!' She looked helplessly at Billy. 'Troubles certainly dinna come alone . . . We shall be fortunate if we get one good man, but two!' She shook her head. 'Even so, we're fortunate in comparison with young Anna MacFarlane . . .'

'I suppose so.' Billy muttered flatly. He had felt more trapped at Fairlyden than ever since Nick died. Now he felt smothered. He would never get away. Thomas knew the farm like the back of his hand, even if he was not and never would be, of the same calibre as Nick Jamieson. He was honest and hard working; he never grumbled; he would have worked for Logan when the time came. They would have managed . . . Logan was a born farmer, or would be in a few more years. Nick had said that often; so did Grandfather Logan.

A week had passed since Thomas broke the news that he was leaving Fairlyden. Sarah worried about him. He was not eating and she suspected he was not sleeping well either. He worked as hard as ever, but he also worked at Highmuir on Saturday afternoons and all day on the Sabbath.

Crispin Bradshaw had come up to Scotland for a visit before the winter weather set in, or so he said. Sarah knew he wanted to assure himself that Mrs Bunnerby was taking care of herself after a bad attack of rheumatism – or at least that was the only complaint she would admit to having. Sarah invited him to Sunday lunch. She looked forward to his company and his news

162

of the world beyond their own parish and it would save his elderly housekeeper. She had also asked her father and Beatrice, Alex and Meg to join them. It seemed ages since they had all been together and she knew it might be the last opportunity for some time, what with winter coming on and new men to train into the ways of Fairlyden.

Beth and Logan had been busy gathering sticks and chopping small logs which they had piled into a large box for Sarah's convenience so that she could light the fire in the dining room. Sadie had been more than willing to polish the silver cutlery and serving dishes which had once belonged to the first Sarah Munro and which Sadie insisted on calling the heritage from her genteel ancestors. Sarah brought out her own old favourite, the blue and white Chinese bowl which her mother had brought with her from Galloway. She filled it with autumn leaves, a few lingering Michaelmas daisies and the first sprigs of winter jasmine.

Sarah felt quite proud of the room with its gleaming mahogany table and the long matching sideboard which looked so much better in the dining room than it had as the kitchen dresser when she was a child. The beeswax and elbow grease had worked wonders on its solid wood. She smiled as she saw Sadie admiring the effect of their combined handiwork too, but then Sadie liked to consider herself a lady.

She turned her attention to the food. She had made a large pot of cock-a-leekie soup to warm her guests. The November day had an insidious chill although there was no wind; it had taken some time for the morning fog to clear and even now the hills were invisible, lost in a grey mirk so that the fields seemed to merge into an endless, colourless sky. There was roast lamb with rosemary and a stuffing made with apricots and herbs and breadcrumbs to follow, parsnips, sprouts and boiled and roasted potatoes. Mrs Bunnerby always maintained that Crispin's favourite dessert was bramble and apple pie made with a sweet crust and served with cream so she had opened one of her jars of preserved brambles and Beth had peeled and chopped the apples.

Almost inevitably the talk turned to the changes which were taking place at Fairlyden.

'Maggie told us about Thomas's proposed move,' Sandy remarked. 'She's a bit concerned about him. After all he is her only brother and they were quite close when they were young and working at Fairlyden together.'

'She says her mother doesna think they'll make enough tae keep the three o' them up at Highmuir, let alone pay the rent.' Alex joined the conversation.

'Thomas is a hard worker,' Billy mused. 'But he admits he canna make decisions. Even after all these years he never kens when the pigs are fat enough for killing, or when it's time tae cut the hay, or if the oats are ripe for harvest . . .'

'Aye weel, there's many a good worker like that,' his grandfather agreed. 'And it's a good job tae or they'd all be wanting to farm themselves and we need labourers. Janet kens her ain son's limitations; that's why she's afraid he will be worse off.'

Logan and Beth listened anxiously. They hated the thought of Thomas having to leave, especially as the thought of it made him so unhappy.

'I wouldna want tae leave Fairlyden either, not ever!' Beth announced vehemently. 'Why can't Anna come back and live in the cottage? She was born there, just like me and Thomas. Surely she must like it tae . . .' There was a sudden silence. Beth's face flushed a bright pink. 'I-I'm sorry. I ken it's nothing tae dae with me . . .'

'No, it is not!' Sadie snapped. 'Ye shouldna even . . .'

'Whisht, Sadie! Ye shouldna be sorry, lassie. I do believe ye've probably found the best solution any of us have thought of yet! If Anna was willing to earn her own living as a housekeeper, then I'm sure she'd be willing to move back to the house where she was born and look after Thomas and Jamie there. What do you think, Billy?'

A wry grin spread over his handsome face. 'I dinna ken why I didna think o' that! Ye're a genius, young Beth!' Sadie scowled as Beth's embarrassed blush turned to pleasure. 'I'd certainly be a lot happier if we could keep Thomas, and I think he'd be happier tae.'

'Of course we shall have to make sure Anna is willing to give up Highmuir . . .' Sarah reflected cautiously, 'but Anna is used to rearing chickens. She could help me with the poultry. She could even bring her chicken brooder . . .' Sarah's enthusiasm increased. 'We could try rearing our chickens without broody hens and all the fuss of chicken coops; maybe we could even rear for other people . . . That way Anna could earn some money too. I read in the paper about poultry instructresses from the new agricultural college; they travel round the country areas, teaching folks about the new methods of rearing and feeding and suchlike. Now that we have a village hall at Muircumwell maybe we could have meetings with an instructress too. Anna and Sadie and I could go . . . Maybe you too, Beth? When you leave school?'

'Maybe I'll come tae if the instructress is pretty . . .' Billy chuckled.

'I'm serious, Billy!' Sarah frowned severely. 'Everybody knows men havena any patience with hens! Anyway you've little enough interest in any o' the animals . . .'

'I'm interested in the animals though!' Logan piped in. 'If Thomas and Anna live in the cottage we'll not need a man for the bothy. I'll soon be leaving school, and Beth will tae.'

'Logan is certainly strong for his age,' Alex agreed. 'And ye ken what tae dae better than most hired men, don't ye, little brother?' Alex's dark eyes twinkled. Then his expression sobered. 'Of course, Mother, if ye would agree tae make the byre bigger so that ye had extra stalls and room for all the cows at once, the milking would be easier and quicker . . .'

'And the cleaning and bedding and feeding!' Billy grimaced.

Sarah's face lost some of its bright glow. 'It's a good byre! I've told you before, it served well enough for the old Earl when he built it.'

'Oh, Mother!' There was anger and frustration in Billy's protest. 'Everything was different then!'

'We canna afford to build another byre,' Sarah said flatly, 'and there's no room to extend the one we have.'

Alex met his grandfather's eye and received an almost imperceptible nod. Crispin Bradshaw, a silent observer, noted the gesture with interest.

'I've had some good luck with the horses these past two years, Mother . . .' Alex grinned, reminding Sarah of his father.

'I suppose you're going to tell me you've sold another Baron of Bucklyvie!' she scoffed. 'I don't believe any horse could be worth nine thousand five hundred pounds!'

'Ach,' Sandy shook his white head, 'there's no other horse will fetch a price like that.' He turned to Crispin. 'Two men were determined tae get him. Though he is a good stallion by all accounts. Alex does well enough with his own prices – and he has a filly foal by the Baron, haven't ye, Alex?'

'Aye, and a fine wee beast she is tae. But I could have built ye a whole new farmsteading and bought the land to go with it, Mother, if I had the money the Baron himself made. As it is I could give ye the money tae build a byre, or loan it tae ye, if ye prefer,' he added quickly, seeing his mother stiffen with pride.

'You'll do no such thing!' Sarah exclaimed sharply. 'I want no more debts!' She caught Crispin's eye and remembered that her father still knew nothing of the debts she had inherited after William's death. She went on more calmly, 'I thank you for your offer though, laddie. You've worked hard for your money and you deserve it, but there's no telling what you might need before you're as old as your Grandfather Logan!'

Alex glanced at Sandy affectionately. 'Seventy-five and still going strong! There's no hope o' me lasting that long!'

'Ach, ye dinna ken!' Sandy chuckled. 'I didna think I'd ever reach three-score years and ten when I broke my leg sae badly, and look at me now . . . But then I've been lucky . . .' His blue eyes twinkled as they moved from Sarah to Beatrice on the opposite side of the table. 'Ye're awfy quiet, lassie . . .'

'I'm fine,' Beatrice smiled her sweet, faintly sad smile. 'But listening to Sarah's problems, it amazes me . . .' She looked at Sarah affectionately. 'Ye're still as fresh as ever. Ye seem tae thrive on challenges. Maybe Alex is right though, ye ought tae have things a bit easier . . .'

'I agree.' Crispin joined the discussion for the first time. 'It seems to me that a larger byre would make the work much easier and quicker for everyone, especially if it is properly planned with piped water and ventilation. If you find a local builder I will pay . . .'

'I think we should discuss this later,' Sarah interrupted hurriedly, afraid that her father might begin to suspect that Fairlyden was no longer hers, as he fondly believed. But she knew by the determined glint in Crispin's eyes that he would not forget the matter for all he nodded so obligingly.

Two days later Crispin drew up in his motor car in front of Fairlyden and strode towards the door with a look of determination on his face.

'Dress up warmly, Sarah,' he instructed after the briefest of greetings. 'I have come to drive you to Highmuir. You will explain things to Anna far better than Thomas, I'm sure.'

Ten minutes later, with Sarah warmly dressed in her winter

jacket and with her woollen cloak over the top, a fine shawl over her hat and round her shoulders and a rug tucked around her legs, Crispin turned to her with a small triumphant smile.

'Now we shall have peace from interruptions, even if it is a little cold and maybe a little noisy in my motor car. It will give me a chance to talk over other matters with you, Sarah.'

'Aah!' Sarah grimaced wryly. 'I should have known you had an ulterior motive.'

As they bowled along it was not easy to discuss any serious topic over the noise and splutter of Crispin's motor car. He waited until they were on their way home again before he drew into the shelter of a high hedge protected from the winter wind.

'Anna seemed as relieved as Thomas when you offered her the chance of returning to the cottage at Fairlyden,' Crispin observed.

'Yes. Poor Anna. She has had so little time for happiness.'

'But she has her son . . .' Crispin reminded her almost wistfully, 'and she had all the love of her husband while he lived.'

'She has a strong character too, like her mother. I remember how brave Janet was when Louis died. I know Anna thinks she has cause to be grateful to me just now, but I do believe she will be a great asset to Fairlyden someday.'

'And speaking of Fairlyden, Sarah, remember I am your landlord; it is my duty to keep the buildings up to date and in good order.'

'Oh, Crispin, it is not your duty at all.' Sarah sighed. 'You know how grateful I am to you. You came to my rescue when I needed help so badly . . .'

'Well, I intend to build a new byre for you and I wish I had realised earlier how inconvenient the present one is.'

'We didn't even have enough cows to fill the present stalls when the dreadful abortions kept recurring after William died. I only hope the present buyers will continue to take all the milk we can produce now that we are making progress again. They simply reject it for the slightest reason if they have too much, and of course we get no money at all then.'

'Well, if you have a better byre at least it will be easier, and while we are discussing improvements, it is time we installed the bath and water closet in the bathing room at Fairlyden.'

'Oh no! You canna do all that, Crispin. Billy and Sadie will wonder why you're being so generous as it is!'

'Then tell them, Sarah. It's time they understood what burdens you have carried, how you have shielded them . . .'

'I couldna . . .' Sarah whispered. 'Billy would be sure to tell Alex. I . . . they might tell Father – even if only accidentally – during a conversation. It would upset him. He is so sure that Fairlyden belongs to me, that I have security for the rest of my life . . .'

'Well, so you have.'

'How can you be so sure?'

'Of course I'm sure.'

'Fairlyden is a part of your estate now – just like your woollen mill; just like Fairlyside. They will all belong to your nephew one day and . . .'

'Not Fairlyden! Nor my house here, in Scotland. Trust me, Sarah!' Crispin's tone was almost harsh.

'I know you would never treat us unfairly but the law is the law and . . .'

'Marry me then! There would be no disputing your right to Fairlyden if you were my wife.'

Sarah frowned. 'Are you . . . are you blackmailing me into marrying you, Crispin, to keep Fairlyden . . .?'

'Well . . . now I come to think of it, I have always believed you would do anything for Fairlyden, Sarah.' There was a twinkle in his eyes but Sarah did not see it.

'Not quite anything.' Her voice was quiet, a little hurt, but she took a deep breath. 'Crispin . . . I – I want you to know that – that if ever I do marry you it would never be for Fairlyden . . .'

'No?'

'No. If ever I marry you it will be because I respect you more than any other man I have ever known – including William.'

'Respect . . .' Crispin repeated the word. He gave a crooked smile. 'Respect – but not love . . . eh, Sarah?'

Sarah bit her lip. 'Maybe it would be – be that too,' she said almost under her breath. 'Certainly it would be because we wanted to be together more than anything else in the world . . . You must be honest, Crispin – neither of us is prepared to give up our – our life's interests right now – today.'

'Perhaps you're right,' Crispin sighed softly. 'But at least I can believe there is some hope for us. I shall not wait forever. Take that as a warning, Mistress Fairly,' he said sternly, but his eyes were gentle and he leaned forward and, cupping her chin in his hands, kissed her gently as though sealing a pact between them. Then he jumped down and proceeded to swing the handle of the engine until it throbbed into life once more. The moment of intimacy was over – though not forgotten.

Twenty

The new byre at Fairlyden was almost completed by the end of January, nineteen hundred and twelve. Crispin had left nothing to chance. He had travelled up from Yorkshire several times to make sure the work was going ahead as fast as the December gales and subsequent frosts would allow. Sarah enjoyed his visits more than she cared to admit; his wry wit and his conversation stimulated her; his attention made her feel cherished and at the same time young again.

Anna MacFarlane had arranged her affairs at Highmuir with the landlord's cooperation and she and Thomas settled into the cottage which had been their childhood home. If Anna looked a little wan, at least she was surrounded by friends. Beth became one of her most frequent and welcome visitors now that she had left her schooldays behind; she loved the antics of young Jamie MacFarlane and he in turn chortled merrily at the sight of her.

'Ye should have seen the pair o' them, Mistress Fairly,' Anna smiled, 'Beth marching round the kitchen singing that new song, "Alexander's Ragtime Band", with Jamie waddling beside her trying tae keep time.'

The bitterly hard frosts at the beginning of February postponed all the work for a while but by the end of the month the cows were moved into their new quarters, and very skittish they were too. In the old byre each cow had been used to its own familiar stall, some preferring the partition to one side, some to the other.

'How stupid they are!' Sadie yelled in annoyance.

'Don't rush them,' Sarah calmed her impatient daughter. 'You should know by now they have their own order of precedence — from the old boss cow down to the most timid heifer. If we can get old Queenie into the new byre the rest will follow.'

Eventually they succeeded, but once inside the sole aim of the whole herd seemed to be to get out again; then three cows would decide to wedge themselves firmly in a stall for two; it took a long time before each one had been allocated her new stall and chained in place. The new byre had stalls down both sides with a wide passage up the middle and troughs in front and even a vent for air, all according to Crispin's plans; there was room for even more cows if the herd should continue to grow.

'Well, now the mêlée's over, that's a great improvement!' Billy declared with satisfaction. It was the first positive expression he had uttered since Nick Jamieson's death, Sarah realised. The cows had been fed with hay and the centre walk swept clean once more. 'I dinna ken how we shall ever repay Mr Bradshaw though . . .?'

Sarah did not reply; she was still dubious about the wisdom of allowing Crispin to pay for so many alterations, yet inwardly she was jubilant about the improvements, and even more so if they meant Billy being more content.

Unfortunately Crispin was not present when the changes were completed. He was deeply concerned for his workers and the Yorkshire woollen mill. The miners' strike was causing chaos; their demands for five shillings a day for men and two shillings for boys had not been met. Coal supplies were running perilously short and factories were being forced to close when they ran out of fuel. If they could not fulfil their orders on time the trade would be lost; there was not a single worker who could afford a cut back on his wage, let alone lose several days' pay if the mills were shut down.

Moreover Crispin was well aware there were always some workers who would cause trouble on the slightest pretext, even in his own mill. It had taken all his tact and diplomacy to avoid a nasty scene after Robert Smith, his own nephew, inflamed the anger and frustration of a small group of men.

'He shouted at them to get back to their looms, while he flaunted himself in checked plus-fours and blasted the horn of his new motor car.'

Crispin had written in his letter to Sarah.

'They knew he was on his way to join a shooting party while they spend their days in the mill. Now he is heading for warmer climes in Europe. Frankly, Sarah, though it pains

172

me to say it about my own sister's son, it is a relief to know he will be out of the way for some weeks. I pray the unrest will be settled before his return. Ted Forbes agreed with me most fervently. I have felt for some time that he would ensure harmony between every department, and bridge any gaps from myself down to the newest young sweeper. It is not an easy task in these times of stress but he is justifying all my faith in him. So much so, in fact, that I find myself making all manner of plans for the future – our future, my dearest Sarah.'

Sarah felt a glow of happiness at Crispin's words, but she was concerned by the news of the increasing industrial strife. She followed events closely now that she understood more about the Bradshaw Mill and some of the problems. She clearly recalled Crispin telling her about Ted Forbes, the young man he had promoted to foreman six months earlier. He had been orphaned when he was six years old; Bert Bradshaw had tried to help him, even offering the boy an education which would have allowed him to escape from his industrial northern roots. Apparently wool and the mills were in the boy's blood and he had pleaded with Crispin to give him a job as soon as he was old enough to leave school. Gradually he had worked his way up through the mill until he understood the various processes, the difficulties of buying quality wool at the right price, of marketing the cloth, the faults, the people . . .

'My father once said he wished he had a grandson with half Ted's potential and personality.' Crispin had sighed when he told her. 'I daresay he might have been a bit disappointed that the lad didn't make better use of his education, but he would have been proud of him in the mill. The men, aye and the women, respect him. I just wish Fanny's son had his ability and his understanding of human nature. I would happily leave everything in his hands. You know what that could mean for us, my dear . . .'

Sarah's own dreams for the future were forgotten when she read the news in Ellen's weekly letter. The page fluttered from her fingers. She bowed her head in her hands.

'Mama!' In his anxiety Logan addressed her as he had when he was a child. 'Mama, are ye all right?'

'Yes.' Sarah heard him as though from a great distance.

173

'What does Ellen say in her letter? Is she coming home this week?' Logan always enjoyed his elder sister's visits. She was interested in everything and she always went with him and Beth for a walk round the fields, or to see the young animals; she never failed to pay a special visit to Peggotty. The old sow had never forgotten her either and she would lie down on her side and wait as meekly as a baby for Ellen to scratch her. Then there was always cake for tea or a special pudding if Ellen was home. He looked at his mother sitting so still and staring into space. 'Is Ellen coming?'

'Yes . . .' Sarah sighed and her voice quivered in spite of her effort to control it. 'B-but she's going away . . . away to America. I expect you've forgotten Brad Leishman, the . . .'

'The American doctor who writes letters to her? Is Ellen going to see him?'

'Yes,' Sarah nodded but her voice was no more than a whisper. She cleared her throat with an effort. 'He's sent the money for her passage. They're going to be . . . married.'

'Married! In America?'

'Well, Brad canna leave his mother and she refuses to come with him. She's sick . . . Ellen is to travel on that new ship we were reading about. At least she will be safe. They say it's unsinkable.'

'Ellen's going tae sail across the ocean on the *Titanic*?' Logan whistled incredulously. Then he stopped short, frowning, staring uncertainly at his mother's white face. She always had colour in her cheeks. 'When – when will she come back?' he asked in a low voice.

Sarah shook her head. She could not trust herself to speak. She had missed Ellen's company terribly when she first went to work at the hospital, but there had always been her visits home to look forward to, and her letters. Sarah shivered. We may never see Ellen again. I must not think about that. She sounds so happy. She smoothed out the letter and read it again. I canna spoil her joy. I must be calm and strong. I must!

'There'll be a lot to do,' she said aloud. 'Maybe Beth will help us with the sewing . . . Nightdresses, petticoats, day gowns and gowns for afternoon . . . so many things . . . She sails on the tenth of April, but she has to travel to Southampton . . . We shall never be ready!'

★ ★ ★

174

Ellen had one full week at Fairlyden. Sarah's head buzzed with anxious thoughts, but she was determined to present a bright, cheerful face to the world as she prepared Ellen's favourite meals. She had arranged a family gathering for the day before Ellen was to catch the train to London and then Southampton. All too soon the day arrived, but almost before it had begun, Alex rode into the yard. Sarah hurried outside.

'Grandfather Logan has caught a chill, Mother.' He was tethering his horse to the hitching rail rather than taking him to the stable.

'You're not staying, Alex?'

'Aunt Beattie thinks he is developing a temperature. He's finding it difficult to catch his breath, though he says it's only a cold.' Alex followed his mother into the kitchen.

'A cold can be serious enough at your grandfather's age, but I hope that's all it is . . .?'

'He doesna want to bother Doctor Kerr. Aunt Beattie is worried, though. She says it would be madness for him to leave his ain bed, but she thinks ye'll have done a lot o' cooking for the party. She . . .er, she wondered if you and Ellen could come tae the Mains instead . . .?' Sarah had been watching him closely.

'Beatrice is really worried, isn't she, Alex?'

'Aye. I dinna like the look o' him either. I thought I'd ask Doctor Kerr tae look in at the Mains when I ride back through Muircumwell . . .'

'Mmm, I'm sure that would be wise,' Sarah agreed. Then she forced herself to smile brightly at her eldest son. His face relaxed slightly. 'Ellen and I will pack some of the pies and the baked ham into a basket. We'll bring them with us in the trap. If Father is well enough we shall enjoy a small family gathering at the Mains. We can have a little feast here when Ellen and I return to Fairlyden tonight.'

'I can scarcely remember Grandfather Logan being ill,' Ellen mused as Sarah took up the reins and clicked her tongue at the pony a couple of hours later. 'He's aye been one o' the healthiest men I know, even for his age.'

'He has enjoyed good health,' Sarah agreed, 'except for the accident when he broke his leg. It's hard to believe he'll be seventy-six next September.'

'He would say, "I was seventy-five last September!" He always says it makes him feel a year younger,' Ellen chuckled.

Privately Sarah wondered if the thought of saying goodbye to Ellen was troubling her father. Her own anxiety, and her grief at the thought of parting from her elder daughter, felt like a heavy stone in her chest. She knew her father loved all his grandchildren but she had always suspected Alex and Ellen were his favourites. He seemed to share a special, inexplicable bond with them which was lacking with the others. Since Nick Jamieson's death, and Crispin's more frequent visits, a similar bond had begun to develop between Logan and the man who was his natural father . . .

'Ye're very quiet, Mother,' Ellen remarked gently. 'Surely ye dinna think Grandfather is really ill . . .?' She shivered suddenly. 'I hate the thought o' saying g-goodbye to him as it is . . .' Her voice shook and Sarah realised that Ellen was feeling the strain of parting as much as she was herself, even though she was going to the man she had loved for so long. She reached out a comforting hand and patted her daughter's arm.

'This is the beginning of a new life for you, lassie. Your grandfather would be the first to tell you he's nearing the end of his.'

'I – I canna bear tae think that I might not see him again,' Ellen whispered.

'We must face facts, lassie,' Sarah sighed. 'But I daresay we'll find your grandfather sitting by the fire sipping a hot toddy, and no doubt keeping everybody in order,' she added brightly. Ellen knew it was a forced brightness, just as her mother had kept up her cheerful chatter all week.

'Ye'd think I'd get used tae accepting death,' she sighed. 'We see it often enough . . . But it's dreadful even tae think o' it when someone belongs tae ye . . .'

'Yes. I suppose it is different – people you know and love . . .' Sarah mused. Then she sat up straight and her voice was brisk. 'All this talk of death! Your grandfather would be in a fine old rage if he could hear us, and him with no more than a sneeze or two!'

'Yes, he . . . Aah, here's Meg, running tae meet us! Goodness, she never seems tae grow any older, and she's as pretty as ever . . .'

Sarah did not reply. She often prayed that Beattie's beautiful, empty-headed daughter would not cause any more heartache than she had already. For some reason her thoughts turned briefly to Emma Braidwood and she wondered whether the girl would ever return to the Mains. As she drew the pony to a halt her thoughts were distracted by Ewan Donnelly coming to hand her down from the trap and lead the pony away.

'How's Maggie, and the boys?' she asked him.

'Fine, Mistress Fairly, just fine,' Ewan smiled. 'Donald is nearly thirteen now, ye ken; just waiting tae leave the school.'

'How time flies!' Sarah exclaimed in genuine surprise.

'Aye. Master Alex has promised the laddie a job here at the Mains when he's ready. He's real keen on the horses tae . . .'

'Aunt Sarah, have y'brought me a kitten?' Meg's high voice interrupted petulantly.

'Brought a kitten? Of course not!' Sarah's tone was sharper than she intended and Meg looked like a child who had been slapped.

'How are ye, Meg?' Ellen asked kindly.

'I've lots of kittens. I wish they could run and dance and sing with me.' Meg did several twirls across the Mains yard, then came back to them. 'Alex was cross with me. I don't like him when he's cross.' She pouted like a little girl. 'I don't like it when things die . . . Will he die?' She glanced back at the house.

Ellen caught her breath. 'Dinna talk like that, Meg!' She followed Sarah into the house but Meg skipped away as blithe as a carefree child again.

Sandy was not sitting by the kitchen fire as Sarah had half expected, nor was he in the small cosy parlour which opened off the Mains kitchen. Sarah went through to the hall and Ellen followed. Beatrice was coming down the staircase carrying a small tray with a cup and saucer and an empty glass. Her face looked pale and strained, but Beattie often looked like that these days, Sarah reflected. Today her hair, now almost pure white, was escaping from her cap giving her a distraught air.

'Beattie . . .?'

'Och, ye startled me, Sarah. I didna hear the trap arrive. Alex said ye were coming . . .' She hurried down the few remaining steps. 'Ellen! It's lovely tae see ye!' A gentle smile relaxed her facial muscles, reminding Sarah once more of the lovely girl she had been in their youth. She hugged Ellen.

'Ye look a bit weary, Aunt Beattie,' Ellen smiled. 'Is Grandfather tiring ye out?'

'Och, he's a good patient for such an active man,' Beattie answered. 'But I'm glad Alex called in at Doctor Kerr's and I'll be glad when he's been for I dinna like the sound o' your grandfather's chest at all. But maybe ye'll ken better than me what tae dae for him, Ellen?'

'Shall I just go up?'

Beatrice nodded. 'He'll be that pleased tae see ye,' she said warmly.

'I'll come up in a minute, Ellen,' Sarah called and followed Beatrice through to the kitchen. 'You seem . . . disturbed, Beattie. Is it more than a chill? When do you expect Doctor Kerr?'

'He was attending a birth at one o' the cottages on the road tae Bentira village when Alex called. His wife said she would tell him to drive down here as soon as he returned. It's a long way for him tae come, but we dinna often need a doctor . . .' Beatrice pushed a wisp of hair under her cap and turned to look at Sarah.

'What's really worrying you, Beattie?' Sarah asked softly.

'He – he reminds me o' Dick – the way he was before he died . . .'

'Oh, surely not . . .?' Sarah frowned. There was no mistaking Beatrice's anxiety. 'I'll go up and see Father now.'

Sandy Logan did not look so very ill at first sight with his high colour and his blue eyes twinkling up at Ellen, but he did seem to have some difficulty getting his breath and his hand, when Sarah clasped it in hers, was hot and dry. When Ellen turned away from the bed Sarah saw that her expression was grave. It was almost as though her daughter had donned an invisible nurse's uniform, she thought; even Ellen's manner was different – calm and reassuring, yet Sarah had an uneasy feeling that it was all a mask to hide her daughter's real thoughts and feelings.

As the afternoon wore on and still Doctor Kerr had not come, Sarah grew more and more tense. She knew her father was suffering from more than an ordinary chill; she also knew it was imperative that Ellen should get back to Fairlyden soon; she had to pack the rest of her clothes ready to catch the early morning train.

When Doctor Kerr eventually arrived he looked tired and drained himself. He examined Sandy with his usual care but Sarah felt he was reluctant to commit himself.

'Ye look dreadfully weary, Doctor. Would ye like a cup o' tea before ye leave?' Beatrice asked. Doctor Kerr shook his head.

'No, but thank ye, Mistress O'Connor. I must be getting back.' He sighed heavily. 'The babe was dead. The mother is vera sick . . . I've two calls tae make, then I'll need tae get back tae her, puir lassie . . .' He bit his lip. He had seen death often enough but he still hated to lose a patient, especially a young mother. The two women nodded silently, understanding.

'I'll see ye out tae your motorcar, Doctor,' Ellen offered quietly, obeying the slight beckon of his head.

'Grandfather's chest is bad, isn't it, Doctor?'

'I think you know, Ellen, that his age is against him,' Doctor Kerr answered indirectly. 'But your grandfather has one big advantage over most of my patients.'

'His will tae live, ye mean?' Ellen frowned.

'You, my dear. I've met Miss Morrison several times at the Manse. She's told me more than once that ye're a born nurse – an excellent nurse, she said. She doesna strike me as a woman who praises lightly.' Doctor Kerr hesitated, then looked Ellen squarely in the eye. 'I'm feart for pneumonia, as I think ye've surmised. He'll not reach a crisis for some hours yet, but at his age . . .'

'I understand, Doctor.' Ellen's voice was calm, reflecting nothing of the upheaval in her mind and heart. The doctor nodded.

'Thank God ye're here, lassie. I feel torn in twae right now.'

'Forgive me for saying it, Doctor,' Ellen summoned a grave smile, 'But I think ye're in sore need of rest yourself.'

'Aye . . .' Doctor Kerr nodded. He moved to the front of his car and swung the starting handle. 'I'll be back as early as I can in the morning!' he called over the noise of the engine, knowing nothing of Ellen's plans to journey halfway across the world.

Even when the little car was out of sight Ellen still stood outside, alone, staring at the flat fields which surrounded the Mains; gazing at the scene which her grandfather must have viewed hundreds of times, the woods to the east, the hills to the southwest rising into the pale grey of the April sky on the other side of the Solway Firth.

Ellen straightened her slim shoulders. Her mouth was firm as she turned her back on the panorama of fields and hedgerows which would soon be bursting into new life. She returned to the house, knowing her mother would be waiting.

Twenty-One

Sarah jumped to her feet the moment Ellen returned from seeing out Doctor Kerr.

'I know it is a dreadful way for us to part, Ellen.' Sarah's voice was husky with tears. 'But I must stay here . . . I – I canna leave your grandfather . . . not now . . . not tonight.'

'I understand, Mother,' Ellen said quietly. 'I am not returning to Fairlyden either.'

'But you must! Your trunk . . . you must finish packing . . . you'll have to be at the station early . . .' Sarah's mouth trembled. It was even harder than she had imagined.

'I canna leave Grandfather like this, Mother. I should never forgive myself if he died. I am a nurse . . .'

'B-but Beattie and I . . . we shall take care of him, Ellen . . . You must go to Brad. You have waited so long . . .'

'Brad is a doctor. He – he will understand.' Ellen's voice shook in spite of her determination to keep calm.

'But will he, lassie? Your grandfather would never want to deprive you of your happiness.'

'I wouldna be happy if Grandfather died and I had not tried to help him.' Ellen's voice was firm. 'I shall rest a while now, Aunt Beattie, if I may? Later, we shall all need strength.' Sarah and Beattie watched her slim, erect figure disappearing up the stairs.

'I'm sure Brad does love her. He will understand, Sarah,' Beattie soothed gently.

Sarah shook her head in distress. 'Maybe I shouldna have brought her here today.'

'Ellen would have come anyway. There has always been a special bond between her and her grandfather. I'm sure Brad will forgive her. Didn't you tell me he came to Scotland to train as a Minister originally? When William died he showed compassion and understanding, although he was very young . . .'

'But they have waited so long . . . and he sent the money for the best passage he could afford for her . . .'

'Maybe they will refund the money, or some of it . . .? Maybe Alex could send a wire to cancel the passage?'

Doctor Kerr held out little hope for Sandy's recovery when he returned to the Mains early the following morning.

'He is an old man, Mistress Fairly. There is nothing more I can do for him.'

'But he is so hot!' Sarah protested. 'And he keeps calling for m-my mother . . .' Sarah's voice choked to a halt. She knew there was no more any of them could do.

'There is nothing I can do,' the doctor repeated patiently. 'He couldna be in better care than your daughter's. I think ye ken that, Mistress Fairly.'

'Yes,' Sarah whispered. 'Poor Ellen . . . He doesna even ken her . . . if it is all for nothing . . .' She shivered. She was tired and low in spirits. She had spent hours with Ellen, bathing and changing, bathing again, taking turns with Beatrice, but Ellen had never left her grandfather since the fever had robbed him of his senses.

'I'm sorry if I caused her to ruin her plans. I didna ken until Alex told me.'

Sarah shook her head. 'Ellen made her own decision, Doctor.'

Late in the afternoon of the following day Sandy Logan tried valiantly to raise his head from the pillow. He was extremely weak. Even his voice was no more than a whisper and he looked very old.

'Oh, Father,' Sarah choked back a sob as she fell on her knees beside the bed, clasping his hand in both of hers. 'You're going to be all right. Thank God!'

'And thank Ellen while ye're at it,' Doctor Kerr said behind her. He came forward and stood looking down critically at his patient. 'Aye, ye'll do,' he nodded. 'I dinna think anyone else could have pulled ye back frae the arms o' the devil, Mr Logan, except an angel like your granddaughter.'

A ghost of a smile curved Sandy's pale lips. ' . . . Tired . . .' he whispered faintly.

Doctor Kerr nodded. 'Sleep now then. I shall go home and do the same. Mistress Fairly, ye'll see that daughter of yours gets some rest now? I shall call again tomorrow, but I know I shall not be needed. Ye're a lucky man, Mr Logan – either that or the devil decided he hadna got room for ye after all . . .'

Despite his weariness there was a flicker of humour in Sandy's blue eyes and he gave a faint nod at the Doctor.

Ellen stayed at the Mains and Beatrice was grateful for her help and calm assurance in those first difficult days. For her own part Ellen had had time to reflect on her hasty decision. She had written a brief letter to Brad, but she knew he would not receive it until after the ship docked, for the new *Titanic* was expected to be one of the fastest liners as well as the safest yet built.

'I'll never forget what ye've done,' Alex murmured, his dark eyes filled with concern at the sight of his sister's pale, tired face. 'Sometimes I wonder what I'd dae without Grandfather – though I ken he's an old man now, and he canna live forever . . . He has such a lively mind . . . and he's been more than generous tae me. I dinna think anybody but you could have nursed him back tae life. I pray Brad will understand . . .?'

Ellen smiled wanly. She had always been close to Alex. They had a lot in common.

'I just feel so . . . lost. Adrift . . . I've no job. No plans . . .'

A few days later came news that shocked the world.

'The *Titanic* has sunk!' Beatrice whispered hoarsely, staring at Ellen. 'On her maiden voyage . . . aah, tae think ye would have been on it, lassie! Those poor bairns drowning in the icy water! And men and women tae . . .'

Ellen shook her head in disbelief. 'Brad said . . . he believed the *Titanic* was unsinkable . . .'

Sarah drove down to the Mains as soon as she heard the news of the disaster. She wept at the sight of her daughter, pale but alive and well, when so many others were lost for ever in the great Atlantic Ocean. Speechlessly, she enfolded Ellen in her arms.

'It must have been God's will, Mama,' Ellen whispered tremulously.

'You're right, lassie. "For in Him we live, and move, and have our being . . ." There *is* a power beyond our ken.' Sarah's voice was muffled against Ellen's shoulder.

'I shall never, never ask you to make the journey across the Atlantic again, my dearest.' Brad wrote fervently. 'I shall come

183

to you the moment I am released from my filial duty.' Brad went on to profess his undying love, and Ellen, alone in her room at Mains of Muir, pressed the letter to her heart. What was time and distance when they were both alive and in love?

'I shall wait until the end of time for you, my love,' she whispered softly and read again the lines of the poem Brad had adapted to express the feelings in his own heart.

'I love you with a love that is more than love . . .'

Three weeks later Ellen received a letter inviting her to visit the hospital in Edinburgh where Brad himself had worked. There was work to be done in plenty if she could bring herself to move to the city. Ellen knew at once that Brad had sensed her yearning to be needed, although she had made no mention in her letters except to say Grandfather Logan was almost recovered and had little need of her skills. Evidently Brad had written to one of his ex-colleagues and here was the call to duty – the summons she needed.

Sarah accepted Ellen's move to Edinburgh without protest, thankful only that her beloved daughter was alive. Besides there was an added warmth in her own heart. Crispin Bradshaw had travelled to Fairlyden as soon as he heard the news of the *Titanic*'s sinking. He had not even stopped at Fairlyside to speak to Mrs Bunnerby.

'Sarah, my dear.' He had come to her, arms outstretched. 'Ellen . . .'

'Ellen is safe. Thanks be to God,' she had whispered fervently.

'You have heard already? Surely the survivors . . .'

'Ellen did not sail on the *Titanic*. She stayed to nurse my father . . .' Sarah had looked up and seen the loving concern in Crispin's grey-green eyes. He had come to her at once. He had left his own business instantly because he believed she needed comfort and support. Just as he had come to her on the night of the fire all those years ago. 'I can never repay you, Crispin,' she whispered huskily. 'But I'll try, if you have need of me.'

Crispin had returned to Yorkshire on the first train the following morning, but Sarah knew she would not forget how he had considered her own need before everything else, or the silent promise in his eyes.

As the spring weather improved, Sarah cleaned the house at

184

Fairlyden from top to bottom, beating rugs, washing the feathers in the pillows, airing the mattresses, brushing away the cobwebs when the sun shone on smoke-blackened beams.

Anna MacFarlane had little spring cleaning to do; it was less than six months since she and Thomas had moved into the Fairlyden cottage and she had cleaned it thoroughly then, but she was restless, eager to begin work with Mistress Fairly and her poultry. She turned her attention to an old tin trunk which was full of McFarlane memorabilia. Jamie had once told her it had belonged to his father, and before that to his grandfather. He had never got around to examining the musty papers which had always made him cough and wheeze whenever he opened the lid. But the trunk was taking up precious space in the little cottage, for it was too big to push under Thomas's bed and it would not go through the small hole into the rafters either, yet Anna was loathe to burn the papers without inspecting the assortment of yellowing certificates, dog-eared cuttings, tenancy agreements and rent roups, valuations and receipts.

One afternoon at the beginning of May, while young Jamie-Tam enjoyed an afternoon nap on the rag rug in front of the fire, she began to sort through the pile, planning to have a bonfire later in the day. As she had surmised, most of the papers meant nothing to her. She knew little about her husband's family except that they had been connected to the McFarlanes of Nithanvale, the wealthy farming family near Dumfries. Anna knew there had been some sort of family feud. When Jamie had questioned his father about it he had nodded at the tin trunk and grunted, 'It's all in there.'

Anna's pile of rubbish grew and Jamie-Tam wakened up and began to scrabble happily amongst crumpled sheets.

'Ach weel, Jamie-Tam, ye'll have tae make your ain history,' his mother sighed, and began to gather the papers up ready for the bonfire. There were still several layers in the bottom of the trunk. She lifted them out and flung them with the rest. A stiff-backed journal fell apart. Anna picked it up curiously. It was almost like a life history – a sort of account of daily life at Nithanvale. It must have been written by one of Jamie-Tam's ancestors, Anna decided. Jamie had had no close relatives, or at least not a single McFarlane had attended his funeral. Anna put the journal aside. Maybe Jamie-Tam would be interested in his roots someday. She carried the rest of the rubbish into the garden and set it on fire, much to her young son's delight.

At Mains of Muir, Sandy was recovering slowly from his illness, and observing the doctor's warnings more closely than either Beatrice or Sarah had dared to hope. He had plenty of time to follow the events in the outside world now, but these caused him some concern as the summer of nineteen hundred and twelve progressed.

In June the government had agreed that all men over twenty-one, with the exception of lunatics, should have the the right to vote, yet some of the suffragettes were still suffering the dangers and humiliation of being forcibly fed.

'Surely even Mr Asquith must realise how inflammatory such a situation must be!' Sandy remarked when Beatrice brought him a cup of tea. He was thinking of the women he knew, and Ellen in particular. He shuddered at the thought of her being manhandled in such a brutish fashion. Beatrice made no response. She had little interest in politics.

'My main concern is Meg,' she sighed. 'She is growing more and more difficult to understand; she wanders off and no one kens where she is – or she clings tae Alex like a limpet. It's a wonder he doesna lose patience with her.'

'He's aye been protective towards her,' Sandy mused, but his blue eyes were faintly anxious.

'Aye, and he thinks it is his duty tae be responsible for her now he kens he's related, but she's no longer a bairn and she's growing more possessive with him than ever . . . A man with Alex's intelligence must surely be sick o' her prattle.'

'Have ye ever heard how Emma Braidwood is getting on?' Sandy asked, following Beatrice's own thoughts with uncanny accuracy.

'She writes whiles. Her mother will never recover frae the stroke, but Emma works three days a week for the neighbouring farmer. I'm sure her sister and her sister-in-law could nurse Mistress Braidwood between them now. Maybe Emma doesna want tae return . . .'

Billy and Logan cycled to Mains of Muir to discuss the news of an outbreak of foot and mouth disease which had forced the closing of the Royal Show at Doncaster on the very eve of opening.

'The ports have only just been opened, and now they're closed again!' Billy was feeling disgruntled.

'Aye, they say the imported Irish cattle are tae blame.' Alex frowned at his younger brothers. 'I hope the pair o' ye havena been near the markets? I dinna want ye bringing trouble here.'

'Of course we havena!' Billy snapped. 'Ye should ken that. Ye ken how fussy Mother is . . .'

'She says the markets are tae be shut and all the shows are being cancelled . . .?' Logan looked at Alex with troubled eyes.

'Aye, it's the only way tae stop the spread o' the disease.' His grandfather joined the conversation. 'The movement o' animals must be restricted.' He fixed his blue eyes on Billy and his bushy white brows drew together. 'And if ye take my advice ye'll stay at home until the trouble is clear. Your mother can well dae without that sort o' heartbreak.'

Billy's face darkened, but he did not argue with his grandfather. He knew the old man was right, but he resented his activities being curtailed. He liked going to the markets and meeting other farmers and merchants, hearing what was going on in the outside world. He felt more and more hemmed in at Fairlyden.

'Even Mr Bradshaw isna coming tae visit,' Logan announced. 'He has nae contact with Yorkshire farmers but he wrote tae say he understood how anxious Mother will be until the foot and mouth epidemic is over.'

'Aye, Mr Bradshaw's a business man, even if he kens little about farming,' Alex agreed. 'I expect he understands how long it has taken tae rebuild the Fairlyden herd after all that trouble with the infectious abortions.'

'Mmm, Mother says oor economy is still too fragile tae contemplate another scourge like that,' Logan quoted knowledgeably, bringing an approving twinkle to his grandfather's eyes.

'I'm glad ye're taking an interest in such matters, young man!'

'Oh I am, Grandfather. So is Beth, now we've left the school. Mother tells her all sorts o' things when they're making the butter on a Friday morning.'

'Mmm, I expect your mother is preparing the lassie tae be a good wife tae some lucky man . . .' his grandfather mused. Logan frowned.

'She says she feels almost a grown woman . . . She isna though! Beth canna get married yet!' Billy and Alex suppressed a chuckle, earning an angry glower from their earnest young brother.

Strife and discontent were affecting more than men in the docks and mines and factories.

'It is rumoured in the city that some doctors have contributed as much as twenty pounds each to funds to oppose the government's new National Health Insurance Scheme,' Ellen wrote indignantly from Edinburgh as the summer progressed. 'If only they could witness the poverty and near-starvation amongst some of the children in this area, and their mothers. Many of the fathers too might have been helped if only they had come to us earlier, without fear of getting into debt to pay for their treatment. Why, oh why do women not have a voice in the governing of our people?'

'Ellen is completely absorbed in her work again since she moved to the hospital in Edinburgh,' Sarah remarked with a mixture of relief and admiration.

'Humph! I hope she doesna bring any o' the diseases here when she comes tae visit,' Sadie grumbled. 'She's not sharing my bed. It's time Beth Jamieson moved intae the maid's room and learned tae ken her place. Ellen can have her room then.'

'Beth will stay where she is. This is the bairn's home as well as her place of work, Sadie.'

'She's not a bairn. She was fourteen last May. Did ye see her putting her hair up on Sunday? Preening herself in front o' the mirror!'

'Yes, I did notice as a matter of fact,' Sarah said slowly. She had felt a little sad that Beth seemed to be growing into a woman already, but she was mature for her age in her thoughts and speech, and she had looked startlingly pretty. Both Logan and Billy had noticed, and even Alex had teased her when they met outside the Kirk. Sadie had been disgruntled by their admiration, although they were her own brothers. Even Meg had seemed more possessive than usual when Alex had given his attention to Beth, however briefly. Yes, Nick, your bairn is almost a young lady, Sarah reflected silently, and a lovely one too.

Twenty-Two

Logan stood with his arms folded along the top bar of the gate which led from the rickyard into the main part of Fairlyden's farmyard. His stance gave him a clear view of the house on this cool March evening. He looked up at the grey clouds scudding rapidly across the sky. They seemed as restless as Billy, he thought and glanced at his elder brother's profile as he joined him. Billy rested his chin on his hands but there was still a faint droop of discontentment around his mouth.

'So ye're fifteen now then, Logan,' he remarked. 'Ye'll soon be a man . . .'

'I am a man!' Logan straightened his shoulders. He had grown rapidly in the last eighteen months; now he was broader than Billy, though not quite so tall. 'I'm as strong as you are, and I can do most o' the things you and Thomas do now – except drive the binder and the mower.' He grinned suddenly; it was not his nature to be sullen or argumentative. 'I expect I could work them as well as ye can yourself – if I had a chance . . .'

'Maybe.' Billy's agreement surprised Logan.

'Och no, I was teasing ye! I'm not interested in machines, Billy. Anyway, even Grandfather admits ye understand them better than anybody else . . .'

'Well, that's praise indeed, coming frae Grandfather Logan!' Billy smiled wryly. 'Ye've spent a lot o' Sundays down at the Mains with him this past year, haven't ye?'

'Och well, he seems pleased tae see me since he was sae ill. Anyway I like tae listen tae him talking about his ain life, how he came tae Fairlyden, all the things he's learned . . . He doesna mind how many questions I ask him either.'

'Ye've missed Nick Jamieson nearly as much as Beth, haven't ye? I suppose it's because ye never kenned our ain father . . . What does Beth dae when ye take her tae the Mains? Ye'll ken Sadie disapproves o' her going with ye . . .?'

'Och, Sadie thinks Beth should work all the time, even on

189

Sundays! Mother says she needs tae get away now and then. I reckon Sadie is jealous because Beth is prettier than she is and she's a better shape . . .'

'Shape, eh!' Billy crowed with laughter and Logan's fair skin flushed a little.

'Well, ye ken what I mean! It's the way Beth walks and laughs and . . .'

'Aye, I ken all right! Beth's a real beauty, or will be in a year or two. Maybe I should start walking with her tae the Mains on a Sunday after the Kirk . . .' Billy's brown eyes glinted.

'You leave Beth alone!' Logan growled darkly. Billy had a reputation with the girls in the village. They all liked him and Logan had recently become aware of these things. 'She belongs tae me . . .'

'Does she now?' Billy asked more seriously. 'Does she ken that, and does she agree?'

'I'm going tae marry her when she's old enough!' This was the first time Logan had ever thought of such a thing as marriage. He shouldn't have let Billy provoke him, he thought ruefully. Even so he couldn't imagine his life without Beth for company, Beth to confide in, to share his dreams, talk away his troubles . . .

'Neither o' ye are old enough tae think o' marriage.' Billy's voice was serious now, the teasing gone. 'Dinna rush intae things. Sadie would make life hard for any wife either o' us might bring tae Fairlyden, but she'd be worse wi' Beth. She's aye been jealous o' her. And she has high ideas – our sister! She thinks Beth's not good enough tae be part o' the Fairly household, just because her father worked here and she was born in the cottage.'

'Och, I wouldna care what Sadie thought! Neither would Beth!' Logan announced with all the confidence of youth.

'Dinna be sae sure, Logie,' Billy said softly. 'Sadie's not like Mother, or Ellen. She never tries tae see any good in anybody – only bad. It's like a flaw in her mind . . . A sort o' poison . . .'

'Well, there's no bad in Beth . . .'

'Maybe not, but Sadie would make Beth's life hell if she thought either o' us were going tae marry her and make her Mistress at Fairlyden.'

'I'm not worried about Sadie,' Logan repeated. He glanced sideways at Billy. 'I'm more bothered about you. Beth told me how ye comforted her when her father died, and I ken she likes ye . . . But ye've lassies in the village . . .'

'Dinna worry about me, young Logan.' Billy's voice was crisp. His dark eyes took on a faraway look. 'In another year ye'll be looking after Fairlyden better than I ever could – not just the machines, but the cows and pigs, the horses and the crops. I'm not going tae be tied down tae marriage – or tae Fairlyden much longer either. I'm going tae travel, but dinna tell Mother yet, mind! It would only upset her before there's need . . .'

'Travel? Ye mean ye'd really leave Fairlyden!' Logan stared at his elder brother incredulously. 'Permanently?'

Billy nodded. 'First chance I get. I mean tae seek my ain fortune, but not in farming. Ye're welcome tae Fairlyden, at least as far as I'm concerned, though Sadie wouldna agree! She's resented ye since the day ye were born. But it would break Mother's heart if one o' her sons didna carry on here, and Alex is settled at the Mains – happy with his horses. Did ye ken he's sending two more tae Canada?'

'Aye, Grandfather told me. He doesna think we should send all our best British horses away. He's worried in case there's a war. He keeps talking about the Germans building ships and such-like . . .'

'Och, there'll no' be a war!' Billy scoffed. 'The Germans wouldna dare! Mind ye, I'd be there tae fight if they did!' His dark eyes gleamed, then he shrugged and straightened up, pushing himself away from the gate. 'I'm going inside for a seat by the fire. It's getting chilly standing out here blethering.'

When he had gone Logan still leaned against the gate, gazing at the house that was his home, the only home he had ever had or ever wanted. He couldn't contemplate leaving Fairlyden. He just didn't understand Billy's restlessness.

In the evening light the sandstone of the old house glowed a warm reddish brown. The windows seemed to wink back at him as the low rays of the sinking sun caught the glass – two up and two down at the back and front with a little window, still protruding from the roof, at the end where the new bathroom had been made, using part of the maids' room. Even after fifteen years it was still possible to see the faint line where the newly hewn stone had been used to build the walls higher after the fire. His mother had talked a lot recently about the way the house had looked before he was born, with all the windows sprouting out of the roof and all the bedrooms with sloping ceilings, and a big room for the maids over the kitchen.

'Agnes had a double bed up there, and when Maggie Whiteley came as a nurse girl she had a little truckle bed of her own under the eaves. Now it's little more than a store room with scarcely room to stand up without a bump on the head! I thought the house was wonderful, just the way it was . . .' she had said almost wistfully.

Logan knew it had been his father's idea to raise the roof, make a bathroom, and convert the bothy into the dining room. Well, the bathroom had been completed at last.

It's certainly a great improvement on the tin bath in front o' the fire, he thought with a grin. As for the water closet, it's a real luxury these cold mornings. Fleetingly he wondered why Mr Bradshaw was so generous to them; they could never have built the new byre and made the bathroom without his help . . . But at fifteen he had boyish dreams of his own and he did not pursue this line of thought.

His gaze was drawn back to the house as though it was a magnet. He could not see the front from here. Doctor Kerr and the Reverend Morrison were the only people who ever used the front door. A pity, he reflected. Mother takes a pride in her garden. There had always been snowdrops and daffodils under the apple trees as long as he could remember, and the jasmine, climbing up the sheltered corner behind the dairy. It always had flowers like golden stars, even on the dreariest winter's day. He smiled again, recalling his mother's protest when Mr Bradshaw had suggested pulling down the earth closet at the bottom of the garden.

'But Billy and Thomas and Logan canna go upstairs in their boots and muddy leggings every time they want tae use the closet!' She had flushed a bright pink. 'We must leave the earth closet for them.'

Despite Mr Bradshaw's quiet manner he was a man used to having things his way, Logan decided with a feeling of respect. He had not argued, but on his next visit he had suggested installing a water closet in the bothy. So now we have two closets, and everyone is happy. Everyone except Sadie, he remembered with a silent groan. She had demanded to know who was to limewash the bothy and clean the toilet. Beth had taken on the chore in her usual matter of fact way.

Beth never grumbles, he mused, yet she has a mind o' her ain. I'm sure she loves Fairlyden as much as I do. He took a deep breath of the cold evening air and expelled it slowly. I'll never leave, he thought happily. He loved everything about the farm, even the smell of old Peggotty, he thought with a grin, remembering how angry the sow had made Sadie two days ago when she decided to push her way out of her pen and take a wander round the yard – all sixteen stones of her with her latest litter squealing around her feet and running everywhere.

Of course I like the scent o' the lilac better than Peggotty, and the lavender . . . the half-smile still tugged at the corners of his mouth. Beth often picked the lavender and made little embroidered sachets to perfume the bed linen and her own clothes. In fact Beth herself often smelled of lavender . . . She loves the garden and the flowers almost as much as Mother does, he thought. Mr Bradshaw thought so too; he had sent two climbing roses for Beth and his mother. Logan had planted them and he had been as delighted as Beth when they had covered the porch in a shower of pink and white blooms last summer. Billy had laughed at him; he considered it unmanly to take such an interest in flowers, but Logan didn't care how much Billy teased. Grandfather Logan was a fine old man and he was interested in everything.

In the autumn Sarah, Anna, Beth and Sadie set out for the village hall in Muircumwell for the first of the talks by the new poultry instructress, Miss Eleanor Brownwell. Sarah had asked Beatrice to join them for these weekly meetings but she had declined.

'Och, I'm too old for such things.'

'Of course you're not too old!' Sarah insisted. 'Old Mrs Wright is going and she must be almost seventy. Besides I'd welcome your company. We'd have time for a chat afterwards . . .'

'I canna, Sarah.'

'Why not?'

Beatrice bit her lip. How could she tell Sarah that she was finding her own daughter such a sore trial. 'I've no energy tae bike four miles tae the village by the end o' the day!' she said instead.

'Beattie!' Sarah was filled with remorse. 'Father must be tiring you out. Why didn't you say so before? I wonder if I could persuade him to come to Fairlyden for a month or two. Logan

193

would enjoy his company. He's always telling me he learned this or that from Grandfather . . .'

'No! No, please dinna dae that, Sarah!' Beattie pleaded urgently. 'Truly, he is no trouble. He is almost as well now as he was before the pneumonia, except that his chest is a bit weaker of course, but he goes out for a walk every day with Alex, unless it's raining.'

'Perhaps you need another maid . . .?' Sarah suggested anxiously.

'Och, it's not the work! Well, not really work, but Meg's changing, Sarah. Sometimes I think she's more of a worry now than when she was a bairn!' Beattie muttered in exasperated tones.

'I've noticed she's . . . different sometimes,' Sarah said hesitantly. 'Is it Alex's fault for spoiling her?'

'Och no! Nae other man would be as kind tae her! Or as patient. Sometimes she makes me so angry and frustrated – and then I feel guilty because she's ma ain bairn and Dick thought the world o' her. But only last week we thought she was lost or lying injured somewhere. She's taken tae wandering away on her own lately; she didna come back at midday, nor at teatime. Alex and the men had tae search for her in the evening. Ewan found her down on the moss land – the furthest corner o' the farm! She'd jumped across one o' the ditches but she couldna get back again.'

'But surely the ditches are dangerous!'

'Aye, if she'd slipped . . . But she just doesna think!'

'I'm sure Alex could afford to hire an extra maid. He told me he received two hundred guineas for one of the horses he sent to Canada, and a hundred and eighty for the other. You must ask him to get you a maid, Beattie, so that . . .'

'No, it's not another maid I need. Maggie comes in most days and she does all the dairy work, and we've a washer woman twice a week. No, Sarah, I'm getting older, I suppose,' Beattie smiled faintly. 'But I'll ask Maggie if she wants tae join ye all at the poultry meetings. I daresay she'd enjoy a change o' company and it would be a good chance for her and Anna tae see each other.'

Alex and Ewan were busy cutting and laying hedges at Mains of Muir. Most afternoons Sandy enjoyed a stroll, taking a basket of tea and a buttered scone to sustain them until the evening meal; he enjoyed a chat with them as they ate.

'We could survive without the tea if it's a trouble tae ye, ye ken,' Alex had told Beatrice with a crooked smile after the first afternoon, 'but we're grateful for a hot drink and I think Grandfather likes tae have a purpose for his walk.'

'Aye, he likes tae feel useful, even now,' Beatrice smiled. She was very fond of Alex. Even as a small boy he had been kindly and considerate; she wished with all her heart that one of her own children had been like him.

A fortnight later the hedge-laying was almost complete.

'We shall be raking up and burning the thorns today. It's bitterly cold and the wind's rising. I dinna think it would be good for Grandfather,' he added in a low voice, 'what with the smoke and the bite in the wind.'

'I'll see he doesna come tae the field then,' Beatrice smiled.

But when the time approached for his usual walk Sandy was adamant that Alex and Ewan should have their tea.

'It's thirsty work with all that smoke,' he insisted and Beatrice recognised the determined glint in his blue eyes.

'Aye and smoke's bad for anyone with breathing troubles,' she reminded him gently. 'Doctor Kerr warned us. I'm sure Alex would rather be without tea than have ye . . .'

'I'll take tea tae Alex, Mama,' Meg piped up unexpectedly, in a voice as meek and light as a child's.

'Will ye, Meg?' Beatrice was surprised. Recently she was almost ashamed because she had found her only daughter's unpredictable behaviour such a heavy burden. This was something useful she could do for once. 'Ye'll take the basket and the can o' hot tea tae Alex and Ewan? At the field?'

'Yes, Mama.' Meg was in biddable mood today, Beatrice thought with relief. Sandy looked surprised too for he had noticed how vacant-minded Meg had been lately.

'They're up in Laneside field,' he told Meg.

'I ken. I saw the sparks flying intae the air.' Neither Beatrice nor Sandy noticed the excitement in her blue eyes.

Alex was stoking the fires with a long-handled fork while Ewan, being quicker on his feet, raked the thorns and trimmings into small heaps and carried them to him. Alex piled on another heap of thorns, pressing them on to the fire with the tines of the fork until they were alight, releasing them as fountains of

195

red-gold sparks rose into the air, then adding more. He moved round the fire, keeping the heavier branches in the centre. Alex was tidy and neat by nature and it vexed him to see the fires spreading and wasting the grass.

He was facing the wind and the billowing smoke when Meg approached so she had almost reached him before he saw her. He licked his dry lips and grinned. His throat felt dry and parched and he was longing for a drink of tea, despite his instructions to Beatrice.

Meg saw his mouth as a scarlet slash in his smoke-blackened face; she saw the gleam of his strong square teeth as he smiled a welcome. But in Meg's fanciful mind it was not the familiar face of Alex Fairly she saw, but that of a fire demon.

Alex threw on another bunch of thorns and moved round the fire, taking the basket from Meg's hand.

'Thanks, Meg. Ye're a welcome sight on such a day. Come and sit beside us in the shelter o' the hedge while we drink our tea.' He smiled kindly as he would have done at a small child. 'I'm glad ye've brought a drink for us after all. Ewan!' he raised his voice, and called to Ewan who was some distance further down the field. Then he turned and limped towards the grassy bank in the lee of the hedge. His ankles and calves ached and he settled himself comfortably on the brown grass of the bank and poured tea into one of the enamel mugs. He savoured the hot sweet brew gratefully.

He did not notice Meg skipping lightly to the other side of the fire. He could not have guessed she was searching for a fire demon, longing for the mythical figure to dance with her. One of the thicker branches had fallen a few inches from the fire. Meg picked up the blackened end and began to poke the red heart of the burning wood.

'Where are ye?' she muttered in her childish voice. 'Come and dance with me! Dance like the sparks up there . . .' She raised her head and stared up at the red-gold sparks glowing richly against the dull grey of the November sky. She prodded vigorously at the fire and watched in delight as more sparks shot into the air. She squatted on her haunches, pulling the hood of her woollen cloak more closely round her head, oblivious of the heat of the fire on her cold cheeks, barely aware of the stinging smoke bringing tears to her eyes as she peered closer into the heart of the fire. 'Where are ye, fire demon? Come and dance with me!'

She poked impatiently, dislodging a small burning branch. It fell on to her skirts. Meg brushed it aside carelessly, intent on making more sparks fly into the sky. Only when she felt the searing heat against her leg did she jump to her feet. The sudden movement fanned the smouldering cloth of her skirt into flames.

Meg's piercing screams filled the air. Alex dropped his mug at the unearthly sound. He jumped to his feet.

'Meg . . .? Meg! Where are ye?'

Further down the field Ewan could see both sides of the fire. His first thought was that it had spread out of control over the dry grass. Then amidst the flames he saw the slight figure break away and begin to run – not to him, or to Alex, but wildly up the field, back towards the house.

Alex had seen her too. He tried to run. 'Come back! Meg! Aah, Meg!' His voice was hoarse. His feet, in their thick-soled boots, tripped one over the other in his haste. Suddenly he found himself flat on his face.

'Wait, Meg!' he called desperately and scrambled clumsily to his feet. 'Lie down! Roll on the ground!' But Meg ran on in panic. Behind him Alex heard Ewan running hard. He pulled off his jacket and held it out. 'Smother the flames with it!' he gasped. Ewan snatched the jacket as he passed. 'If ye can . . .' Alex whispered hoarsely. 'If ye can . . .'

Twenty-Three

Alex knew he would never forget the sight of Meg's ravaged face. The shock and pain made her lose consciousness as he and Ewan carried her back to the house and for that small mercy he was thankful. He blamed himself. He could scarcely face Beatrice as she focused her stunned gaze on her daughter. Meg's lovely face was unrecognisable, her clothes charred.

Ewan was dispatched for Doctor Kerr.

'I should have watched her!' Alex's head was bowed, his face drawn.

'Nae, laddie,' Beatrice whispered hoarsely. 'If there's blame at all, it's mine – her ain mother! Fire aye fascinated her, even when she was a bairn . . . I should hae remembered . . .'

But Alex could only shake his head in remorse. 'I promised tae take care o' her but I didna protect her when she needed me most . . .'

Meg's burns were extensive; the shock and pain too great to endure. When death released her from suffering, Beatrice's initial reaction was one of thankfulness that God had shown His mercy and given Meg peace.

Richard did not return for his sister's funeral, or even acknowledge his mother's letter. Beatrice was not sure whether he had received it. At the funeral she stood a little apart from Alex and Sandy and Sarah while Meg was buried in the family grave beside her father. Only when it was over did reaction set in. Beatrice's relief gave way to guilt.

'I should have loved her more, had more patience when she behaved like a bairn . . . Dick would have loved her . . .' She could not stem the tears of grief and remorse.

'Hush, Beattie,' Sarah soothed gently. 'Even my father blames himself because he did not take the tea that day; Alex thinks he is responsible because he was not diligent enough, because he could not reach her in time. You cannot blame yourselves. Meg

199

was happy . . . free from care because of you, free from want, surrounded by warmth and love . . .'

Beattie groaned softly. 'Ye dinna understand, Sarah. Sometimes she made me so exasperated . . .'

'And sometimes she made you smile. And when she was a bairn you loved her and cared for her . . . You must remember her blithe spirit and be glad she cannot suffer any more . . .' Sarah insisted softly. 'For Alex's sake too . . .?' she pleaded. 'Though I know you need time . . .' Beatrice realised Sarah did understand; had she not suffered too?

'I'll try . . .to remember the happiness o' her,' Beatrice promised tearfully.

So Christmas came and went almost unnoticed and the new year of nineteen hunded and fourteen dawned.

The winter was mild and the spring work relatively easy at Fairlyden, as on most of the farms. Sarah was pleased to see Crispin when he came for another short stay with Mrs Bunnerby at Fairlyside. He always helped to put things into perspective when the newspapers made everything seem grim and uneasy in the wider world beyond the green fields and woods and burns which made Fairlyden seem like a peaceful sanctuary in comparison.

'The suffragettes seem to be more militant than ever,' Sarah commented the afternoon Crispin accompanied her to Mains of Muir to see her father. 'But Prime Minister Asquith offers no hope at all to them.'

'I fear he and his cabinet have problems enough. The threat of civil war in Ireland is increasing now the Home Rule Bill is going through parliament.'

'According to the newspapers we have troubles even nearer home than Ireland, don't we? I thought the railway workers and builders and the miners were banding together to force the issue of minimum wages. Will the disruption affect your factory, Crispin?'

'It is already affected, but we have had several warnings before; this time I have made sure we have good stocks of coal, but I can do little to combat the transport problems. I pray it will all be over before we are forced to put men and women out of work, as some of the other mills have done already.'

'How can Great Britain remain great?' Sandy Logan de-

manded with a touch of his old spirit, 'with two million people out
o' work, and women and children starving?'

'I don't know, Father, but I'm pleased to see you're taking an
interest again. I think it will help Beattie adjust to Meg's death
too, if you and Alex can get back to normal.'

'Aye, I suppose ye're right, lassie . . . We've a lot tae be
thankful for. Maybe God has His ain way o' sorting things out
tae, for I dinna ken what Meg would have done without Beatrice
tae look after her . . .'

'I had a letter from Ellen last week.' Sarah gently changed the
subject.

'Aah, is there any word o' Brad coming . . .?' His voice was
eager.

'No, not yet, but Ellen is engrossed in her work and she seems
happy.'

As time passed most British people were too preoccupied with
the workers' strikes and the effects on their own families to pay
much attention to the launching of yet another ship by the
German Kaiser, even though it was claimed to be the biggest
battleship in the world.

The assassination of the Archduke Franz Ferdinand and his
wife was shocking, but it seemed too far away to have any effect
on the everyday lives of men and women in Britain.

Then suddenly Austria and Serbia were at war. The Czar and
his cousin, Kaiser Wilhelm II, issued warnings, and ignored
warnings. The Czar ordered the mobilisation of more than a
million troops.

Still it all seemed very remote from Fairlyden and the fight to
make good hay before the weather changed. 'I see the government are setting aside their plans to grant Home Rule to
Ireland.' Billy's voice quickened, his dark eyes scanned the
newspaper eagerly. 'On account o' the troubles in Europe. I
wonder what it means . . .?' Sarah did not answer. She was
looking at her son, but she was seeing another pair of dark eyes
sparkling at the prospect of adventure. She felt uneasy without
knowing why.

Ever since Sandy's illness Sarah had visited the Mains once a
fortnight and she made her visit as usual but she still felt
troubled.

'Billy is so excited about the news. I know things seem very uncertain in Europe, but why should it affect him?'

'The Kaiser is powerful — too powerful.' Sandy frowned. 'He could be a dangerous enemy. Billy's not stupid. He follows events closely these days, I believe.'

'But surely the Kaiser would never harm Great Britain,' Beatrice joined the conversation. 'He and the King are related!'

'Mmm, relations can be terrible enemies,' Sarah mused, thinking of the Fairly ancestors, and even Sadie, her own daughter. 'But we have more ships than Germany . . . We are an island so we are protected by the seas . . .'

'Maybe . . .' Sandy said slowly. He sighed heavily. 'Maybe . . .'

Sarah remembered her father's wary reply the following day.

'The Kaiser has declared war on the Czar, his own cousin!' Billy exclaimed. 'He has scorned Britain's offer to mediate . . .'

Twenty-four hours later the Royal Navy was being mobilised. The whole country seemed to be holding its breath now. Would Great Britain fight? This was the question Billy asked repeatedly, along with thousands of other young Britons. He could not concentrate. It was left to Logan to organise the horses, while Thomas and the women gathered in the hay.

'Germany has declared war on France tae! The Kaiser must be mighty sure o' his ain power tae fight at his front door and his back door at the same time!' There was no doubting the tension and excitement in Billy. Sarah's heart felt cold and heavy in her breast.

'Your grandfather thinks Germany has too much power for everyone's good!' she snapped.

This proved only too true. Germany invaded Belgium. Billy jumped on his bicycle and pedalled off to the village. The doctor had a crystal set. There was a gathering outside his gate as people waited for news.

'We're tae join the war!' someone cried.

'Britain is joining the war!'

'Hurrah! Hurrah. We'll put the old Kaiser in his place!'

'Rule Britannia!'

It was not the news of war which struck such a chill in Sarah's heart so much as the sombre words of the foreign secretary, Sir Edward Grey.

The lamps are going out all over Europe. We shall not see

them lit again in our lifetime. How ominous it sounds, so melancholy, she thought with a shiver.

As the warm days of summer continued, it was still hard to believe that the peaceful tenor of life at Fairlyden could be affected by events so far away. Yet Sarah had only to visit Janet at the Muircumwell Store to sense the excitement of the young, the apprehension of their parents, the new wariness of fathers who might yet be called to serve their country. Sarah tried to ignore the gleam of excitement in Billy's dark eyes, the eagerness with which he waited for Thomas to return from the station each morning and bring him the latest news.

'Some of them say the war will be all over by Christmas,' he announced flatly one evening after a visit to Muircumwell.

'And a good job too!' Sarah retorted with some asperity. 'If you don't forget about the war and concentrate on getting the corn cut we shall have no harvest!'

A few days later it was Logan who announced, 'It says here that General Kitchener thinks the war will last much longer than until Christmas. He is calling for more men to volunteer to fight. He intends to train a new army . . .'

'Here, let me see!' Billy almost snatched the paper from his younger brother. There was a restlessness about Billy which no one at Fairlyden could fail to notice.

It was Logan who brought out the binder, who checked the canvasses and set Thomas to sharpen the knives, and it was Logan who took out the scythe and opened up the fields in readiness for the machine.

'It is a good crop this year and we canna afford tae lose it,' he declared with a new maturity. 'Besides, they say the soldiers will be wanting hay for their horses and corn tae, as well as wheat for their ain bread. We can help the country by doing our ain work well, Billy. The folks at home still have tae be fed.'

'Och!' Billy scoffed impatiently. 'Ye've been listening tae Grandfather Logan! That's the way for auld men and cowards — tae stay at home!' Logan's youthful face flushed. 'Anyway,' Billy went on, 'there's plenty o' food in the country, and plenty of British ships to bring all we need.'

'Why, Billy Fairly! That's a change of tune! When the dockers were on strike you said the government should have looked after the British farmers instead of importing so much that they were out of business . . .'

'Och, that was different, Mother. It's fighting men Lord Kitchener needs right now. Have ye no' seen the posters, Logan?'

'Why should he have seen the posters? He's too young to fight. Anyway, somebody has to supervise the harvest and see the cows are fed and milked. You spend too much time running to the village, Billy. We must get the harvest started!'

'Mother's right,' Logan agreed. 'We need the harvest, even if the rest o' the nation doesna. The pigs and cows have still tae be fed – and all Anna's hens. But I hope ye're right about the power o' the British navy, Billy, because Grandfather says we shall starve if the ships canna get through. He says we only produce enough food in Britain tae feed everybody at week ends . . .'

'That canna be true!' Billy argued.

'Grandfather says it is. And ye ken how much is imported – even the cake to feed our ain cattle. Grandfather says it's because the government has only believed in free trade and other countries have been keeping their larders in better order. He says that's why half the farms in Britain have run wild and gone tae waste.'

'That's scaremongering!' Billy declared angrily. 'Dinna let me hear ye talking like that again, Logan. Grandfather's an old man and he doesna ken any better.'

'Your grandfather is a very wise man!' Sarah intervened. 'And he studies all the news reports. All of them! Not just the ones he wants to believe. He reads the *Scottish Farmer* too, and the farming reports. There's more than him concerned about the food situation in Britain, my lad!'

'Grandfather hasna anything else tae dae but read! He never leaves the Mains now. He doesna ken what's really going on . . .' Billy argued stubbornly.

'Well, you canna say the same about Mr Bradshaw, Billy, and in his last letter he said a lot of people in London queued to exchange their bank notes for gold; he said something about the bank rate rising to ten per cent as well – whatever that means. He thinks Britain would be in a poor way if ever the ships canna bring in food too. He says the Germans have been protecting their farmers against imports for years. He thinks we should produce all we can at Fairlyden from now on!'

'The sooner we win this war the better!' Billy replied jauntily, 'before you two, and Grandfather Logan, scare the life out o' everybody! I'm going tae volunteer for Kitchener's army.'

'Oh, Billy . . .' Suddenly the fire went out of Sarah and she sank on to a chair beside the kitchen table as though her knees were too weak to hold her. Her face had gone a deathly white. Deep down she knew this was the moment she had been dreading – the moment when Billy decided he was leaving Fairlyden – but never in her darkest moments had she thought of him leaving to go to war! I should not have argued, I should not have provoked him, she thought dully. Billy looked at his mother's stricken face with contrition. He had not really believed she would care so very much if he left Fairlyden, not now that she had Logan.

'I – I'll wait until we've gathered in the harvest then . . .' he offered with the gentleness few people except Beth Jamieson had ever seen. 'Maybe we shall ken better what's happening by then . . .' Sarah had to be content with this reprieve, however short it might prove to be.

The weather was kind, making the harvest easier and quicker than usual. An uneasy peace settled over the fields and valleys around Fairlyden.

Then all too soon it was over. On the twenty-third of September, Billy returned from the village with news that three British cruisers had been sunk by German submarines. Sarah saw the determination on her son's face and her heart jolted sickeningly.

'There's rumours that the Germans are laying mines in the shipping lanes tae,' he reported grimly. 'I'm going this time, Mother. Britain needs me more than Fairlyden ever will.'

Sarah bowed her head in silence. How could she protest when so many thousands of mothers and wives must feel just the same as she did.

The evening before he went to join the army, Billy cycled to the Mains to say goodbye to Alex and his grandfather.

'There's a wee thing I'd like tae discuss wi' ye, afore I leave, Alex . . .?' Billy's voice was low. Alex knew at once that his brother wanted a private word.

'I'll walk wi' ye tae the main road then. Wait 'til I get my jacket.' A few minutes later they walked side by side, Billy pushing his bicycle, slowing his pace to Alex's.

'Ye seem a wee bit down in spirits tonight, big brother!' Billy tried to sound a cheerful note. 'There's nae need tae be worrying about me. Ye ken the devil aye looks after his ain!' He gave a wolfish grin, but Alex did not respond. 'Aw, come on, Alex! Even Grandfather didna blame me for going – though I thought he might, me leaving Mother and Fairlyden and everything . . .'

'Of course he doesna blame ye! If he'd been young he'd have gone tae fight for his country himself! Just as I should hae been doing if I'd been a – a real man, instead o' a cripple!'

'Aa-ah . . . . So that's what's wrong! But, Alex, ye've never wanted tae leave the Mains! Any more than Grandfather would have wanted tae leave Fairlyden . . .'

'This isna a matter o' what a man *wants* tae dae! It's a duty! I ought tae have been able tae dae my bit for the land that I love!'

'Och, Alex, ye've aye had too much sense o' duty! Too much conscience. There's plenty o' men tae fight, but they canna farm as you can! Ye were the same wi' Meg, taking her on as your ain responsibility! She wasna . . .'

'Meg was my responsibility!' Alex's voice was harsh. 'If I'd been able tae run she'd have been alive now and . . .'

'And scarred for life! Miserable as hell! Aye and probably still suffering pain!' Billy was angry now, and impatient with Alex. 'Man, ye've got tae get things intae perspective. I tell ye Meg wasna your responsibility anyway. Ye were aye far too protective! Nae wonder Emma Braidwood went away home and never came back!'

'Emma!' Alex's face went white. 'What has Emma tae dae with anything?'

'Och, ye must have been blind if ye couldna see she liked ye well – but what chance did she have with Meg aye dancing round ye, and her as pretty as a picture. Mind ye, Emma wasna bad tae look at . . . but she'd sense enough tae ken she couldna hold a candle tae Meg!'

'Meg was just a bairn!'

'She didna look like a bairn! And ye never seemed tae see anything wrong wi' her . . . I never could understand ye, Alex.'

Alex's face was pale and he walked in silence, frowning down at his twisted feet.

'I always had a tender spot for Meg,' he muttered, 'but not as a woman – never like Emma! Meg was a freak o' nature like me. I thought o' marrying her once – tae protect her frae men who didna understand her. Aunt Beattie was horrified. She told Grandfather. I don't suppose ye ever guessed he's Aunt Beattie's father tae . . .?'

'What!' Billy stopped in his tracks and stared at Alex. 'Ye mean . . .? Ye canna mean . . .'

206

Alex nodded. 'Mother and Aunt Beattie are half-sisters. Meg was my ain cousin – well almost.'

'Well!' Billy whistled through his teeth. Then he began to laugh. 'Imagine Grandfather Logan! Why, the old rascal! And I thought I'd inherited all ma wicked ways frae Father!' He thought of the 'wee thing' he'd meant to discuss with Alex and changed his mind.

'I hope ye'll no go blethering about all this?' Alex demanded irritably. 'I was only explaining the situation with Meg, and why I feel responsible for Aunt Beattie tae. They have as much right tae Gradfather's money as I had . . .'

'Aah, but ye've made it grow for him. Anyway ye aye got on well with Aunt Beattie so she'll not be a problem. Meg's gone now, Alex. She's at peace.' Billy's voice was softer, gentler than Alex had ever heard it. 'Forget the past and look tae your ain future. Take my advice and go up tae Lockerbie some day to see Emma Braidwood. Now,' he straddled the bicycle, clapped Alex hard on the shoulder, 'it's time I was on my way. Dinna forget tae write me a letter!'

Alex watched until he was out of sight. As he turned back to the Mains he remembered Billy had forgotten to discuss his own affairs. Couldn't have been that important, he thought with a shake of his head – and his thoughts moved on to Emma Braidwood.

Billy had not forgotten. He had decided Alex had enough responsibilities, and in any case his sense of duty might make him over-zealous. After all, Polly Loveday was known to be free with her favours; even if she did have a bairn, there was no guarantee it would be his. Some said she had a way of preventing such things. Still . . . Billy frowned as he bowled along, he wouldn't like to think of any dark-haired, dark-eyed waif suffering because of him. He resolved to write to Ellen and enclose a letter for her to open if he didn't come back from the war. He knew he could trust Ellen. He would tell her about Alex's low spirits too. She would know how to cheer him up, see his own worth.

The following day everyone gathered outside Fairlyden to see Billy off. He kissed his mother on the cheek and bid her not to worry, he nodded at Sadie, aimed a playful blow at Logan's broad young chest.

'Dinna forget tae write and tell me how things are going,

Logie, and tell me how many piglets old Peggotty rears in her next litter.' Then he turned to Beth.

'Will ye miss me then, Beth?'

'Och, Billy, ye ken we'll all miss ye . . .' Beth's smile was wobbly, her voice choked.

'Ye'll write tae me then? All the soldiers have a girl back home tae send them letters, ye ken!'

'Aye, I'll write tae ye, Billy.' He smiled then, kissed her first on one cheek and then on the other, winked at Logan's frowning face, and jumped on his bike.

'Remember tae ask Thomas tae collect the bike at the station in the morning!' he called cheerily as he cycled down the track to catch the train for Annan to join the queue of young men eager to fight for their country.

Sarah could only pray they would all return home safely; that the war really would be over by Christmas as many of the politicians believed. She refused to think about the work that was to be done at Fairlyden. Somehow they had to manage. Already one of Alex's men had gone to war and another one was considering volunteering.

'Thank goodness Ewan has no need to think of fighting,' she said to Anna as they fed and watered the hens together.

'Ye think they'll not take men as old as Ewan?' Anna asked.

'The Prime Minister was appealing for those between nineteen and thirty-eight – unless they had been soldiers before.'

'Aah, well Ewan must be forty, I'm sure,' Anna said with relief. 'Though he doesna look it . . .'

'He's nearer forty-five, I think,' Sarah mused.

'I suppose he could be . . . after all, Maggie's laddies are fifteen and thirteen now . . . How time flies! It's a good thing they're too young tae volunteer!'

'I dinna think Donald would want to leave the Mains,' Sarah smiled. 'Both Alex and Ewan say how much he loves the horses.'

'I'm sure he wouldna *want* to go to war . . .' Anna said soberly. 'But Mother said there was an awfy lot o' pressure on the young men in the village and round about. She says some o' the laddies are just volunteering because their friends are going.'

'Let's just pray it will be all over soon then,' Sarah said firmly.

Twenty-Four

The war proved to be very different to any that had gone before. Soldiers were not fighting hand to hand and face to face; battles were not decisively won or lost; men dug trenches in the earth and lived there, behind barricades of barbed wire – like rats, many of the returning wounded declared. Each side tried to outflank the other and the battle fronts spread wider.

In October a different development was reported.

'It seems impossible! Beyond imagining! An aeroplane flying over the heads of the soldiers, dropping a bomb over Paris!' Sarah exclaimed, looking up into the innocent pale blue sky above the Solway Firth. No one at Fairlyden, or anywhere in the parish, had ever seen an aeroplane.

There was certainly no end to the war in sight when Christmas came. Feelings against Germans grew. Everywhere men who had any connections, or the slightest possible sympathy, with the enemy were shunned or hounded or even rounded up and imprisoned. The purge did not end with ordinary men and women either.

'Prince Louis of Battenburg has resigned his position as First Sea Lord!' Sarah's tone reflected her bewilderment. 'People seem to be wary of their own shadows these days.'

'Aye, Mother was saying some o' them speak in whispers when they're in the shop!' Anna MacFarlane said gravely. 'Worse than that though, she said some o' the locals had smashed all the windows o' the old clockmender in Bentira village, for all he's lived there more than twenty years, and never done anybody any harm. Now the authorities have taken him away.'

'Poor old man,' Sarah sympathised. 'But maybe he will be safer away from hot-headed young men. I do wish Billy would write more often. He's not a good correspondent at all . . .'

Sarah was more worried about Billy than she cared to admit. At first he had seemed so jubilant and enthusiastic, describing his training, the barrack room, the food, new friends, even mentioning local girls near the training centre. Later he had travelled by train and then by boat to France. He had described the scenes there, the towns and villages, the land and the people. But as the weeks passed Sarah sensed a change of mood. The letters were more formal, even stilted, thanking her for a food parcel, or Beth for her knitted socks, Logan for his news of Fairlyden and the village – yet saying nothing of his real life – or death. It was as though a door had closed between him and his family and friends at home.

Women everywhere were knitting socks for the soldiers in response to Queen Mary's urging. Anna frequently joined Beth, Sadie and Sarah round the fire in the Fairlyden kitchen for an hour or two in the evenings. Once Jamie was asleep, his Uncle Thomas was content to settle down to a quiet half-hour by the cottage fireside, with a book or the weekly newspaper, but neither he nor Logan had much time or energy by the end of their labours.

'They say the war is costing a million pounds every day,' Anna remarked one evening as the needles clicked busily.

'Well, Billy says there's thousands and thousands of men tae feed, as well as the horses.' Beth's needles ceased their rhythmic clicking for a moment and a slight frown creased her forehead. It was some weeks since Billy had written to any of them and she couldn't help wondering if he was all right. Sarah had never lifted her eyes from the four needles and the sock she was knitting but she read Beth's thoughts with uncanny accuracy. 'I just wish he would write to let us know how he is – and where he is!'

'He'll be enjoying himself too much tae have time tae write!' Sadie muttered. 'While we dae all the work as well as paying for the war. Mr Jardine reckons income tax is tae be doubled! One and six in every pound!'

Sarah sighed. They all had to do extra work to make up for Billy's absence, but Sadie grumbled constantly. It had been a great relief when all the turnips were lifted and safely carted home; it was a cold hard job, even for the men, and Sarah would have sympathised if Sadie had not been so loud in her complaints. In comparison, Beth and Logan made the best of even the most laborious tasks – so long as they were together. Their youthful laughter and occasional bursts of song were like balm to her spirits these days.

210

At Mains of Muir the tragedy of Meg's death, while not forgotten, had certainly been overshadowed by the war and the changes which were constantly taking place. Alex and Ewan had been deeply upset when army officials commandeered some of their best horses. 'They think money is the only thing that matters. They dinna understand that our horses are almost like brothers tae us,' Alex complained to his grandfather. 'And there's nae telling when we'll get the money anyway.'

'Aye, Beatrice was saying old Mr Mathias has shot his two mares and the old gelding. He couldna bear the thought o' them being taken away.'

'Well, he is a widower and he hasna any family,' Beatrice sympathised. 'I expect his horses are like kin tae him.

'I could almost agree with him now that I've seen them taking Bess and Flash away . . .' Alex muttered huskily.

'Aye, it's a sorry business,' Sandy sighed. 'I reckon this war will affect every man, woman and child in the realm before it's finished, whether they're fighting in a foreign land or biding at home.'

Beth wept when the army commissioners arrived at Fairlyden to review their horses and Sarah almost joined her. They took away a fine young gelding, barely broken to the shafts. Logan was silent and brooding for days afterwards. He was sure the men knew little about horses and less about handling them; it also meant the old mare would have to do far heavier work than he would have asked of her, but there was no choice; it took several years to breed, rear and break another gelding.

Two months had passed without any letters from Billy.

'Well, they say nae news is guid news,' Janet Whiteley said to Sarah, 'but I ken it's little comfort tae ye. Jim Braid has delivered plenty o' bad news these past months. I reckon the very sight o' the telegrams is getting him down . . .' Sarah nodded but she still worried about Billy. Then at the end of April Beth received a postcard, but it bore only a brief pencilled greeting and told them nothing, except that Billy was alive. Her mother's instinct told Sarah that all was not well with her son.

She was right. At the beginning of May, nineteen hundred and fifteen, just when Sarah was getting desperately anxious and wondering where to apply for news, Billy appeared, walking slowly up the track. She could scarcely believe her own eyes.

'Oh, Billy!' It was impossible to restrain her tears as she enfolded him in her arms. But Billy was stiff and awkward, there was no glint of laughter in his dark eyes, no rueful smile tugging the corner of his mouth. Even his dark curly hair seemed to have faded. 'Why didn't you send word you were coming? I would have sent the trap to the station. We should have . . .'

'I dinna want any fuss, Mother.' Billy's tone was harsh and Sarah drew back in dismay. She saw the lines of strain on his dark face, the shadow of beard accentuating his lean jaw. He crossed the kitchen and dropped on to one of the high-backed wooden chairs, but not before Sarah had noticed his limp. He had been injured! He had never mentioned it in his letters . . .

'I'll make some tea,' she said quietly, and moved to the fire, poking it up before she shoved the swey over the flames, setting the iron kettle swinging gently. She heard Billy let out a long sigh and glanced over her shoulder. He was staring round the familiar kitchen, his dark eyes almost drinking in each copper pot and pan, each jug and bowl and ornament. He was flexing his right hand too . . . Sarah busied herself making the tea.

'Logan is finishing drilling the turnips today. They're up in High Meadow . . .' she said conversationally, striving to sound normal.

'Aye,' Billy nodded. 'I thought it would be about time for't.' He frowned fiercely. 'Mother . . . I couldna write for a while. I was wounded. No!' He held up a hand as Sarah opened her mouth to speak, her dark eyes anxious. 'I just dinna want everybody asking questions! Most of all, I dinna want tae talk about . . . about anything . . .' His voice trailed to a halt, his mouth set in an uncompromising line.

'Very well,' Sarah agreed soothingly.

'Dinna humour me! I'm no'a bairn! I'm . . .'

'A wounded soldier who acts like a bairn . . .?' Sarah suggested mildly, but her face was gentle.

'I'm sorry . . .' Billy heaved a sigh, but his knuckles clenched tightly. How tense he is, Sarah thought anxiously, and how painfully thin!

'Drink up, laddie.' She poured the tea from the big brown pot.

'Still the same old teapot, I see . . .' Billy summoned a smile and sipped gratefully at the hot sweet tea.

'You'll feel better after a good sleep,' Sarah advised. 'But I canna tell you how glad I am to see you. The rest o' them will be too, when they come in . . .'

'I-I think I'll rest first. Er . . . ye'll – maybe ye could tell them – I dinna want tae discuss the bloody war . . .' He stopped and bit his lip. 'I'm sorry, Mother.'

'I think I understand, Billy,' Sarah nodded. 'How long can you stay?'

'Three weeks, I think.' He grimaced. 'They reckon I'll be good as new by then . . .'

Everyone, even Sadie, seemed pleased to see Billy again, but he seemed most at ease with Beth. Gradually he began to relax and eat with more enjoyment, and take short walks in the fresh damp air. No one questioned him about the war. Sarah had warned them all. In any case they all heard Billy's unearthly yells on his second night at home. They could only guess at the memories which triggered off the spine-chilling nightmares.

Sarah wrote a note to Alex at Mains of Muir. She had been concerned about his moodiness in the weeks following Billy's departure.

'I think he feels guilty because he's still safe at home when so many o' the young men he kens have gone tae France,' Beattie had suggested when she mentioned it on one of her visits to the Mains. Sarah knew she was right.

'Janet says some of the men in Muircumwell have received white feathers because they haven't volunteered . . .' she mused aloud.

'That's not what I meant! Alex isna a coward!' Beatrice had exclaimed in distress.

'I know, but I suppose he feels he's less of a man because he canna join the army. All because he's lame . . .' Sarah muttered miserably.

'I ken ye still blame yourself for that, Sarah, but if ye ask me it's a blessing in disguise now! We need some o' the farmers tae stay at home and look after things.' Beattie declared firmly. 'Anyway, I think Alex has been more resigned since Ellen sent him that poem frae Brad. Did ye see it?'

'No.'

'It's pinned on the wall i' the wee room where Alex does his accounts. Away and read it while I make some tea.'

★ ★ ★

213

They sing about the glories of the man behind the gun,
And the books are full of stories of the wonders he has done;
There's something sort of thrilling in the flag that's waving
    high,
And it makes you want to holler when the boys go marching
    by;
But when the shouting's over, and the fighting's done some-
    how,
We find we're still depending on the man behind the plow.

'Alex didna comment on the poem when he showed it tae us,'
Beatrice told her later, 'but I'm sure it helped him accept his
limitations. He's planning tae help "the cause" in his ain way
now – growing as much hay and corn as he can – even though he
willna need it all for the Mains' animals. He says the horses that
have gone tae war will need tae be fed, as well as the men,
especially if oor navy doesna stop the Germans sinking sae many
ships.'

Alex came over to Fairlyden the day he received the news of
Billy's return and it pleased Sarah to see her two eldest sons
together on such friendly terms, teasing and arguing almost as
though Billy had never been away.

It was on a Sunday at the end of Billy's second week that Alex
drove into the Fairlyden yard again. This time he was driving
the Mains' trap and Ellen was beside him.

'I wasna sure I could get away frae the hospital,' she chuckled,
even though a few emotional tears trickled down her cheeks at
the sight of Billy. 'Alex offered tae meet the train in case I was on
it.'

'And here she is!' Alex announced jubilantly. 'All the way frae
Edinburgh to see the biggest rogue of a brother a lassie ever
had!'

'Ye'll be referring tae yourself, nae doubt!' Billy responded
with something of his old teasing smile, but he hugged Ellen
with unexpected fervour and his voice was gruff. 'But it's grand
tae see ye again. All the lads fall in love with the nurses but I've
told them ye're the prettiest, as well as the best – even though
they're never likely tae see ye . . .' For a moment Ellen was
absolutely still in the circle of his arms.

'Dinna be sae sure . . .' she whispered softly. Billy was startled, especially when Ellen met his dark gaze so steadily, but

before he could ask any questions she tossed her shining head and laughed up at him. 'I'm starving and I can smell Mother's broth simmering away on the swey.'

'It was Beth who made the broth,' Sarah smiled, 'while I was at the kirk. Did you know about this surprise, Beth?'

Beth blushed shyly as all eyes turned towards her and she looked at Alex.

'Just a wee note with Jim Braid, the postie,' he admitted. 'We didna want anybody tae be disappointed if Ellen couldna come. I kenned we could depend on Beth tae make sure there was plenty tae eat though.'

Sarah knew she would never forget the happiness of that Sunday afternoon with all her family together under one roof. After dinner was over and the dishes washed, they all gathered into the front parlour and persuaded Beth to play the piano. Even Sadie joined in the singing without a grumble. After the hymns and a few well-known songs which Beth could play by heart, Billy hummed some of the latest tunes and Beth, with her quick ear for music, soon picked them up. The parlour rang to the sound of 'Hello, hello, who's your lady friend?' and 'Alexander's Ragtime Band'. Only Sarah noticed the returning shadows in Billy's dark eyes when Beth played 'Keep the home fires burning', the song which the Minister's young wife had taught to nearly everyone in Muircumwell.

Twenty-Five

Billy's wounds had not healed as quickly as the doctors had expected and his leave was extended for another week. On the twenty-second of May, the very day he was to have travelled to Liverpool, en route for France, a terrible tragedy occurred. Three trains crashed at Quintinshill Junction on the border between England and Scotland. One of them was the troop train.

'Thomas says the lines are blocked. He heard it at the station. They're saying there's more than two hundred dead!' Sarah's face was taut with distress. 'He says a lot of the survivors are badly burned . . .'

Billy's face paled. 'I would have been on that train if the doctor hadna given me extra time!' He put his arm around Sarah's shoulders. 'It lets ye see, Mother, any of us could be killed, at any time – not just in the war. So promise ye'll try not to worry when I go back tae France . . .?'

'I do try not tae worry . . .' Sarah whispered huskily, 'but war seems such a dreadful thing and some o' the stories . . .'

'I'll no' deny I'm petrified whiles . . .' Billy's voice was low. 'But somehow I have this feeling that God is watching o'er me . . . And I ken ye'll be praying for me, eh . . .?'

Sarah's eyes widened. Of all her children Billy had always been the least religious, the most reluctant to attend the kirk each Sunday. As though sensing her surprise Billy gave a wry grimace. 'I've seen lots o' things in a different light since I went away, Mother . . . and since I came home tae . . . "For thou art with me; thy rod and thy staff they comfort me." ' He quoted the lines from the twenty-third psalm with a faintly mocking smile. 'I didna ken I felt like that – but I do now . . .'

Sarah nodded. 'I understand, laddie,' she said huskily. 'And I'm thankful for that at least.' But she knew she would worry just the same. Dreadful though the train crash had been, it had been an accident – or perhaps even human carelessness – but war was killing by intent; cruel and heartless and without mercy. Sometimes she had been driven to question God's will herself when so many young men had died already.

All too soon Billy was ready to leave once more. Logan had brought the pony and trap to the door and all that remained was the final goodbyes. This time even Sadie got a kiss on the cheek. Sarah hugged Billy hard, compressed her lips to stop them trembling and gave him a gentle push. She was determined not to shed any tears. As usual Beth stood a little aside, ever mindful that she was not really a member of the family even without Sadie's constant gibes and reminders, yet her young heart grieved for Billy returning to unknown horrors in a foreign land. She was beside the pony and trap when Billy came to her. She held out her hand, but Billy clasped her shoulders and stared earnestly into her face. His dark eyes were serious.

'I've always said I'd never be tied down with a wife – but ye could surely tempt me, Beth . . .' He bent his dark head and kissed her cheek. For a moment he hesitated, then he cupped her face in his hands and kissed her lingeringly on her soft, surprised young mouth. Beth was seventeen and it was her first real kiss.

'Oh, Billy, please, please take care . . .' Her voice was husky with tears.

'You can be sure I shall – and if ye're no' married when I come back the next time, young Beth . . .' he glanced up at Logan's glowering face with an unrepentant smile, 'then the young men around here will have missed their chance!'

The power of the German navy became more and more apparent with the sinking of the *Lusitania* and the destruction of several houses on shore, killing people in their own homes. In London four people were killed by a German Zeppelin. It was becoming increasingly clear that this was a war which knew no boundaries and no mercy. Every day men were killed in hundreds. There were appeals for more volunteers. The British Government drew up a register of men over eighteen years old. There was growing fear that this was a preliminary to enforcing conscription.

As the summer progressed, Sarah detected a restlessness in Ellen's letters.

'I feel I ought to be working where I am needed most,' she had written. 'I have heard reports of hundreds of wounded soldiers in desperate need in France and Russia.' Then more recently,

'Many married women who trained as nurses are returning to the hospitals while their husbands are away. Hundreds of women, married and single, are manning the munitions factories and even working on the buses and trams as conductors. I feel it is my duty to do more, Mother – to use my skills to help the men who are fighting for our freedom. I have mentioned this to Brad. I think he understands. He is restless – and he longs to use his skills to help our soldiers too. His mother no longer recognises him, or anyone else, and she is growing increasingly frail in body as well as mind.'

Sarah guessed it was only the possibility of Brad's return which had kept Ellen in Edinburgh so long.

'I know it's selfish of me,' she confessed to Janet Whiteley when she collected her groceries at the Muircumwell Store, 'but I hope Ellen bides in Edinburgh waiting for Brad until this war is over.'

'Well, I hope it will be over soon tae, or they'll be taking Maggie's laddies before we ken.'

'I pray it willna come to that!' Sarah said fervently. 'Logan will be eighteen next March and I don't know how we should manage without him as well as Billy . . . Donald is a year younger. Surely the war canna go on that long.'

'They're men already – in a' but years,' Janet sighed. 'Sae many pleasures they've missed . . .'

'And yet I believe they are happy with their responsibilities and their work,' Sarah mused. 'Alex tells me Donald is proving to be an excellent horseman and he shows promise as a ploughman too. Maybe he has inherited Louis's skill with the plough as well as Ewan's instinct with the horses.'

'Aye, weel I hope the government leaves him be!' Janet muttered darkly. 'We need workers on the land as well as soldiers at the front if we're no' tae starve. Supplies are getting harder tae get and the prices are rising every day. There's nae wonder Jardine's aye complaining o' pains in his stomach. The very thought o' missing a wee bit trade, and losing a shilling or twae makes him ill!'

Sarah smiled faintly at Janet's wry expression. Her employer was well known for his parsimony.

'At least Ray Jardine only has his money to worry about! Most families in Muircumwell seem to have somebody in France.'

Crispin Bradshaw made an unexpected visit to Fairlyden to see his housekeeper, Mrs Bunnerby. He was concerned about the shortage of food too.

'We're supposed to grow more corn and less grass and turnips next year,' Sarah told him, 'but I don't know how we'll manage to harvest what we have this year without Billy. Some of the farms are even worse off where two or three men have gone to fight. Alex is short o' two men at the Mains and three of the women have gone to work in the munitions factory so they are short of milkers too.'

'There's a shortage of labour everywhere,' Crispin agreed gravely. 'I hear a lot of the town dairies have stopped keeping cows since the men went to the war?'

'Yes, I think that must be true. We get more money for our milk now, because it is in short supply, but it will get scarcer still if we have to grow less turnips and grass for the cows, and we canna buy imported cattle cake for them either.'

'The country is not in a happy situation.' Crispin frowned. 'I'm told many English farmers do not even possess a plough since the prices of grain were so depressed, and there is neither the steel nor the men to make new ones. Some of the farms in the south and east do not even have tenants. The government is taking over neglected land, but who is to farm it?'

'Mmm, well, maybe the government should have foreseen such things,' Sarah replied dryly. 'But let us forget about farming and troubles for a wee while,' she smiled brightly. 'How is Mrs Bunnerby today? You didna tell her I had mentioned how tired she is in my letter, did you, Crispin?'

'No, but I'm glad you keep me informed, Sarah. I know how independent she is, but she does appreciate your care – and Beth's frequent visits. She will not admit to feeling ill. Yet she tells me she is not afraid of death – which shows she has been considering such things . . .'

'Don't worry, Crispin. We shall keep an eye on her. She's a good woman and she has been very kind to Beth.'

'Yes . . . She imagines Beth is in love . . .'

Sarah smiled. 'I think Mrs Bunnerby may be right.'

'You do?'

'Well, when you see Beth and Logan together . . .'

'But they're so young! Not yet eighteen!'

'Aye,' Sarah's brown eyes darkened. 'As Janet says, all the

young folks are being forced to grow up too fast. It's the war! It has changed everything!' She sighed. 'How are things at the factory?'

'Frantic.' Crispin accepted the change of topic but he guessed Sarah was more concerned about Logan and Beth than she cared to admit. 'All our machines and all our efforts are concentrated on making uniforms for the soldiers. Of course I miss Ted Forbes – remember the young man I was training to take my own place so that I could spend more time up here? He was an excellent foreman . . .' Crispin sighed and frowned, then he looked searchingly at Sarah. 'I miss our meetings . . .' he said softly. 'Our discussions – even arguments . . .'

'Oh, Crispin! We never quarrelled!'

'Of course we didn't.' He smiled, reminding her of Logan. 'But you have too much spirit to agree with me all of the time, my dear. It is one of the things I respect you for – your intelligence, your integrity . . . You do look very charming too – when you get a little angry . . .' His eyes sparkled so that they looked more green than grey.

'Well, I'm not getting angry today. Our time is too short to disagree. I shall make tea for you instead.'

Only when Crispin had gone did Sarah allow herself to admit how much she had missed his company and his frequent visits. The war! she fumed irritably. It is upsetting the lives of everybody!

Reports had filtered back from Brussels that Nurse Edith Cavell had been imprisoned by the Germans. She was accused of spying despite the help she had given to wounded soldiers from both sides. If she was found guilty the penalty was death.

As Sarah read Ellen's letter it was clear that her beloved daughter was particularly distressed and indignant that such a fate should fall to a fellow nurse, especially one who had dedicated her life to her profession, regardless of faith or politics. This was the final spur and Sarah's heart quailed as she read her letter.

'I cannot wait any longer. It is my duty to go where I am needed most, to help those who are fighting for our freedom. Many other nurses are not free to go. I am – and I must go now. I have asked Matron to find someone to take my place.

Not all the women are willing to work in a hospital where poverty abounds and fever is often rife and I shall not neglect my young patients, but as soon as a replacement has been found I shall travel to France, or wherever my services are required. Please try to understand, dearest Mother. If Nurse Cavell is prepared to give her life, then I must offer whatever help I can. Surely this dreadful slaughter cannot go on forever?

'Brad is very frustrated but I am sure he would not forgive himself if his mother died alone in the company of strangers – even though she rarely recognises him.

'He believes there will be work which we can do together, even when the war is past and forgotten – helping the wounded, the limbless and the sightless. He has seen the same cruel waste of men in America.

'Please pray for me, and give me your blessing, so that I may have the strength and the will to do what is needed.

'Please Mama?'

Sarah's hand trembled as she folded the letter, but she knew Ellen was determined to do her duty for her country and her fellow men, even if it meant postponing her happiness with Brad a little longer. When she goes I shall give her all the support she craves, Sarah resolved, however much my own heart aches when I think of the danger and difficulties she will face. Billy might have died without the skill of the nurses who tended him; how can I try to prevent Ellen helping some other mother's son?

Twenty-Six

It was becoming alarmingly clear that more men would be needed to take the place of the thousands who had been killed or maimed for life. No one was more aware of this than Logan, even without the snatches of first-hand information he had gleaned from Billy. He had no desire to leave Fairlyden, he had even less desire to kill his fellow men; but he had inherited a strong sense of duty as well as the conviction that every man and woman was entitled to freedom – freedom to work, to worship where they pleased, freedom to laugh, and to love.

As the weeks passed the newspapers continued to print long lists of those killed in battle, some of them young men Logan had known; he knew he could not stand aside if the war continued. The prospect made him quiet and subdued. He looked at the familiar scenes he had known throughout his seventeen years and he saw them all with new eyes. He had a fresh appreciation of everything from the simple, sun-warmed grassy knoll to the wild-eyed kitten, from old Peggotty's ageing and ungainly bulk to the trim young Clydesdale mare which was his pride and joy.

His heart sank at the prospect of leaving all that was dear and familiar, everything that represented his dreams for the future. Like his mother, and thousands of ordinary men and women everywhere, he prayed that the war would soon be over, that the world would return to normal and let everyone live their lives in peace again.

'What's wrong, Logan?' Beth asked quietly, one afternoon in late August. They were walking back from the cornfield in silence. Logan had been scything the outer rows of corn in readiness for the binder while she bound the sheaves. Sadie had been helping too but she had left the field early on the pretext of rounding up the cows for milking. 'Are ye worried about getting in the harvest without Billy? Your mother said two o' the farmers frae Strathtod parish have offered tae help. They dinna grow any corn themselves . . .' Logan did not answer. 'I ken they're not young anymore,' Beth persisted gently, 'but Mr Jenkins says he can build the corn stacks and . . .'

'It isna the harvest I'm worried about, Beth – at least not this year . . .' He stared across at the field of waving corn gleaming golden in the afternoon sun, at the young heifers grazing contentedly in the field below; he saw the brambles ripening from red to darkest purple and the beech hedges which would soon be turning to bronze. He sighed deeply. 'I keep wondering if I'll be here for next year's harvest . . .'

'Why wouldn't ye be here?' Beth's voice rose involuntarily.

'I shall be eighteen in March, remember – old enough tae join the army . . .'

'But ye've never wanted tae leave Fairlyden before!'

'I dinna *want* tae leave it now!' He looked down into Beth's startled blue eyes. 'I dinna want tae leave you either . . .' Logan surprised himself as much as Beth, but he held her gaze almost defiantly. The delicate flush which coloured her cheeks delighted him, but she lowered her lashes shyly. He had always known what Beth was thinking by the expression in her eyes. Her gaze was always clear and honest.

'But surely ye dinna have tae go if ye dinna want tae fight . . .?'

'I dinna want any white feathers pinned tae my jacket either. I'm not like Jake Dodds.'

'Jake Dodds is idle – and he's a coward and a bully. He . . .'

'He refused tae volunteer,' Logan finished flatly. 'I'm no coward, Beth, and I wouldna give any man the chance tae say I am. Besides I think the government will be forced tae bring in conscription in spite o' all the denials. There'll never be enough volunteers tae take the place o' the thousands o' men that have been killed already – and it's getting worse.'

'But ye're a farmer!' Beth protested tearfully. 'Surely the government must realise we need people on the farms if we're all tae have enough food?'

'People? Aye, women and old men – and conchies. They'd likely say one man at Fairlyden was enough and we have Thomas. He's too deaf and past the age for soldiering. Anyway, I'd rather go willingly,' he added proudly. 'But dinna ye worry, Beth . . .' He sighed and reached for her hand, drawing her closer to his side as they walked.

'I dinna ken what I'd dae if ye went away . . .' she murmured huskily. Logan glanced down at the bright honey-gold head which just reached to his shoulder. Beth would not meet his gaze; her eyes were bright with tears at the very thought of Logan going away – especially going away to fight in this dreadful war.

'Och, ye'd soon forget me . . .' Logan had meant to sound blithe but his voice croaked miserably.

'I'll never forget ye!' Beth retorted vehemently. 'Never . . .' she repeated in a trembling whisper.

Logan stopped, so Beth was forced to stop too. Very carefully he removed the scythe from his shoulder and laid it on the grass beside the hedge, then he turned to face her. He lifted her little pointed chin almost diffidently. For several seconds he stood there in silence, gazing down at her. She thought his eyes looked more green than grey as he searched her upturned face.

'I love ye, Beth . . .'

'Aah . . . Logan!' Her voice trembled. 'Do – d'ye really mean it. .?'

'Have I ever told ye a lie, Beth? Maybe I'm no sae much of a man as Billy, but I ken that ye're the only one I'll ever love.'

'I didna think ye would ever love me as I love you . . .' Beth said breathlessly. 'I-I . . .'

'You . . .love me?' Logan stared at her incredulously, his earnest face flushing with pleasure. He looked very young, but to Beth he was everything she had adored for as long as she could remember – except that recently it had been more than childish adoration that made her heart beat faster and her knees feel weak.

'Surely ye must have guessed?' She peeped up at him uncertainly.

'No. I scarcely dared tae hope . . . Oh, Beth . . .' Logan's smile slowly transformed his boyish face until he was grinning with happiness. Suddenly he put both his arms around her and swung her off her feet, spinning her round and round until they were both breathless with laughter. Then the high spirits drained away as swiftly as they had risen and Logan stared down at Beth. 'I love ye!' he muttered and pressed his lips to her soft mouth in a hurried, clumsy kiss. Then he bit his lip in an agony of embarrassment. 'I-I'm sorry.'

'Dinna be sorry, Logie,' Beth said softly, shyly. 'I-I liked it.'

'But it wasna like Billy kissed ye! When he went away. He . . .' Logan broke off, miserably aware that he had probably revealed the burning jealousy he had felt since his brother's departure.

225

'Billy?' Beth gave him a puzzled frown. 'I dinna understand. Billy kissed everybody goodbye – even Sadie.'

'It was different though – the way he kissed you . . .' Logan mumbled.

'Ye mean because I'm your mother's maid?' Beth's eyes were wistful. 'Sadie keeps reminding me o' my place. I-I think she's guessed I love ye.'

'Aah, Beth!' Logan's voice was choked with emotion and he pulled her close, pressing her bright head against his chest. 'That's not what I meant at all! Not at all! Billy kissed ye like a man kisses a woman! A real woman! The woman he – he admires . . .wants . . . Oh, God forgive me, but I've been jealous o' Billy since the day he went! I was glad – glad he had tae go back tae France! Now I'm sorry . . .'

Beth raised her head but she did not move from the warm circle of Logan's arms. She smiled up at him shyly. 'I dinna remember Billy's kiss being special.'

'Ye dinna?' Logan asked earnestly and his heart was in his eyes as he stared down at Beth with youthful passion. 'I'm glad then, because I'm going tae marry ye . . .' Logan broke off, and the colour rushed up under his fair skin. 'I-I mean I'm going tae marry ye if – if ye'll . . . er, consent . . .?'

'I'd like tae be your wife, Logan,' Beth said shyly. 'I've dreamed about it,' she added honestly, 'b-but I thought it would always be just a dream. Sadie . . .'

'I dinna care what Sadie says. Ye mustna listen tae her either. I told Billy ages ago that I was going tae ask ye tae marry me!' Logan declared with increasing confidence. 'I kenned then that he admired ye, Beth . . .'

'Well, maybe he'll not mind then, if ye make me his sister. He's aye been kind tae me since Father died . . . but I think Sadie hates me . . .' Beth shuddered as she thought of Sadie's cold eyes.

'Ye dinna need tae worry about Sadie! She doesna like anybody except herself. Anyway, we'll not tell her, or anybody else, that we're going tae be married until I come back frae the war. Then I shall be here and Sadie willna dare vent her spite on ye. I'm sure Mother thinks o' ye as part o' her family already, Beth. I think she'll be pleased when ye have the Fairly name tae.'

'Oh, Logan!' Beth shivered in spite of the warmth and strength of his arms. 'I canna bear the thought o' ye going tae war. Let's not talk about it until . . . unless it really has tae happen.'

'Ye're right!' Logan agreed promptly. 'Now I ken ye love me, it doesna matter about anything else. We'll just think about each other, shall we?'

'Oh yes,' Beth murmured fervently, 'just each other.' She looked up into his face and the love shone in her blue eyes – youthful, innocent love. Logan bent his head and this time his kiss was more confident, slow, experimental – infinitely, mutually satisfying. Beth was so soft and warm, her young body moulded to his instinctively, guilelessly. Logan felt her tremble as his kiss deepened but he was unprepared for his own sudden arousal. He blushed furiously, holding Beth away from him. He saw her eyes widen in astonishment.

'D-did I make ye f-feel like that?' she asked with awe.

Logan bit his lip and frowned. 'D'ye mind?' he gulped.

'Not if it means that ye love me like a real woman – I mean really l-love me . . .?' she stammered uncertainly.

'Ye're a real woman all right,' Logan said gruffly, 'and ye make me feel like a real man . . . Too much like a man,' he muttered softly. He looked down into her face, saw the trusting innocence in her blue eyes. 'I'd never want tae hurt ye, Beth . . .' He sighed with a mixture of happiness and regret. 'We'd better get back. It's almost time for the milking.'

Beth nodded and smiled up at him, glowing with the happiness of young love.

The harvest was half finished when Ellen returned to Fairlyden for a few brief days in September and to Sarah it seemed no time at all before she was bidding her goodbye again. Ellen had made a point of visiting Mains of Muir to see her grandfather and Alex before she left for France but she had been dismayed by her grandfather's appearance.

'He seems tae have aged several years since I last saw him,' she confided huskily and Sarah refrained from telling her it was the news that she was going to work in such dangerous places that had shaken him so badly. She knew how much it had distressed Ellen to say goodbye to him.

'I pray this war willna last much longer, lassie,' he had muttered gruffly. And I hope I'm still here tae see ye return, he thought silently.

So Sarah strove to control the tears which burned behind her own eyelids when she kissed Ellen goodbye. Sadie remained as cool and unmoved as if Ellen had been travelling no further than Jardine's Store but Beth could not restrain a few tears as Ellen gave her a sisterly hug and murmured softly, 'I know ye'll look after Logan and Mother, Beth. I see now that ye love them both – and I'm glad . . .' She smiled wistfully into Beth's face. 'Seize your happiness while ye can,' she whispered hastily as Logan drove the trap to the door.

'I dinna ken what ye were greetin' for,' Sadie sneered contemptuously the moment Logan had driven Ellen away in the trap. 'Anybody would think she was your sister.'

Ever since her father's death Beth had visited Mrs Bunnerby, the kindly Yorkshire woman, every day, but in the past few months she had noticed the old lady growing frailer and it saddened her. She knew Mistress Fairly had noticed it too because she had formed a habit of taking milk to Fairlyside herself every morning as early as she could and Beth guessed it was an excuse to make sure the independent old lady was well.

Logan accompanied Beth whenever he was free. Mrs Bunnerby looked forward to their visits with gratitude, reliving her own youthful memories as she basked in the love which seemed to shine from every smile and glance they exchanged. She knew how little time they had to spare from the eternal round of cutting the corn and setting up stooks, loading and unloading carts and all the other work of the farm. Yet Beth and Logan scarcely noticed the hard work, or the showers that frequently prolonged the harvest and made so much extra work. They were happy just to be together.

If Logan was detained in the harvest field, or attending to a sickly animal, then Beth went alone to Mrs Bunnerby's, but she knew Logan would be waiting for her by the gate when she left the house. They treasured these precious moments alone together when the evening shadows crept over the land and the birds flew back to their nests; just for a little while it was possible to make believe that all the world shared the peace of Fairlyden's meadows and fields. Logan always drew Beth aside before they reached the yard gate so that he could steal a kiss in the shelter of the old ash tree.

In October Sarah was shaken when she read the report that

228

Nurse Edith Cavell had actually been executed – shot by a German firing squad.

'Please God,' she prayed fervently, 'protect Ellen from such heathens.'

Three weeks later she felt her prayers may have been answered when she received a letter from Brad Leishman. Ellen had been forced to make several moves at short notice and he was uncertain how to contact her directly.

'Mother is at peace at last,' he had written. 'Many times I was tempted to seize my own chance of happiness with Ellen. How glad I am that I waited, supported by your daughter's love and understanding. I think you will understand, Mrs Fairly, how grateful I am now. Mother died in my arms – and not alone. For a few precious minutes she recognised me, her only son. She spoke to me lucidly and with all the loving kindness of the mother I had known and respected.

'I feel free now in mind and in spirit – free to follow my beloved Ellen to the very ends of the earth. I pray that you will bless our union, and I hope you will forgive us if we cannot wait to return to Scotland for our wedding.

'As soon as I can procure a berth, I shall be on my way to Britain. If you are able to communicate with Ellen, could you please tell her my news and my plans? I enclose a letter and I shall be eternally grateful if you can send it to my beloved.'

There were a few more sentences enquiring after members of the family, especially her father. Sarah finished the letter and folded it with a contented sigh. Ellen deserved happiness after all this time and Sarah had no doubt that Brad would make a loving and loyal husband now that he was free; in addition, he and Ellen shared a mutual love for their work in healing the sick.

Sarah realised from Ellen's brief letters that there was little time to spare for leisure, and few facilities or comforts either for the wounded or those who attended them.

'Sometimes – indeed often – we dress the wounds of more than a thousand men in a single day,' she had written. 'They must lie on straw as we have no beds. They are not even as clean, or as warm and comfortable, as the cows in the byre at Fairlyden. Some of the soldiers seem even younger than Logan. I am so very glad I came – though often I feel helpless and the need is so very great.'

She had added a postscript.

'I received Brad's letter this morning with your note, Mother. It makes me so very happy to know we shall soon be together at last. I shall write a letter, as he requests, and send it to the Liverpool office to inform him of my present station. He intends to travel direct to London to offer his services, but he hopes we shall be near enough to see each other and we plan to marry without further delay. I thank you for all your love and good wishes to us. It saddens me that our wedding will not be in our own wee kirk at Muircumwell with my loved ones at my side, but we shall look forward to the day when we can celebrate with you all – when there is an end to this dreadful suffering.'

It grieved Sarah to think of Ellen being married in a foreign land with not a single member of her family present but nothing was normal any more since this dreadful war had spread to almost every corner of the globe. She prayed fervently for her daughter's happiness. She busied herself making a wedding cake containing a dozen eggs and fresh butter, with all the fruit she could persuade Janet to sell from Ray Jardine's meagre hoard.

'It's a waste o' time and guid food,' Sadie muttered impatiently. 'It will be nought but a parcel o' crumbs by the time it arrives in France – if it ever gets there!'

'I shall wrap it in layers of paper and sew it in calico so that it canna be torn apart,' Sarah insisted firmly. 'There's little enough I can do to make Ellen's wedding day the happy occasion it ought to be.'

For Logan and Beth it was a time when each new day brought fresh news of war and strife, danger and death – and each shy smile, each new discovery, was a moment to be treasured as the golden days of autumn moved to winter.

230

Twenty-Seven

Ellen and Brad Leishman were married quietly in a small French church at the end of November.

'We had one whole day and two nights together,' Ellen had written, 'and dearest Mama, the cake arrived in beautiful condition; it reminded us of Fairlyden and all your love and kindness. Brad and I thank you from the bottom of our hearts. The nurses, and even some of our patients, toasted our health with Scottish cake and some French wine which one of the doctors had commandeered from a local château. One of the officers, a very cheery fellow who seems to have taken a great liking to us, borrowed a motor bicycle so that we could get away on our own for a few hours. It was rather frightening at first and Brad said I clung to him so tightly that he could scarcely breathe. However, we arrived safely at a small cottage which the officer had arranged for us. It was beside a wood and only a few yards from a wee burn with crystal-clear water, just like ours at home. It was wonderful to light the fire and be able to bathe. Everything seemed so peaceful after the sounds and smells and constant bustle of the Casualty Station.

'The next morning we had to rise at dawn to get back to our respective posts and return the motor cycle. We are back in the endless routine of dressing wounds again but the memory of those precious hours spent together will stay with us for ever.'

'There's no doubt Ellen is very happy to be married to Brad,' Sarah announced with a tender smile as she looked up from reading the letter. 'In spite of the dreadful conditions out there.'

'What is Brad doing now then?' Logan asked as he finished his porridge. 'He canna be in the army, can he?'

'Ellen says they are in desperate need of doctors. Brad is spending most of his time at what she calls the Advanced Dressing Station. She writes "Nurses are not supposed to work nearer to the front than the Casualty Posts but some of my new

231

friends – one makes friends very quickly in these circumstances – drive ambulances as far as . . ." '

'Humph!' Sadie interrupted derisively. 'It sounds as though they're all enjoying themselves with the . . .'

'Whisht, Sadie!' Logan frowned impatiently. 'Ye wouldna go out there to work! Ye ken nothing about it. Jimmy Short said the nurses were wonderful and he should ken after the weeks he spent in hospital. Go on, Mother, what else does Ellen say?'

'You're very interested, Logan . . .' Sarah frowned questioningly, but when Logan made no reply she read on. ' "Drive ambulances as far as the Advanced Dressing Station to collect the wounded soldiers and bring them in to us. There is a constant stream of patients. No one gets much time to sleep but there is a wonderful spirit of camaraderie. Brad . . ." Oh dear, she says Brad spends most of his time between the Advanced Dressing Stations. Surely that's bound to be more dangerous . . .? Ellen says he feels he may be able to save some lives, or at least prevent some of the men from losing badly severed limbs, if he can clean them and bind them while they are waiting for the ambulances to take them away.' Sarah shivered. 'It all sounds so cruel and dangerous.'

Beth's face was pale as she rose to clear away the breakfast dishes. There was no sign of the war ending and if it went on much longer she knew that Logan would feel it was his duty to fight for his country. Even Alex had joined the local volunteers to keep a lookout for spies and help with defences at home, and he was doing his best to grow as much corn and hay as he could despite the extra work and trouble it caused. He had had arguments with members of the new local agricultural committee. He felt the government was not paying enough attention to home-grown food supplies, even though the Germans were sinking so many cargo ships.

The new year brought little consolation. There were heated debates in parliament but by the end of the first week of January nineteen hundred and sixteen it seemed that conscription must be enforced. As the weeks passed feelings ran high; government ministers resigned; the Miners' Union, and later the Labour party, voted against a policy which compelled men to fight.

When the sinking of British ships was intensified, concern increased even in government circles.

232

'Don't the men in London realise that we canna depend on the ships bringing enough food from the other side o' the Atlantic anymore, Logie?' Beth asked, half-angry, half-pleading. She followed the news with a sort of desperation as Logan's eighteenth birthday drew nearer.

'Ach, they talk about oor ain farms producing more, but they only talk!' Anna MacFarlane exclaimed. 'They're going tae recruit four hundred thousand women to grow the crops and harvest them while the men fight.' Anna's face was pale. 'D'ye think that means Maggie's laddies will have tae go tae, Mistress Fairly? And Master Logan! How could we manage? Thomas couldna organise things, or dae all the work . . .'

'I don't know, Anna. I just don't know what will happen!' Sarah shook her head.

Mrs Bunnerby's strength was ebbing fast and Crispin had made several brief visits recently. On his last visit he had not tried to soothe away Sarah's increasing anxiety about Logan and she sensed he was just as concerned as she was. He cared deeply for the son he had never been able to acknowledge as his own and time was running out. There was no end to the war in sight. Sarah knew Logan well enough to realise he would not wait to be taken by force.

Mrs Bunnerby died peacefully at the end of February and both Sarah and Beth were with her. Crispin came the following day in response to Sarah's wire but he looked harassed and tired.

'I shall close the house. There are no maids to spare for housework at such a time as this. I have little time for leisure and the government is asking us to use our motor cars only if it is essential.'

'We'll help you close up, Beth and I,' Sarah offered quietly, 'and you know you are always welcome to stay with us at Fairlyden whenever you do have time to spare . . .' Her eyes spoke the words her lips could not utter – to see our son.

'Thank you, Sarah. It is comforting to know I shall find a welcome in your home,' he said gravely.

'How is Ted Forbes?' Logan asked. 'The man who was foreman at your mill? Mother said he had been badly wounded.'

'Yes, he was.' Crispin was surprised and pleased at Logan's interest. 'He is still in hospital. He has lost his left arm and the wound on his leg is still very painful. I visited him when I was in

233

London to see Fanny. I have arranged for him to be transferred to a hospital in Yorkshire as soon as he is fit to travel by train.'

'Will he be able to work again?' Logan asked and his voice was strained.

'Yes,' Crispin answered decisively, sensing that it was important to Logan. 'He can still use his head. We need men like Ted Forbes – with knowledge and foresight; he understands the men and women from the mill towns, and I know they will respect him more, rather than less, because he has lost a limb. I think it gives him a purpose to know there will be work and a place for him when he is well.'

'I'm sure it does,' Sarah said, her dark eyes glowing with admiration. 'It was kind of you to visit the laddie and give him an incentive to recover.'

'It was not just kindness which prompted me, Sarah, I have to confess,' Crispin grimaced wryly. 'It was selfishness too. I know he will make an excellent manager – better than Robert ever would.'

'Has Robert volunteered to join the army yet?' Sarah asked curiously.

'Oh, yes, but he works in an office, in safety,' Crispin remarked dryly. He had little respect for his nephew and he changed the subject. 'What about Ellen, how is she getting on in France? And Brad?'

'Working hard, but very happy when they can snatch a few hours together,' Sarah smiled tenderly.

It was Beth who felt most bereft by Mrs Bunnerby's death, although she knew the old lady had declared herself 'ready for the next life' many times during the past year.

'I ken she wouldna want us tae grieve for her,' Beth whispered huskily as Logan held her in his arms. 'But I felt she was a friend, although she was old, and I aye liked going to Fairlyside. It was a sort o' refuge.'

'Ye mean we were safe frae Sadie's ill temper!' Logan agreed ruefully. 'But we're not bairns now and we dinna need tae be afraid o' Sadie.' Beth did not answer. She thought she might always be a little wary of Sadie; she had never quite forgotten Aunt Agnes's warning as she lay dying and that strange look in her eyes – as though she was staring at someone . . . Beth could not suppress a shudder. Logan's arm tightened instinctively.

234

Every evening Logan bedded the horses and made a last round of the cows and pigs, to make sure they were all right for the night. Beth always accompanied him. It was the only opportunity they had to be alone together. Soon the lighter evenings would be here again. Soon . . . Beth shivered in spite of the warmth of Logan's embrace.

'Are ye cold, Beth?' he asked with concern, turning her to face him and locking his strong young arms more firmly beneath her shawl.

'N-no, I'm not cold!' But she clung to him with a feeling of desperation. It was the first of March, the evening of his eighteenth birthday. 'Your mother . . . she looked so anxious about ye tonight,' she whispered. 'She's kind, sae very kind tae me, but oh . . .' Her voice cracked, 'I dread tae think o' ye leaving . . .' She glanced up. Logan's eyes held a wistful, far away expression in the flickering light of the storm lantern.

'But ye understand I have tae go tomorrow tae register, don't ye, Beth? I must dae my duty now that I'm of age . . .'

'I ken.' Beth's voice choked with sudden tears.

'I've heard they're delaying taking some o' the farm men, at least until the spring sowing is done. Alex says the government wants extra wheat and oats and potatoes.'

Beth guessed he was trying to comfort her but she knew in her heart that Logan would never plead for his freedom; from now on each day was only a temporary reprieve. Almost as though he had read her mind Logan pressed her closer.

'I canna bear the thought o' leaving ye either, Beth,' he groaned softly and laid his cheek against the crown of her head.

'Dae ye think they'll k-keep ye when ye g-go tomorrow?' She could not help trembling at the thought that he might never hold her in his arms again if they sent him away. She felt Logan stiffen and his arms tightened.

'I dinna ken what happens exactly, but they say that every man will be trained before they send him tae the front . . . Oh, Beth . . .'

She felt the passion rising in him, and the desperation in her own heart was echoed in his ragged voice.

'I love ye more than anything on earth,' she whispered against his chest. Then she raised her head and for the first time she pressed her lips hard against his mouth without waiting for Logan to kiss her first. His response was instant. He kissed her eyes, her cheeks, her throat, even her earlobes. Beth experienced a tide of desire which swamped all reason. She fastened her arms round Logan's neck and returned his kisses in a frenzy of passion. When he lifted her in his arms and carried her to the pile of sweet-smelling hay at the end of the stable she made no objection. He set her down gently and knelt beside her, staring into her face by the dim light of the lamp.

'Beth . . .?' His voice was hoarse.

'I love ye . . . I *want* tae belong tae ye.'

Later Beth felt she wanted to tell the world that she belonged to Logan; she was Logan Fairly's woman and he was her man – now and forever. Their love was a beautiful, precious treasure.

Logan helped her pick the bits of hay from her shining hair and brushed it from her skirts, then he cradled her face in his hands and studied it beneath the lantern.

'Ye're the most beautiful girl in the world, Beth Jamieson,' he smiled tenderly, 'and ye're mine . . . my one and only love . . .' He kissed her gently, without passion, but with all the promises his young heart could make.

Sarah chewed anxiously at her lower lip when Logan and Beth returned to the house. There was an unmistakable radiance about them despite the strain they must be under now that parting was imminent. Beth went into the scullery to wash her hands before pushing the kettle over the fire to make the bedtime drinks. Her cheeks were flushed and her eyes bright with happiness. Sarah's misgivings increased. She knew Beth and Logan were in love and she knew the temptations they must face, living and working together as they did; now there was the uncertainty of Logan's future – the possibility, indeed probability, of parting.

Maybe I shouldna have allowed them so much freedom . . .? Yet they had always been together since they were in the cradle. Beth was such a willing, cheerful lassie, and Logan had too much responsibility for one so young. He needed Beth's companionship. The sight of Beth's bright eyes and flushed cheeks, the tenderness in Logan's gaze as his eyes followed her graceful movements, only increased Sarah's uneasiness. She was as responsible for Beth as she was for Logan and she did not want either of them to be hurt.

'Sadie's gone to bed,' she said. 'Ye seemed tae be longer than usual at the byre tonight. Was everything all right, Logan?'

'Aye, the cows are settled and the horses are fed and watered,' Logan answered. 'Peggotty's a bit restless. I think she'll farrow in a day or two.' This was true but Logan saw his mother relax a little as he had hoped she would.

'Aah, so that's what took so long?' The strain eased and she smiled. 'Peggotty's getting old – like me.'

'Och, Mother, ye'll never grow old!' Logan's grey-green eyes sparked with humour. 'Peggotty's nine though and that's certainly old for a pig,' he added seriously. A small frown creased his brow. 'She's too old to have any more litters, but I hate the thought o' killing her. I could never eat any bacon if it came frae dear old Peggotty – not even if I was starving.'

'Oh, Logan! Dinna even think about it!' Beth gasped, turning from the swey.

'I feel the same myself about Peggotty,' Sarah agreed slowly. 'I never thought I'd be sentimental about a pig! But I dinna think any of us would want tae send her tae the butcher's yard. She can stay in her old pen in the orchard after she's reared this last litter. She's earned a rest. We've never had a sow rear as many piglets – at least not in my lifetime.' Logan nodded, glad to know that Peggotty would be cared for when he had to leave Fairlyden, glad too that he had distracted his mother's attention from Beth and himself. Yet he found his own eyes continually drawn to Beth's slender figure as she poured cups of tea for them all.

Logan returned to Fairlyden with a khaki armband embroidered with a gold crown – proof that he was willing to fight for his country when called.

'The recruiting officer seemed tae understand a wee bit about farm life,' he announced with a grin of relief. 'He said, "I'm instructing you to get back to your farm and plant some bloody seeds. If we dinna get more food soon, the bloody Huns will starve us into surrending." So here I am!'

'But for how long?' Sarah asked, ignoring the language. Logan's expression sobered.

'Until the spring sowing is finished. Maybe even until the harvest is in,' he added with a glance at Beth's anxious face. 'I suppose it depends what they need most. The officer said the Germans are just as short o' food as we are, for all their farmers were growing such a lot more on every acre o' land.'

237

'How can they do that?' Sarah asked with a faint note of disbelief.

'Grandfather said they used chemicals to make better yields even before the war started.'

Even Sadie seemed happy that Logan had been granted a temporary reprieve, but they all knew it was because she did not want any extra work to do in his absence. Most of her attention was taken up with the call for less extravagance in women's dress. New fashions were being tried.

The following week Sarah received a letter from Ellen at last. Her happiness at Logan's reprieve evaporated and her heart plummeted as her eyes read the words.

'. . . and Brad was injured.' The words were stark. They seemed to leap from the page. It was some time before Sarah could collect herself enough to read the rest of the letter.

'Is – is something wrong?' Beth asked diffidently, noticing her white face. They were alone together in the kitchen. Silently Beth boiled the kettle and made some strong tea. It was the most comforting remedy she knew. Sadie was waiting for her to clean out one of the hen houses but she could not leave Mistress Fairly in a state of shock. Sarah looked up blankly when she set the tea in front her.

'Is – is't bad news?' Beth whispered gently. She longed to put her arms around the white-faced woman who had been a mother to her in all but name. 'Is it Billy?'

'Billy?' Sarah looked at Beth with empty eyes.

'Drink this tea,' Beth prompted softly. 'Ye've had a shock, I think.'

'Brad's been injured.' Sarah said flatly.

'Oh, no!' Beth gasped aloud. 'Poor, poor Ellen!' Her young face crumpled. She had always liked Ellen Fairly. Surely she deserved happiness? Sarah glanced at her as she sipped at the tea. 'Thank you, Beth. I'll be all right in a minute. It's the shock . . .' Her voice wavered into silence. After a few more sips of the hot sweet brew, however, her eyes moved back to Ellen's letter and the short brave sentences. 'Oh God, she has such courage!' Sarah almost sobbed, 'and You've granted her so little happiness so far . . .' Sarah looked up at Beth. 'She is staying with him in France.'

Sarah drove to the Mains that afternoon to break the news to

238

her father and Beatrice and Alex. Sandy Logan was deeply upset.

'If Brad dies the lassie will have missed her chance o' happiness because o' me,' he grieved and Sarah was dismayed at the sight of his drawn face. 'I've lived longer than ma time. If only Ellen had gone tae America when Brad wanted her tae go. She might have had bairns by now . . .'

'Dinna distress yourself, Father,' Sarah pleaded helplessly. 'You know Ellen would have drowned if she had gone on the *Titanic* for she would never have left the ship while there were women and wee bairnies still on board . . .'

But Sandy just shook his white head in silence.

'I'll make him a cup of tea in a wee while, Sarah,' Beatrice said gently. 'And I'll see he gets to bed early . . .'

'He's taken it worse than I expected,' Sarah said wearily as she followed Beatrice into the big Mains kitchen.

'Well, he is an old man. He'll be eighty this year. I suppose Ellen will let ye know if Brad is out o' danger?'

'Aye,' Sarah sighed heavily. 'There's nothing I can do except pray . . . If only they weren't so far away!'

Crispin arrived at Fairlyden three days later, after receiving Sarah's letter.

'I can only stay two days, I'm afraid, but I wanted to see you, Sarah. Have you any more news?'

'Thank you for coming, Crispin,' Sarah's voice was husky. 'I didn't expect you to come, but I'm glad now you're here.'

'There are so many fine young men sacrificing their lives . . .' Crispin's voice was low, almost bitter. 'I know Ellen has great character and courage. I'm sure she will help Brad if anyone can.'

'If God is willing . . .' Sarah shivered. 'Ellen says there are so many who have lost loved ones.' Sarah straightened her shoulders. 'But I must not lose hope. Logan says he will sleep in the kitchen boxbed so that you may have his room.'

Crispin nodded, accepting the change of subject. 'You know I wanted to see him too, of course? I don't think it can be much longer now before they send for him – for training at least. I've heard rumours that there's to be a big offensive . . . though it would be better if you did not repeat that,' he added hastily.

'Robert's office . . .?'

'Yes,' Crispin's reply was terse. His nephew liked to pass on such news. It made him feel important. Yet he had never been in danger or seen fighting of any kind.

Twenty-Eight

Weeks passed before Ellen could send any really positive news of Brad. His injuries had been extremely severe and infection was Ellen's greatest worry. Sarah was able to report that he was holding his own by the time Crispin returned to Fairlyden again at the beginning of May and for this she was doubly thankful when she saw the strain in his face and the dark circles beneath his eyes. His thick hair was completely grey now and she remembered that he had had his sixtieth birthday more than a year ago.

'You look dreadfully tired, Crispin,' she remarked with sympathy.

'Yes, I am, but Ted Forbes returned to the mill on Monday. He is very lame and he's self-conscious about the hook they have given him for a hand, but he has a fine understanding of what is needed. He will be a tremendous help to me. There is so much work to do and not enough people to do it all. The demand for uniforms for the soldiers is increasing every day.' Sarah's face paled.

'Yes. I – I read the news. All men between eighteen and forty-one are to be called to serve our country, I see.' Her voice was low. Crispin nodded. They were both silent, thinking of Logan.

'How is he?'

'Busy.' Sarah grimaced. 'I think he lives from day to day. He tries to keep all the work up to date. We have ten acres of extra oats sown, as well as four acres of potatoes. I canna imagine how we shall harvest them if he is not here.'

'Beth will miss him.'

'Yes. Oh, Crispin, it's so hard to know what to do! I'd hate to see Beth getting hurt; happiness seems so elusive these days . . .'

'There is nothing we can do to keep Logan at home, my dear. He would not want us to interfere, even if we could . . .'

'I didna mean that. I meant Logan and Beth . . . they are so young, and the strain of knowing they must part must be

241

terrible. I feel responsible for Beth. She has no mother of her own. Yet I canna keep them apart. They work together, eat together, live in the same house . . . They have always been together . . .'

'They've been like brother and sister.'

'Yes, but things have changed. I-I'm sure they have. Remember Mrs Bunnerby thought they were in love. I think she was concerned for them. S-supposing they . . . What if Beth were to have a child . . .?' Sarah looked up at Crispin, her dark eyes wide and troubled. He frowned.

'Do you think there is such a possibility.'

'I don't know. I only know that Beth is a sweet, kindly lassie and she would do anything for Logan . . . I would not like her to be hurt – yet what am I to do?'

'Certainly *we* could never condemn them,' Crispin said slowly, 'if they were to succumb to temptation – yet they are so young . . .'

'Logan is eighteen, remember. He works like a man; he's had all the responsibilities of a man twice his age this past year – and Beth helps him with everything . . . She loves Fairlyden as much as he does . . .'

'Are you saying . . .' Crispin frowned. 'Are you thinking Logan should marry Beth now, Sarah? She is only seventeen!'

'She'll be eighteen soon.' Sarah sighed heavily. 'But it is not just their age! Life is so uncertain!' There was a note of anger and bitterness in her voice.

'I know, my dear, I know,' Crispin soothed. 'But even without the war life has never been smooth. I feel it must be their own decision.'

'I suppose you're right.' Sarah sighed softly. 'But Beth is like a daughter to me and . . . Sometimes I think I willed Ellen not to go with Brad when he went to America . . . She had to wait so long for her happiness, and it was almost snatched away; indeed even now it is uncertain.'

'I know, my dear,' Crispin's voice was gentle. He moved to her and put his hands on her shoulders, looking down into her face. His earnest gaze reminded her of Logan. 'You cannot blame yourself and I can assure you that even the briefest happiness is better than none at all.' His voice was low and intense and Sarah wondered if he was referring to that one night they had spent together, and to the friendship that had blossomed between them over the years. 'I am more grateful to you than you will ever know,' he said almost under his breath, confirming her thoughts. 'I am sure Ellen will always remember the joy she has had with Brad – and we must think positively; even if Brad is physically crippled, he and Ellen share so much more. Their minds have always been in tune . . .'

'Oh, Crispin, you're a great comfort to me. You have always been here when I needed you most.'

'I hope I shall always be here if you need me, Sarah.'

It was a Sunday afternoon. The spring sun was shining and the hawthorn hedges were white with dainty blossoms, filling the air with their sweet perfume.

'Mr Bradshaw will keep Mother company today,' Logan whispered in Beth's ear as she carried the dishes to the scullery. She blushed shyly and glanced back to the table, but no one was taking any notice of Logan helping to carry the rest of the dishes for her. 'I must see the calves in the top meadow. Come with me, Beth? We have a couple of hours before milking time . . .' His grey eyes were pleading. Beth had sensed the increased tension in him ever since they had read the news of the government's new conscription policy. Even men who had been exempted on grounds of ill health were to be re-examined. Beth shuddered. In her heart she knew Logan's time at Fairlyden was running out.

'I'll meet ye by the burn as soon as we've washed the dishes . . .'

'Make sure that Sadie does her share, then!' Logan warned softly. 'Or it will be milking time before ye're finished!'

Sadie seemed to be deliberately slow with the washing up and Beth waited impatiently to dry each plate and bowl, putting them away methodically. Sadie always preferred to wash the dishes rather than dry them.

'I ken why ye're in a hurry!' Sadie sneered. 'Running after Logan again! Ye're nothing but a cheap strumpet, Beth Jamieson! Mother thinks ye're still an innocent bairn, but I ken better!' Beth's fair skin coloured hotly and then paled. She had long since learned that it was better to keep silent when Sadie started her vicious criticism, but today she had no other option. She had no defence. Sadie ranted on, her insults increasing when she found Beth would not argue. 'Strumpet's too polite a word for what ye are!' Sadie fumed. 'Dinna think ye can stay here if Logan gets ye a bairn! I ken what ye're after! But maids dinna marry the master at Fairlyden! Remember that! All Ellen thinks about is Brad and her nursing. She'll never come back here, any more than Billy will. He never wanted Fairlyden. It will be mine – mine dae ye hear, if *dear* Logan gets himself killed!'

Beth gasped in horror. 'How can ye say such a thing, Sadie! It – it's almost as though ye're wishing Logan dead!'

'And what if I am? He should never have been born anyway. Mother was never meant tae have any more bairns after Katie and me. She might have died because o' him!'

'B-but she didna, a-and it wasna Logan's fault he was born. He's your ain brother!' Beth was dismayed by these new depths to Sadie's resentment and jealousy.

'Is he?' Sadie sneered and gave Beth a strange, fathomless stare from her pale cold eyes. Beth shivered, but Sadie went on viciously, her voice low and intense. 'I'm warning ye, there'll be no place here for ye if he gets ye a bairn. I saw the way ye made up tae Billy as weel before he went awa . . .' Again Beth gasped but Sadie went on relentlessly. 'But ye needna think he wad help ye even if he doesna get killed by the Germans – and I dinna expect he will. He aye looked after himself!' she finished bitterly.

Beth stared at her. Sadie sounded like the old gypsy who told fortunes at the Fair – but Sadie didn't look like any gypsy Beth had ever seen and these were the lives of her own brothers she was forecasting. It sounded almost as though Sadie was wishing Logan and Billy dead. Yet she hated the work and the animals so why should she want Fairlyden all to herself? Beth felt sick as she dried the last of the dishes in silence.

It was a relief to escape from Sadie and get out into the cool fresh air. Beth ran down to the burn to meet Logan as though all the witches in all the stories she had ever read were after her. Logan was waiting, his grey eyes sparkling, his smile wide and happy and Beth's heart did a little somersault with love for him. She would not allow Sadie's vicious words to spoil this precious afternoon together, she vowed silently, and neither would she burden Logan with tales of his sister's spite.

Gradually the magic of the spring afternoon and Logan's company helped Beth to push the scene with Sadie to the back of her mind as she and Logan strolled together hand in hand beside the burn, following its winding course up to the northern boundary where Fairlyden's land rose in a gentle slope to the small upland farm of Westhill.

'Shall we sit by the burn for a wee while before we go back?' Logan chose a cushion of soft springy moss for Beth as though she were a queen. He pulled a long stem and began to chew, staring dreamily at the distant hills for a little while. Beth was content just to be with him. Each day was a gift to be cherished. Today she refused to consider Sadie's sordid remarks, or think about the war and partings. Beth knew she would remember the beauty of the precious moments in Logan's arms, even when she was old and grey – the sweetness of Logan's early kisses, the wonder of discovering a greater, deeper love that made every bone in her body melt with desire . . . She turned to look at Logan and found his eyes already fixed on her, tender and with such an awful, aching yearning in their grey-green depths.

'Oh, Logie!' she groaned softly and turned into his arms with an instinct as old as the hills around them, finding comfort in his arms, giving comfort in the only way she knew – in sweet and complete surrender.

Some time later Logan raised himself on one elbow and gazed down into Beth's blue eyes. He traced the line of her pointed chin with a gentle finger.

'I love ye, Beth.' His voice was husky. She smiled dreamily up at him, loving him with her eyes, her smile, the touch of a finger.

'I don't want tae wait until the war is over tae marry ye, Beth. I think we should be married now.'

'Married!' Beth stared at him and her blue eyes darkened. The scene with Sadie flooded back into her mind. 'H-has S-Sadie been talking tae ye?'

'Sadie? No . . .' Logan's tone was puzzled. 'Why, Beth?' But Beth was silent, frowning. 'What has Sadie been saying tae ye?' Logan demanded.

'N-nothing really . . . but oh, Logan, I think she kens about . . . about us . . .' Beth's face flushed. It was one thing to give herself to Logan in love, it was another thing to discuss such things.

'Sadie couldna possibly ken . . . everything!' Logan protested.

'M-maybe she's j-just guessing but . . .'

'And maybe she's just jealous!' Logan interrupted angrily. 'No man would want tae love her with her vicious tongue and her narrow mind. She only wants cardboard men with golden hair and blue eyes like she reads about . . .'

'Hush, Logie, please! She's your ain sister . . .'

'Well, she doesna act like my ain sister! Never has, if ye ask me. Sadie has always resented me. Now I expect she's trying tae turn ye against me tae . . .'

'No, no! Nothing could ever dae that. I love ye, Logan!'

'Let's get married then, Beth . . .' Logan said more gently, staring moodily at Beth's troubled face. She shivered. If only Sadie had not been so spiteful, not insinuated she was trying to make Logan marry her to make sure of a place at Fairlyden . . . She shook her head. 'We canna marry, not yet . . .'

'Why not . . . What if our loving makes a babe?' Beth shivered – not at the thought of having Logan's child – but because he was echoing Sadie's own words.

'I ken we havena made one yet, and your mama would think we're too young . . . I wadna like tae hurt her, Logan. Neither would you . . .'

'I dinna care what Sadie says, and maybe Mother would understand . . . I want tae marry ye, Beth!' Suddenly it seemed the most important thing in the world to marry Beth before he had to go away to war.

'Ye ken I'll wait for ye,' Beth said softly. 'I'll never love anybody else . . .'

'And I'll never love anybody but you, Beth . . . But it's not just that,' he said urgently.

'What is it then . . .?'

'What if I was killed? What if I never come back?'

'Logie!' Beth's blue eyes were wide with horror. 'Dinna say such a thing! Dinna think such a thing! I-I couldna bear it! I-I think I'd die tae . . .' she whispered hoarsely and flung herself into his arms, clinging to him as though she could protect him from Sadie's ill wishes, and from the Germans and their guns and shells.

Logan returned her embrace but he could not rid himself of a feeling of urgency; it communicated itself to Beth and they clung together until passion flared anew. They were powerless to resist, even if they had wanted to. Afterwards they lay exhausted, staring up at the pale clear blue of the spring sky. Somewhere a blackbird sang to his mate. Beth sighed softly.

'I love ye, Logan.' Logan turned on his side and smiled at her, gently stroking the honey-gold hair away from her temple.

Presently they turned into each other's arms, holding each other, gently this time, with infinite tenderness.

The following day Logan drove Crispin to the station to catch the train back to Yorkshire. They rode in silence, each deep in their own thoughts until they reached the bridge and skirted the high wall round the Manse grounds. Suddenly Crispin spoke, surprising Logan.

'It seems every able-bodied man under forty will be in the army soon, Logan . . .'

'Aye. I expect I shall get word any day now . . .'

'May God protect you.' Logan was taken aback by the emotion in Crispin Bradshaw's deep voice.

'I pray He will, Sir. I've a lot tae live for.'

'Indeed you have, Logan,' Crispin said with feeling. 'I hope you will always have consideration for your fellow men and women, especially your mother . . . but don't miss the chance of happiness when it comes your way . . .' Logan looked at his companion in surprise.

'Isn't that somewhat contradictory advice, Sir?' he said slowly.

'Contradictory . . .?'

'Aye . . . you see, Sir,' Logan frowned. 'Maybe I shouldna be telling ye this but . . .'

'Go on. If you wish to speak in confidence I can keep my own counsel, Logan – now, and at any time in the future – indeed I would be honoured to think you would come to me, if ever I could help you . . .'

'I dinna think anybody can help right now, Sir,' Logan grimaced wryly, 'but thank ye anyway.'

'What was so contradictory then . . .? I am curious now.' Crispin smiled the winning, almost boyish smile which seemed strangely familiar to Logan, though he could not think why it should be so. Suddenly he felt very much at ease with Crispin Bradshaw.

'I want Beth tae marry me – that's where my happiness lies . . . But,' Logan sighed and smiled wryly, 'ye also say I should consider Mother. In truth I dinna want tae upset her, neither does Beth, but we ken she'll think we're too young tae marry, especially when everything seems so uncertain.'

'I do not think your marriage would upset your mother, Logan. She is very fond of Beth.'

247

'Aye, she never thinks o' Beth as just another maid – that's Sadie's idea! She'd make Beth a slave if she could! Beth thinks we should wait.'

'But she loves you – as you love her?'

'Aye!' Logan said simply.

'Then follow your heart, lad. Your mother would never stand in the way of your happiness. Or Beth's,' he added as the trap drew to a halt. 'The train is in! I must hurry. Goodbye and good luck, my s . . . Logan.'

There was no time to follow Crispin Bradshaw's advice. Sarah was looking out for him when he returned to Fairlyden.

'I'll unyoke the trap, laddie. We heard ye returning. Peggotty's farrowing. Beth's with her but she's having trouble. The first four piglets are dead . . .'

'Poor old Peggotty. She's too old for this,' Logan muttered with feeling. 'I'll go right away.'

It was some time before Beth and Logan returned to the house carrying two very weak piglets.

'She has four live ones,' Logan announced quietly. 'We'll wrap these two in a bit o' blanket and keep them beside the fire, Mother, until we see how Peggotty fares. She's sick . . .' In his concern for Peggotty he did not notice how pale and strained Sarah's face was but Beth saw.

'Are ye all right, Mistress Fairly?'

'Aye, lassie, I'm fine.' Sarah summoned a smile but it was an effort. She took a deep breath but before she could speak Sadie came through from the scullery.

'There was a wire for ye, while ye were at the station. Ye're tae report tae Annan by four o' clock today . . .'

'Sadie!' Sarah protested.

'Well, he's got tae ken, hasn't he!' Sadie retorted but there was no doubting the gleam of satisfaction in her narrowed eyes. She's glad I'm going, Logan thought, his face paling. Even though the call had been expected it was still a shock. Beth's hands shook uncontrollably as she handed him the second piglet to set beside the fire. He looked up at her and saw his own misery reflected in her blue eyes.

Sarah helped Logan pack the few private possessions he would be allowed to take; he had already been issued with a uniform. It

248

almost broke her heart to see his youthful face beneath the tam o' shanter; his ears seemed to protrude more than they ever did beneath his own cloth cap, but it was the earnest expression in his grey eyes as he looked at her which made her want to weep.

'Take care o' yourself, Mother,' he murmured huskily before he gave her a brief, hard hug that reminded her he was a man now and a strong one at that.

'God be with you, son . . .' she whispered hoarsely, struggling valiantly to hold back her tears.

Sarah had already suggested that Beth should drive him to Muircumwell station.

'He should walk! It's what he'll be doing soon anyway. She'll only dawdle and be late for the milking.'

'Thanks for all your good wishes, Sadie,' Logan said with a bitterness which was alien to him. 'Come on, Beth.'

They were driving along the track to Muircumwell before Logan broke the silence.

'I dinna want ye tae drive me tae the station, Beth. I couldna bear tae say goodbye tae ye there. Stop the trap under the last o' the beech trees before we reach the bridge.' Beth nodded but her throat was too full of tears to speak. Her head ached and her eyes burned with the effort of holding them back but she knew she had to be brave for Logan's sake.

Under the beech tree beside the track, he jumped to the ground and tethered the pony, then he turned and lifted Beth to the ground, but he did not release her.

'I dinna want tae make ye miss the train . . .' she whispered hoarsely. Logan shook his head and removed the new tam o' shanter, then his jacket. Silently he drew Beth into his arms again. They did not speak much; he covered her face with kisses, but Beth could not restrain some of her tears from squeezing under her closed eyelids. Then, all too soon, Logan was buttoning up his jacket again and she was clinging to him, kissing him urgently. At last he held her gently away from him and with one last, lingering kiss he bid her goodbye. Beth waited until he was out of sight; she saw him turn at the bend in the track and raise his arm in a last salute, then she threw herself down on the grass where they had lain together and sobbed as though her heart would break.

Twenty-Nine

That evening of Logan's departure Beth could not bear to stay in the house, especially not in Sadie's gloating presence. As soon as the milking was finished she made her way back to the sty where Peggotty still lay prone. The old sow tried to lift her head, but the effort was too much. She blinked her sandy-coloured lashes and gave two soft little grunts. Beth crouched beside her and scratched her side gently, just the way Peggotty had always enjoyed.

'Ye ken he's gone, don't ye, old girl?' Beth murmured wistfully. The four remaining piglets tugged relentlessly first at one teat and then another but they had little success. 'Poor Peggotty, ye canna even feed your wee ones, can ye . . .?' The two weaker pigs had not survived either. It was late before Beth could bring herself to leave the sty. She was half afraid Peggotty might be dead by morning.

She slept only fitfully that night and as soon as dawn broke she rose and went back to the sty. Peggotty had scarcely moved. Her long ungainly bulk was stretched almost across the inner part of the sty. The four piglets were ravenous. Peggotty gave a weary grunt to acknowledge Beth's presence then closed her eyes once more. Presently Sarah joined them.

'I'm afraid this is the end o' the road for Peggotty,' she said gently. Beth nodded but she could not speak for the knot of tears in her throat. 'I'm afraid we shall have to take the piglets away or they'll starve. We'll ask Thomas to try fostering them onto Little Peg. She only has seven of her own this time and she's a grand mother . . .' Again Beth nodded. Little Peg was a grand-daughter of Peggotty's and she was proving an excellent young sow, but right now this was little consolation to Beth. After breakfast Thomas removed the four piglets, which squirmed and squealed vociferously. At any other time Peggotty would have bounded to her feet and charged in pursuit. Today she opened her eyes and looked at Beth as though she understood her end

251

was near. Beth scratched her comfortingly and Peggotty managed one last soft grunt in response.

That night Beth wrote to Logan. She told him of Peggotty's death, but she did not tell him how much she had wept for him, and later for the ugly old sow who had meant so much, for so long, to both of them. She tried hard to banish the feeling that Peggotty's death, so soon after Logan's departure, was an ill omen.

'We have tae move the clocks forward an hour, on the twenty-first of May,' Sadie announced sullenly as the evenings grew lighter. 'The hens will never gang tae roost!'

'The government hope it will save hundreds of tons of coal,' Sarah said patiently. 'They think it will increase the hours of daylight – though I canna see how that can be. It just makes it light at a different end of the day.'

Sadie grumbled even more than she had in previous years and Beth volunteered to take over the task of gathering the hens in to roost. She did not mind as she wandered from one small hut to the other, shooing in the last of the stragglers as the evening shadows settled over the distant hills, but she missed Logan's company dreadfully. He was constantly in her thoughts, but especially in the evenings.

The dry weather of May gave way to a cold wet June which did nothing to lift the spirits of anyone at Fairlyden. When the *Hampshire* was sunk off the coast of Orkney, with Lord Kitchener aboard, the feeling of gloom in the rest of the country intensified also. Even the gentry were complaining about the scarcity of food, the high prices, the lack of servants.

Sarah and Beth waited anxiously for letters.

'Logan is certainly a better correspondent than Billy,' Sarah said ruefully when she saw Beth opening yet another letter from Logan.

'But Logan is still at the training camp. Maybe it's more difficult tae send letters frae France?' Beth dreaded the day when Logan would be moved across the Channel.

'Billy doesna say much even when he does write,' Sarah frowned anxiously. 'Sometimes I think this war has knocked all the spirit out of him. He has never managed to see Ellen again. He mentioned something about operating a big machine gun in his last letter . . .' She shuddered. 'It's impossible to imagine what it must be like out there.'

At Fairlyden it was a thankless task hoeing the turnips; the weeds seemed to sprout again as soon as they were knocked out since there was no sun to wither the roots. Sadie grumbled continuously until even Sarah lost patience with her.

'We all have to work in the fields whether we like it or not! Think yourself lucky ye're not in Belgium!' Beth and Anna MacFarlane worked on doggedly. Anna's son Jamie, now a sturdy six-year-old, tagged along trying to help his mother whenever he was not at school. Thomas struggled valiantly with the machine for hoeing between the rows of potatoes.

'I dinna ken how we shall get the hay in,' he said repeatedly to Anna each evening, shaking his greying head in near despair. 'I never worked yon mowing machine afore, ye ken . . . And as for the harvest and yon binder!'

'Ye'll manage somehow,' Anna encouraged. 'I'll try tae sharpen the knives for ye if ye'll show me how tae dae it.'

'I'll sharpen some tae, Thomas,' Beth offered. 'And maybe I could learn tae scythe for I see the rain has flattened some o' the crops already. Logan and Billy said the knives o' the machines just clog up if the crops are tangled and laid.' She had taken to visiting Anna in her little cottage since Logan went away. There were times when she felt the need to escape from Sadie's constant carping and grumbling. Anna and Jamie welcomed her company, especially when they could persuade her to sing for them. Thomas's hearing had deterio-rated further and he paid little attention to what he called women's chatter as they knitted socks and gloves for the soldiers.

As the year went on there were reports of more ships lost and warnings of increasing food shortages. The continuing wet weather did not help and it became clear that, unless there was a swift and dramatic improvement, the hay and harvest would not be good, especially with so few men left on the farms to help snatch in the crops.

'Mother says it really worries Mr Jardine because he canna get enough groceries and meat, especially sugar and tea, tae sell to his customers,' Anna remarked one evening when she appeared for a knitting session at Fairlyden at the end of a particularly dismal day.

253

'I expect he's feart he's missing a chance tae make money out o' the war!' Sadie commented acidly.

'Och, I ken he's mean, and he's a bit strange at times,' Anna said, 'but I dinna think it's just the money. He doesna like tae let his customers down and Mother says he keeps getting bad pains in his stomach when he doesna eat regular meals. She's worried about him – and about her own work and Lizzie's. I dinna ken what would happen if Mr Jardine decided tae give up.'

'I didn't think of that aspect . . .' Sarah mused, peering over the spectacles she had recently begun to wear when knitting or sewing.

It was almost the end of June when a letter from Logan made Beth's heart quicken in alarm.

'We are all preparing to move out soon. There seems to be something special afoot judging by the excitement. No one in our camp really knows what to expect but we have been warned that we must be ready to move at short notice. There is certainly an air of tension and tempers are beginning to fray. Some of the men think we shall be sent to France for a massive attack on the German lines.

'No one really knows though, my dearest Beth, but I am taking this opportunity to write to you as I do not know when I shall be able to write again, or whether there will be anywhere to post my letters. I miss you, Beth. All the things I said to you in those last wonderful months, I repeat a thousand times. I wish I could write poetry and put into words all the things that are in my heart. Instead I must borrow the words of Robert Burns, our own great poet and lover. When you play the piano be sure to play, "My love is like a red, red rose". And as you play the music, think of me, Beth, and know my heart is singing the words to you wherever I may be . . .

> 'Till a' the seas gang dry, my dear,
> And rocks melt wi' the sun:
> And I will luve thee still, my dear,
> While the sands o' life shall run.'

'Please try not to worry, Beth. I pray you will keep on writing, even if you do not hear from me for a while. I live for your letters and all the news of home.'

Beth could scarcely read the rest of the letter; her eyes were blurred with tears.

'Please God, keep him safe,' she prayed fervently.

There was only one piece of news she had not told Logan. As each day passed she was becoming more and more certain that she was carrying his child. Her monthly cycle had never been reliable so she had not paid much attention until she wakened with a dreadful sickly feeling several mornings in succession. She had begun to rise earlier each morning so that she could sip a cup of buttermilk in the scullery, willing it to ease the sickly feelings before Sadie or Mistress Fairly came down. It was a relief to sit down on her milking stool and rest her head against the cow while her nimble fingers milked automatically. Usually the feeling had passed by breakfast time but each morning it returned again.

As the weeks passed there were other signs to add to her conviction. Beth knew she ought to feel shame; she was young and unmarried; she was expecting a bairn without a father to provide for it. But I love Logan with all my heart, she protested silently, and I shall love our babe.

Even so she tried not to think about the future. She was loathe to worry Logan: he was not free to do as he pleased anymore; he could not come to her; he had discomforts of his own to contend with, and dangers to face . . . It was when Beth thought of the dangers that her heart quailed. Mistress Fairly had always been kind to her, but would she forgive her if she brought shame to Fairlyden? Or would she consider her cheap and unworthy as Sadie did? Mistress Fairly was getting older, and she had so many worries with Billy and Ellen, and now Logan away – and old Mr Logan growing more frail every day. Beth shuddered and prayed that the war would soon be over so that Logan could come home again. Sadie would show her no compassion, or charity.

'Aah, Logie, I should have listened tae ye,' she muttered into her pillow when her fears threatened to overwhelm her. 'I shouldna have listened tae Sadie's spite, but I ken she would hate me even more if I was your wife . . .'

Gradually news filtered through the newspapers of a massive assault by the British and French troops on the Western Front on the River Somme in Picardy.

'Dae ye think that's what Logan meant, Mistress Fairly?' Beth asked, white-faced. 'He said they were all preparing tae move out and there was great excitement, and I havena had a letter . . .'

'I don't know, Beth,' Sarah smiled wanly. There had been no letters from either Logan or Billy. 'We can only pray they are safe.'

As the days passed more news filled the papers – bad news of wounded men, men slaughtered like herds of cattle in their thousands and acres of mud. Beth could not sleep or eat. Each day the news seemed worse than ever. It was true that many German soldiers had been killed too and hundreds had been taken prisoner, but the promised victory had not been achieved.

The dismal weather made matters worse. At Fairlyden, and on farms throughout the country, the hay crop had been cut and was now lying in the fields and meadows, too wet to gather into the barns or even to build into haycocks. Beth worked automatically, turning the swaths with Anna and Thomas, and Sarah and Sadie helped too when they could be spared from the dairy and hens, but her heart felt leaden in her breast. She no longer cared about the babe. If Logan was amongst the thousands who had been killed then nothing mattered.

'You must eat, Beth,' Sarah urged with growing concern. 'No one has had any news. I asked if there were any letters at the post office when I was at Jardine's Store this morning. Mary Braid said they'd had some telegrams, but the only letters they'd had were local ones. They canna be getting through . . .'

'Telegrams?' Beth repeated. 'Would ye have had a telegram if – if . . .'

'If there was bad news we should have had a telegram,' Sarah said quietly. She did not add that there were rumours of hundreds, maybe thousands, of dead and wounded men still waiting for help on the battlefield. 'All we can do is pray. But you need strength even for that, so eat up your dinner . . .'

'Och, let her starve if she wants tae!' Sadie snapped impatiently. Sarah frowned. Recently she had wondered if Beth was pining for Logan or if something more serious ailed her as well.

'One day you will love somebody, Sadie, then you will understand how Beth feels . . .' Beth looked up, startled out of her lethargy and her cheeks coloured faintly. Sarah looked at her kindly.

'Surely you knew we had all guessed, Beth?'

'G-guessed?' Beth's colour fled, leaving her whiter than before.

'Why, we guessed you and Logan are in love. I canna think of any other reason for those long letters.' Sarah was striving to lighten Beth's spirits despite her own anxiety.

'O-oh . . .' Beth gulped, then burst into tears of relief. For an awful moment she thought Mistress Fairly had guessed her secret.

'Why, lassie! I didn't mean to upset you!' Sarah gasped, rising from the table to put a comforting arm round Beth's trembling shoulders. Sadie glared sullenly at her mother embracing Beth Jamieson.

'For goodness' sake! Why must ye make such a fuss, Mother! She's only a maid. It's . . .'

'Beth has never been "only a maid" to me, Sadie,' Sarah said quietly, but there was a hint of steel in her voice. Sadie's eyes narrowed.

'She is a maid – and she's . . .'

'She is in my care – at the request of her own mother! My promise to Sally would have been enough, but Beth is also the girl your brother happens to love – the girl your brother will probably marry.' Beth gasped and rubbed her tear-stained face as she stared up at Sarah, but she went on speaking to Sadie. 'Now will you please put an end to this childish resentment and let us all live in peace – if this dreadful war will allow such a thing as peace.'

'Logan disna ken his own mind! She,' Sadie glared contemptuously at Beth, 'she never gave him a chance tae look at other lassies, but I'll bet he's looking at them now!'

'Sadie!' Sarah's voice was cold with anger. 'Logan has gone to fight for the freedom of our country! Don't let me . . .' But Sadie did not wait to hear any more. She scraped her chair back furiously and left the kitchen. Sarah sighed.

'Eat up your dinner, Beth, and try not to take any notice. I'm sure Sadie must be as worried about her brothers and Ellen as the rest of us.'

The following morning Jim Braid pedalled slowly up the track, his sack still half-full of letters.

'Three for Fairlyden today,' he announced sombrely. Sarah eyed her letters anxiously but Jim Braid seemed unusually weary today. 'You seem to have a lot more mail to deliver yet, Jim. Would you like a drink of buttermilk – or a cup of tea maybe – to help you on your way?'

'I canna stop, Mistress Fairly, but thank ye. I'm taking the short cut over Fairlyden tae Strathtod, if ye dinna mind? The postie there isna weel and I'm tae deliver the southern half o' the parish for him. There's nae other men tae spare. The puir man has lost two o' his sons and his younger brother in this latest battle.'

'Oh no!' Sarah's face paled and she glanced involuntarily at her own letters.

'Aye,' Jim Braid sighed. 'I canna tell ye the number o' letters and telegrams I've had tae deliver lately – and most o' them wi' bad news o' one kind or another.' Jim Braid was usually a bright, cheerful little man but being the bearer of sad tidings was evidently getting him down. Again Sarah glanced anxiously at her own letters but Jim was talking still as he turned his red-painted post bike. 'Some folks reckoned this last assault over the Somme was going tae finish the Germans once and for a' but noo. I hear we only gained a few hundred yards and they're still bringing back oor wounded men – at least that's what some folks say,' he added as jumped on his bike and pedalled across the yard to the Strathtod track.

Before Sarah could take her letters into the house, Anna MacFarlane came hurrying up the track.

'Did Mr Braid tell ye the news, Mistress Fairly? D'ye think we'll be working at the hay today?' Sarah glanced up at the overcast sky.

'I don't know, Anna. The hay will not dry much unless the wind gets up. There's no sign o' the sun coming out. And what news? You look a wee bit pale . . .?'

'Mr Braid just brought me a note frae Mother. Mr Jardine died during the night. Mother fetched Doctor Kerr but he was vomiting blood . . .'

'Oh dear!' Sarah was shocked. She was fifty-seven herself and Ray Jardine was only a few years older . . . 'I didn't think he was as ill as that, Anna – though I know he has been worrying about the shortages and things . . .'

'I'd like tae go down tae the Store and see Mother and Lizzie if ye think I'll not be needed tae rake up the hay? I expect they'll be worried about what's tae become o' them. Mr Jardine had no relations that we ken o'. I expect they'll miss him tae – for all he was such an auld miser at times. He was aye quite guid tae Lizzie . . .' Sarah nodded.

'I'm sure your mother will be pleased to have your support, Anna. You can always come back earlier if you think the hay will be drying. There's nothing we can do but snatch it in a few swaths at a time.'

'I ken. Thomas keeps worrying about it and wondering if there'll be enough tae feed the cows and the bullocks and horses all winter.'

Sarah chewed her lower lip. She had wondered the same thing herself. 'Tell your mother I'm sorry to hear about Mr Jardine and ask her to let me know if there is anything I can do, Anna.'

'I will, and thanks, Mistress Fairly. I often wonder what we Whiteleys would have done without ye.'

Sarah turned into the house, inspecting the letters as she went. 'One from Ellen,' she murmured . . . Her heart sank as she saw the postmarks on the other two.

Thirty

Beth hurried across the yard. She had seen Mr Braid cycling down to Strathtod.

Sarah glanced up as she came into the kitchen, her face pinched and tense.

'There's letters from Logan, lassie – but he must have written them before they sailed for France,' she added cautiously as she saw the blaze of hope in Beth's blue eyes.

'Thank you.' Beth's hand shook. Was it one of those letters left behind to be posted if a man did not return? Was that why it had an English postmark when Logan was in France? She opened it with trembling fingers.

' . . .and there are six of us in this section excluded, but we are under strict orders not to discuss movements of any of the regiments, so don't be surprised if I cannot post this letter for a while.' Beth read the words twice before she could take them in. Logan was not in France! He had not been sent!

'I am being dispatched to shore defences.' Beth glanced at the date. It had been written more than two weeks ago. 'All six of us will be sent back eventually to help with the harvest. The Government officials are said to be alarmed at the loss of so many British ships. It is important that our own harvest should be gathered in if the nation is not to starve – at least that is the story I have heard.

'As soon as I can return to Fairlyden I want you to marry me, Beth. Please, my dearest love? I have been so anxious about you. I sense something is troubling you, despite your cheerful letters. We know each other too well to hide what is in our hearts and minds.' Beth smiled dreamily for a moment, then she read on.

'My first thoughts were that Sadie must be making you miserable now that she can no longer use me as a butt for her spite, but I suspect it is more than that. Am I right? I have learned a great deal about life, and men and women in particular, since I came here.

'Mother expressed concern for your health in her last letter. I shall write to her as soon as I finish this. I shall tell her it is my most earnest wish that we should be married as soon as I return. Do not be afraid, my love. Mr Bradshaw seemed to think Mother would give us her blessing – even if she does think we are too young to be married, or that our lives are so uncertain at present. She knows how much we have always meant to each other.'

Beth looked up anxiously, but Sarah had only just opened Logan's letter and she returned eagerly to her own.

'In truth there are many here no older than myself who are married and have children of their own already. Most of them are deeply concerned for their loved ones despite the payment offered by the government in their absence. A few of them married hastily hoping to escape conscription, (single men being the first in line for the call to duty). You know, Beth, that such a possibility has never been my intention; indeed there is no longer any escape through marriage as there are not enough men to replace the thousands who have been killed or wounded. I am not afraid of my own call to duty, and I shall return to fight for the freedom of my country as soon as the harvest is safely gathered in. But I shall return with an easier mind if I know you are my wife, Beth. Already you toil so willingly for Fairlyden's future. I shall be happier when I know you are secure there as Mistress Logan Fairly.

'I believe Billy is concerned for you too in your present position – and this time I am not jealous of his interest in your well-being, my love. He wrote to me recently – a long letter for Billy. I was dismayed. On his last visit home Sadie, with her usual cruel candour, had informed him that she would sell Fairlyden if neither he nor I returned . . .' Beth shuddered. How could Sadie even contemplate such things! Her soft mouth tightened but she read on.

'Apparently my sister feels she is a slave at Fairlyden; she resents her position in life. Billy says he understands her desire to be free, but he has never understood her jealousy and spite. It troubles him. He says our father once warned him of a flaw in the characters of some of his own ancestors – sometimes it is an obsession, or an irrational desire – even unreasoning hatred or jealousy. Billy believes Sadie has inherited such a flaw. Certainly he believes she would not grieve if he, or I, were killed while fighting for our country . . .' Beth stiffened. Aunt Agnes's warning about Sadie Fairly echoed in her mind, but she pushed it aside with an impatient frown. Billy must be under a great deal of strain to write such warnings about his own sister; she had read of the effects of life in the filth of the trenches, the shells and gas, the squalor and suffering.

'I hope that Billy is wrong in his harsh assessment of our own sister's character,' Logan had written, 'but if such a flaw does exist in my family, dearest Beth, then you have a right to know of it now. Our marriage may inflame Sadie's jealousy, yet still I beg you to marry me, Beth. When this dreadful war is over I promise we shall live together in peace and harmony. I will even take you away from Fairlyden and Sadie's spite, if that should be your wish.

'Please write soon and tell me of your decision.'

There were a few more endearments which brought a delicate flush to Beth's cheeks and a sparkle of happiness to her blue eyes. She folded the letter neatly and put it in her apron pocket, knowing she would read it at least twice or thrice before she went to sleep that night. She looked up to find Sarah's dark eyes on her; Logan's mama was smiling – a sweet tender smile.

'You have read your letter, Beth? You know Logan is coming home . . .?'

'Yes.' Beth could not hide her happiness. It was shining in her eyes, in the brightness of her young face. 'Oh, Mistress Fairly, I'm sae very thankful he didna have tae go tae France.'

'So am I, Beth, so am I. At least he doesn't need to go yet, anyway. Will you marry him as he hopes, Beth?' Sarah looked down at her own letters. 'He tells me it is what he wants – more than anything in the world.' Beth blushed.

'I love him, Mistress Fairly,' she said simply, softly.

Sarah nodded. 'It will make me very happy to know you are Logan's wife, my dear – very happy indeed.'

'Oh, Mistress Fairly . . .' Beth breathed and tears of joy and relief filled her eyes.

'So!' Sarah said with satisfaction. 'We have many plans to make if we are to have a wedding so soon . . .'

'Oh no!' Beth gasped. 'I dinna want . . . I – I mean I just want tae be married quietly . . .'

Sarah looked at her shrewdly, at the delicate colour ebbing

263

and flowing in her thin cheeks, at the shadows beneath her expressive eyes.

'Well . . . we shall see, Beth. First I must tell you Ellen's news. She has had a brief visit from Billy. He has had a very stressful time operating machine guns; apparently he has aquitted himself very well.' Sarah could not keep the pride out of her voice.

'I'm sure he would!' Beth murmured warmly.

'Now he is to return to England for a period of training with some sort of new weapon. Ellen says he will be writing shortly but he hopes to spend a week with us when he arrives.'

'That's wonderful news!' Beth declared happily.

'But that is not all. Ellen has written to Alex . . . They have always corresponded regularly, especially since Brad was injured. They've always been very close, but I do hope Alex will not take offence . . .' Sarah frowned, then she went on. 'You knew Emma Braidwood had returned to work at Mains of Muir of course, Beth, but did you know Alex went to see her? To ask her to return as soon as he learned of her mother's death?'

'I didna ken that, but I'm glad Emma did come back tae the Mains. I aye liked her.'

'Mmm, she's a fine person. She and Alex would make a splendid couple – if only he would forget he is lame and ask Emma if she will marry him! Anyway Ellen has written to tell them of Billy's plans. She hopes they will arrange to be married during his leave.'

'Oh, that would be marvellous!'

'Indeed it would. I'm sure Emma would never have returned to the Mains if she had not cared for Alex. Let us hope he takes Ellen's advice. It would be a pity to waste any more of their precious young lives!'

Beth thought Mistress Fairly sounded mildly exasperated, for all she was so fond of her eldest son.

'Will Mistress O'Connor mind Alex having Emma for his wife?'

'No, I'm sure she will be pleased. She likes Emma. Maybe we should have a double celebration.'

'Oh no, Mistress Fairly. Please . . . I – I dinna deserve a grand wedding . . .' she added almost under her breath.

'You shall be married exactly as you wish, lassie – so long as you and Logan are both happy?'

264

'Yes, oh yes!' Beth agreed with a heartfelt sigh of relief.

Sarah looked out of the window at the drifting clouds. 'There will be no hay made today,' she sighed. 'I think I shall drive to the Mains later this morning. It is a fortnight since I visited my father.'

Beth nodded. 'I'm sure Mr Logan will be pleased tae see ye, especially now he canna get out much himself. But what about Ellen, Mistress Fairly? How is she?' she asked diffidently. Sarah's dark eyes shadowed momentarily.

'She says she is in good health and that she is almost asleep before she falls into bed each night. Brad is making good progress, even though he canna walk . . . Apparently the number of wounded soldiers is increasing every day. There are not enough nurses to go round.'

Beth could scarcely believe her own eyes when she saw Logan striding up the track from Muircumwell in the late afternoon only six days later. She dropped the two pails of meal which the squealing pigs were waiting to devour and ran to meet him. She was breathless, laughing and crying at the same time as he caught her jubilantly in his arms. He hugged her tightly and hid his face against the warmth of her neck. Beth felt dampness on his roughened cheeks and knew that a tear or two had squeezed beneath his own eyelids, despite the manly image he presented in his unfamiliar uniform.

'Oh, Logie,' she breathed tremulously, 'Ye'll never ken how glad I am tae see ye . . .'

'I'd forgotten how lovely ye are, Beth . . .' His voice was deep and husky with emotion as he held her slightly away from him.

'I'm not even c-clean . . .' Beth protested weakly, trying to brush the dampness from her cheeks and tidy her hair. 'If only I'd kenned . . .'

'Ye're beautiful! Tae me ye're the most beautiful woman in the whole world . . .' Logan's voice was low and intense and he bent his head and kissed her with all the pent-up passion of the past weeks. When he lifted his head at last, Beth clung to him. 'Ye'll marry me then, Beth?' Logan asked urgently.

'Yes, oh yes . . .' She drew back a little then and looked anxiously into his face, her cheeks burning. She could not tell him about the wedding dress as it was supposed to be a secret from every groom, Anna said.

'What is't, Beth?'

'Y-your mama . . . she's been sae kind . . . And Anna . . . They want us tae have a proper wedding . . . b-but I c-canna . . .' Beth's voice had dropped to a distressed whisper. 'I-I'd feel shamed in the kirk . . .' Logan stared at her, then slowly his eyes widened.

'I was right then! I've given ye a babe, Beth?'

'Y-yes . . .'

'Aah, Beth! My ain sweet love . . .' He cradled her against his chest as tenderly as though she were a bairn herself. Tears sprang to her eyes at his gentleness. 'Thank God I've been spared for this day!' Logan breathed fervently. 'But dinna be shamed, Beth. I love ye more than life itself; surely a babe born frae a love such as ours must have God's blessing . . .'

'I dae hope sae!' Beth whispered earnestly.

A week later, with the help of a good drying wind and Logan's extra muscles, the meadow hay was gathered safely into the lofts in fine condition, and the other little weathered ricks were brought from the fields one by one.

Billy had arrived home two days before but, as Alex had asked him to be best man at his wedding, they had gone to Emma's home at Lockerbie. Both Emma and Alex had wanted a quiet wedding so Sarah was pleased that Billy would be there to represent Alex's family.

There was excitement in the air at Fairlyden.

In spite of her earlier misgivings, Beth was pleased by all the preparations and good wishes, especially at a time when so many people were worried about their own loved ones, and when food and clothes were in short supply. Anna MacFarlane had been extraordinarily kind. Beth had intended to wear her best blue gown for her wedding but Anna had generously offered to alter her own wedding gown. At first Beth had demurred but Sarah had added her own persuasion. She wanted Beth to have a day to remember and she wanted Logan to carry the memory of his bride with him wherever he had to go in the months ahead. She guessed why Beth was so reluctant to have a big celebration and she blamed herself for her lax supervision and lack of guidance.

Anna's gown was oyster satin and when Sarah had pinned in a

few extra tucks and taken up the hem, Beth did the stitching herself.

'Logan will be pleased you've made an effort for him, despite the difficulties and the short time we had to prepare,' Sarah smiled approvingly.

'It's old-fashioned,' Sadie sneered when Anna left the room. 'Dresses are supposed tae be short enough tae show your ankles and far lower at the neck than that!'

'It's beautiful!' Beth protested, stroking the thick satin material with a gentle finger. 'And it's kind o' Anna tae let me wear it.'

'It is a wedding gown, Sadie, not a cheap afternoon dress!' Sarah was irritated by her daughter's criticism.

'Humph, well it didna bring Anna much luck,' Sadie snorted and flounced out of the room. There was a silence but Beth could not suppress a small shiver of apprehension. Surely Anna's dress was not unlucky . . .?

'You look beautiful, Beth,' Sarah assured her quietly. 'Logan will be so proud.' There was warmth – and even love in her voice, Beth thought gratefully. It was a long time now since she had addressed Logan's mother as Mama Fairly, but she had always thought of her as akin to her own mother.

Beth was glad the dress was not too tight as she dressed for the drive to the little Muircumwell Kirk. It was true she had felt happy ever since she knew Logan was coming home; she had lost the dreadful sickly feeling too and regained her former appetite; but secretly she was convinced that her waist was beginning to thicken already.

'My, but you're beautiful, lass!' Crispin Bradshaw exclaimed involuntarily as he watched Beth descending the stairs at Fairlyden. 'Pretty as a picture!' He had volunteered to escort her to the church and give her away in the absence of any male relatives of her own. Beth had thanked him shyly, though she had not expected so many formalities. Now she blushed, a little overwhelmed as she took the arm which Crispin extended with a wide smile and a gallant bow. Sarah had also waited behind with Anna, partly to make sure everything was in order with the meal and with Beth's dress, but also because she guessed Beth might be a little nervous and it saddened her that neither Nick nor Sally had lived to see their only child as a beautiful bride.

★ ★ ★

After the ceremony everyone returned to Fairlyden for the meal which Sarah had prepared with Beth's help and the gift of several precious items of food from Janet. Anna's sister, Lizzie, had baked a wedding cake but she could not leave the Store to join them for the meal so Janet had come alone. She watched the young bride and groom take their places at the head of the dining table. Sarah had extended it, using all the leaves, and it stretched the full length of the room.

'I never kenned the table was as big as that, Mistress Sarah,' Janet remarked. 'It all looks sae nice, for all there's a war and sae many things are scarce.'

'We never had space to extend the table until we had a dining room,' Sarah smiled. 'The leaves were always stored in a frame in the hall.'

Crispin joined them. 'I believe condolences and congratulations are in order, Mistress Whiteley,' he greeted Janet with a smile. 'I was sorry to hear about Mr Jardine's death, but I'm glad he showed his appreciation of all you did for him.'

'Aye. Ye could have knocked Lizzie and me down with a feather when the lawyer read oot the Will after the funeral!' Janet declared. 'I can hardly believe it's true even now – and I was sair worried when Jardine died, I'll tell ye, Mr Bradshaw.'

'Well, you looked after him very well.' Crispin smiled. 'I'm sure everyone will be relieved to know you and Lizzie will be carrying on the Store, as well as the bakery and tearoom. Are you going to change the name?'

'Och, we havena thought about that,' Janet frowned. 'I suppose we'll just be kenned as The Muircumwell Store . . . Aah, look at Beth and Logan . . . They look sae young and happy,' she added almost tearfully. Sarah felt a lump in her own throat as she looked at the radiant young faces of her son and his bride. When Emma and Alex came to stand beside her she thought their quiet happiness was beautiful to behold, too.

'Thank you, dear God, for bestowing such happiness on my little family.' She offered her silent prayer with all her heart. When she looked up she found Crispin regarding her with such infinite tenderness in his steady grey eyes that she knew he understood. He smiled and took her hand, drawing it through his arm as he escorted her to the table with all the courtesy of a true gentleman. Only Sadie noted the gesture and her thin mouth tightened with disapproval, but Sarah was too happy to notice.

Thirty-One

Although the nineteen sixteen harvest was a constant battle against the elements, and every bit as bad as many of the government and county officials had forecast, Logan and Beth seemed to be bathed in their own aura of sunshine. It was not that they worked less than anyone else, indeed they toiled from morning to night whatever the weather, moving stooks to dry ground after drenching rain, erecting damp and bedraggled sheaves blown awry by the wind, carting in the half-dried corn whenever there was an opportunity. Beth's arms stung with scratches from the straw and her fingers were constantly throbbing with lethal daggers from the thistles, but each day in Logan's company was a memory to treasure, each night a precious gift.

Sometimes they lay in each others arms, too weary even to talk, happy just to be together. But there were nights when they clung together in desperation, almost overwhelmed by the impending separation, until passion mounted and carried them beyond the shadows and threats of the outside world, filling them with a joy which even Sadie's bitter resentment could not mar.

The jealousy of Logan's sister had increased alarmingly, inadvertently inflamed by her own mother, on Beth's very first night as Logan's wife. Sarah had cleaned and painted Logan's room as soon as she knew he and Beth were to be married. Even that had vexed Sadie.

'I dinna ken why we have tae bother. He'll only be here until the harvest is finished!' Beth had winced at her malevolent sneer.

'This is the room I slept in when I was a bairn,' Sarah had murmured. 'I've always liked it.' She had continued with her plans, ignoring Sadie's grumbles at the extra work. Only when her wedding day was almost over had Beth realised Mistress Fairly's real intentions. She had gone to her room to change out of Anna's lovely wedding gown in readiness for the afternoon milking. Logan's mama had followed her.

'There will be two of you now, Beth. It will be better for you and Logan to have the largest bedroom.'

'B-but we canna dae that! It's your ain bedroom . . .' Beth had felt overwhelmed by such a gesture.

Sadie, coming out of her own room, had paused on the landing, only to overhear her mother say, 'Well, it's your room now, my dear. It's the bedroom where all Fairlyden's bairns have been born since the house was built.'

Beth had blushed hotly. Had Logan's mama guessed her secret? She had drawn in her breath instinctively but she saw nothing but kindliness in the dark brown eyes of the woman who was now her mother-in-law, the only mother she possessed.

'Th-thank you . . .' Beth had whispered brokenly. 'I . . .'

'I was born in that room myself. I like to think there'll be another generation of Fairlys when . . .'

'Ye're giving *her* your bedroom!' Sadie had interrupted explosively. 'It's the best bedroom in the house and she's just a-a . . .'

'That is enough, Sadie! Remember Beth is your brother's wife now. Dinna spoil their wedding day, lassie . . .' Sarah's brown eyes pleaded for her daughter's charitable understanding. Her plea was in vain.

'My brother!' Sadie had been furious – angrier than Beth had ever seen her and she had slipped away, her new joy overshadowed by Sadie's jealous hatred.

Logan had been inordinately pleased by his mother's unselfish action. 'I always liked Mama's room. When I was young it always seemed warm and peaceful tae me . . . I shall think of ye in this room, Beth. Maybe Mama guessed you might need a pleasant refuge frae Sadie's company . . . Somehow I ken ye'll be safe in here – you and oor bairnie.'

'Oh, Logan, ye're sae good tae me – and your mama is sae very kind . . .'

'Ye make folk want tae be kind tae ye, Beth. Ye're sweet and tender . . .'

It was sometime later when Logan, lying on the big bed with his arms behind his head, had murmured, 'When ye paint it, will ye make it the colour o' the primroses down by the burn, Beth? I think I'd like that . . . sunshine even in winter.'

Every minute of Sarah's spare time was spent either knitting for the soldiers or writing letters to her sons and Ellen, as well as regular letters to Crispin. It was Crispin himself who had initiated this habit soon after Logan had joined the army. She had sensed his need for regular news of the son he longed to claim as his own, but she had begun to look forward to his letters with an eagerness which surprised her; she enjoyed his news, his dry humour and cryptic comments, his views of the men and women whose lives were so different from her own. She knew Crispin liked to receive her letters in return because he often told her so, and was therefore surprised when three weeks passed in September without any word at all.

Maybe he is not so interested in my letters after all when he knows Logan is safely at Fairlyden, she thought, and she could not help a small feeling of pique. Her father also liked to hear news of Crispin's life in Yorkshire when she made her regular visits to the Mains. Despite his advancing years he still retained a lively interest in the outside world, and the Bradshaws in particular. Both he and Beatrice had had reason to be grateful to Crispin and his father.

'Och weel, I expect he's busy,' Sandy excused Crispin readily when Sarah explained that she had had no further news from Yorkshire since her last visit to the Mains.

'It will soon be your birthday though, Father. Crispin always remembers that, doesn't he? I expect he'll write you a letter then.'

Although it was Sandy's eightieth birthday Crispin did not write and neither did he reply to Sarah's letters. Her concern grew.

Then at last Jim Braid brought a letter with a London postmark and she recognised Crispin's writing at once.

'Have ye had bad news, Mother?' Logan asked a few seconds later, prompted by the sight of his mother's shocked face. 'Not Billy?' he asked sharply.

'It's Mr Bradshaw's sister, and her husband . . . Both killed.'

'Killed, but how? Did they go tae their house in France after all?'

'No . . .' Sarah scanned the two sheets of Crispin's copperplate writing before she looked up. 'Do you remember we read about the German airplanes flying across the Channel?'

273

'Zeppelins? Aye, I remember. Some people were injured . . . Surely that wasna . . .'

'Crispin's sister and her husband were visiting friends. Robert too. His mother and father were trapped . . . and a child. Apparently Robert tried to save them and ended up under some masonry himself. They – the rescuers – thought he was dead too at first. He was unconscious. They had to cut off his leg . . .'

'Dear God!'

'It is a dreadful world . . . dreadful.'

'How is Mr Bradshaw's nephew now? And Mr Bradshaw himself? Is that why ye hadna heard frae him, Mother?'

Sarah nodded. 'There's not much more news. Robert is in hospital, getting along fairly well – but shocked of course. It must be awful to wake up with only one leg . . . Crispin has been with him.'

Later, when she was alone in the kitchen Sarah read Crispin's letter again and her heart went out to him.

' . . . I feel so guilty for misjudging Robert and thinking him a coward. He saved a child's life at the risk of his own. I have to say, Sarah, he is very depressed, or at least bewildered. The accident has altered his whole life – as so many of our brave soldiers have already discovered.

'I am sorry there has been so little time to write to you, indeed I was scarcely aware of the days passing. I realise I have forgotten your father's eightieth birthday and must try to make amends although I know he will understand. I shall write again as soon as I get back to Yorkshire. I thank God for Ted Forbes, who has kept the factory working in my absence, although there is urgent business which needs my attention now. Robert says the telephone is a great invention and I think I shall install one so that I can speak to Ted when I am away. As it is I must make a visit to the factory soon. Afterwards I feel it is my duty to be with Robert whenever I can. It will be many months before he is fit to leave the hospital – and he has no family, except myself, to care for him now.

'I do not think I shall be able to see Logan before he leaves again. You will know how that grieves me, dear Sarah. I pray that God will be with him. Have you received delivery of the photographs taken at his wedding? I should like to have one.'

Sarah raised her eyes and stared unseeingly into the fire. She

274

knew how Crispin would feel, how much he would want to see Logan again; instead he would do his duty and visit his nephew. She went to the desk and took out two photographs. She had a similar one with only Logan and Beth on it in a frame on top of the piano. Beth had one too. Crispin had arranged it all; it had been a great surprise when the man had arrived at the wedding with all his strange equipment. There was a group photograph too, showing herself and her father, all her children except Ellen, and Crispin and Beatrice. How stiff we look in the picture, Sarah thought, yet how pleased I am to have it. She resolved to send Crispin a photograph and a letter that very day.

Slowly the harvest progressed; one by one the fields were cleared of their bedraggled stooks.

'I think even the harvest moon is looking down on the world through a mist of tears . . .' Beth's voice was soft and wistful as she stood at Logan's side, painfully aware that time was running out for them.

'Aye, the year's moving on. I hope they dinna send for me until the tatties are gathered, though . . .'

'Oh, Logan, I hope not too!'

'According to the newspaper, some o' the officials who're supposed tae ken about such things are predicting shortages of wheat and potatoes, for all sae many o' the farms have planted extra acres.

Billy had returned to France after completing a spell of training on the new tanks. Sarah was very proud of him, even while she feared such monstrous machines. She had seen a picture of one during the local Tank Campaign when the Scottish Savings Committee were encouraging people to buy either War Bonds or War Savings Certificates to help purchase these great new machines which were expected to end the war. Beth had used her own precious savings to purchase some Bonds. She felt she would do anything in her power if only it would end the war and leave her and Logan to live their lives in peace.

The potato crop at Fairlyden was small in comparison to farms on the eastern side of the country and the potatoes were almost all harvested and safely pitted by the time the weather improved. For several days there was no wind, no rain – just a uniform sky neither grey nor blue; the autumn days were surprisingly mild although there was little sign of the sun.

'It seems as though the whole world is holding its breath. Even the leaves are clinging to the trees as though they're reluctant tae die.'

'Ye've a wonderful imagination, Beth.' Logan smiled tenderly, then he sighed. 'I shall remember all this when I'm in France – the brown and bronze and yellow of the sturdy old beech tree, the trembling wee leaves o' the silver birch . . .'

'Aye, the birches are sae very dainty,' Beth smiled. 'But even the birds are gathering and chirruping as though they dinna want tae say goodbye either. Oh, Logie . . .' Suddenly her voice choked with tears, taking her unawares. Logan drew her against him and stroked her shining hair. Over her shoulder his pensive gaze travelled over the familiar countryside, coming to rest on the old house sheltered by the sloping fields behind. The smoke from the kitchen chimney was spiralling lazily into the autumn air.

'There's not a breath of wind . . .' he murmured. 'Not a sound to disturb the peace . . .' He bent his head and brushed Beth's temple with his lips.

Two days later the dreaded wire arrived. There was a quiet desperation in their loving during that last night before Logan set off to join his comrades. Once more it was Beth who accompanied him in the trap to the station. This time they did not halt beneath the last of the young beech trees on the track; their passion had been spent and the love in their hearts was too deep for mere words. They rode in silence, Beth's hand tightly clasped in Logan's. He released it briefly as the high wall surrounding the Manse garden came into sight. Gently, reverently he brushed Beth's swelling young body.

'So if it's a laddie ye'll call him Nicholas, Beth . . .?'

'Aye, if ye're sure ye dinna mind us calling him after ma father. Nicholas Logan Fairly . . .'

'And Kirsty if it's a lassie.'

'I expect ye'd prefer a son . . .?' Beth glanced anxiously at his youthful face. His skin was still so smooth . . . He turned his head and met her eyes. His gaze was clear and earnest. 'I dinna care about anything else so long as ye're all right, Beth. Ye will take care . . .?'

'I shall be fine. Dinna fret about us, Logie – just come back safely . . .' Her voice thickened but she blinked back her tears, determined not to make this parting any harder for Logan than it was already. He slipped his free arm around her shoulders and kissed her tenderly. Then he turned his attention back to the pony and flicked the reins, speeding the pony into a gentle trot.

The day after Logan's departure there was still no wind to stir the leaves from the trees, but as the morning wore on the grey skies grew duller, mist shrouded the distant hills, thickening until they were lost to sight. Gradually, almost imperceptibly, the damp white mist turned to rain; it fell silently, unceasingly.

And now the world is weeping with me, Beth thought.

It was a busy winter with little respite from the endless tasks of lifting and carting turnips, feeding the cows and bullocks, the pigs and hens. There was only Thomas left to do the heavy work, filling the dung cart and taking it to the field. Anna helped him spread the little heaps ready to plough.

'You will need to start the ploughing early, Thomas,' Sarah spoke loudly to make sure he heard correctly. 'I pray you will keep in good health.'

'Dinna fret, Mistress. I'm luckier than most. We have plenty tae eat and a warm dry bed of a night. We'll all dae our best for the sake o' the soldier laddies.'

Sarah nodded, but she wondered if Sadie would ever do her best. She grumbled continually.

'I'm thankful I'm not with them. I'll tell ye,' Thomas nodded vigorously. 'I thought it was wet in oor ain wee bit o' Scotland but at least we dinna have tae stand in mud up tae our backsides and live i' trenches.'

'We're very fortunate, Thomas . . .' Sarah's face was strained as she thought of her own two sons out there. Logan wrote regularly but his letters rarely mentioned the conditions in which he was living, except to say how greatly he appreciated the parcels which she and Beth packed with such loving care. Their love for Logan had strengthened the bond between them, but Sadie's jealousy was now focused solely on Beth.

Beth's condition could no longer be disguised despite the loose gowns she had taken to wearing. Sarah was anxious in case she worked too hard, but without her help it would have been impossible to manage.

277

'When is the bairn due, lassie,' Sarah asked quietly, one morning when they were alone together in the dairy. Beth had just straightened wearily and put a hand to her aching back. She flushed painfully at Sarah's question and lowered her eyes. Sarah watched her chewing her lower lip nervously. 'I don't want to pry, Beth,' she said gently. 'Indeed I'm pleased one of my sons is going to give me grandchildren . . .' Beth looked up then, but her blue eyes were still troubled.

'The – the babe will be born in J-January, I th-think.'

Sarah nodded. 'I dinna want you or the babe to suffer any harm because there's so much work to do. Maybe I should ask Anna if she could help me in the dairy. She has less work with the poultry now we are into winter weather . . .'

'Oh no, please, I-I'm fine,' Beth stammered quickly. Already Sadie grumbled when she was slower than usual with any of her work. Logan's sister would be even more unpleasant if she thought she was shirking. 'I-I'd rather be busy anyway, and I'm feeling fine, truly I am . . .'

'Very well, Beth. But please take care. Logan would never forgive me if anything went wrong, you know.' Sarah smiled encouragingly and slowly Beth's anxious young face relaxed and she smiled back.

This conversation brought Beth unexpected relief. Logan's mother knew everything now and she had not condemned her. She told Logan about it in her next letter.

'And now I don't feel so guilty when I knit the tiny vests and hats and boots that our babe will need. I believe your mother is happy for us. Last night she brought out a bag of new white wool and told me she intends to knit a shawl. She is so good to me, Logan. Anna is also very kind, especially when her own life has been so sad. She has promised to make two nightgowns and she has given me some of Jamie's baby clothes – although she said she could not bear to part with them until now. She is a good friend to me. I do confess our babe is becoming more of a burden; he prevents me doing my work as quickly as I would like to do it – but I must not grumble. I know your own hardships must be many, for all you say little about your life in the trenches. I am so sorry your new friend Sammy was killed. How cruel war is and how I wish it would all end and send you home to me again . . .'

Thirty-Two

General discontent with the Government's leadership had reached a crisis. The war was dragging on without any end in sight, people were hungry, prices were rising. At the beginning of December Lloyd George was chosen to replace Mr Asquith as Prime Minister of the new Coalition Government.

'Maybe the war will end soon,' Beth voiced her own secret hopes wistfully.

'Let us pray it will. There is no possibility of Ellen and Brad being with us for Christmas, though. Not even anyone from the Mains will be here this year.' Privately Sarah was more disappointed than she cared to admit. Neither Billy nor Logan would be home for Christmas and Crispin would not be with them either.

He had travelled up to Fairlyden early the previous week but his visit had been brief. He had brought lengths of fine woollen material for herself, Sadie and Beth as well as a large bag of coloured knitting wools for Beth to knit into small garments. He had also brought gifts for the Mains which he had delivered himself. Sarah felt she had scarcely seen him at all.

'Robert is so lacking in spirit I scarcely know what to do to interest him,' he had admitted. 'I have ordered one of the new bathchairs which are being made for crippled army officers.'

'I'm sorry, Crispin.' Sarah looked at him helplessly, noting the new lines of strain on his strong face. His thick hair was pure white now, but he still stepped out briskly, his broad shoulders erect. 'Maybe they will fit Robert with a wooden leg?'

'The doctors have tried already. He persevered manfully but I think it was too soon. The stump of his leg became badly inflamed. He says he will not try again, and instead insists he will learn to walk on crutches. He needs company to cheer him. Ted Forbes has been very good. He calls at the house and chats about the factory and his ideas for the future, but Robert never showed any interest in such things before his accident so he cannot share Ted's enthusiasm. Yet Ted says he has made one or two helpful suggestions about organising the supply of raw materials, and marketing our cloth – but like everything else we must obey the government's rules.' Crispin heaved a sigh. 'Maybe he will develop an interest in time, after all the factory will be his one day. But he has other problems too . . .' He hesitated, frowning a little. 'He will never be able to sire a child to take over his inheritance – even if he were to meet a woman who cared enough to marry an invalid.'

'Poor Robert. Perhaps a change of scene would be good for him, Crispin. You are welcome to bring him to Fairlyden if he wants to come.'

'You're very kind, Sarah.' Crispin smiled down at her with deep affection. 'I might suggest that to Robert in a few months' time, when the weather is better perhaps. It is years since he came to Scotland . . .'

'Years since who came to Scotland?' Sadie asked, coming into the kitchen.

'Crispin's nephew – Robert. He is having a difficult time adjusting to being an invalid. I was suggesting that he might like to visit us . . . have a change of scene – and company.'

Sadie glowered and made no more than a token response as she passed through to the scullery. Crispin's grey eyes followed her thoughtfully.

'Maybe it would not be such a good idea to bring him to Fairlyden, Sarah. You all have more than enough to do already with such a shortage of men. Maybe I shall open up Fairlyside when the war is over, and women are released from the munitions factories . . . At least Robert has plenty of money to pay for his comforts, and a choice of houses – London, Yorkshire, Scotland – France too, if the house is still standing by the time the war is over! He is more fortunate than many of the men wounded in the trenches.'

Neither Crispin nor Sarah were aware that Sadie was standing behind the scullery door, eavesdropping unashamedly. There was no one to see her calculating expression. 'As for children, Robert never seemed very fond of them anyway,' Crispin mused, speaking his thoughts aloud, 'but I don't like to think of him growing old all alone . . . Maybe he will meet a homely young widow who would be content to settle for companionship.'

'I hope so. At least as his wife she would have a nice home and servants to help with the work. I'm sure when the war is over, Robert will make a new life of his own.'

'I hope you're right, my dear, but I'm not sure Robert has your brand of courage. On the other hand I've got to know him better since he was ill and sometimes he does remind me a little of my father, although he bears no physical resemblance to him at all.'

Christmas was a subdued affair at Fairlyden. Sarah and Beth had prepared Christmas parcels of food and warm clothes for Ellen and Brad, Billy and Logan; they had received sepia-coloured Christmas postcards in return.

'I suppose there must be thousands of families feeling just as sad as we are,' Sarah sighed. 'Young Jamie MacFarlane is the brightest spot around Fairlyden just now.'

'Aye, Anna says he is looking forward tae Christmas Day,' Beth smiled. She was very fond of Jamie. 'Thomas has been carving a wee wooden horse with moving legs. He works on it at night when Jamie is in bed.'

'Well, I suppose we must all put on our own bright smiles. It wouldna do to spoil Christmas for everyone.' Sarah cast a fleeting glance at Sadie but her daughter made no reply. She made no secret of the fact that she did not want to spend Christmas Day at Mains of Muir.

'I expect Emma and Mistress O'Connor will have taken a lot of trouble,' Beth murmured gently, seeing Sarah's anxious expression. 'Anna says her mother and Lizzie have been pestered with folks at the Store, all wanting dried fruit and extra tea and sugar, but they canna get enough themselves.'

'No, even a loaf of bread costs ten pence now,' Sarah frowned. 'I don't know what will happen if this war goes on much longer. It's costing such a lot of money, apart from causing such a shortage of food.'

In January Sarah found herself spending another whole day at the Mains. She was reluctant to be away so long when Beth's time was drawing near, and with so much work to be done, but Sandy Logan had been suffering from a particularly bad cold. It had settled on his chest and she knew Beatrice was concerned about him when Jim Braid brought her letter.

Sandy had brightened visibly at the sight of her and Sarah was pleased she had made the effort to visit him, even though he seemed to need frequent rests between conversations. It was during one of his sleepy spells that Alex and Emma joined them.

Almost inevitably the conversation turned to the government's proposed new powers which were to affect farmers in every part of the kingdom.

'It is bad enough the way they come and commandeer our hay; the stable loft at Fairlyden is more than half-empty already and it's a long time until the spring grass will be ready. We've received no payment yet either!' Sarah added. Privately she was all in favour of supporting the cause of the soldiers in any way she could but she had not taken kindly to the manner of the two men who had demanded hay for the army. 'Do you mean to say, Alex, that men in suits are going to interfere with everything we do? Tell farmers which fields we must plough? Which crops to plant, and how much and when and where . . .?' She stared at her eldest son incredulously, but she knew both Alex and Emma followed all the farming reports very closely, and neither of them would jest about such radical suggestions.

'Well, it's not official yet, Mother, but Lord Rhondda is the new food controller and his attitude seems tae be the very opposite o' Lord Devonport's. They're proposing tae set up District Agricultural Executive Committees tae advise the Scottish Board of Agriculture. I expect they'll dae the same for England and Wales. Mind you, if government officials do tell farmers what crops they have to grow, they say they'll also be responsible if there's a glut when the war ends. They reckon there's going tae be a guaranteed minimum price when the crops are sold. At least the government can control the amount o' imported food tae suit the situation each year which is more than ordinary farmers can do.'

'It's because they're worried about bread and things being sae scarce,' Emma said in her quiet, thoughtful way. 'They want things tae be more evenly distributed and at fairer prices. They seem tae think there's a shortage o' milk already.'

'Mmm, but there's little wonder milk's getting scarce when cattle feed is costing so much, and it's difficult to get too . . .'

'Aye, and sae many o' the men have gone tae fight. A lot o' the women milkers have left the farms tae. There is one good thing about the new proposals,' Alex added with satisfaction. 'They say no more farmworkers should be taken for military service without the approval o' the Board of Agriculture. I pray they'll bring that in soon. Young Donald has received his papers already. Ewan and Maggie are upset. Indeed I'm vexed myself. He's a grand laddie.'

'Janet never mentioned it when I called at the Store on my way here . . .'

'No, she'll no' ken yet, Mother. Better let Maggie tell her.'

'I thought ye'd come tae see *me*, lassie, not tae talk over the world's troubles wi' these two young folk.' Sandy Logan's faded blue eyes twinkled as he looked at Sarah. She smiled back at him fondly.

'You were bored with my company, Father! You dozed off! Alex and Emma were only keeping me entertained. Beatrice has gone to make a cup of tea before I set off home. It's a raw day outside.'

'Aye, so Alex was telling me. It's guid o' ye tae come all this way in such weather, Sarah . . .'

'Och, it's not good of me at all! You know I usually come every two weeks or so. I've just come a wee bit earlier.'

'Aye,' Sandy nodded wryly. 'I suppose Beatrice thought I'd a wee bit o' a cough so she just happened tae send ye a wee note with Jim Braid, eh?'

'Something like that.'

'Aah, ye're a grand lassie . . .' Sandy sighed contentedly.

'I'm hardly a lassie anymore, Father,' Sarah chuckled. 'I shall soon be a grandmother!'

'Aye, aye, so ye will! It only seems like yesterday since ye were a bairn yourself. And how's young Beth getting on? Is she well?' His expression grew grave. 'I remember her mother nearly died when Beth was born, didn't she? I suppose there's no word o' Logan getting home?'

'No, unfortunately. He is stuck in France. Beth seems fine, but then she never grumbles. I think she works too hard, but she insists she is all right, though she's ready for bed as soon as the milking is finished . . .'

It was true that Beth was tired by the end of the day but she had kept remarkably well and she managed to do most of her usual work, even if she was a little slower. She had learned to be firmer with Sadie, usually insisting that she do her own neglected tasks, though sometimes these were so trivial it was easier to do them herself than waste energy arguing with Sadie. Either way

283

her sister-in-law's malice continued to increase.

Thomas Whiteley and Anna were well aware that Sadie evaded the most unpleasant or heaviest work whenever the opportunity arose, especially on days when Sarah was visiting the Mains.

On this particular day Thomas returned from the ploughing barely an hour after he had set out. He found Beth cleaning out the byre and wheeling the barrow of manure to the midden.

'The Mistress told Miss Sadie tae dae that!' Thomas exclaimed indignantly when Beth straightened to speak to him, unconsciously holding her aching back.

'I know, but Sadie volunteered tae throw the hay down frae the loft in the stable for the horses. I dinna like climbing up the ladder sae much now . . .'

'No . . . but surely she should dae that anyway!' Thomas frowned uncertainly. 'Anyway I dinna think ye should be handling that heavy barrow. I'll empty it for ye now I'm here!' Before Beth could object Thomas had wheeled away the barrow and brought it back again. I'll be glad when I'm as quick as that again, Beth thought ruefully. My back has never ached so much as it does today! Not even when we were gathering the potatoes frae the muddy drills . . .

'Just ye sit on yon wee stool for a minute and I'll have the rest o' this muck oot in a jiffy,' Thomas declared. 'I'm sure it wadna have hurt Miss Sadie tae do it . . .' he muttered. Beth silently agreed with him but she knew Sadie was taking advantage of her mother's absence; she was probably reading one of her penny novels.

'We didna think ye'd be back frae the ploughing until late, Thomas . . .?' Beth tactfully changed the subject.

'I've just come back for a spanner. There's something wrong with the plough.' His brow furrowed. 'Aah, but I'll be glad when this here war's over and Master Billy and Master Logan get back . . .' Beth smiled wanly. So will I, Thomas, so will I, she echoed silently.

Sarah was a little late returning from the Mains but she always insisted on milking her own cows. Consequently she was still milking the last one when everyone else had finished.

'You must be tired, Beth. Dinna wait for me. I will wash the milking buckets myself. Sadie, you can make the supper for once.' Sadie's mouth tightened but she made no comment. Beth gave a sigh of relief. She could not stand any arguments with Sadie tonight. All she wanted was a drink of hot tea. Then she could stretch out her weary back. She nodded gratefully at Sarah and took one of the lanterns from its hook on the byre wall. She felt more tired than usual tonight and she knew it was on account of the dragging ache which had increased as the day wore on.

Sadie followed her. 'Dinna forget ye've the horses tae feed.'

'I havena forgotten.' Beth made her way to the stable with dragging feet. Usually she enjoyed looking after the horses. She had helped Logan often and she had promised to take special care of them while he was away. She hung the lantern up, grasped the fork leaning against the wall and turned towards the spare stall at the far end of the stable. But there was no pile of hay waiting for her. She groaned aloud.

'I forgot tae get it down frae the loft this morning,' Sadie announced behind her. Beth turned ponderously.

'Ye couldna forget! You offered tae get it while I cleaned the byre. I saw ye come tae the stable . . .'

'Aye, and I saw Thomas wheeling the muck frae the byre for you instead o' getting on with his ain work!'

'He only wheeled the barrow tae the midden for me. Anyway that's no reason for ye not tae keep your promise. I'd have got the hay myself while it was daylight if I'd kenned! It's dangerous taking the lamp up there.'

'Aye, it is. I'll come up after ye and hold the lamp while ye push the hay through the trapdoor.'

'But . . .' Beth stared at Sadie's defiant face in the dim light. 'I'll hold the light if ye . . .'

'Oh no! Logan thinks nobody else can look after his precious horses as well as you. After all ye spent plenty o' time i' the stable with him,' she added slyly. 'Now ye'd better get on with it – or the horses can dae without their hay, but dinna blame me if they whinny half the night. Dae ye want me tae light the way for ye or no?' Beth looked at Sadie's unyielding features and her heart sank. She felt she had scarcely the energy to climb the ladder, even less get the hay. But she could not go to bed and leave the horses hungry.

'Very well. Hold the light for me.'

Beth went up the ladder first. It was very dark when she

pushed her head through the trapdoor into the hayloft, but Sadie was nimble and she soon followed with the lamp. She stood by the hole in the floor of the loft while Beth carried a forkful of hay from the far end.

'That's not enough!' Sadie announced critically.

'I know.' Beth was breathing hard with the exertion. 'It's not easy tae see in the dark. I'll hold the lamp while you bring another forkful.'

'No, thanks.'

'But you . . .' Beth sighed resignedly. Pride would not allow her to plead with Sadie Fairly.

'Hurry up. I havena got all night! Remember I've tae make the supper!' Beth began to make her way to the far end of the loft where the remaining hay was piled. She had her back to Sadie when the flickering shadows of the lamplight jumped erratically. She glanced over her shoulder.

'Sadie!' But Sadie's head and the lamp were already disappearing through the trapdoor. Beth groped her way as fast as she could towards the faint square of light shining up from the stable below. Before she could reach it Sadie's arm reached up and grasped the iron ring of the trapdoor, pulling it shut behind her. The loft was in darkness. Absolute and complete darkness.

'Sadie!' Beth almost screamed in panic. 'Sadie! You canna leave me alone!' There was no reply. Beth fell to her knees and began to scrabble her way in the direction of the trapdoor. The darkness was intense. A sharp splinter shot under her fingernail. She cried out at the stab of pain. 'I canna open the trap door frae this side anyway,' she muttered. 'Sadie kens that.' She slumped wearily to the floor and tried to suck the minute wooden dagger from beneath her nail. Surely she'll come back in a minute. She must! 'I ken ye're just trying tae frighten me, Sadie!' she called aloud. 'I ken ye're just playing a stupid prank!' There was no answer. Sadie would push up the trap any minute now. She must. She must . . . Beth bit hard on her knuckles in a desperate bid to control her rising panic. How could she have been stupid enough to fall for Sadie's trick!

Thirty-Three

In the firelit kitchen Sadie set out the plates and cups. Beth had made potato and leek soup earlier in the day, in readiness for the evening meal. Sadie pushed the iron pot over the fire to reheat.

'Mmm, that smells appetising, Sadie,' Sarah sniffed in appreciation as she came in. 'It's a bitterly cold night. I expect there'll be a keen frost.' She rubbed her chapped hands in front of the fire. 'Where's Beth? Has she had her supper already?'

'Och, she's probably resting. Again! Ye ken she never waits tae wash the dishes!' Sadie's tone was full of spite and Sarah sighed.

'Och, Beth works hard all day! She's bound to be tired. But the bairn'll not be long now, then . . .'

'She hasna been married long enough tae be having a bairn yet.' Sadie stared challengingly at her mother. Her pale eyes were hard and mocking. Sarah grimaced.

'There's no need to be provocative. You know the circumstances are not normal – what with Logan going off to the war and . . .'

'Oh, I ken ye never see anything wrong with Logan, or his – his . . .'

'His wife! I'm not condoning their behaviour, Sadie.' Sarah's tone was mild. 'There's more than Logan and Beth in the same predicament. At least they love each other – and they'll love the bairn when it comes too.'

'Oh aye!' Sadie sneered furiously. 'And I expect ye'll make a fuss over it tae – just like ye did with Logan!'

'Oh, Sadie, there's no need for you to be jealous of Logan, or his bairn. Dish the soup, will you please. Beth has probably taken hers to her room. We'll have our supper and leave her to sleep in peace until morning.'

Sarah did not see the smirk of satisfaction on her daughter's face.

★　★　★

287

Beth's thoughts had winged back over the years, dispelling the loneliness and fear of the darkened hayloft until exhaustion claimed her and she fell asleep.

She wakened suddenly, trembling, gripped by pain. Had she screamed? Her breath came in little gusts. Gradually the pain abated and she breathed more slowly, gathering her senses with an effort as memory flooded back and the insidious fear returned. She lay still, listening intently to the noises in the stable below – faint muffled fidgeting. Had something startled the horses? What time could it be? How long had she slept? There was not even a lighter shade of darkness – just deep, inky blackness.

Suddenly pain engulfed her again. It caught her unawares. When it passed she felt weak, shattered; she drew the back of her hand over her brow and felt beads of perspiration there. Her throat was parched. She longed for a drink of tea – even water would do; she lay back staring unseeingly into the empty blackness. The pain came again, convulsing her in its severity. She could not fail to recognise its cause. My bairnie! She felt the panic rising in her. What if the baby was born in the loft? She was completely alone. No one to help her babe into the world. The thought terrified her.

'Please, God, help me! Help our bairn.' She sagged back against the hay. 'Please, God, dinna let my bairnie die!' Had Sadie sensed her time was so near? The intense backache – had she guessed what was the cause? Beth remembered Anna MacFarlane telling her that some women suffered backache for several days before the babe got himself into position . . . Sadie had been there too, knitting in sullen silence . . . Beth shuddered. Did Sadie want the baby to die? Did Logan's sister want her to die too?

'Dinna panic!' she admonished herself aloud. Sadie would enjoy that! Dinna let her beat ye. Keep your head, Elizabeth! Horses and cows prefer to be alone when they give birth. They . . . The pain came again. Beth bit her lip until it bled. She was unaware of it. At length she lay back, panting, trying to think what she ought to do. When the pain came again, quicker, fiercer, her limbs thrashed away the covering of hay. Beth could not stifle the scream. It seemed to echo in the rafters of the loft. Down below one of the horses whinnied. The others pulled on their halter blocks, nervous and uneasy, their great hooves moving restlessly on the cobbled floor.

Thomas shivered in the cold night air. He held the lamp aloft as he made a last round of the animals before he went to bed. He had done this every night since Logan went back to the army. Tonight he was later than usual. Queenie II was due to calve and he had dozed beside the fire for a while. He gave the pigsties a cursory glance. None of the sows was due to farrow. He moved on to the loose box. He had put the young cow in there after milking. He opened the top half of the door and lifted the lantern. His heart gave a little leap of joy. Queenie II had given birth unaided. Her gangly-legged offspring was already struggling unsuccessfully to its feet while its mother licked the damp curly coat with her rasping tongue. She looked up sharply as Thomas opened the door. She gave a low, warning moo and moved between her calf and the door in a protective gesture as ancient as time.

'It's all right, old girl,' Thomas murmured soothingly. 'I didna mean tae disturb ye.' He closed the door again and moved on, thankful that the cow did not need his help tonight. He welcomed the cosy warmth of the byre, even the smell of ammonia which stung his eyes a little. Most of the cows were lying contentedly in their stalls, chewing their cud. He hung up the lamp and moved down one side of the byre and back up the other, easing the dung from the stalls to the channel, knowing the cows would be cleaner in the morning. It took some time but Thomas did not mind. He liked the byre at night – warm, peaceful, the cows fed and contented. When he had finished he unhooked the lamp and latched the door. He was slow, methodical. He looked in at the horses. He could not hear the faint moans from the loft above but he sensed that the horses were uneasy. The hay racks were empty. His mouth tightened.

'That wad be Sadie!' he muttered giving the rump of the nearest mare a gentle slap and a firm stroke or two. 'Lazy young wretch she is! She should have brought more hay frae the loft when it was light. Now ye'll have tae wait until morning . . . Whoa, boy!' he called, startled by the nervous dancing of the gelding in the end stall. He walked quietly behind each of the horses, wondering if something had disturbed them. 'Rats likely!' He closed the door behind him, resolving to make sure they had extra hay in the morning. 'I canna see tae everything!' he mumbled to himself. 'That idle . . .'

289

'Thomas? Thomas? Is that you? Can you hear me? Have you seen Beth?' Sarah lifted her lantern and hurried across the yard towards Thomas's shadowy figure. He could not hear but he saw the lantern.

'Queenie has calved, Mistress. They're both fine. We can gang tae bed now.'

'It's Beth, Thomas! She's not in bed! I've just been to the cottage. Anna says she's not been there all evening . . .'

'Beggin' yer pardon, Mistress . . .?' Thomas bent towards her, cupping his good ear. Sarah expelled a shuddering breath.

'Have you seen Beth? Is she out here?'

'Beth? What would the lassie be doing out here in her condition? Anyway I tell ye Queenie has calved.'

'I took her a glass of hot milk. She was not . . .'

'No thank ye. I dinna like hot milk . . .'

Sarah controlled her impatience and her anxiety with an effort. What could Beth be doing outside until this time on a cold winter night? Unless she had fallen, hurt herself . . .

'Help me look for Beth!' she commanded and pushed past Thomas, opening the stable door herself. 'Beth! Are ye here?' In her anxiety Sarah had raised her voice and it startled the horses, setting them on edge. The youngest gelding tried to rear and his hoofs came down hard against the wooden stall. In the loft above Beth heard something of the commotion.

'Is someone there?' She summoned her strength in a desperate call for help before the pain swamped her once more.

'Listen! What was that?' Sarah looked wildly at Thomas. He shook his head in bewilderment. He thinks I'm mad! Sarah thought. 'Beth? Beth, answer me if ye're up there!' She raised her eyes to the loft. Thomas followed her glance and shook his head.

'There's naebody up there, Mistress,' he muttered pityingly. 'There's no' even a ladder and the trap's shut.'

Sarah nodded and turned to the door. 'The byre then . . . .Or did Beth shut in the hens?'

Sarah was just about to close the door when she heard a faint but unmistakable sound. Surely it was a groan? From the loft?

'Wait, Thomas! Put the ladder up and hold the lamp. I must look up there.'

'I'll gang up,' Thomas sighed patiently. He was tired and he didn't understand what the Mistress was about, but he propped the ladder up and pushed open the trap. Sarah heard then the unmistakable moan of someone in pain. She tugged Thomas's trousers.

'Leave your lamp up there and come down.'

'But, Mistress . . . Ye canna go up there! In the dark . . .'

'Thomas . . . go back to the cottage. Get Anna. Do you hear me?'

'Anna! Aye . . . Aye!'

'Hurry then!'

Despite her fifty-seven years Sarah was still nimble and she hauled herself into the loft the moment Thomas had disappeared through the door.

'Beth . . .?' she called gently. 'Beth, are you up here? Answer me, lassie. There's no need to be frightened – or shamed. Beth . . .?'

'Ooh . . . Mama Fairly . . .' Beth uttered a shuddering sob which ended in a stifled groan.

'Oh, Beth!' Sarah hurried into the darkness of the loft, holding her lamp high. Suddenly she saw Beth writhing on her bed of hay. 'Oh, dear God! Whatever possessed you to hide, lassie?' There was alarm and fear, exasperation and pity in Sarah's voice. Beth didn't answer. She was too busy battling with the waves of pain. The threatening blackness. Sarah moved closer, stepping carefully. 'Dear Beth,' she whispered hoarsely. 'Why didn't you tell me, lassie? We must get you down the ladder and into bed . . .'

'Can't . . .' Beth gasped. 'Too late . . . Sadie shut the trap . . . Couldn't get out . . . Aa-agh, help me, Mama Fairly! Help me-ee . . .'

Sarah's heart seemed to stop as she realised what Beth was saying. Sadie! Had she shut the trap deliberately? Her own daughter! What had she done? If the baby died . . . If Beth . . . Sadie would be a murderer! Her blood ran cold.

'I think . . . the bairn's coming . . .' Beth gasped, calmer already. Mama Fairly would help her. She thought of Logan. He had said she would be safe in the big bedroom at Fairlyden. She had painted it just as he had wanted – the colour of primroses.

Swiftly Sarah scanned the beams until she saw one with a bit of old rope. She tied the lantern safely, then she stripped off her flannel petticoat ready to wrap up the baby, then one of her cotton petticoats. She used her teeth to tear it into strips.

291

When Anna popped her head into the loft and saw the lantern and the shadowy figure of Mistress Fairly bending over the hay at the far end she realised Thomas must have heard correctly after all.

'Anna! Thank goodness you've come. Bring some blankets frae the house please! And a kettle o' hot water . . . and . . .'

'Is the bairn coming already? Up here!'

'Hurry, Anna! Bring what you think we'll need, but hurry!'

It took Anna a little time to boil the kettle over a dying fire and gather a clean bowl and blankets, scissors, tape. Her heart was pounding from her haste and her fear for Beth. She'd heard often enough from her mother that Sally Jamieson had almost died when Beth was born, and she had never really been well afterwards. She muttered fervent prayers for Beth and her babe as she ran hither and thither.

Sarah gazed down at Beth's waxen face with a feeling of near despair. It was plain the girl was exhausted. She must have battled alone with the pain for the past two or three hours at least. That was enough to unnerve a woman experienced in motherhood, let alone an eighteen-year-old girl. She smoothed back the damp tendrils of hair from Beth's brow with a gentle hand. Her forehead felt clammy, her hair was dark with perspiration. Sarah wiped her face with a piece from her own petticoat and Beth opened her eyes.

'It's coming! I k-ken . . . .' Her words were lost in a mammoth groan as she made one last supreme effort, summoning all the strength she had.

As Anna hurried breathlessly up the ladder with her awkward bundle a faint wail echoed into the shadows. Then another.

'My goodness!' She scrambled upright and grabbed her lantern. 'It really is the bairn! Oh, Mistress Fairly! Is – is . . . Are ye all right, Beth? Oh my, oh . . .'

Sarah straightened, holding her first grandchild, rolling it, hastily in its improvised red flannel shawl.

'It's a girl, Beth.' She smiled down into Beth's face, so pale and tired in the dim light. She watched the relief and happiness erase the fear and pain as though by magic. 'You have a daughter.' She knelt in the hay and placed the baby in Beth's arms. Anna knelt too, shaking her head in bewildered disbelief.

'I'd never have had the courage tae hide away on ma ain like that!' she exclaimed in awe. 'But what if anything had gone wrong? What if Mistress Fairly hadna found ye in time? Oh my! I've left the kettle o' water and the bowl at the bottom o' the ladder . . .' She shook her head, bereft of speech, and hurried back to the trapdoor.

'I didna hide away . . .' Beth began. She raised her eyes to Sarah. In the lamplight their eyes met. Beth saw pain and shame in the brown eyes which had been shining with joy a moment ago. 'I came up for more hay for the horses and fell asleep,' she whispered and met Sarah's eyes steadily. Sarah bit her lip, but she understood that Beth was telling her silently she would never condemn Sadie in public for her evil deeds this night. After all, Sadie was the babe's aunt, Logan's sister, her own daughter . . . Sarah shivered. She knew Beth would never forgive Sadie – and neither could she.

Anna came back with the water.

'Ye've looked exhausted for days, Beth.' She bent closer and touched the tiny cheek with a gentle finger. 'Jamie will be thrilled when we tell him in the morning!'

'I believe ye're almost as excited as I am, Anna,' Beth smiled. She felt tired and happy. She looked up and saw the love and gratitude and understanding in the eyes of her mother-in-law.

'Thank you . . . Mama Fairly.'

'Thank *you*, Beth . . .' Anna looked at them strangely, but Sarah was smiling down at Beth, hoping she would not see the sheen of her tears in the dim light.

Thirty-Four

A week later Anna MacFarlane called at the Muircumwell Store.

'I'm tae take the groceries for Mistress Fairly tae, Mother. She says she'll be down tae see ye when Beth's out and about again.'

'Aye, aye,' Janet nodded absently. 'But tell me again about Beth and the bairn. I canna understand her going tae sleep in the loft – or staying up there . . . I mean . . .' She frowned. 'Most women would have been frightened tae go up tae the loft . . . It's a wonder Beth didna panic . . . It doesna make sense.'

'No, I ken. Anyway Sadie was supposed tae be getting the hay down for Beth tae feed the horses. I didna understand it either. I ken Sadie has made plenty o' nasty remarks about Beth and Logan only being married in the summer, but I've never heard Mistress Fairly utter a word o' reproach. She seemed ever sae pleased tae have a wee granddaughter . . .'

'She's a good woman – Mistress Fairly . . .'

'Aye, weel I didna ask Beth any questions. She said her legs were a bit wobbly the next morning when we helped her doon the ladder and up tae her bedroom, but she seems ever sae well. She's working in the kitchen a bit already . . . There is one thing though . . . she'll no' let the babe out o' her sight when Sadie's around!'

'I shouldna think Sadie would want anything tae dae with the babe anyway. She never had much time for bairns and she was jealous o' Logan frae the minute he was born. She's jealous o' her ain shadow, if ye ask me.'

'Aye, I ken. She snaps at Jamie tae even when he's nowhere near her. She's going around with her thin lips pursed up! An' her eyes! Well, ye can scarce see them, they're that screwed up. She's hardly speaking tae her ain mother! I expect it's because she has a wee bit extra work tae dae until Beth's fit again. Mind you, Mistress Fairly's gae cool wi' Sadie just now . . .'

'Och, I expect Sadie'll have been complaining about the extra work. I've always thought Mistress Fairly tried too hard wi' her.

Sometimes I'd have given her a good skelping if she'd been mine . . .'

'Ye didna skelp Lizzie and me . . .' Anna chuckled.

'No, but neither o' you two were as sullen as Sadie Fairly – even when ye werena pleased about things.'

'Well, I dinna ken what Beth's going tae dae with the babe when she's working outside again. Logan showed her how tae harrow in the corn with the horses last spring – in case he wasna here for this year's sowing. Thomas is depending on her being able tae help. Ye ken he canna dae everything. Besides, Mistress Fairly says he has tae plough one o' the grass fields. She says it's the regulations – to plant more corn.'

'Well, it wadna hurt Sadie Fairly tae harrow in the corn and let Beth nurse her ain bairn, but I ken she'll no' dae that.'

'The puir horses would have sore mouths if Sadie were driving them all day!'

'I'll tell ye what!' Janet exclaimed suddenly. 'Ye ken the bairn frae the Loandale cottages – Lucy Craig. Maybe Mistress Fairly would give her a trial at Fairlyden? She could keep an eye on the babe for Beth and help with the dishes and cleaning and suchlike . . . Her mother is wanting her fixed up with a job. She doesna want her tae go tae the munitions depot . . .'

'Mary Craig's lassie? But surely she's no' old enough tae work yet? She's just a wee thing . . .'

'Aye, she's small for her age and she's a bit delicate . . .' Janet agreed doubtfully. 'Maybe if she had some fresh air and a bit o' Mistress Fairly's cooking she'd be a bit healthier. She's thirteen, but she's an awfy shy, willing wee maid . . . Will ye mention her tae Mistress Fairly, Anna?'

Only Sarah understood the reason for Beth's excessively protective attitude towards her baby. Her first reaction had been to banish Sadie from Fairlyden completely, but it was almost impossible to get through the work as it was and it would be impossible to hire a replacement. Despite Sadie's constant grumbles she was an experienced milker and she knew the household and dairy routine.

'How was I tae ken she would have the bairn sae soon?' she had demanded sullenly when Sarah had tackled her.

'You knew it could not be long. You must have known the shock could bring on the birth.'

296

'Aye, well as far as I'm concerned it's just another mouth tae feed! Another body tae clothe!'

The confrontation had been the most unpleasant scene Sarah could remember since her marriage to William Fairly, but she clearly recalled the day she had tackled his half-brother, the late Sir James Fairly. He had had just that same vicious streak as Sadie, the same ruthless desire to destroy other people's happiness. Sarah had been awake for most of two nights mulling over her daughter's treacherous behaviour.

The second night she had risen, taken out her writing materials and written to Crispin Bradshaw. She had told him of the safe arrival of Kirsty Elizabeth, of Beth's amazing resilience, her joy in her baby daughter – and her protectiveness. Sarah could not bring herself to set out the details of her daughter's perfidy in black and white, but she did admit that she was ashamed of Sadie's behaviour.

Three days later she had received a brief letter from Yorkshire.

'I plan to visit Fairlyden during the second week of February, if the weather allows. Robert would like to accompany me but I understand how busy you must be, dear Sarah, believe me. Please let me know if I am asking too much. Ted Forbes's aunt is willing to come with us to Fairlyside but I think it would be even more trouble for you to air the rooms there, especially when our visit must be so short.'

Sarah had lost no time in assuring Crispin of a welcome, no matter how busy she was. She felt a great sense of relief. She needed to confide in someone she could trust, someone who would understand . . . Even to herself Sarah could not admit that she shared Beth's fear for the baby's safety.

When Anna related her mother's request concerning Lucy Craig, Beth was relieved and delighted by the idea of hiring the girl as Kirsty's nursemaid – her young guardian. Sarah agreed instantly. Privately she felt it must be God's guidance. Two days later Lucy was installed in the tiny maid's room above the Fairlyden kitchen with her scanty possessions. Almost from the moment she arrived, Lucy attached herself to Beth and her baby with a shy, dogged loyalty.

Crispin duly arrived in a hired cab with his nephew and a very bulky package on wheels. It was his gift for the baby.

297

'Why, it's a perambulator!' Beth gasped in astonishment. She was clearly overwhelmed by Crispin's generosity. He longed to tell her that she had given him a far greater gift – his own granddaughter; he wanted to tell her he was almost as relieved and delighted as herself and Logan . . . Instead he smiled down into her shining eyes and smiled his kindly smile.

'Now you'll be able to take the little lass with you wherever you go if you wrap her up in plenty of woollen blankets. This here keeps out the wind and rain see . . .' Crispin proudly demonstrated the hood. 'And this clips on the front . . . And inside there's a mattress. You can lift it up, look, and there's this flap underneath so you can use the bottom of the pram to store . . .' He paused, frowning. 'Well . . . store whatever babies need I suppose . . . Later on she will be able to sit up with her feet in the well.'

'Oh, Crispin . . .' Sarah began to laugh. Beth looked at her. It was the first time Mama Fairly had laughed – really laughed – since the night Kirsty was born. Sarah was unaware of the sudden transformation. 'It's a lovely gift, isn't it, Beth? B-but you're like a little boy with a new toy yourself!'

'Mmm . . . well I rather like the idea of babies on wheels . . . I'm sure they must enjoy it . . .?' Crispin's tone was defensive but there was a twinkle in his eye as he looked at Sarah. The look of intense strain which had been on her face five minutes ago seemed to have vanished like magic.

'I-I thought only ladies in big houses had perambulators,' Beth said softly. 'It's wonderful, Mr Bradshaw.' Suddenly she reached up and kissed him fleetingly on his cheek. Crispin's eyes were infinitely tender as he viewed her flushed face.

'Logan is a lucky man, my dear.'

'I shall write tae him again tonight and tell him how very generous ye are tae us.'

'Well, I must say it will be a lot easier than carrying the baby everywhere in a shawl,' Sarah agreed. 'Why, you'll be able to wheel her to the byre while we're milking, Beth.'

'Aye, aye I shall!' Beth's blue eyes reflected relief.

'Well, if all the excitement of the baby's carriage is over . . .?' Crispin's nephew, Robert Smith, came swinging into the kitchen on his crutches. 'What shall we do with the rest of the luggage? The coachman is wanting to get back to Muircumwell . . .'

★ ★ ★

298

It was three evenings later before Sarah found herself alone with Crispin. The household seemed to be bursting at the seams. Robert had a bed in the dining room since he could not climb the stairs. Amazingly it was Sadie who had organised that and she had spent a lot of time keeping him entertained.

'Sadie seems in remarkably good spirits, Sarah? I was rather anxious when I received your letter . . .'

'Mmm, I'm surprised at the trouble she is taking with Robert's comforts . . .' she admitted. 'And he seems to enjoy her talk of ladies' fashions. Is he becoming interested in such things?'

'In some aspects which might benefit the factory eventually, I think.' Crispin frowned thoughtfully. 'He certainly has some radical ideas, but maybe he and Ted Forbes will make a good partnership when the war is over . . .'

'There seems no end in sight.'

'No, but it must end sometime. No country can go on using up young lives for ever. There are reports that Germany is recruiting lads as young as fifteen. Then, there's the crippling costs of war.'

'Let's try to forget about the war, Crispin. Your visit is so short, and I'm so pleased you managed to come. Tell me about Robert and the factory?'

'Well, the Bradshaw Mill has always had a reputation for fine-quality cloth, but we've never made it up into garments. Robert believes there will be a market for made-up suits and ladies' skirts and such things, after the war. He thinks women will not want to go back to sewing their own clothes at home by hand.'

'He could be right there. I don't think anything will ever be the same again. And I'm sure even the most blind politician must see that women have earned the right to vote after all they have done to help.'

'Yes, many women have discovered a new freedom, despite the sorrow and hardships.' Crispin sighed. 'So, Robert may be right. Anyway he spends a lot of time making sketches of the kind of clothes he thinks our cloth would be most suited for. At least it keeps him occupied. Maybe Sadie's ideas will help him – the woman's point of view. Why were you so ashamed of her, Sarah?'

Slowly, suddenly reluctant, Sarah began to recount the events leading up to the birth of Beth's baby.

'You mean the child was actually born in the hayloft?'

Crispin's face paled visibly. 'Surely it was an accident? No one could be so cruel? So heartless as to . . .'

'To shut Beth up there deliberately . . .' Sarah's face was strained again as she thought of what might have happened if she had not discovered Beth's empty bed that night. 'I couldna tell anyone else. I am still ashamed that my own daughter could be so – so callous – vengeful even . . .' she whispered hoarsely. 'I shudder every time I think of it. Now you will understand why Beth will not leave her bairn alone with Sadie . . .?'

'Surely she would not harm the child now?'

'No-o. No, I don't think she would . . . but how can I be sure . . .? She shows no compunction for what she did . . .' Sarah shivered. 'I'm sorry, Crispin. I should not say such things. It hurts me to think them! Sadie is my own flesh and blood – but aah, I was sorely tempted to put her out of this house that night.'

'But you need her help.'

'Yes. It would leave too much for Beth to do if Sadie went away just yet, though Beth can tackle almost anything in the dairy or in the fields. She feels she is doing it for Logan – and Billy and Fairlyden.'

'And now there is another generation at Fairlyden . . .'

'Yes. You are very generous, Crispin. I know the perambulator will give Beth peace of mind. I think Lucy will be very loyal and reliable too . . . Somehow none of my problems seems so big when you are here to share them . . .'

'Maybe it will not be too long before I can come more often now that Ted Forbes is back, and Robert beginning to take an interest. It's strange how often things turn out for the best in the end. You know how much it pleases me, Sarah, to have your company.'

Thirty-Five

Kirsty proved to be a happy and contented baby, despite the trauma surrounding her birth. Beth derived great joy in feeding and caring for her in the long dark days while her own activities outside were curtailed. Her strength and energy had returned quickly, no doubt helped by Sarah's determination to provide her with the most nourishing food available.

'I remember lying in this very room and longing for a substantial meal, instead of being treated like an invalid,' she had declared with a wry smile.

Beth wrote long letters to Logan describing every detail of their daughter's progress. Later she was able to send him a photograph of herself with Kirsty in her arms. Once again it was Crispin who had arranged this and paid for the man and his little black tent to travel all the way from Dumfries.

'I shall write to thank Mr Bradshaw this very day,' Logan wrote jubilantly. 'I cannot tell you how proud I am of you both, dearest Beth. The photograph arrived the day before my birthday too – a wonderful surprise. The other chaps are almost as pleased as I am! There is a tremendous sense of friendship here – even if we do suffer some discomforts. We all share our parcels and everyone – even the C.O. – toasted your health and wee Kirsty's with bars of chocolate and lukewarm tea!

'I keep you and Kirsty next to my heart all the time.'

Tears sprang to Beth's eyes as she read. Logan always made light of the hardships. It had never been his nature to complain and Beth guessed he did not want to worry her, or his mother, but they had heard many tales of the squalor and misery. Some of the men who had been discharged on account of their injuries were still unable to talk of their time in the trenches, but there were others, like Jake Dodds's brother, who revelled in recounting the horrors. He had supposedly been discharged, too sick to serve his country, yet he seemed to have no visible injuries, except for a scar over his eye which he maintained gave him

301

violent headaches. Beth was sure he had wriggled out of the unpleasantness of war under false pretences. She looked forward to Logan's letters but she longed to see him again, to be able to show him his daughter in the flesh, to feel the strength of his arms around her.

As the weeks passed Beth gradually relaxed her protective guard over Kirsty but she had warned Lucy, her devoted nursemaid, never to leave Kirsty alone with Sadie. The girl had nodded obediently. She had not asked any questions. She had experienced Miss Sadie Fairly's sharp tongue on her second day at Fairlyden and she had been wary ever since; she resolved to guard her small charge with her life if necessary.

Although the days grew longer and lighter the weather was cold and wet and the spring sowing dragged on alarmingly. Beth was frequently too weary to complain as she trudged behind the horse, harrowing in the seeds which Thomas had sown. She was always pleased to see Lucy Craig struggling to push Kirsty's little carriage over the bumpy headland and it was a welcome relief to sit in the shelter of the hedge to feed her baby daughter.

'The Mistress has sent ye some oatcakes and cheese, Mrs Fairly,' Lucy reported shyly. 'And a bottle o' milk and a piece o' gingerbread. She says it's important for ye tae eat if ye're tae feed the bairn as well as doing a man's work in the fields.'

'Thanks, Lucy. I must confess I'm ready for it!'

'She gave me some tae. She's nice, isn't she, the old Mistress . . .'

'Mistress Fairly is very kind,' Beth smiled as she cradled Kirsty to her breast. She never thought of her mother-in-law as old.

It was well into April before all the spring corn was sown.

'It looks like being a late harvest again at this rate,' Thomas mumbled anxiously as he and Beth finally closed the gate on the last smooth brown field. Beth nodded but her mind was not on Thomas, or the sowing. It was more than two weeks since she had had a letter from Logan. Sometimes it took his letters longer to come, but he always wrote regularly.

'I know you can't help worrying, Beth,' Sarah said kindly as they watched Jim Braid on his bicycle turning on to the track to

302

Strathtod instead of coming up to the house. It had become part of his regular round to cut across the back of the Fairlyden steading on to the track for Strathtod. 'I expect they'll get another postie in Strathtod when the war is over,' Sarah mused aloud.

'Oh, I wish it was over now!' Beth exclaimed vehemently.

'Well, at least we haven't had a telegram,' Sarah comforted. 'I confess I dread the sight of wee yellow envelopes. They never seem to bring any good news.'

Two days later Jim Braid brought Beth the longed-for letter and a postcard for Sarah. As soon as she saw the address of one of the field hospitals Beth's face paled, but as she scanned the first few lines she relaxed a little. Logan had written very cheerfully and his first words were to tell her not to worry. Sarah looked up.

'Logan says you will give me the rest of his news, Beth, but he says I have no reason to worry for all he is in hospital . . .?'

'He says he took too big a puff of the German gas.' Beth frowned. 'But he says he wouldna be writing himself if he was really ill . . . D'ye think that's right?' Beth asked anxiously.

'I – yes, I think so, Beth. Ellen sometimes mentions writing letters for men who are too ill to write their own, or if they have lost an arm . . . Yes, I suppose we should find comfort if Logan is able to write himself. Read your letter, lassie, and enjoy it. You can tell me the rest of Logan's news later.'

Logan had described the crowded building and some of his fellow patients but he said little of his own condition.

'Although we can hear the shelling in the distance, it all seems relatively peaceful here, clean too! Though probably not according to your own standards, dearest Beth, or Mother's. How I long to be home again! Do you remember a poem we learned at school? While I am lying here thinking of you, some of the lines keep going round in my head. They remind me a little of Fairlyden.

> 'I remember, I remember,
> The house where I was born,
> The little window where the sun
> Came peeping in at morn;
> He never came a wink too soon . . . .

★   ★   ★

'There was more. Perhaps you can write it down for me so that my mind will stop going round in circles, if you have time to humour me, Beth? There was another verse too about roses, red and white. It makes me think of the roses we planted in the garden.

> 'The violets, and the lily-cups,
> Those flowers made of light!
> The lilacs where the robin built . . .'

Beth's heart ached for Logan so far away from the home he loved. In spite of his efforts to write cheerfully she sensed a homesickness in him that had not been so evident in his earlier letters.

Two days later she was amazed when Jim Braid delivered yet another letter from Logan, as well as one to his mother and her hand shook so much she could scarcely open it in case Logan was worse.

'My dearest Beth,I do believe I have had a most wonderful stroke of luck. Yesterday we had a new doctor doing the inspections. He read out my name twice – Logan Brad Fairly. He did not say anything else except that I am coming along nicely. Certainly breathing is a little easier.' Beth bit her lip. He had not mentioned any difficulty in his earlier letter.

'He – Doctor Fisher – looked at the photograph of you with Kirsty for a long time. He asked if I had seen her. I fear I was a little short. I mean, how could I see her when I have been stuck out here!

'Very late last night he came back to see me. Wakened me up in fact. He looked exhausted, but he had taken time to make enquiries. He sat on the edge of my bed and looked again at your photograph. Then he said slowly,

' "I know a fellow named Brad – an American volunteer. He was already out here when I joined this hellish war! He married one of our nurses. They'd known each other for years apparently. Strange really . . . she was Scottish too, and her name was Fairly . . ."

'I just gaped at him. "Ellen . . .?" I asked, though I scarcely believed such a coincidence.

304

' "The same. One of the best nurses we have, and they're all angels. So . . .? She really is your sister, then? She married Doctor Brad Leishman?"

'I could only nod. He nodded too and closed his eyes as though he was too weary to talk anymore. I was afraid he was going to fall asleep beside me. Then he opened his eyes and muttered. "It's a rotten bloody war!" (I'm sorry about the language, Beth, but it's exactly what he said – and he's right too). "They're a lovely couple. Just wonderful. Your sister is a courageous woman, Fairly. The best. She wouldn't let Dr Brad give up. She willed him to live. Did the same for Lord Willowman's younger son too. His father is mighty grateful, I'm told. His eldest son and heir left Oxford to join up as soon as war was declared. He was killed in the first month. Anyway, Lord Willowman would like to repay that sister of yours if he can find a way but she's working herself to death – do you know that, eh!"

'He sort of barked at me in his anger and frustration. Of course I didn't know anything about Lord Willowman. "Right then," he muttered gruffly. "I'll get it all arranged. How would you like to see that pretty little wife of yours, Fairly? And your brand new daughter?"

'I just stared at him. "We have to convince your sister that you need her to get you safely home. She needs a break, but she'll not leave Doctor Brad. You're about the only thing that'll take her away from that bloody hospital! It will not be for long, mind you, and I'm trusting you to look after Ellen and see that your family do too. I don't know whether Doctor Leishman will ever walk again, but he can use his brain and his hands; his courage and your sister's are the best example our wounded men could have. Of course troubles are a bit easier to bear here you know! So many others in the same bloody boat. So, Fairly! Prepare yourself for a visit to Scotland . . . A short one!" '

'He's coming home!' Beth gasped aloud, 'Logan's coming home! Oh, thank God!'

Sarah looked up from her own letter and her smile was tremulous. 'And Ellen too . . . but not for a little while yet, Beth. I pray nothing will happen to prevent them coming,' she added cautiously, looking at Beth's joyful face, at the tears of joy glistening in her blue eyes.

★ ★ ★

305

In many ways that late spring proved a blessing to Beth. Of course there was always the routine care of the animals, the feeding, cleaning and milking to be done, but the turnip hoeing had not started when Logan and Ellen arrived in the middle of May and the prospect of two precious weeks together seemed like a holiday in heaven.

Sarah was dismayed at the sight of Ellen. Her thick brown hair was almost as grey as her own and the skin was stretched tightly over her cheekbones. She had always had fine strong white teeth but now they seemed too big for her thin face. Sarah could not prevent a few tears as she embraced her beloved daughter.

'I'm so pleased – so very pleased to see you, lassie. Your grandfather is looking forward to a visit from you too – just as he always did!' She summoned a smile and was rewarded by the lightening in Ellen's shadowed eyes, then the old gentle smile which had always transformed her face.

'I'd almost forgotten how green . . .' She sketched a wide arc with her arm, her eyes drinking in the sloping fields and the distant hills. ' . . . How green and peaceful it is,' she finished huskily. 'I'm glad I've come, Mama . . .' They both turned to see Logan clasping Beth and his baby daughter to him as though afraid to let them go. Beth was laughing and crying all at once, while Kirsty cooed beguilingly.

'She's scarcely seen any men, except Thomas and Jim Braid, the postie, but you would think she knew Logan is her father,' Sarah marvelled.

'I believe ye like being a granny, Mama?'

'Yes. Kirsty seems to give us all hope for the future.'

'Is that my daughter ye're talking about?' Logan grinned, tearing himself away from Beth to hug his mother.

'I can hear the breath rasping in your chest like a rusty saw, Logie!' Sarah exclaimed involuntarily, echoing Beth's concern.

'Och, there's a lot o' soldiers worse than me. Tell them, Ellen . . .' Ellen regarded her youngest brother affectionately.

'Aye, there's a lot who have suffered badly frae the gas.' She did not add that many of them had been discharged from the army on account of it though. Ellen was concerned about Logan, despite his stoicism, but it would not do to let her mother or Beth suspect he could suffer from the effects of the dreaded gas for the rest of his life. She sighed. There was a desperate shortage of

306

fighting men; many would never survive, but many more would suffer from this dreadful war for as long as they lived, including her own dear Brad – but at least she still had him.

Wherever Beth went, whatever work she had to do, Logan was at her side. Whenever possible they took Kirsty with them, but Ellen enjoyed looking after her young niece. Sarah wondered if she and Brad would be able to have children, but she would not pry.

'I'm going to visit Grandfather tomorrow,' Ellen announced on her third evening. 'Are you and Beth coming with me in the trap, Logan? Mother had a letter frae Mr Bradshaw this morning. He would like to come up next week to see both of us before we return to France.'

'That's decent of him! Mr Bradshaw has been remarkably kind, especially tae Beth and me – Kirsty tae, bringing her a perambulator, just like the gentry! And I really appreciated the photograph of wee Kirsty with Beth . . . Aye, we must be here when he comes tae stay, but I'd like tae have a day at the Mains with Grandfather and Alex. What d'ye think, Beth? Shall we go tae the Mains tomorrow? The days seem tae be flying now I'm home. I wish . . . Och well, never mind what I wish . . . Maybe we could take Kirsty in her shawl if it's dry.'

'Shall we be back for the milking . . .?'

'Och, you enjoy yourself with Logan while you can, Beth.' Sarah smiled warmly at the two earnest young faces. 'We can manage the milking without you for once.'

'Indeed we cannot! She should dae her share! I shall be busy enough getting the rooms at Fairlyside opened up for Robert and Mr Bradshaw.'

'Oh, Sadie, dinna spoil Logan's visit! I thought you were really beginning to consider other people when you offered to open up some of the rooms at Fairlyside.'

'That's different.' Sadie pursed her thin lips in the way Logan remembered so well from their childhood. He grimaced but before he could say anything, Ellen intervened peaceably.

'I'll help ye with Mr Bradshaw's house, Sadie, and I'm sure Logan will help us move the furniture to make a bedroom downstairs for Robert . . .?'

'Of course.'

'And I could milk some o' Mrs Fairly's cows tomorrow,' Lucy Craig offered shyly. 'I'm no' feart o' them anymore.' She was so quiet they had forgotten her presence. Now Sarah turned to her with a smile. 'Of course! That would be a great help. Lucy didn't like cows when she first came to Fairlyden but she is becoming quite a good milker now.' The young maid flushed with pride. 'I'm sure Anna will milk a few extra too. So, that's settled . . .' Sarah broke off with a sigh as Sadie flounced out of the kitchen without a word. 'I know your grandfather will be really pleased to see you all, but remember he's eighty-one now. He's getting very frail for all his mind is still so alert. I'm surprised Sadie is being so uncooperative over the milking. She was unbelievably pleasant and helpful with Crispin's nephew and she has visited the Mains regularly these past few weeks.'

'Has she?' Ellen's eyebrows rose. 'She used to detest the long drive to the Mains.'

'We-ell, perhaps she's growing up at last.' Sarah glanced at Beth. Logan knew nothing of his sister's malicious trick on the night of Kirsty's birth. Beth had had no desire to worry him and Sarah had expressed her own relief, and gratitude, at her reticence. But she knew Beth would never forget her fearful experience, nor Sadie's treachery. Sadie's moods had changed as often as the weather in recent weeks.

'You'll see the German prisoners when you turn off for the Mains. They're billeted in the old mill and the officers in charge of the prisoners stay in the Mill House. They march down to work at the peat every morning. I've seen them several times when I've been to the Mains. They look so ordinary. Some of them seem very young . . .'

'They are ordinary, Mama.' Ellen's voice was quiet, and strangely sad. 'And many of them are young too – but so is Logan. I'm sure most of them dinna want tae fight this dreadful war . . .'

Logan nodded agreement but made no comment as he accompanied Beth and Lucy to the byre.

'I thought I would feel so bitter if any o' the Germans were brought to us for nursing . . .' Ellen's voice was no more than a whisper, but Sarah halted on her way to the door. She sensed the time had come for Ellen to put aside her mask; she recognised her need to talk.

'I thought I should want to kill them all after . . . after what they did to Brad and – and after seeing our ain brave soldiers suffering so terribly. But they lie there with pain etched on their gaunt faces, their eyes pleading for help, and even . . . even for death. They're human beings, Mama – just like you and me. They feel the same pain . . . suffer the same loss, miss their ain loved ones . . .' Her voice cracked suddenly. 'Oh God! Sometimes it's terrible . . .' She began to weep, silently, her too-thin body shaken by shuddering sobs. Sarah moved to her then and held her in her arms, waiting quietly for the storm to subside, knowing that the tears would wash away a little of her tension. What a wise man that Doctor Fisher was, Sarah thought with a flash of insight. Ellen had been driving herself continually, but the unrelenting work had brought her almost to breaking point . . .

At length Ellen raised her tear-drenched face and scrubbed her eyes with the back of her hand as she used to do when she was a child. Her long dark lashes were stuck together in little spikes. She looks so vulnerable! Sarah felt tears burning the back of her own eyes. Her heart ached for the daughter she had borne and could no longer comfort. 'I didna want tae leave . . .' Ellen confessed brokenly, 'but Brad insisted that Logan needed me more than he did for a week or two. Oh, Mama . . . I'm so glad I came home tae ye . . .'

'So am I, lassie, so am I . . .'

Thirty-Six

The second week of Logan's and Ellen's visit was even more pleasant and relaxed. Sadie, to everyone's surprise, volunteered to look after Mr Bradshaw and his nephew at Fairlyside and the atmosphere seemed lighter in her absence.

The grey skies cleared and the birds sang as they darted backwards and forwards between the rickyard and the hawthorn hedges, with their trophies of straw to build yet another nest, or to feed their fledglings. Kirsty shook her chubby fists at them and gurgled with delight from the sheltered depths of her brown perambulator. The moment Jamie MacFarlane arrived home from school he became Logan's shadow.

'Mistress Beth says ye used tae ken where all the birds had their nests when ye were young. Tell me where tae look for a wren's nest . . .?' he pleaded. Or, 'Are there really trout up the burn, Master Fairly? Is't true ye can catch them with your hands?'

'Jamie makes me feel as though I'm old and wise!' Logan chuckled late one evening as he lay beside Beth in the big bedroom at Fairlyden. Beth turned into the circle of his arms and smiled.

'And are ye – wise I mean?'

'Right now I feel neither old nor wise . . .' His voice thickened as he looked down into her dreamy eyes. Beside the wall Kirsty slept peacefully in the crib where Logan and his brothers and sisters had once slept. 'But I do feel a very happy man, Beth . . .' After the first passionate reunion their loving had become tender, almost reverent – each night a precious gift.

'It's very good of you to take on extra work looking after Uncle Crispin and me, Sadie. You must have been up at the crack of dawn to milk your cows and be back here to cook our breakfast . . .?' Robert Smith manoeuvred his crutches and sank on to a chair, leaning his elbow on the table. 'I'm getting better with

311

these wooden props of mine, don't you think?'

'Aye, ye're managing fine. Ye seem in good spirits this morning.'

'I am. I had some great ideas for sketches last night. I know you're interested in the changing fashions. I'll show them to you later – if you have time, that is?'

'Of course I'll make time!' There was more warmth and enthusiasm in Sadie's tone than usual.

'You really don't mind coming down here to look after us then?'

'No, I dinna mind. I told ye. As a matter of fact I like it here. It's a far easier house tae look after than Fairlyden – more compact, and yet all the rooms are big and light and the carpets and furniture are lovely. Anyway it's a relief tae have peace frae crying bairns and washing napkins, drying clothes . . .'

'You sound as though you don't like babies anymore than I do . . .?'

'I dinna. They're aye demanding attention! If they dinna want tae be fed, they're wanting tae be cleaned or changed or put tae bed or lifted up . . .'

'But most women want their own babies, even if they don't like other folks – don't they?'

'Well, I'm different tae "most women" then.'

'Do you mean that, Sadie? You really wouldn't mind if you married and your husband couldn't give you children?' Sadie heard the tension in his voice and she knew the reason. She turned away in case he detected a gleam of satisfaction in her eyes. She knew he couldn't sire any bairns. She'd overheard his uncle discussing his injuries, hadn't she?

'If I marry it will be because o' the man himself – not for the sake o' what he can give me – least of all his bairns.' She cast a sly glance over her shoulder and saw a thoughtful expression on his lean face.

'I'm glad you like this house,' he said as though changing the subject. He paused. 'I have two houses which belonged to my parents, then there's Grandfather Bradshaw's Yorkshire house, where Uncle Crispin and I stay just now . . . I have plans for it when Uncle Crispin is finished with it. It's very handy for the factory so I would have to keep it now that I'm getting involved . . . I must say I like Fairlyside better than I expected. Maybe I could keep it as a country retreat – when I'm needing inspiration. Uncle Crispin always seems to return refreshed, almost rejuvenated you might say, after he's had a visit to Scotland.'

'But Fairlyside is his own house, isn't it?' Sadie remarked, her tone deceptively casual. 'It never belonged to your grandfather.'

'I expect it will be mine one day, along with everything else, including the extra money he has invested in the factory. After all, I'm Uncle Crispin's only relative. Of course I don't know much about his private affairs, but I believe he still owns some land around here. Isn't it part of Fairlyden? I seem to remember your parents owned the house and buildings and some of the fields . . . but they rented the rest from my grandfather?'

'Aye. Your Uncle Crispin kept it when he sold the rest o' Strathtod Estate. It all belonged to my ancestors once.' There was a hint of bitterness in Sadie's tone. Robert Smith eyed her speculatively.

'Well, my father didn't own a thing! But he married well . . .' There was wry amusement in his tone. 'He lived like a gentleman before the war – on the money Grandfather Bradshaw allowed my mother . . .'

'Did ye approve?'

'I did at the time.' He shrugged. 'But I've had plenty of time to think . . .' He grimaced towards the empty, pinned-up leg of his trousers. 'I shall never be as philanthropic as Uncle Crispin . . . but I think I needed a challenge. I've certainly got one – learning to cope with this! But maybe I shall make something of my life after all. Who knows, Sadie Fairly, once this bl . . . Sorry! Once this war is over and we can get servants to work in the houses again, maybe I shall persuade some young woman or other to marry me and help me on the road to success.' He caught Sadie's hand briefly. 'Of course it would have to be a woman who was interested in clothes and fashions, a woman with ambition who didn't want to spend her time in the nursery . . .' He grinned. 'Who can tell what the future holds . . .?'

Sadie looked down at him, her pale eyes shrewd, but less hard than usual. 'Indeed, who can tell?' she echoed.

A little while later Sadie was thoughtful as she washed the breakfast dishes. If I marry Robert I shall be mistress of his house in Yorkshire – and I shall be mistress of all this too, she decided with satisfaction. When he inherits the land belonging tae Fairlyden we shall be the landlords! There'll be no more piano playing and singing, and acting the 'my Lady Elizabeth Fairly' then . . . It could all be mine – if I marry Robert! Yet something in Sadie quivered restlessly. If she married Robert Smith she might never know the wonderful sensations that were hinted at in the romances she read so avidly . . . Unless she embarked on a little adventure of her own, as all the best heroines did . . .? Her pulses quickened as she thought of the handsome young prisoner with the infectious grin who waved and smiled whenever she passed the peat works on her way to the Mains . . . Once he had lifted his cap at her and she had seen the gleam of his golden hair. When the war was over he would go away . . . Sadie frowned. Everybody expected Great Britain to win the war, but supposing the Germans won? It might be wise to have a friend on the other side then . . .? A foot in both camps . . .?

There were only three days left before Logan and Ellen were due to return to France. There were reports that large numbers of Americans had enrolled for military service.

'Surely such combined strength will end the war soon?' Beth voiced a hope that would find an echo in thousands of hearts.

'It canna go on much longer, surely?' Sarah agreed. 'If the newspapers are right it is costing seven million pounds a day. That alone must bring it to an end . . .'

'But until there is peace we must all return tae our duties,' Logan reminded them quietly. His face had grown pale and strained as the days flew by. Sarah's heart went out to him.

Her anxiety for her own son was temporarily set aside the following day when Thomas returned from taking the milk to the morning train. He had formed a habit of calling in at the Store, mainly for a newspaper, but partly because news of the village and the parish filtered in to Janet and Lizzie and was mulled over and discussed by all who entered the Store, but the scattered community also had a wealth of sympathy and compassion to offer for those in distress. This morning the distress was Janet's and her family's.

'It's M-Maggie and Ewan's l-laddie,' Thomas stammered, white-faced. 'They've had a telegram tae say he's been reported missing, p-presumed d-dead.'

'Oh, Thomas! Surely not young Donald! It seems no time since he went. I – I . . . Alex hoped they would release him for essential work . . .'

'Aye, I ken, Mistress.' Thomas looked hopefully from Sarah to Logan and Ellen. 'It does just say missing though . . . Maybe they'll find him yet . . .? Anyway I'd best go and break the news tae Anna.'

When he had gone Sarah turned to Logan and Ellen. 'Is there much hope, do you think? That they will find Donald alive?'

Ellen met her brother's eyes. Logan was deathly pale. Donald Donelly was a year younger than himself and had been just as full of life; he had loved his work . . . 'There's scarcely a hope in . . . scarcely any hope at all!' he exclaimed bitterly. 'It's just the kindest way o' telling the families back home that their lads have been blown tae bits and there's no body – or that they've drowned in the b . . . in the mud!'

'Logan . . .' Ellen's voice was quiet but she looked pointedly at Beth and her mother.

Logan followed her glance, instantly regretting his outburst. Billy could be reported missing any day and they would all cling to straws . . . 'I – I'm sorry. Of course there's always hope. We'd all be dead without hope . . . It's just that – well, Donald was younger than I am.' Sarah noticed the past tense in silence.

'Poor Maggie . . .'

'Ye didna bring many clothes with ye, Ellen.' Sadie was watching her sister pack her bag ready to leave early the following morning.

'Clothes were the last thing on my mind when I heard that Logan was sick enough to be posted home.'

'He's not that bad!'

'The gas can have such longterm effects, especially if he gets any more – or even if he has to suffer the chillingly damp conditions of the trenches.' Ellen straightened up and looked at Sadie. 'Do you know that some of our soldiers work for stretches of twenty-four hours or more up to their waists in mud and water when it rains, or where the land is without drainage . . .?'

'Well, dinna look at me like that! It isna my fault! I didna ask them tae go tae war.'

'They didn't ask to go to war either.'

'Billy did! He wanted a war. He wanted tae get awa' frae here!'

315

'He would have had to fight anyway when they brought in conscription.'

'Well, I think he enjoys it, especially now he's driving a tank. Though he hardly ever sends more than a postcard.'

Ellen sighed and changed the subject. 'I dinna expect Grandfather will last much longer. Mind you, there's worse things than death and at least he is prepared . . . I feel he's almost longing to go now he's so frail. Mother says ye've visited him regularly lately . . .' Ellen was astonished to see Sadie's pale face flush bright crimson. She looked . . . guilty? Ellen frowned. 'Come to think of it . . .' she murmured slowly, trying to recall the exact words, 'Aunt Beatrice said they hadna seen . . .'

'Ye've nae right checking up on me wi' Aunt Beatrice! She's not our real aunt anyway. Grandfather pays her to look after him so why should I c—?'

'For goodness' sake, Sadie! Calm down! I havena been checking up on you! Why should I? It's just that Aunt Beatrice said you stay such a short time, yet Mother thinks . . .' Ellen broke off, frowning at her younger sister's expression. Her pale face was convulsed with anger and guilt. But why? Suddenly Ellen's heart went cold. 'Not the prisoners? Surely ye're not one o' the – the women Alex was talking about . . .? Hanging round the prison camp or the field where they're digging peat? Women like . . .'

'Ye've nae room tae talk! Or tae lecture me! I remember ye going off tae Edinburgh tae be with Brad Leishman before he went tae America – and ye needna pretend tae be innocent! I found the letter ye wrote tae Mother! "Please trust me, Mama!" ' Sadie mocked scornfully. 'Ye might hae fooled the Reverend Morrison with all that talk about staying with Sir What's-his-name and his Lady wife – but ye didna fool me! Not when I'd had time tae think about it!'

'Stop it!' Ellen's face had grown deathly white as she listened to her sister's tirade. 'Brad and I did nothing to be ashamed of in Edinburgh. If you want the truth I sometimes regretted being sae chaste when he was sae far away and it seemed he'd never come back. But at least I loved him and he loved me! Ye dinna even ken the prisoners, much less love one o' them! Prisoners, Sadie! D'ye no' understand the shame ye'd bring on Mother – and everybody connected tae ye – if ye were caught associating with a prisoner o' war! And your ain brothers out

316

there fighting! I'd die before I'd . . .'

'Och, spare me the Saint Ellen bit! If ye must ken I'm going tae marry Robert Smith when the war's over!' It was an impulsive, even desperate, attempt to divert her sister's attention, and it succeeded. Ellen's eyes widened and then filled with relief. She always had lovely big brown eyes, Sadie thought enviously.

'Does Mother ken? When did he ask ye? Do ye . . .?'

'He hasna asked yet! But he will . . .'

'I see . . .' Ellen sat down on the bed with a thump. 'I'll never understand ye, Sadie. Do ye mean . . .?' She thought of Sadie's romantic notions, the ideas gleaned from the novelettes she devoured, her dreams of marrying a golden-haired Adonis like the hero in one of her magazines . . . 'D'ye ken Robert Smith canna have children or . . . or be a real husband . . .?'

'So? That's all the more reason why I should have a wee bit romance before I'm a respectable matron. Anyway who told ye, about Robert, I mean?'

'Mother did. She says Mr Bradshaw is vexed for him. After all he'll never have a child to inherit, and he will be quite wealthy one day . . .' Ellen broke off. Suddenly she knew why her sister wanted to marry Robert when she had spurned the attentions of many of the local boys – all except the Reverend Morrison. Sadie had always wanted a position – with servants to do her bidding . . . the best silver . . . ribbons and laces . . . Her aspirations to be a lady . . .

'Dinna stare at me like that!'

'Like what?'

'As though ye'd never seen me before!'

Maybe I never have seen the real you before, little sister, Ellen thought sadly. Aloud she said quietly, 'I hope you and Robert will be very happy.'

'Ye'll not tell Mother, Ellen?' Sadie's voice was sharp, but it was probably as near to pleading as it was ever likely to be, Ellen decided wryly.

'No . . . no, I shallna tell Mother. I shall wait for her to write and tell me your news.' Ellen remembered the prisoners of war and their guards. She had seen them on her way to the Mains. Their barracks, at the old mill, were not so very far from the bottom of Fairlyden's Low Meadow. 'Dinna play with fire though. Remember Robert's no fool, Sadie, even if he is housebound when he's at Fairlyside. If he ever heard . . .'

'What d'ye mean?' Sadie demanded sharply, but Ellen had already opened the door, indicating all too clearly that she had no desire to continue this particular conversation. Inwardly she felt sick with contempt – and even fear – for the silly, selfish girl who was her own sister.

It was some time before Beth could bring herself to eat a proper meal after Logan's departure. Saying goodbye had been every bit as heart-breaking as she and Logan had feared, despite their resolve to be calm and cheerful.

'I know the King asked us all to eat a quarter of the bread we're used to eating, Beth, and to cut out meat once a week, but you're not eating enough to keep a sparrow alive,' Sarah protested anxiously.

'I ken, but I just feel it would choke me . . .'

'I understand you're tense and anxious, lassie, but for your bairn's sake – and Logan's too – you'll have to keep your strength up. After all the war may be over soon. They say the American soldiers received a hero's welcome when they landed in France and surely . . .'

'But they're not the ones who're heroes!' Beth bit her lip. 'I-I'm sorry, I didna mean tae snap. I'm glad they're going to help. If only I could be sure Logan will keep well and come back safely . . .'

Sarah nodded. 'Well, if nothing else, we must do our bit for the country. It will take us a long time to hoe the turnips. You'll need all your strength. We canna manage without you, Beth. And at the rate the grass is growing the hay will be ready to cut before we know it!' Beth nodded but she still felt utterly bereft.

Ellen wrote to them as soon as she reached the Field Hospital in France.

'I hated leaving you all and the peace of Fairlyden, but I returned to the most wonderful surprise. I realised the break had given me new strength, but I also know now that it was engineered as much for my benefit as for Logan's. Brad travelled to England the day after I left. He has had an operation to remove a piece of shell which was lodged near his spine. We knew it was the cause of his paralysis. Brad did not want me to know about the operation until it was over; it could have gone so dreadfully wrong. Even now I shudder to think of it. Dearest

318

Brad, he knew how worried I would have been. In fact I do not think I could have borne it. Lord Willowman has been corresponding secretly with him and it was he who paid for the services of one of the most eminent surgeons in Britain. Brad is still in London, where he is learning to walk again. He has so much courage! I can scarcely concentrate on my work when we are apart, but I know how badly every pair of hands is needed here. I can only pray the fighting will end soon so that we may all live together in peace. Brad sends his love to you all and promises we shall visit Fairlyden together the next time.'

Logan had further to travel and another week had passed before Beth received a letter. Even then she worried. She guessed Logan had been too weary and sick at heart to dissemble much when he was writing. His misery was clear to her despite the ordinary sentences telling her he had arrived safely, though cold, wet and damnably weary. She knew he was missing her as much as she was missing him, probably more, she thought despondently. At least I have Kirsty and a roof over my head and enough to eat and a dry bed . . .

She realised that in his weary state he had probably been less careful with his choice of words than usual, yet the censor must have passed his letter.

'It must have rained every day and every night while I have been away, judging by the mud. The duck boards are floating in some of the trenches. Worst of all is the absence of so many familiar faces – young men no older than myself, men whom I had learned to value as true friends. Now they are facing their Maker and this world's joys are lost to them. I have been absent so short a time – or at least it seemed a short time to me. But then I was in heaven with you, dearest Beth. My comrades were not so fortunate.'

Gradually Beth summoned all her energy for the tasks which were so essential to Fairlyden's survival, and her appetite began to improve. Thomas was fully occupied with the horse hoe and keeping the potato drills clean. It was vital to the country, as well as to Fairlyden, to see that every crop yielded as much as possible. The new Agricultural Committees had brought in several new regulations. Some of the landlords and farmers were dismayed at the extent of the government's interference but not all the regulations were bad. Regular farm workers were to receive increased pay with a minimum wage fixed by the government. Wheat was to have a guaranteed price and the millers were instructed to extract more flour despite the grumbles of the people.

'Better to eat black bread than have no bread, I suppose,' Anna remarked philosophically. 'I think Mother would like the government to go ahead with their plans for rationing everything. Some people are so disagreeable if she canna supply what they want.' Beth was grateful for Anna's easy chatter as they worked day after day at the turnip hoeing with Sadie and Lucy. Sarah frequently joined them in the afternoons and evenings, when the dairy work was done. Kirsty sat up in her pram now, sometimes she cried when they were a long way down the field, sometimes she slept. Everywhere women were doing their best to help on the farms as well as in the factories and hospitals, on omnibuses and in offices – places where women had scarcely been allowed to venture before the war. Many of them had been reared as genteel young ladies so even Sadie refrained from grumbling too often.

Everyone at Fairlyden had noticed how attentive she had been to Robert Smith during his stay at Fairlyside. Beth had gained the impression that Robert was not averse to her either, so she was surprised when she accidentally discovered that Sadie was meeting another young man, apparently in secret.

Kirsty was teething and reluctant to sleep one evening. Consequently it was almost dark by the time Beth went to shut in the hens. She was walking slowly back to the house, her thoughts with Logan, her body longing for the familiar feel of his arms, her heart aching at the memory of their walks together as the evening shadows lengthened. She stood still for a little while, breathing in the fresh night air, gazing up at the blue-black of the midsummer sky and the darker shadows of thickening cloud. The night silence was broken by the unexpected sound of a woman's stifled laughter, followed by the deeper chuckle of a man. Beth blinked in astonishment. Then she heard Sadie's voice – low, faintly muffled, but quite distinct – indeed more distinct than usual because she was pronouncing each syllable slowly and with extraordinary care. 'I would have come to the hollow. You are taking a risk.'

Her companion's voice was indistinct but the voice was deep. Beth wondered why he couldn't have come to the house to speak

to Sadie? Maybe she had a secret assignation with one of the
soldiers home on leave? Yet I've never heard Sadie's name linked
with any of the village boys. She always gave the impression
they were beneath her notice, Beth thought. But she was too
tired to ponder Sadie's peculiar arrangements. Certainly she had
no desire to eavesdrop on other young lovers. She wanted Logan
and she cared nothing for anything else! Silently she made her
way back to the house. Tomorrow Thomas planned to start
scything the outer edges of the hay fields ready for the mowing
machine. She would need a good night's rest if she was to be any
use. Could Logan have given me another bairn? she wondered
vaguely. Is that why I feel so listless?

Thirty-Seven

Two nights later Beth was shutting in the hens again when she saw the shadowy figure of a man creeping stealthily from the darkened stable. She had just met Sadie on her way indoors so she could not be meeting her secret lover tonight. Her heartbeat quickened, but even as she watched the man left the shadows and ran swiftly across the rickyard, vaulted the wall and disappeared from sight. Slowly Beth's heart resumed its usual rhythm. Whoever he was he must be very agile. Probably a poacher, she thought, hunting rabbits for his family now that meat had become scarce and expensive.

Several times during the next few weeks Beth thought there were fewer eggs than there ought to be, and twice she thought she glimpsed the figure of a man gliding away into the deepening shadows. Och, it's your ain imagination playing tricks, she told herself sternly.

Making hay was a slow process with the continual showers and Fairlyden seemed to get more than its fair share of rain when the wind was in the west. On the other hand even Logan had mentioned the heavy rain several times in his letters. Beth sensed the weather was depressing him more than usual despite his efforts to write cheerfully of food parcels and trench humour, of Jocks and Macs, Tommys, Taffys and Paddys. She longed to be with him, to warm him, hug him tight . . . to love him.

She was convinced now that she was expecting another child but the tired, sickly feeling which had dragged her down almost since Logan's departure was beginning to lift. She would never be truly happy until the war was finished and Logan was home again with her and Kirsty, but for all that she was aware of a lightening of her spirits. Maybe it would cheer Logan too, if he kens we're tae have another bairn, she thought. Maybe it will be a laddie this time; he'll like a son tae talk tae as he talks tae Jamie MacFarlane. I will write tonight and tell him, but I will ask him to keep it as our very ain secret. I dinna want Sadie tae ken . . . Beth shuddered involuntarily; she could not help reliving a little of the terror she had known the night Kirsty was born, the long hours alone in the darkness of the loft with only the mice for company.

Haymaking dragged on into August. None of it was good because of the constant wetting and drying but at least they had managed to cart a large part of the crop into the two lofts. Some of it had been built into hotts to be brought in at a later date. Only the Low Meadow remained.

'It's the bottom half o' the meadow that's the problem,' Thomas mumbled gloomily as they halted for their midday meal one day in the middle of August. 'It's such a steep slope down into the hollow, the horses would never pull the cart back out when it's sae wet.'

'We shall just have tae concentrate on getting the rest safely home then,' Beth suggested, 'and leave the hollow until last.'

'Aye, I suppose sae. I'll awa' for ma dinner then. Look, who's that riding up frae Muircumwell? I dae believe it's the Reverend Morrison.'

'Mmm, ye're right, Thomas. Sadie has already gone for her dinner so I'd better hurry and wash my hands . . .' Beth wondered what could be bringing the Minister to Fairlyden today. He must know they would all be busy at the hay.

'We were just going to have a bite to eat. Would you care to join us?' Sarah invited cordially after the Minister's initial greeting.

'No thank you, Mistress Fairly. Mine will be ready when I get back and I know how busy all the farmers are today.' His thin face was grave. 'I'm not here with good news, I'm afraid. Doctor Kerr was on his way up to Fairlyden after he called at the Manse so I volunteered to come instead. He thought you ought to know – or at least Mistress O' Connor thought you would want to know – that Mr Logan is not too well today . . .'

'Not too well . . .' Sarah repeated slowly, her brown eyes fixed on the Minister's face. 'My father has been going downhill ever since Ellen went away. He has no fear of dying, as I'm sure you know, Mr Morrison . . .'

'I do. He has told me several times that he has had a good life. Not all sunshine of course, but he considers he has been truly blessed for all that. He does not want anyone to grieve for him . . .'

'No . . . but I would like to be with him . . . What did Doctor Kerr say exactly?'

'Your father is sleeping a lot. Doctor Kerr thinks he will gradually fall into a last long sleep . . . It could be a day, or three or four days, he cannot tell, but he said I was to assure you that Mr Logan is in no pain. He is at peace. Mistress O'Connor thinks you will wish to be with him if you can. I am going to the Mains myself this afternoon. I could give you a lift in the Manse trap if you wish to visit today?'

'Thank you . . .' Sarah's voice was soft, wistful. More than anything on earth she wanted to be with her father now, one last talk perhaps . . .? A gentle smile . . .?

Young Lucy stared at her in awe. Death was a dreadful thing, a thing to be feared. How could the kindly Mistress be so calm? Surely she must care if the old man was her father . . .?

'Wouldn't ye like tae stay at the Mains, Mama Fairly?' Beth asked gently, sensing Sarah's yearning to be with her father now the end was so near.

'Yes, I would like to stay . . . until the end. But the hay . . .' She looked across at Sadie. Her daughter's mouth was thin.

'I dinna see what good ye can dae now. Alex is there, and Emma and Mistress O'Connor.'

'Perhaps I should wait until the hay is finished . . .'

'That may be too late, Mistress Fairly.' The Reverend Morrison's face was troubled. 'At least come with me this afternoon?'

'We can manage the rest of the hay, I'm sure.' Beth looked impatiently across at Sadie. Surely she knew her mother needed their support and cooperation now, today, before it was too late! 'I could take Kirsty with me,' Sarah said suddenly. 'If you're agreeable, Beth? It would be a wee bit less work for you, and Lucy would be able to help you and Sadie . . .? Emma would be pleased to look after her.'

Beth hesitated. She and Kirsty had never been apart for more than an hour or two . . . But she knew Emma loved children. She would have one of her own in another month or two, God willing. And if Mama Fairly was away from home Sadie would be sure to seize every chance to stay in the house instead of working in the fields . . . 'Aye, it would be a great help if I kenned Kirsty was being looked after, if ye're sure she willna disturb Mr Logan?'

'She will not disturb anyone. Even if she cries the Mains house is big enough to make sure my father has peace. Besides I think he will be happy to see Kirsty once more . . .' She turned to the Minister. 'He is very proud to be a great-grandfather. He says he can die in peace now that he knows there will be another generation at Fairlyden . . .'

'I'm sure you're right, Mistress Fairly. So you will accompany me this afternoon . . .?'

'I will drive ye down tae the Manse in the trap,' Beth offered, 'but first I must pack some clothes for Kirsty. I hope Mistress O'Connor willna object to all the extra baby washing . . .'

'Beatrice loves children, always has,' Sarah assured her. 'And in my heart I know it will not be for long . . .'

The Minister nodded agreement and turned to the door but then he hesitated, frowning. 'I don't wish to frighten any of you but there have been rumours in the village that one of the German prisoners from the Mill has been seen about several times in the evenings, after they have finished work.'

'One of the prisoners? Surely they are not allowed to wander freely in the district?' Sarah's tone held consternation.

'The officer in charge was very indignant at the suggestion. He has strongly denied that any of his prisoners could escape the vigilance of his guards, but he admits that one of them is a particularly daring young man and not one to resist a challenge, or a wager. Two of the men at the peat works believe his fellow prisoners challenge him to steal fresh eggs from the neighbouring farms, or butter from the dairies. Apparently some of the local girls have been seen from time to time around the peat works too. But the prisoners probably converse in their own language and I doubt if our own men understand a word of it! I am simply warning you all to be on your guard. After all, there is only Thomas here to protect you . . .'

Beth drew in her breath. Her eyes seemed drawn to Sadie, studiously concentrating on moving a tablespoon from one place to another for no particular reason.

While Sarah was away Beth and Anna and Lucy worked hard, helping Thomas bring in the hay. As Beth had suspected Sadie found plenty of reasons for remaining in the house, at least during the day, but when evening came she washed her face and put on a clean white apron to take a stroll around the yard. This was a matter of some amusement to Anna.

'Does she think the chickens and hens appreciate her clean pinny! She doesna even shut them in at night for ye, Beth.'

'Och, I dinna mind shutting in the hens . . .' Beth said slowly. 'Usually I enjoy a stroll in the peace of the evening, before the day dies away, but last night when I was down at the burn shutting in the pullets, I'm almost certain I saw a man darting frae the rickyard and intae the Low Meadow. There's another thing too, I ken there were eggs in the nest in the barn at milking time but they had gone last night . . . unless ye brought them in, Lucy . . .?'

'No, Mrs Fairly, I didna collect them. D'ye think that German prisoner has been up here at Fairlyden?' she asked, her eyes round with sudden terror.

'No, no, I'm sure he wouldna dare – even if he did escape frae the guards.' Beth reassured the frightened little maid instinctively, but she could not prevent a frisson of fear shivering down her own spine at the thought of the terrible, ruthless enemy living so close to Fairlyden. Then she chided herself for being silly. The German prisoners might be dangerous but the guards would never allow them to escape. It was more likely that one of their own men was shirking his duties, even stealing from the farms perhaps . . .? And throwing suspicion on the German prisoners? Few of the local people would be brave enough to tackle such a dangerous adversary.

Beth did not tell Lucy or Anna of the simpering laughter she had heard coming from the loft above the stable, or the grunts and sighs and whispers which had followed. She was certain it was Sadie. She was surprised that Logan's fastidious sister would stoop to clandestine meetings, especially so soon after she had set out to win the admiration of Robert Smith. She remembered Sadie's snide remarks about herself and Logan. At least we loved each other, we did not hide from the world, Beth thought.

It had been a temptation to take her revenge and remove the ladder, leaving Sadie and her 'friend' trapped in the loft all night as she had been. Then she considered how shocked Mama Fairly would be if she ever discovered her daughter's odd behaviour. Who could the young man be who was too ashamed to come openly to Fairlyden? Did he already have a wife? Was that the

327

reason for Sadie's secrecy? Could he be one of the English guards from the mill?

The following night the same thing happened again and this time Beth knew there was no mistake. She saw the figure of the man melting away into the shadows. He was too far away for Beth to see his face but before he disappeared over the wall into the field he paused and waved to someone. Beth turned her head and saw Sadie Fairly standing in the open door of the stable returning the salute, a smile of satisfaction on her thin face. As though sensing someone's presence she peered into the shadowy yard. Beth continued walking and would have proceeded into the house, but as she drew nearer Sadie snarled, 'So ye have been spying! I suppose it was you we heard the other night!' Her narrow face twisted with such hatred that Beth momentarily recoiled.

'Spying? I've nae desire tae spy on anyone, but . . .'

'But ye think ye'll just mention it tae "Mama Fairly"!' Sadie mocked. 'Well, I'm warning ye, if ye sae much as mention Kas . . . mention anybody being here I shall tell her he came tae see you, that ye couldna wait for your ain husband tae come hame frae the war, that . . .'

'Stop it! Stop it!' Beth almost screamed. 'You ken I'd never look at another man beside your ain brother! As for telling your mother ye're ashamed o' the company ye keep, I wouldna hurt her with such tales, though I've nae doubt she'll hear soon enough if ye carry on, but that's your business.'

'Aye, it is my business! See and remember that or ye'll pay for your spying and your tales! You and your brat!'

'Don't threaten me, Sadie.' Beth's firm, quiet voice held none of the contempt which showed so plainly on her expressive face. Sadie's eyes narrowed. There's something evil when she looks at me like that, Beth thought, and she could not suppress the shiver which ran down her spine. 'I'm away tae bed!' She turned away impatiently, annoyed with herself for bandying words with Sadie tonight, annoyed that she had allowed herself to feel upset . . . aye and frightened . . . She shivered again, yet she was not cold.

That night Beth had difficulty sleeping. When she did she had a terrible nightmare and she felt exhausted when she wakened. Even then she could not shake off the memory of the nightmare

– or the fear which had gripped her.

Logan had been calling for her and she could not find him. She turned this way and that but wherever she turned there were bodies and arms reaching out to her, grotesquely long arms, arms covered in mud, arms without hands – even arms severed from bodies still groping towards her, calling . . . calling for help with Logan's voice. Even sitting on her milking stool in the familiar byre, with her hands working mechanically, Beth still shuddered at the memory of the dreadful nightmare. If only she had found Logan before she wakened up . . .

When Thomas returned from taking the milk to the train he handed Beth a note.

'The carter frae the Mains gave me this frae Mistress Fairly.' He looked at Beth hopefully, evidently waiting to hear whatever news it contained.

'Aah . . . Mr Logan died just before dawn . . .' she reported sadly. 'He died very peacefully, though, and . . .'

'Ye should have given that letter tae me, Thomas Whiteley!' Even Thomas winced at Sadie's loud, harsh voice.

'It's really just tae let us ken what is happening . . .' Beth protested, flashing Thomas a sympathetic look, which did nothing to endear her to her sister-in-law. 'Your mother simply says she may be home later this afternoon, but more likely Alex will bring her tomorrow morning, when she has helped Mistress O'Connor make arrangements . . . Here, you can read it yourself. The rest is just about Kirsty.' Sadie snatched the letter ungraciously, her malevolent gaze following Beth as she walked out of the kitchen.

Lucy followed hastily.

'I'll help ye finish up i' the dairy if ye like, Mrs Fairly,' she offered breathlessly. 'I'm a bit feart o' Miss Sadie when she's in one o' her moods. She seems even worse this morn . . .'

'I expect she will feel better when Mistress Fairly returns,' Beth assured the girl gently. She knew Lucy often bore the brunt of Sadie's sharp tongue. 'If the weather stays dry until tonight we should finish carting in the hay before dark, then I think we shall all feel better.'

'Aye, and it'll be nice tae hae wee Kirsty home,' Lucy said shyly.

They all worked hard to finish the hay but it was clear that rain

329

was in the air as the day wore on. The distant hills were obscured in mist and the sky slowly turned a uniform grey, darkening as the afternoon wore on. Beth brought in her load and positioned the cart beside the stack.

'There's only another few swaths tae bring out o' the hollow, Thomas. I expect Sadie and Lucy will bring it on their cart. I'll bring in the cows ready for milking.'

An hour later Beth was carrying a pail of milk across to the dairy when Lucy caught up with her.

'We didna bring all the hay oot o' the hollow, Mrs Fairly,' she whispered hastily, her eyes round and fearful, even though Sadie was safely in the byre. 'Miss Sadie said we couldna get it all on the cart, but we could hae done easily. We only brought half a load.'

'Then why did she leave some?' Beth asked with a frown. 'The mist's coming down. We're in for a wet night . . . I could have gone back with the other cart if ye'd told me earlier, Lucy.'

'Miss Sadie said she was tired o' carrying the hay up that steep slope oot o' yon hollow, but she's going back wi' the horse and cart herself after we've had oor supper . . . She told me tae give the horse some oats and harness him tae the cart for her after milking. "I dinna want ye wi' me, snivelling . . ." she said, but I wasna snivelling, Mrs Fairly! I – I thought she was leaving it for you tae bring . . . playing another o' her nasty tricks on ye . . . and . . . and she slapped ma face . . . That's what made me greet.'

'Poor Lucy,' Beth sympathised. 'Miss Sadie seems to have had a bad day, but dinna worry, ye'll not need tae go back down to the field with her.' Beth shook her head. 'I canna think why she left sae little when it's so far away – almost as far as going tae Muircumwell. Still, ye'd better just do as she says and leave Prince ready in the cart.'

As soon as the milking was finished Sadie hurried to the house on the pretext of preparing the supper, leaving Beth to feed the pigs and young calves, while Anna attended to her chickens. Lucy chased the cows back to their field so that Thomas could get on with cleaning up the byre ready for morning.

Beth was still feeding the last of the pigs when she saw the red post bike on the track to Strathtod. It always gave her a shock to see it at this time of the day for it meant there was a telegram to deliver to someone, and telegrams rarely seemed to contain good news. She had no premonition that the boy, who sometimes helped the Braids at the post office, had already been up to the house.

Lucy had finished her own tasks so she was on her way indoors when the telegraph boy thrust the little yellow envelope into her hands, jumped back on to his bike and cycled away to deliver two more in Strathtod before the damp mist turned to drenching rain.

'Was that Jim Braid I saw going past the window on his bike?' Sadie called sharply.

'N-no, Miss Sadie. It was Jimmy Mackenzie. He brought a letter. I think it's for Mrs Fairly.'

'Give it to me!' Sadie almost snatched the envelope from Lucy's fingers. She turned the envelope over in her hands, then back again.

'Maybe it's for Mother. I'd better open it . . .'

'But it says . . .'

'Never ye mind what it says! Ye're as bad as Thomas Whiteley – handing over letters tae her as though she's the Mistress here! Ye'd best remember that I'm in charge now and . . .'

'But it's printed Mrs L. Fai—' Lucy broke off at the sound of Sadie's indrawn breath. Sadie read the words to herself again.

'Reported missing. No further details available. Will keep you informed.'

Her eyes narrowed. 'It usually says missing, presumed dead,' she muttered to herself. 'What's the difference . . .? Presumed dead . . . Dead!'

'What did ye say, Miss S-Sadie!'

'Dead! I said dead. What's the difference?'

'M-m-master F-Fairly? B-but he canna be dead. He's wee Kirsty's dada . . .'

'Of course he can be dead! He's a man like any other, isn't he!' Sadie snapped and watched Lucy's remaining colour ebb from her young face. Death was such a final, dreadful thing to her. Sadie's cold, colourless eyes regarded the girl speculatively. Logan probably was dead by now. Nobody could blame her if the stupid little maid got things muddled or jumped to conclusions. 'Well? Aren't ye going tae tell "Mrs Fairly" about Kirsty's dear "dada"?' she mocked callously.

'I – I, y-you . . .?'

'I'm going upstairs tae wash ma face and change ma pinny. Your supper is on the table if ye want it.'

'Sh-shall I take the l-letter tae Mrs F-Fairly first . . .?'

Sadie glanced down at the flimsy paper in her hand, then stuffed it into her apron pocket. 'I will take care o' this for now,' she said and with that she flounced out of the kitchen and up to her room. Lucy stared after her, her young heart thumping painfully, then she turned and ran from the house, the hot tears streaming down her face. She had thought Mr Logan was a wonderful dada, a beautiful soldier. Now he was . . .

'Whatever's wrong, Lucy?' Beth had stopped to stroke Prince, the gelding waiting patiently between the shafts of the cart until Sadie was ready to drive back to the field. Lucy stumbled towards her across the yard. 'Lucy? Has Miss Sadie been shouting at ye again . . .' She caught the girl by the shoulders. Lucy glanced up into Beth's kind, concerned face with tear-drenched eyes and began to sob. 'Tell me what ye've done tae displease Miss Sadie this time?' Beth said gently, stifling her own weariness.

'O-oh, Mrs Fairly, 'tis Kirsty's dada. He's dead!' Lucy sobbed harder than ever. 'He was a lovely man. He loved wee Kirsty . . . a-and n-now . . .'

'Stop it! Stop it, Lucy!' Beth's face had turned a deathly white. She shook the girl fiercely. 'Kirsty's father canna be d-dead . . . I would have had word . . .' Her voice sank to a whisper. She remembered her dream. It had haunted her vaguely all day. She couldna find Logan. She had searched and searched. She had never found him. She had woken up without finding him. She began to shake violently. 'The post bike . . . I saw it earlier . . .' she whispered hoarsely. Lucy looked up at her helplessly through her tears. 'Where is the telegram? Tell me, Lucy!' Beth heard her own voice rising hysterically. She took a deep breath, striving for control.

'Miss Sadie put it in her pocket. She opened it! I told her it was yours. She . . .'

'Did she tell you what it said?'

' "He's dead! Dead!" She said it twice. K-Kirsty's dada! I told her he canna be dead.'

'Wh-what else did she say?' Beth demanded tensely.

'She said he was a man like any other so he of course he was dead . . . O-oh, Mrs Fairly . . .' Lucy's voice rose in a wail. 'She seemed g-glad! What will wee Kirsty dae without her dada . . .? Miss Sadie's wicked!'

'Glad.' Beth breathed, releasing her hold on Lucy's trembling shoulders. 'Glad . . . yes, Sadie would be glad.' She sagged. Lucy's description convinced her more effectively than anything else could have done, except reading the printed words herself. 'Oh, Logie!' She turned blindly, almost colliding with the horse and cart. A great shuddering sob shook her.

'Mrs Fairly . . .?'

'G-go back t-to the house, Lucy. Eat your supper . . .'

'Where are ye going . . .?

'Where . . .? Anywhere! Go in, Lucy!' Almost instinctively Beth climbed into the cart, lifting the driving rope from the hook. In her mind she could see the triumphant smile on Sadie's thin mouth, the malice in her pale eyes. 'I must get awa' frae her . . . I must get awa' . . .'

Beth had no recollection of driving the horse and cart through the narrow gate in the rickyard wall, or down the mist-enshrouded meadow. She lifted her face to the weeping skies and felt the fine rain like tears on her cheeks. But her own eyes were dry, burning with a pain the rain could not wash away. 'Dear God, help me!' she prayed aloud. Prince pricked his ears at the sound of her voice but Beth did not notice. The guide rope hung limply in her hands and the horse plodded on, moving slowly over the damp earth, heading instinctively to the bottom of the field where he had worked earlier in the day.

Thirty-Eight

The horse halted instinctively at the edge of the steep little hollow. He eased his strong-boned legs and prepared to wait, head down, patient. The lack of movement brought Beth's attention back to her surroundings. The evening was closing in as the clouds hovered ever closer over the humps and hollows, turning the field into a ghostly grey sea. She shivered, but not with cold. She did not feel the chill of the damp evening air; she did not feel anything.

She got down from the cart, automatically reaching for the hay fork which lay along the bottom. Its two prongs were long and slightly curved, shiny and sharp from recent use. She grasped the long handle firmly, her numbed brain telling her hands what to do. She gazed woodenly at the few weathered haycocks, all that remained to gather in. Her mind was blank. She would not, could not, accept Lucy's news. She must gather in the hay. She must go down into the hollow and carry the hay up to the cart.

The meadow tapered to a funnel-shaped point forming a basin. The sides were fairly steep and the wet grass was slippery. Beth found herself sliding, propelled out of control. She landed at the bottom in an undignified heap. She looked around dazedly.

In wet weather the little hollow was often waterlogged. It had provided many a frozen pond in winter. Beth forced herself to think of the past. The burn was the boundary between Fairlyden and the small fields belonging to the blacksmith, the mill, and old Mrs Mackenzie. The doctor had a field too where he grazed his horses, but it was on the other side of the glebe land. She remembered other children from the village scrambling through the hedge to skate when the burn was frozen.

Once, when the snow had been deep, her father had made a toboggan for her and Logan. Neither of them had considered their aching legs as they toiled to the top of the slope and whizzed to the bottom time after time, clinging to each other on their little sledge. Beth lifted her head, a tender smile curving her lips. She could almost feel the ice-cold air rushing past her stinging cheeks, she remembered sheltering behind Logan, clinging to his sturdy little figure and squealing with delight as the sledge careered madly down the slope. It had seemed such a great adventure when they were ten . . . Suddenly Beth's face crumpled as the present rushed back, washing away her happy memories.

'Oh, Logie! Logie . . .' she cried piteously. Then she lifted her face to the damp mist, staring up at the endless, impenetrable grey sky. 'Why?' she screamed aloud. 'Why? Why? Why?' She clenched her fists until her ragged fingernails dug into her palms. 'Oh, God, I love him! I've always loved him! Dear God, d'ye no' ken how I love him?' she raged, throwing her arms wide, staring wildly at the lowering clouds. Then finding no response, no relief from her outburst, she flung herself face down on the wet earth and beat the ground. When her energy was spent she lay with her face buried on her arms while harsh, tearing sobs wracked her slender body. The dampness from the soil penetrated her clothes and her cheeks were streaked with earth, but Beth cared nothing for her condition. All her thoughts were centred on Logan. 'Did they make him suffer? Did he cry out as he did in my dream?' In her tortured, confused state the enemy became devils, not ordinary men. 'Did he die in pain? Alone . . .?' A riving sob burst from her lips and she pressed a fist against her mouth, shuddering.

'Fräulein?'

'Maybe it is a dream . . .' She rubbed her eyes and stared around the sheltered hollow. There was no one there of course. She raised her eyes despairingly and saw the horse and cart. Was there someone there? The figure of a man? Everything looked ghostly in the the grey mist of evening. Prince moved restlessly. Beth thought she heard a man's deep voice soothing him. A figure moved, standing away from the cart now. She could see his dark shape through the mist. Was it Thomas . . .? No, Thomas was not so tall.

'Fräulein!' Beth heard the voice more distinctly. But the words? She could not understand them! Guttural words spoken in the throat. She scrambled to her feet, her heart pounding.

'This is the way the Germans speak,' Logan had said, trying to imitate the strange guttural sounds. The figure paced backwards and forwards. Beth gasped. Surely it was the man who had jumped over the wall at Fairlyden? He had disappeared into the field – this field, stretching almost to the village! Almost to the old mill! He was tall and lithe . . .

He called again – some gibberish Beth could not grasp. Then, 'You play game? Huh?'

'He is a German!' Beth shivered. He must be an escaped prisoner! A German prisoner . . . The Germans have killed Logan. Has he come to kill me too . . .? Beth's usual common-sense deserted her. The long day's work, her unborn child, the shock of Lucy's news delivered so childishly, so innocently – all combined to try her sanity.

Kaspar Brecht raised his face to the grey mist, welcoming the fresh damp air on his skin, feeling the breeze in his hair, revelling in his temporary freedom. He had not wanted to join in the war, he had no stomach for killing innocent human beings, yet he did not lack courage. His first meeting with the young woman from the farm had been the result of a dare after he and his fellow prisoners had seen her driving by the peat works; he knew he risked the vengeance of the sadistic sergeant if he was caught, but so did she – and she had wanted to know what real life was all about . . . There was a kind of desperation in her . . . Suddenly he gave an exultant laugh. He didn't care. Life was for living and he was young and very much alive.

'I come! I get you!' With a strange yell he started down the steepest part of the slope towards Beth.

'No!' Beth looked round wildly, but there was nowhere to hide; there was no one to help. 'Oh God, keep him away frae me! He killed Logan! Keep him away!' Fear and grief drove reason from Beth's mind as the man's pace increased. In fact the momentum of the slippery slope propelled Kaspar Brecht faster than he desired but Beth only knew he was coming towards her, arms outstretched, menacing, or so it seemed to her distraught mind.

'Keep back! Keep away frae me!'

The dare-devil laughter in the young prisoner's eyes turned to surprise, but Beth could not distinguish his features, only his powerful frame bearing down upon her out of the mist like some ghostly spectre. But this man was alive! It was Logan who was dead! He had died fighting the Germans. They were the enemy. 'Go away!' she screamed. Suddenly she thrust the sharp-pronged fork in front of her and screwed her eyes tightly shut. The young prisoner could do nothing to halt his mad, headlong descent.

'Nein!' he gasped frantically, but the impact sent Beth staggering. The long shaft of the fork reared upright catching her temple with a stinging blow. She lay still, too stunned to move.

Gradually her senses began to return. She opened her eyes. The man was writhing on the ground. Beth stared in horror. He was trying vainly to relieve himself of the fork now swaying above his supine figure. One of the lethal prongs was firmly impaled in his body. Beth scrambled to her feet and moved cautiously closer, her heart pumping with fear. The man opened his eyes. Even in the half-light she could see they were very blue, and dazed with pain. He was wearing a blue uniform with a red stripe, just as Alex had described on the prisoners of war. He muttered something in his own language and the ghost of a rueful smile curved his white lips before his face twisted in pain.

'He's not old!' Beth thought irrelevantly.

'You . . . not Fräulein Sally!' he muttered. 'Help . . .?' He looked at Beth pleadingly. He was a young man – like Logan. Tears filled her eyes. He could not have killed Logan. He was here and Logan was in France. She bent closer, nervous for all that she knew he was badly hurt. He groaned and clawed at the fork.

Beth grasped the long handle and pulled. The young man reared, screamed and sagged back against the earth. Kaspar Brecht was unconscious; blood began to stain his clothes. Beth felt faint. She shook her head, trying to clear it. She had never hurt any living thing in her life. Even the young cockerels were safe in her hands. 'Dear God! What have I done? Have I killed him?'

The Germans have killed Logan. The insidious voice seemed to echo in her mind. But she could not forget the pleading in the young German's blue eyes. If he died she, Beth Fairly, would be responsible! She stuffed her fist in her mouth and bit hard on her knuckles, trying not to scream hysterically, trying to think what to do. She was nearer the village than the farm. She must bring the doctor. He would understand. He would know what to do.

'He came this way, I tell ye!'

Beth jumped as the sound of men's voices echoed through the mist, muffled, but surely not far away. She stared wide-eyed trying to see through the damp grey curtain.

'He must be in the field.'

Beth opened her mouth to direct them. The words died on her lips as a harsh command came from the village side of the burn.

338

'Find him then! And the girl. If she gives you the slip, send some men to the farm. Show her no mercy. Remember she's a traitor. She'll pay the penalty whoever she is! I'll see to that!'

Beth whirled around in horror, her heart pounding with fear. I'm not a traitor, she wanted to scream. But would they believe her? The young German had come to meet someone and in her heart Beth knew it was Sadie – even though he had used a different version of her name. It was almost dark now, and wet. No sane person would be gathering hay at this time, especially a woman alone! Beth knew instinctively that the harsh-voiced sergeant would condemn her without a hearing if she was caught here with the German prisoner. Nothing would save her from prison. She shuddered. If only Mama Fairly had been at home – but would they listen even to her? Sadie would never help her, certainly she would not risk admitting she had met the German prisoner secretly. The sergeant was a stranger . . .

The other voices were coming nearer, muttering angrily. Beth began to shiver. I must get away! The men will find the prisoner. They will attend to him.

'Please, God, help me!' she whispered fearfully. She could make out the figures of two men near the horse and cart now. She looked round. There were two more coming from the top of the field. They were blocking her way back to the house! There was only one way to go. She must jump across the burn and hide in the village until they had taken the prisoner away. Janet Whiteley would shelter her if she could reach the Muircumwell Store. Janet knows I am not a traitor.

She clenched her fists and moved swiftly but silently towards the burn and Fairlyden's boundary hedge. The burn was wide at this point but despite the wet summer the water was not exceptionally high. Beth picked up her damp skirts and scrambled down the bank. She jumped. She did not quite reach the opposite bank and there was a loud splash. She had to scrabble her way up the opposite bank, her boots and the hem of her dress heavy with water.

'What was that?'

The man's voice almost startled Beth out of her wits. She recognised the same harsh tones but the man sounded only yards away now, on the other side of the hedge!

'Och, it wad only be a wee water rat!' his companion answered placidly as Beth held her breath, her heart pounding with fear.

'Dinna fret, Sergeant,' the voice went on, 'your prisoner'll no' get far. The local folk'll find him, even if your guards dinna!'

'Local folk!' the sergeant scorned angrily. 'They're more likely to shelter him than hand him over!'

'I told ye before, there's nae reason tae speak like that, Sergeant Forster!' The genial tone had vanished and Beth recognised the voice of Police Constable Wyllie. 'Mebbe I'm no' an army man masel', but I'll have ye ken there's as many brave soldier laddies fighting for their country frae these pairts as frae anywhere else!'

'That may be so,' the sergeant sniffed, 'but while their men are away the women are fraternising with the enemy! Some of them cannot wait for their own men to return, according to the tales I've heard!' he added scathingly.

'Tales? What tales?'

'One of the prisoners hinted that the missing man has been seen slipping out several times in the evenings and . . .'

'And what were your men doing tae let him slip oot, eh?'

'I have only two English soldiers. The rest are locals!' the sergeant retorted huffily. 'Prisoner Brecht returned to the barracks with eggs on more than one occasion, and sometimes butter, even milk . . .'

'Stolen, nae doot!'

'If they were stolen, surely your loyal local women would have reported the matter, Constable? Anyway the prisoner is known to have made a conquest – a woman from a farm near the barracks.' The sergeant almost spat with anger and contempt. He did not tell the constable that Prisoner Brecht had found the Scottish countryside, and his Scottish guards, so much to his liking that he was contemplating asking for refuge after the war was over. Instead he taunted the constable. 'It's only a matter of time before there'll be at least one little German in this area! You mark my words!' Beth stifled a gasp of dismay. Surely Sadie . . .?

'Ye believe all the prisoners tell ye, Sergeant? Men who tell tales on one o' their ain countrymen? Like as no' they're jesting wi' ye – or stirring up trouble. Maybe they're jealous!'

'I saw the broken eggshells myself! It is no jest, Constable. You would do well to take it seriously! Anyway Brecht is missing. Surely that is proof enough. I expect he's with the woman now. There'll be no place for her in this village when I'm finished with her!'

Beth cowered even lower and bit her lip in an effort to stop her teeth chattering from cold and fear.

'Ye'll need proof first, Sergeant Forster! I dinna believe there's a woman around these pairts would even look at a German prisoner. Why there's scarcely a family that doesna have at least one man in the war, or a relation who has been killed. There's few enough as lucky as yoursel', Sergeant, sent hame tae ride around the bonnie Scottish countryside hounding the locals.'

'I'll have you know I was seriously wounded!' the sergeant retorted angrily.

Beth had never seen the English sergeant who had come to Muircumwell to supervise the care of the captured Germans but she had heard he was not popular with either the guards or their prisoners and she guessed there was no love lost between him and Constable Wyllie. Maybe the constable would help her if she told him everything? Everything? That meant implicating Sadie! Mama Fairly would never forgive her! Or Alex, or Billy – not even Logan. Logan's dead! She almost cried aloud as she remembered. What did it matter if they caught her? What did anything matter without Logan? But there's Kirsty. How would she feel if her mother was branded a traitor? She remembered the German's pleading blue eyes. She hated war. She didn't want anyone to die . . . She stifled a sob. She was cold and wet, hungry and tired, but most of all her mind was half crazed with grief and fear.

Even so she stiffened as one of the men in the field called to the sergeant.

'We've found him, Sir! I think he's dead.' Beth began to shake. Would they accuse her of murder?

'He isna dead!' A second man called. 'Not yet anyway, but we canna see very well. His clothes are sticky. He seems to be bleeding!'

'Let the German bastard bleed!'

'We can't just leave him, Sir! There's a horse and cart on the ridge. We could borrow it to bring the prisoner round to the barracks.' Beth detected sympathy and concern in the man's voice.

'Oh, all right! One of you drive the cart. I'll ride to the doctor's house and bring him to the barracks. The rest of you look for the woman! I'll send some more men to help. Search the fields and the farm. Watch the track. She's worse than the bloody Germans. Show her no mercy.'

Beth shuddered convulsively. She heard Constable Wyllie protest angrily. 'Are ye accusing one o' the Fairlyden women o' being a traitor – and worse – Sergeant?'

'If that's the name of the farm at the end of that track, yes I am, Constable Wyllie!' the sergeant retorted haughtily.

'Ye must be mad! Mistress Fairly is one o' the most respected women i' the district!'

'Maybe she is, but what about her daughters, or is Sally Fairly her daughter-in-law . . .?'

'There's no Sally at Fairlyden.' The constable's voice held a note of triumph.

'What are their names then?'

'There's Miss Sadie Fairly. Young Mrs Fairly's name is Beth. Her mother was called Sally . . . Sally Jamieson. She's dead, though.'

'I believe Sally is just another name for Sadie, or for Sarah, Constable Wyllie! Or maybe the young Mistress Fairly preferred to use her mother's name. They're sly, these young women, but whichever one it is she'll not get away with it.'

'I've kenned young Beth all her life. She'd never look at another man, German or anything else! Master Logan's in France, fighting for his country. His brother Billy's fighting tae. Ye've made a mistake, Sergeant . . .'

'We shall see, Constable. We shall see!'

He made the words sound like a threat. Beth couldn't still her trembling limbs. She was sure they must hear her teeth chattering. Constable Wyllie gave a grunt of disgust and then Beth heard him striding briskly away. A little while later she was relieved to hear the Sergeant mount his horse and ride away too.

Her relief was shortlived however. The men in the field were carrying the prisoner to the cart. One of them would be driving it to the gate leading on to the track, then down to the village. It would take him a little while, but the others would search the field – maybe even all night? They would never, never believe she had not been meeting the prisoner if they found her now – skulking in the ditch. Was there no end to trouble? Sadie would never admit to meeting a German prisoner, especially if she could pass the blame to her . . . Either way it would break Mama Fairly's heart.

Oh Logie, what am I tae dae? Why did ye have tae die in this dreadful war. The hot tears spurted from her eyes once more. She felt utterly weary and bewildered, scarcely knowing which way to turn or what to do. If only she could talk to Constable Wyllie alone . . . If only she could get to Janet's . . .?

Thirty-Nine

Scarcely aware of the sharp thorns, Beth pushed her way through a small gap in the hedge, tearing the skirt of her dress as she pulled it free. There were scratches on her arms and her face but she scarcely felt the pain. A sob rose in her throat. It seemed like a whole lifetime since Lucy Craig gave her the news that Logan was dead – news she had subconsciously dreaded ever since he went to France. What did it matter if the sergeant caught her? Or if he thought her a traitor? What had she to live for without Logan?

Kirsty needs you! Mama Fairly will need you too! Logan's death will break her heart. Beth tried to summon her courage and determination, but the place where her own heart should have been felt cold and empty, her limbs were like lead. She felt sick. What if the young German died?

'Oh God, forgive me. Please give me strength!' she prayed silently.

When she thought the sergeant had had time to reach the village she darted across the stretch of open ground towards the glebe land. Keeping in the shadow of the high sandstone wall, she forced her weary legs to walk. If she was lucky she would find refuge with Janet at the Store before the sergeant returned from the doctor's house. Maybe Janet would send for Constable Wyllie, or maybe she would have a better suggestion . . .

Luck was not with Beth that night though. Sergeant Forster had met Doctor Kerr leaving one of the cottages and insisted that he must accompany him to the makeshift barracks immediately. The doctor resented the sergeant's autocratic manner. Ever since his arrival with the prisoners he had caused ill feeling in the neighbourhood.

'The man has revenge and punishment on his brain – and not just for the prisoners either!' the landlord of the Crown and Thistle had remarked bitterly. 'I dinna think he cares whose

345

blood he spills so long as he can vent his evil spleen on some poor devil.'

Beth knew little of these feelings amongst the local men and she was seized with fresh panic when she saw the sergeant and the doctor coming towards her down the middle of the empty street. There was no place to hide! Nowhere except the little lane leading to the old mill. Without further hesitation she darted up it. She had been to the old mill often when she was a child, and even to the old quarry beyond it once or twice. There were plenty of outhouses and corners to hide in. Too late she remembered the prisoners. The mill was their temporary home – the very last place she ought to be! The sergeant would indeed consider her a woman without morals if he found her near the barracks! But there was no alternative now. Fear lent her speed and she reached the shadow of the old mill buildings just as the two men entered the yard. Her fear increased as she realised there was considerable activity in the millyard. Lanterns lit several of the windows and men seemed to be hurrying here and there. She pressed herself into the deep shadow of the mill wall and edged her way round to the back as the sergeant and the doctor drew their horses to a halt only a few feet away.

Doctor Kerr's personal resentment at the sergeant's aggressive manner turned to astonished disbelief as the man continued his tirade.

'Ye canna be serious, man!' the doctor's voice rose angrily. 'Ye canna accuse the local women of encouraging him and then say one has wounded him and ye'll have her tried for murder if he dies! It doesna make sense! *You* are the man responsible for the welfare of the prisoners – or have you forgotten that?'

Murder! Beth's blood seemed to freeze in her veins. I didna mean tae kill him . . . did I . . .? She was no longer sure. Logan was dead and she scarcely knew what she was doing anymore . . .

The sergeant was well aware of his own unenviable position if a man in his care died – even if he was one of the enemy. He blamed the laxity of the local guards, but they were a clannish lot! He dare not use any of them as a scapegoat. The blame must fall on the unknown woman.

'I know the woman comes from the farm over the bridge, up that track at the end of the Manse grounds. My men will bring her in eventually and then we shall see. First you had better attend to the prisoner. I hear the cart bringing him in now.' He

346

dismounted and bellowed for one of the men to take his and the doctor's horses. Beth pressed herself almost into the hard stones of the mill wall as a man passed within a few feet, swinging his lantern.

She heard the iron-rimmed wheels of the Fairlyden cart draw into the yard.

'How is the prisoner, McNab?' Doctor Kerr asked as soon as the driver jumped from the shafts where he had been taking a welcome ride.

'Not much life in him, Doctor! I couldna see him very well, but I reckon he's lost a lot o' blood.'

'I will just take a look at him before we move him again, then. Bring a light, sergeant, while we examine your prisoner.' It gave him a mild pleasure to issue commands to the arrogant sergeant. He guessed he was nothing more than a bully, probably a coward too.

Beth felt they must hear her heart, it was beating so loudly. It was one thing to know she had probably killed a man, but it was another thing to hear herself being branded as a murderer. Her fingers gripped frantically at the rough stone wall as her legs threatened to give way. Her knuckles began to bleed and tears of desolation and grief sprang to her eyes. It was a long time since she had eaten and the babe inside her seemed to demand extra sustenance for all he was still little more than a bubble. Her head was spinning. It was hard to think coherently.

'Please, God, dinna let me faint!' She prayed fervently. But Beth knew she could not wait indefinitely. Maybe if she could get right round the back of the millyard she could cut across the fields and come into the village from the other end? Her teeth were chattering with cold and fear and her dress was wet and muddy. She needed Janet's help desperately. She could not see the sergeant but from his commands she guessed they were carrying the prisoner into the Mill House where he and his official guards were billeted. She waited a little while but there was no further sound. The sergeant must have gone inside. Beth summoned all her strength to make a swift dash across the corner of the mill yard to the little field behind.

'What was that? Who goes there?' A man's voice shouted tensely and a lantern was lifted high, swinging to and fro. Beth ducked behind the low wall just in time, her heart pounding as she prepared to run along the edge of the field.

347

'Ye're mighty jumpy t' nicht. Did ye see a rat?' There was amusement in the tone. Beth guessed the man was probably one of the local volunteers from the surrounding villages.

'It was not a rat! It was a man I reckon – ran across the yard over there. Or maybe it was the woman . . .'

'Dinna be daft! This is the last place a woman would come tae!'

'Maybe she is anxious about her German lover boy.'

'She canna be that anxious or she wouldna have tried tae kill him in the first place!'

'Well, I'll just take a stroll across there with the lantern and make sure . . .' Beth had been unable to hear all of their conversation but she guessed the guard was coming over when she saw the moving lantern.

'Och, I may as weel come wi' ye then, but there's nought o'er there except a wee field and the auld quarry.'

The quarry! If I can get to the quarry surely I could hide there, Beth thought. She recalled the warnings they had received when they were children. She remembered how the Dodds brothers enticed Logan to the quarry to look for birds' nests; he had fallen on to a ledge . . . Her father would never have found him if he had not called for help . . . There was no time to lose! The men were coming nearer. She could tell by the light. Surely they would not see her in the mist. She gathered up her skirts and ran up the slope of the little field. It was a steeper, longer slope than she remembered from her childhood and she was already exhausted. Behind her she knew the men had gained the wall but the beam of the lantern did not reach her as she sped over the wet grass.

'There is something moving! There is! See over there . . .'

'Och, man, ye're imagining things. There's nought but a swirl o' scotch mist.'

'I may not be used to your bloody mist and rain, but I know when I'm imagining things,' the guard retorted huffily, even more determined to prove his point. 'I'm going over there to take a look. Are you coming, or not?'

Beth felt as though her heart and lungs were bursting as she reached the top of the little field behind the mill but she could see the dark shape of the scrub that had grown over the edge of the quarry. If she could reach it in time they would never find her in the dark and by morning she would have found safety. She groped her way amongst the elder bushes and brambles. When she thought she was reasonably hidden she crouched down to

348

wait. The two men did not seem in any hurry as she watched the glimmer of the lantern emerging out of the misty rain. It gave her a chance to regain her breath; gradually the stitch in her side began to ease too. If only this awful faintness didna keep threatening tae rob me o' my senses, she thought, clenching her fists.

The two men arrived at the edge of the quarry some yards to the west of Beth's hiding place and began to search the bushes which fringed the whole rim of the quarry. It was not an easy task in the dim light of the storm lantern. Beth was scarcely aware that she was holding her breath until she realised they were walking away from her. She heaved a huge sigh of relief and settled down to wait, closing her eyes. Beth didn't think she had dozed off, not even for a second, but when she opened her eyes again the lantern was almost directly in front of her. Instantly she pressed herself back, oblivious to the brambles scratching her hands and face and tearing her cap from her hair.

'What was that?'

'A rabbit likely. Man, ye're nervous as a kitten.'

'It was over here . . .' the man held the lantern higher. Beth could see it plainly. She stifled a sob and pushed herself further into the scrubby growth. Suddenly the ground slipped away beneath her feet. She screamed involuntarily as she hurtled backwards.

'Jesus Christ! That was no bloody rabbit!'

'There's nae need tae blaspheme! Come on . . .'

'That yell was enough to frighten the life out of a man!'

'Let's have your light! Quick now. This quarry's full o' water in the bottom. It hasna been used for years. If the poor devil isna dead when he reaches the bottom he'll drown in the water . . .'

'That sounded like a woman's scream to me . . .'

'More reason tae hasten then. I canna see a thing. Hand me the lamp . . .'

'Don't fall over the edge yourself.'

'It's nae use. I canna see anybody. Whoever it is we'll no' stand a chance o' finding them until daylight . . . It's too dangerous tae gang rumbling about. This summer's rain has been enough tae dislodge many a boulder.'

It was Lucy Craig who worried when Beth did not return as darkness closed in and the mist increased to a steady drizzle.

Eventually she huddled into her shawl and crept through the scullery and the dairy and ran to Anna's.

'Ye mean Logan's dead!' Anna gasped in dismay. 'And Sadie didna even have the decency tae let Beth open the telegram herself?'

Lucy nodded dumbly. 'Mrs Fairly sent me for ma supper and went off in the horse and cart and she's never come back. Miss Sadie was furious when the cart had gone,' she added with a frown.

'Well, the cart's back and Prince is in the field. The army men borrowed it tae cart a wounded man tae the doctor's. Seemingly the sergeant gave poor old Prince a hearty slap on the shoulder and made him jump. He lifted his forelegs kind o' sharp and cracked the sergeant's kneecap so they've taken him and the wounded man off tae the hospital. The men are hoping he'll no come back.'

'Some men came tae the door asking a lot o' questions,' Lucy said slowly. 'Miss Sadie sent me tae ma room so I didna ken what it was all aboot but when I asked what we should dae about Mrs Fairly she just shrugged her shoulders and said tae leave her . . .'

'Well, dinna cry, lassie,' Anna comforted. 'When wee Kirsty was born Mrs Fairly hid in the hayloft. Maybe she needs tae be on her own with her grief tae. Some people are like that . . . They suffer in private.' Anna's eyes took on a wistful look as she remembered her own grief when Jamie died – but at least I was with him at the end, she thought. 'Poor Beth. Sadie Fairly would be nae comfort tae her, that's for certain!'

'Master Fairly's her ain brother, but she didna seem sad.'

'I wish I'd kenned . . . It wouldna have been quite sae bad if the Mistress had been at home. She'll get a shock tae . . . Anyway, Lucy, ye'd best get tae bed. I expect Mrs Fairly will come back soon and she'll be up for the milking, I'm sure. Even when there's death the work has tae go on, and Beth kens that well enough, poor lassie.'

Lucy did not sleep well and as the dawn broke she scrambled down the little stepladder to the kitchen and crept up to the big bedroom which now belonged to Beth and Logan. The bed was neat and undisturbed. Lucy ran to Anna's cottage once more and knocked urgently on the door.

They searched all the buildings at Fairlyden but there was no sign of Beth. Sadie came out for the milking and flew into a rage because no one had brought the cows in from the field. Thomas and Anna stared at her in silent contempt before Thomas turned on his heel. 'I'll take the bike and go tae the village. If Mother hasna seen Beth we'll need tae organise a search party.'

'And what about the milking?' Sadie demanded. 'And carting the milk tae the train . . .?' But if Thomas heard he did not answer. He headed straight to his mother and Lizzie at the village.

It was Janet who sent word of the night's events to Mains of Muir. Alex drove Sarah home to Fairlyden immediately, leaving Kirsty in Emma's care. But there was still no news of Beth when they arrived. Sarah was distraught with grief and anxiety.

'I suppose Beth has taken the telegram with her? Did she say exactly what was in it?'

'No, she d-didna take it,' Lucy sobbed. 'B-because Miss Sadie had it . . .'

'Sadie!' Sarah spun round only to see her daughter's defiant stare. Her heart filled with foreboding. 'Where is it?' Sadie produced the telegram in silence and Alex moved to his mother's side to read over her shoulder.

'But it doesna say Logan is dead! Not for certain!' he exclaimed. 'In God's name, Sadie! What did ye tell Beth?'

'Alex . . .' Sarah's voice was quiet but her brown eyes were filled with pain as they waited for Sadie's reply.

'I didna tell her anything!' she announced triumphantly. 'It was that nosy little wretch! She's always minding other folk's business and telling tales.' Lucy stared at Sadie as though she had taken leave of her senses, then she burst into another flood of tears.

'Dead, ye said! Ye said it twice! As-as though ye were g-glad!' she sobbed. Sadie's face paled. 'Ye told me tae tell Mrs F-Fairly t-tae . . .' Lucy ended in a wail. Suddenly she turned and fled to her room. Sarah's mouth tightened. She felt cold and sick. Never for a moment did she doubt Lucy Craig's story. The young maid was too innocent and too uncomplicated to tell anything but the truth.

'Sadie, if anything has happened to Beth, I'll never forgive you as long as you live!' Sadie stared at her mother, but she saw the face of a stranger – a cold, contemptuous stranger. Sarah turned away from her. 'Will you send a wire to Mr Bradshaw please,

351

Alex? On your way back through the village?'

'What has't tae dae with him?' Sadie's voice rose sharply, despite her mother's clear rejection.

Sarah was tempted to blurt out that he was Logan's father, that he had a right to know. She wanted to say, 'I need him! I need him more than I've ever needed him before. Only God knows how I need him this day.'

'He is coming for Grandfather's funeral,' Alex said impatiently. 'He has had the telephone installed now, Mother. Would you like me to ask Mr Morrison if I can speak to him from the Manse? I could explain better . . . Maybe he would arrange to stay a wee while . . .? I'm sure ye'd be glad o' his company . . .?'

Sarah's eyes filled with tears. 'You were always a sensitive laddie, Alex. I would be glad of Mr Bradshaw's company. Tell him that, will you, if you can speak to him.'

All the old men and the biggest schoolboys and any women who were willing were organised to search for Beth. It was Doctor Kerr who eventually suggested asking some of the guards at the old mill barracks to join the search. Immediately the two guards recalled the incident of the previous evening.

'We thought we heard a scream as if somebody had fallen into the quarry.'

'And ye didna think tae report it?' Doctor Kerr demanded in dismay. 'What kind o' men are ye, for heaven's sake?'

'Tae tell the truth, Doctor, we – we forgot about it until now, what with all that upset over the sergeant, and getting him away tae the hospital . . .' The guard did not add, and celebrating his misfortune with too much whisky.

'Well, there's no time to lose!'

Beth's white cap was still fluttering on the bramble bush like a small brave pennant. It was not long before the men located the exact spot where the quarry edge had crumbled and slithered down the side of the quarry, taking with it a young woman.

Forty

Beth hovered on the brink of death. She had lost her baby, the small bubble of newfound happiness which had welled within her; she had cracked bones in her leg and shoulder, and worst of all she had a serious head wound. The bruises which seemed to cover her slender body, and her broken limbs, were healing nicely, but shock and loss of blood, together with the chilling effect of a wet night in the open, had weakened her resistance. She developed a raging fever. The doctors at the hospital despaired of saving her, but eventually the fever was brought under control. Still Beth showed little recognition of those around her and she had no interest in anything, especially not in food. The doctors reached the conclusion that her head wound had caused permanent damage.

One person did not share their view. The Minister's aunt, Miss Morrison, was still an influential figure at the hospital and Beth received the best care the nurses could give. Ironically she was regarded as something of a local heroine for the way she had fended off the supposed attack of a German prisoner. Kaspar Brecht had also survived and to his credit he had said nothing to implicate Sadie Fairly. Both he and Sergeant Forster had been removed from the area.

Beth knew none of this as she swung between brief spells of reality when she remembered that Logan was dead, and long horrendous nightmares when she was running through endless mud and storms in search of him. These hallucinations were due, in part at least, to the large quantities of morphine which the doctors had administered to relieve her pain.

After several weeks of careful nursing without results, Sarah voiced her increasing concern.

'There is little more we can do for her here, I'm afraid,' Miss Morrison admitted with regret. 'She still needs many weeks of care – but she needs something more . . .'

'What do you mean?'

'I am not sure . . .' Miss Morrison hesitated, then she looked Sarah directly in the eye. 'I feel Mrs Fairly lacks the desire to live. I understand she had just received the news of her husband's death before the accident happened? Personally I wonder if that is still uppermost in her semi-conscious mind. Perhaps if she saw her young daughter again . . .? Perhaps if she was in familiar surroundings? I am not a doctor. These are entirely my own opinions, based only on intuition . . .'

'Sometimes intuition, with experience, is the greatest guide of all,' Sarah murmured. 'Certainly it is so with animals.'

'Aah, I am glad you understand. I think Mrs Fairly needs some kind of reassurance, but we seem unable to give it. Over and over during her dreadful nightmares she repeats the same things. "I'm not a murderer," or sometimes "I didna mean tae kill him".' There were other disjointed phrases concerning Sadie Fairly, but Miss Morrison was too tactful to repeat them. 'Beth does not seem to believe that the prisoner is alive. In any case surely no one could have blamed her if he had died!'

Neither Miss Morrison nor Sarah knew of the sadistic Sergeant Forster and the threats Beth had overheard.

'Beth will blame herself if she still believes she has killed a fellow human being,' Sarah mused softly. 'She was always a gentle lassie. She hated to see any of the animals die.'

Miss Morrison nodded. 'She murmurs her husband's name so often when she is on the verge of sleep. I'm convinced that news of him would provide the spur she needs. I suppose you have heard nothing further?'

'No.' Sarah knew she would never forgive Sadie for the callous way she had led Lucy Craig to believe Logan was dead, or the way she had usurped Beth's right to open the telegram herself – or even to see it – denying her the faint hope which might have helped her even now. Yet as the weeks passed there was still no news to suggest that Logan might be alive. 'His Commanding Officer was killed later on the same day the telegram was despatched. Ellen and her husband have been doing their best to make enquiries in France but there seem to be so many young men killed or missing every single day.'

'Yes, war is a cruel, senseless thing! But don't give up hope. My son tells me you have great faith, Mistress Fairly.'

'It has been sorely tried recently,' Sarah admitted. 'My father

354

was an old man and ready to die, but to lose Logan in the same week, and then to see Beth on the brink of death . . . to watch her suffer like this . . .'

'Well, I'm convinced the good Lord is not ready to take your daughter-in-law yet. If you decide to take care of her at home I can recommend a nurse to help you. Even if you are successful in banishing the demons which seem to impede her progress, it will be some time before her strength returns; she will need help to enable her to walk again. Mistress Wilson is not a young woman, indeed we have been friends since our schooldays, but she is an excellent nurse. She is a widow now and I think she would be a great comfort to you.'

'Very well, Miss Morrison. I will consider your suggestion. Perhaps I should try to talk about it to Beth? Although she makes so little response I think she understands some of the things I tell her, especially when I mention Kirsty.'

In this Sarah was right; Beth did seem to understand, in part at least, but the mere mention of going home to Fairlyden seemed to make her distraught. She thrashed restlessly in the narrow hospital bed as though trying to protest and even her gentle blue eyes flashed wildly. Her few coherent words were even more distressing to Sarah.

'Sadie! Never trust Sadie.' Sarah had no way of knowing that Beth was repeating the warning which had haunted her over the years – her Aunt Agnes's last words to her.

As she journeyed home on the train that October afternoon Beth's words echoed and re-echoed in her brain. So much had happened since the accident. Sarah looked out of the railway carriage at the shorn fields. There were still a few bedraggled lines of weathered stooks to gather in here and there, and large pools of water where the persistent rain had gathered. At Fairlyden the harvest was over. Sarah had not known she had so many friends and helpful neighbours; even the guards at the prison barracks had set up corn stooks and loaded carts when they were off duty.

Lucy Craig was little more than a child herself but she had worked hard too, until Sarah had arrived home from a visit to the hospital one afternoon to find the girl in floods of tears and expressing an urgent desire to leave Fairlyden. Sarah suspected Sadie seized every opportunity to use Lucy as her own skivvy while her small charge was still in Emma's care at Mains of Muir.

She sighed heavily as the train rattled along. It was Emma, with her usual kindliness and good sense, who had solved the problem of Lucy.

'Perhaps she could move to the Mains for a few weeks, until Beth can decide what's best for wee Kirsty? Lucy could look after the bairn and I'll keep an eye on them both.'

Sarah had agreed gratefully. She missed her granddaughter's baby chuckles but her first concern was for Beth. Every night she prayed fervently that she would soon be well enough to return home, then Kirsty could come back to Fairlyden too; but they would need Lucy more than ever, at least until Beth regained her strength – if she ever did. Sarah was beginning to lose hope herself.

After Lucy's departure to the Mains, Sadie insisted on hiring another maid. Sarah paid little attention to anything her daughter had to say now, even if she had not been too anxious and preoccupied with Beth's condition.

Sadie had gone ahead and hired a big, strong-boned woman named Gertrude Brockwood. Gertie, as she called herself, seemed willing to do all that Sadie asked, and she was apparently oblivious to her sharp tongue.

In France Ellen had used every contact she knew to discover news of Logan, but without success. Sarah felt a pang of guilt as her thoughts dwelt on her elder daughter. She had scarcely had time to congratulate Ellen and Brad on their own good fortune. Lord Willowman had decided to turn his country estate into a refuge and rehabilitation centre for wounded and disabled soldiers; he had asked Brad and Ellen to advise him on the equipment and changes which would be required. He hoped they would take charge of it when the war was over – maybe even before, if it dragged on much longer. There were so many disabled men in desperate need. It was exactly the sort of work Ellen and Brad would do well, especially together. Brad's own recovery would be a spledid example to his patients too . . .

As the train chugged along Sarah's thoughts moved to Alex and Emma and Beatrice; they had supported her in every possible way, especially during Crispin's brief visits back to Yorkshire, but Emma would have a baby of her own to care for soon.

'I must make arrangements to bring Beth and Kirsty home . . . I must make arrangements . . . I must . . . I must . . .' Her thoughts seemed to whirl in her head to the rhythm of the train. She felt anxious and uncertain about everything since the mention of Fairlyden had clearly brought Beth renewed distress. Kirsty will soon be ten months old; she's taking notice of her surroundings; she needs to know where she belongs. So Sarah's anxious thoughts churned. Kirsty's place is with me; Kirsty's place is with me . . . until Beth gets well. She must get well . . . she must get well. The train began to slow and Sarah sat up sharply. Sadie will resent Kirsty's return to Fairlyden, just as she had always resented Logan and Beth, she thought bleakly.

'How could I have borne a daughter with such a jealous, spiteful nature?' she asked herself wearily. It was a question she had asked herself many times since Sadie's birth – but now she no longer felt guilty. Sadie had forfeited the right to a mother's love. Sarah's dark eyes were shadowed, but her mouth tightened. I'll never forgive her for the malice she has shown to Beth, she thought. Beth is haunted by her wickedness . . . afraid to return to the home which is hers by right as Logan's wife . . . She shivered. Even in her thoughts she could not say 'Logan's widow'. Deep down she would never believe Logan was dead until she had proof – yet she knew there were hundreds of women who felt the same, and most would wait in vain for the proof that could never be given. The train shuddered to a halt.

'Crispin!' For a moment Sarah's cares fell away and her face was transformed by the warmth of her smile as she stepped down from the train. 'I didn't expect you would be at the station to meet me.'

'You surely didn't think I would leave you to walk?' Crispin Bradshaw looked down into her face with concern, suppressing his own excitement. 'You look tired, Sarah. Tired and rather dejected. Was your visit not as successful as you had hoped?'

'No. Indeed I scarcely know what to do for the best any-more . . . for Beth, or for wee Kirsty. Oh, Crispin, I am glad to see you.'

'Are you, Sarah? It's only a few hours since I saw you off on the train.'

'I know, but it seems like a week. A bad week . . .'

'Would you like to go to Lizzie Whiteley's for a cup of tea?'

'No thanks. Janet and Lizzie are finding it difficult to get

357

supplies. Anyway I'd rather go back home – or rather back to Fairlyside. Crispin . . . I need to talk to you.' He nodded, secretly pleased that Sarah had elected to go back to his house where they could talk in private.

Apart from two quick visits to Yorkshire he had been staying at Fairlyside since Sandy Logan's funeral and Beth's accident. Ted Forbes and Robert were getting on remarkably well at the factory and he sensed that Sarah needed him as much as he needed her. She had clung to him like a child in her grief for Logan, and for Beth when it had seemed impossible that anyone could survive such extensive injuries.

There was Kirsty to consider too, and the possibility of her being an orphan; she was his grandchild – his and Sarah's. There had been no question in Crispin's mind that his place was with Sarah but he had been gratified when she turned to him with all the simplicity and trust of a true wife. Even so he had chosen to stay in his own house rather than the Fairlyden farmhouse. Janet Whiteley had sent him a young woman who had recently lost her own husband in the war; she cleaned and did his washing, but Sarah had insisted on cooking his meals.

Half an hour later he helped her down from the trap and ushered her into the small parlour at Fairlyside. She held out her hands to the blazing fire as though she was frozen, although the weather was mild enough for October.

'I will make some tea,' Crispin insisted. 'Shall I bring the toasting fork so that we can have toast?'

'Very well,' Sarah smiled wanly. 'I don't know why I feel so cold and depressed.'

Crispin brought a laden tray and placed it on a small table before the fire.

'Did Beth understand that you want to bring her home?' he asked as Sarah poured the tea.

'Yes, she understood. I'm sure she did.' Sarah's cup rattled sharply in its saucer and she set it down and gripped her hands tightly together to stop them trembling. 'Crispin, I dinna think Beth wants to come home! The very mention of it upset her terribly! I'm sure it is on account of Sadie . . .'

'I see . . .'

'And I canna blame her!' Sarah's tone was bitter. 'After all the trouble and heartbreak Sadie has caused for her. Yet Miss Morrison is convinced that Beth will recover more quickly if she sees Kirsty every day, and other familiar faces . . . There is only one solution. Sadie must leave Fairlyden this time – even though we need her help with the work so badly – especially with Beth ill and so few men or maids available. But there is nothing else I can do.' Sarah's mouth firmed. 'Beth's recovery must come before everything else.' Crispin was silent for so long that Sarah began to think he had not heard her – or perhaps he was shocked that she was rejecting her own daughter . . .? Then, as though reaching a decision, he set down his own cup and came round to her chair. He knelt beside her, and gently took her hands in his.

'I have waited a long time to make you my wife, Sarah, but if nothing else, these past weeks have brought us closer than ever. Certainly they have shown me that you are more important to me than anything else in this life. I have realised how much I need you – and I think you have needed me. Am I right, my dear . . .?'

'Oh, Crispin, you know how badly I need you. I don't know what I would do, even now, if you go back to Yorkshire. But I canna think of my own happiness when Beth is lying there with only her own private horrors and grief for company . . .'

'I am thinking of Beth, my dear. She is my daughter-in-law too remember, although she does not know it. Also Kirsty is my granddaughter and we must both consider her future. So what better solution than that they should both live here, in my home? In our home, if you will marry me, Sarah? Sadie could stay at Fairlyden for the time being; she would have Gertie Brockwood for company. Perhaps it will teach her a lesson; she will have no one else to blame but herself when things go wrong or don't get done. Anyway, I think Beth could be happy here, at least until she is well again. She always liked this house when she and Logan were children calling on Mrs Bunnerby . . .'

'Aye, they did . . .' Sarah's eyes filled with tears as she thought of the happy days that had gone.

'Don't cry, my dear. Remember Kirsty has all her life ahead of her. The future of Fairlyden lies in her hands. She will grow up loving Fairlyden as Logan and Beth did, with you to guide her. But more than that, if Miss Morrison is right, I think Beth will learn to live and laugh again, here with us. Will you marry me, Sarah?'

Sarah nodded. She could not trust herself to speak.

'Aah, my dearest . . .' Crispin stood up then and pulled her gently into his arms, cradling her head against his shoulder. A little while later he said cautiously, 'I had some news today, Sarah . . .' She looked up, wondering at the strangeness of his tone; the brief happiness faded from her soft brown eyes. 'Unpleasant news . . .?'

'No. Frustratingly vague news, so vague I am almost afraid to raise your hopes – or my own – and yet hope springs eternal.'

'Crispin – you cautious Yorkshireman! What is it?' Sarah chuckled softly and relaxed again. It occurred to Crispin how much he had missed her warm laughter in the past weeks. He drew a torn, flimsy envelope from his breast pocket. Then he sat down close to Sarah. 'This has been written with a copying ink pencil and it has been badly smudged. Sarah . . . There may be a faint chance that Logan is alive . . .'

'Crispin! I – I . . .'

'The writing is hard to decipher but the words Muircumwell and Scotland are plain enough. Jim Braid and his sister think it is meant to say "The house over the bridge", so they brought it to me. It has been some time on the way.' He smoothed the sheet of cheap paper with the utmost care, and they peered at it together – a mixture of bad English and some French. 'Possibly the writer was at a loss to think of an appropriate English word,' Crispin suggested, and now Sarah sensed the tension in him which she had failed to notice earlier. 'I think it has been written by a French peasant, possibly a very frightened one too – and probably with a very poor family of his own. As far as I can decipher they have given shelter to a young soldier found wondering in a wood. He is – or was – very ill. It could be anybody except that he calls for someone called "Beth". Look here . . .' Crispin pointed with his finger, 'and again at the end . . .'

'I wish I had my reading glasses!' Sarah exclaimed impatiently. 'I can hardly read any of this. Why hasn't Logan written if he is alive?'

'That was the first thing I asked myself.' Crispin looked steadily into her brown eyes. 'We must remember it may be just someone who has known him. Someone hoping for money. Perhaps not even Logan at all . . .Or he may be too ill to write.'

'But you said . . .'

'I know – it mentions Beth. I think the writer means the young soldier has a fever and has been calling the name Beth – or it could be Bess . . . But see at the end it says Beth quite clearly and mentions *l'image* – that could be a picture or a photograph.'

'I know Logan kept the photograph of Beth and Kirsty with him all the time. Crispin, do you think . . .? Could it be possible?'

'I don't know, Sarah, but I have taken the liberty of writing to Ellen while you were visiting Beth this afternoon. She may be able to find out more, though even the postmark is blurred. I think we should write again to Logan's battalion.'

'So you really believe there is reason to hope . . .' Sarah breathed, her eyes shining with a mixture of joy and tears.

'Oh, Sarah, my love!' Crispin hugged her close. 'I don't want your hopes to be dashed and see you suffer all over again . . .'

'But I have never quite given up hope . . . I think we must keep this to ourselves though. It would be so cruel to raise Beth's hopes until we are sure.'

'At least we might find out one way or the other – and even knowing Logan is dead and where and how, would be better than this . . .'

'I know my dear, I know.' Sarah reached up and drew Crispin's head against her breast, gently stroking the silver hair at his temple. 'In your heart you have always thought of Logan as your son, haven't you, Crispin?'

'Always.'

Forty-One

Sarah and Crispin were married quietly in Muircumwell Church at the beginning of November. Only Janet Whiteley and Alex were present as witnesses. Emma was still recovering from the birth of her son and Beatrice was taking care of her as if she had been her own daughter.

Alex had expressed sincere delight when he learned his mother and Crispin Bradshaw were to be married, but Sadie had made her disapproval only too plain.

'It was more than disapproval. She seemed almost . . . dismayed.' Sarah frowned. Crispin had reassured her in his usual practical, no nonsense manner.

'Sadie is probably afraid I shall spirit you away from Fairlyden altogether, but she should know by now I could never prevent you from milking those precious cows every morning and evening, even if I tried!' His whimsical smile had temporarily banished the lines of strain which had marred his strong face in the past few months. Sarah knew how much he was looking forward to spending their remaining years together despite the tragic news which had finally convinced them their need for each other was paramount. 'Anyway,' he had added shrewdly, 'I wouldn't be surprised if Sadie and Robert were to get married before long. He has written to say he would like to spend Christmas in Scotland. I don't flatter myself that it's my company he craves!'

A few days after the wedding Nurse Wilson arrived at Fairlyside and Beth's stay at the hospital ended at last. Lucy Craig and Kirsty moved back from Mains of Muir. After their weeks of separation Kirsty no longer recognised Beth as her own mother and Sarah felt deeply saddened; even worse was Beth's apparent lack of interest in the baby daughter she had adored.

Suddenly Christmas was almost upon them but there was still no further news of Logan. Beth's recovery was slow. To Sarah it seemed as though a light had been extinguished, leaving a pale flicker of her former bright spirit. Nurse Wilson was a placid, motherly woman and a great comfort whenever Sarah despaired of rousing Beth from her lethargy.

'At least it will be a happy Christmas for Emma and Alex,' Sarah commented as her needles clicked busily with another small vest. 'Even though wee Alexander William is too small to know what it is all about. Beatrice says she could not love him any more if he had been her very own grandson.'

'Beatrice was always fond of children, and generous in her love for them,' Crispin agreed. 'It is a pity Richard does not keep in touch. He is probably fighting in France too. I can't understand how he can neglect his own mother so completely.'

'I know, it must be heartbreaking – not knowing where he is or whether he's alive or dead . . .' Sarah stopped knitting and stared unseeingly into the leaping flames.

Crispin knew her thoughts were on Logan. He was silent for a while. When he spoke his tone was firm, decisive. 'Sarah, I shall go to France myself as soon as Christmas is over. I have been thinking about it for some time.'

'Aah, Crispin . . .' Sarah's face paled. She set aside her knitting and moved to sit beside him on the chaise longue which he had bought so that Beth could join them during the day. 'You know how often I wonder about Logan, b-but I would rather live in ignorance for ever than have anything happen to you! I don't think I could bear it.' Crispin stretched out a long arm and drew her close. He was surprised to feel she was trembling.

'That is the best Christmas present I have ever had, my dear.' His voice was gruff. 'I knew you must care for me a little when you agreed to leave the old house to move in here with me – but I didn't know you cared quite so much . . .'

'How could you not know, Crispin! I love you, you must know that by now!' Crispin's smile widened almost boyishly.

'I have dared to hope in the past months, but I have never been sure – until now.' He kissed Sarah with great tenderness. 'You can be certain I shall not take any unnecessary risks, Sarah. I have waited too long, and now I have too much to lose, to do anything foolish – even for our son.'

'Billy has promised to use his next leave to find out from the men who were with Logan where they last were before he disappeared and to visit those places. Ellen has sent him details of everything we could decipher from the letter but she says there are many French peasants who live in fear and poverty. I pray that one of them is taking care of him in secret.'

'Then I shall wait to hear from Billy before I make any plans.'

The following morning Sarah had just finished helping with the milking as usual when Sadie waylaid her on her way to the dairy.

'Mother, I've been thinking . . . I'd like tae make the Christmas dinner, here at Fairlyden.' Sarah was surprised. Sadie had never been one to make extra work for herself. 'Robert says ye're expecting him for Christmas . . . He thinks I'm a good cook.'

'Very well.'

Sarah nodded, but she was even more astonished when Sadie went on, almost diffidently. 'D'ye think Beth wad come tae?' She flushed at her mother's incredulous stare. 'Please, Mother, it's important. Ye said I hadna tae visit her at Fairlyside, but Anna MacFarlane does and she thinks it's strange that I never see her. Anyway I dinna suppose she's ever alone there, what with Nurse Wilson and Lucy Craig dancing attendance . . .'

'Alone! Why dae ye want tae see Beth alone? Sadie, if ever you upset Beth – ever again . . .'

'I'm not going tae upset her! I – I want tae say I'm sorry about . . . well about everything.' Sarah knew the effort it must have cost for Sadie even to think of appologising, but it was so out of character she could not help feeling suspicious. Sadie grimaced and turned away, with an air of rejection.

For a moment Sarah felt a brief flash of tenderness and sympathy for the daughter she found so hard to love. 'I'll talk to Beth,' she promised. 'But she is only just beginning to take an interest in Kirsty. I canna promise that she'll even be strong enough to come.'

Sarah reported this conversation to Crispin when they were alone.

'Beth's listless state troubles me,' he mused anxiously. 'She has never lacked courage, I know . . . but it is as though she has lost the will to take up the threads of her life again. Will you let me try to persuade her to go to Fairlyden with us? Maybe it will help her to dispel some of the ghosts which seem to haunt her. I have heard her calling out in her sleep several times.'

'Yes, I've heard her too. Beth has lost so much in her young life

365

though . . . You – you will be gentle with her, Crispin?' Sarah looked up at her husband's firm mouth and steady grey eyes. 'You have such strength and character. I have often been glad you were my friend . . .'

'Dear Sarah, each day I spend with you is like discovering a new and precious flower.' He smiled tenderly and his face softened. 'Do not worry, I shall never hurt Beth.'

Crispin waited until he was sure he and Beth would not be interrupted before he told her of Sadie's invitation.

'No! I canna go tae the hoose! I willna . . .'

'Hush, lass, don't upset yourself so.' In spite of Sarah's warning Crispin was dismayed by the terror in Beth's blue eyes. 'Sadie can't hurt you anymore. I think she wants to say she's sorry for the mischief she caused . . .'

Beth stared at him mutely. Crispin knew he had to help her out of her apathy; she had to overcome her terrors and face the real world again – with or without Logan.

'We shall be with you and Robert will be there too. You are getting stronger now. What harm could it do to dine at Fairlyden with us at Christmas – a time for forgiving and . . .'

'Sadie *wanted* Logan tae die! She wanted tae be Mistress of Fairlyden! She hates me! She'll hate Kirsty! I-I . . .'

'Listen to me, Beth . . .' Crispin bit his lip. This was harder than he had expected. 'We have had no absolute confirmation that Logan is dead . . . but if he is, surely Kirsty needs you more than ever? She is Logan's daughter too. She will need your help and guidance through life. Fairlyden will be her home one day. You must teach her to love it as you and Logan love it . . .'

'Ye dinna understand . . .' Beth muttered wearily. 'How can you understand how much I miss Logan! Nothing matters without him!'

'I do understand, Beth.' Crispin's voice was quiet but insistent. He hesitated, but only for a second. 'I understand because I loved him too. He is my son . . .'

Beth stared, blinked, then shook her head.

'It is true, Beth. I pray Sa . . . my wife will forgive me for sharing our secret with you, without her permission, but I must make you understand that you are not alone in your grief. We must help each other. Logan never knew I was his father. I didn't know myself until I saw him . . .' Crispin added softly, remembering his first sight of Logan and of Beth herself as toddlers. The shock, the happiness . . . 'I could not give him my name even, but I have loved him always. Always.' Still Beth shook her head. She felt confused, utterly bewildered. Crispin went on speaking softly.

'Sadie will never be Mistress of Fairlyden. As soon as you are well again it will be your home, and Kirsty's – if that is your wish.'

'No . . . not without Logan. Ye dinna understand. There's Billy and Sadie and Ellen and . . .'

'Listen carefully, Beth. I tell you this in confidence . . .?'

Beth nodded silently.

'Fairlyden belongs to me now. It is true that the house and steading and fifty acres of the best land belonged to William Fairly at the time of his death, but I inherited the rest when I inherited Strathtod Estate from my father. I sold it to pay death duties – all except the land which had once been part of Fairlyden. When Master Fairly died so suddenly he . . . Well, let us say his widow was left with little money to pay for the alterations he had set in motion before he went to America. Logan's mama is a very independent lady . . .'

'Aye . . .' Beth nodded. 'I ken . . .'

'The only way I could help her was by buying Master Fairly's share of Fairlyden. At least I could make sure she would always have the home she loved, and a living from the farm. She used the money from the sale to pay off her husband's debts, but she insisted on paying a rent for Fairlyden – even though she was the mother of my son . . .' he added almost under his breath. Beth waited quietly, her attention held in spite of herself. 'No one else knew. I always intended to leave Fairlyden to Logan. Now it will belong to you, Beth – you and Kirsty. I hope you will respect my confidences – at least for the time being. But do you understand now how closely we are bound together? You are not alone in your grief, my dear. We need you. The happiness of Logan's daughter – our granddaughter – is in your hands.'

Beth stared at Crispin, scarcely able to take in so many revelations. She was silent so long he thought she had been struck dumb again. Then she whispered, 'I believe ye. I think . . . I understand many things now . . .'

'So, will you help us in our loss, as we shall try to help you and Kirsty?'

367

Slowly, for the first time in many months, Beth's mouth curved. It was only a shadow of her former bright smile but Crispin sighed thankfully; it was a start. 'I'll try, Mr Bradshaw . . . I'll try.'

'I know you will, lass. I'll leave you in peace now.'

When Crispin had left the room Beth slowly swung her feet to the floor and forced herself to walk to the window. She knew Nurse Wilson was right. She had to make her wasted limbs move, she had to regain her strength, but her legs felt so wobbly. She was glad to reach the solid little mahogany table standing within the curve of the window. She clutched the edge for support and then eased herself on to a small chair.

She looked at the blue and white vase. Its reflection shone in the polished surface of the table. She reached out to it, her long, sensitive fingers caressing its smooth surface. The vase was one of the few things Mistress Fairly must have brought from Fairlyden. Logan had told her it had been a wedding gift to his great grandmother. Beth remembered how they had woven wonderful tales about it when they were children. Sadie had thought the dragons and strange figures were ugly. Sadie . . . Beth's fingers clenched and she stood up, restless, uneasy. Her gaze was drawn to the wide window and the track outside – the track to Anna's cottage, to Fairlyden, to the fields, the hills . . .

The front windows at Fairlyside were wide and high, four windows together forming a large curve. Beth moved closer and leaned her forehead briefly against the cool glass. The winter day was fading rapidly. Soon it would be time to light the lamps, to draw the heavy curtains and shut out the world . . . shut out Logan . . . She began to tremble. She tried not to think. She stared fixedly at the trees, shorn now of their leaves. They looked like giant charcoal drawings against the purple blue of the sky. Logan's grandfather had planted them; already they were tall and strong, swaying with the winter winds, offering shelter from the summer sun; they would grow taller and wider as the years passed . . . The trees will still be there when Kirsty goes to school, she thought, and even when she's an old, old woman. Beth drew in her breath. There must be a Power far beyond our ken . . . How else could such might, such strength come from a tiny seed . . .?

Even as she watched, the rays of the setting sun crept from behind a cloud to soften the skeletal branches with a halo of golden light and bathe the room in a rosy glow. The amethyst hills merged with the evening sky. But the day was not ended yet. Beth watched entranced as the clouds parted, revealing the beauty of the setting sun in all its vermilion splendour. She had forgotten how beautiful the sunset could be on a frosty winter evening. Rays of gold and orange and magenta spread across the sky, and as the sun sank lower the heavens were rippled with pink, just as if they had been swept by a rose-coloured sea. As Beth gazed in wonder a softer light gleamed behind a distant layer of cloud; it seemed as though another world waited beyond the clouds – a gentler world of aquamarine and palest gold . . . Had Logan already reached such a world of beauty and tranquillity . . .?

Beth was so enthralled that she did not realise Sarah had entered the room until she stood beside her.

'It's a glorious sunset,' she murmured softly. 'I'm glad you've seen it, Beth.'

'Yes . . .' Beth could scarcely tear her gaze from the magnificence of the evening sky. 'There must be a God . . .' she murmured softly. 'There must be . . . yet why . . .?' She turned and Sarah saw the shadows in her wide blue eyes. 'Did ye ever doubt His presence, Mama Fairly . . .?' Her voice was little more than a whisper, almost as though the words were drawn from her against her will. She was unaware that she had reverted to her childhood name for Sarah; she was almost unaware she had spoken, but the words seemed to hang in the quiet shadows of the room. 'I'm s-sorry. Please forgive me.'

'Don't be sorry, lassie.' Sarah slipped an arm around Beth's thin shoulders, but she was silent as they watched the fiery sun finally slipping away. Then she turned and her face was grave. 'I have to confess – I too have doubted God's presence, Beth. I know what it is like to wander in a wilderness of loneliness and grief – even despair . . .'

'A wilderness . . .?' Beth stared at Sarah incredulously. 'Ye doubted – as Thomas doubted in the Bible?'

'I did. But God has always brought me back to Him and made me see the wisdom of His ways in the end. He never deserts us, Beth, however far we stray from His chosen path . . .'

'But where can His wisdom and mercy be when He sends men to fight each other so cruelly? Logan didna want tae fight . . .' Beth's voice choked with tears and Sarah pulled her gently

369

against her breast and stroked the fine curls which were beginning to grow again now that her wounds had healed.

'I canna understand God's will either, lassie, but I do believe
He will guide us and give us courage to follow the path He has
drawn for each of us – just as He guided His own son through the
wilderness. Even in my darkest hours there has been light, but
only when I opened my eyes to see it.'

Beth sniffed and wiped her tears.

'Ye – ye really understand . . .' she mused in wonder. 'I do feel
as though I'm in a wilderness . . . Yet ye've been sae very good
tae me.'

'No better than you deserve, dear Beth.'

'I-I've promised Mr Bradshaw that I'll go tae Fairlyden on
Christmas Day.'

'I'm glad.' Sarah smiled. 'I never doubted your strength and
courage, Beth. All you need is time, lassie.'

'Time – and you and Mr Bradshaw tae help me.' Beth
summoned a smile. She had a long way to go yet, but she would
not turn her back on a world which contained such wonder and
beauty. She felt a strange sense of peace and strength as she
watched Sarah light the lamps and draw the curtains.

Sadie seized the first opportunity to get Beth on her own when
she visited Fairlyden that Christmas Day.

'I dinna blame ye for being sae wary, Beth,' she admitted with
surprising frankness. 'I did want tae hurt ye, the day the
telegram came – but I never thought sae many things would go
wrong in a single night.' Beth stared at her in silence. 'Honestly.
It's the truth!'

Beth nodded. 'Maybe it is. But I ken ye never liked me, though
I never understood why. I still dinna ken what I've done tae ye.
Aunt Agnes warned me . . .' She shuddered, then straightened
her thin shoulders resolutely. 'There's nothing more ye can dae
tae hurt me now. Logan's gone . . .' Some of her new strength
evaporated as she thought of Logan. Maybe I could bear it, if I
only kenned he didna suffer, she thought sadly.

'I dinna want tae hurt ye anymore,' Sadie interrupted her
thoughts. 'I'm not jealous o' ye being pretty and clever now.
Everybody . . . everybody always liked ye and ye didna even
have to try! All I want is your promise . . .'

'Promise?'

370

'Aye.' Sadie flushed an unbecoming red. She screwed up her thin lips. 'Robert has asked me tae marry him,' she said in a rush. 'I – we're going tae live in Yorkshire. I want tae get away frae the animals . . . the rain and mud . . . the never-ending work!'

Beth looked at her in silence, subconsciously waiting for an explosion of anger over some triviality.

'Will ye promise, Beth? Promise me ye'll never tell Robert what happened that night?' Sadie's voice was low and urgent. 'Or the other nights when Mother was staying at the Mains . . . Please! Robert hates the Germans! He hates all o' them, but I ken they're not all bad, honestly they're not. K-Kaspar – that's the one who came tae s-see me – he's the only young man who has ever treated me like a real woman . . . He didna want tae fight in the war! He told me he didna – and I believed him!' she added with a trace of her old defiance. 'But Robert would never believe that. He'd never forgive me. He'd never marry me if he kenned I'd . . . I'd . . . Will ye promise not tae tell him, Beth? Or anybody else . . .?'

Beth looked at Logan's sister pityingly. She had done her best to blot out the memory of that dreadful night when Sadie had opened the telegram which had been meant for her. Now she saw again the blue eyes of the young German – the glimpse of laughter, the sudden horror, the pleading. She shuddered violently. She was glad he had not died.

'Please, Beth!' Sadie reiterated urgently. Beth looked at Sadie's pale, tense face, then at the colourless eyes which had haunted her dreams, willing her to die.

'I shall never tell Robert Smith, Sadie – or anyone else. Ye didna need tae ask,' she added quickly as Sadie burst into speech. 'I wouldna tell because I wouldna hurt your mother, or shame your brothers.' Sadie stared into Beth's clear blue eyes, then she flushed angrily. So she needn't have humbled herself to plead after all! Her mouth tightened. She turned on her heel and left Beth gazing after her with a mixture of pain and pity.

She had guessed Sadie had an ulterior motive in wanting to see her. Now she understood, but she was glad she had come to Fairlyden – even glad she had met Sadie again; it was another hurdle over. Each day she set herself one small goal, as Mr Bradshaw had suggested, one step towards facing the future . . .

She wandered out into the garden. The winter jasmine was blooming again, but the roses which Logan had planted, and which he had remembered so clearly, were dead now. Would they bloom again in summer?

It was the second week of nineteen hundred and eighteen when the telegram arrived from Billy.

'Found Logan. Still very weak. Family starving. Letter following.'

'I canna believe it! I c-canna . . .' Beth burst into tears. Sarah held out her arms and she rushed into them as she had done as a child.

'It seemed such a frail chance, especially as the weeks passed . . . We didn't dare give you false hope, Beth,' Sarah said gently. 'I couldn't bear to see you suffer all over again. As soon as Billy's letter arrives, Crispin is going to France to bring Logan home. He will take food and money . . . but we can never repay those who have saved his life . . .' Her own voice shook, and her tears mingled with Beth's.

Forty-Two

Beth's blue eyes were luminous with joy as she stood in the doorway at Fairlyden and gazed at her husband for a few moments unobserved. She could never see enough of him, even after all these weeks. Every day they spent together was a blessing to be treasured, she thought happily, as she went to sit beside him on the large flat stone which had stood outside the house at Fairlyden for as long as she could remember.

It was the middle of May, three weeks since Sadie's wedding to Robert Smith. They had moved back to the old house they both regarded as 'home' the moment Mr and Mrs Smith set out for the station. Anna and wee Jamie had been delighted to see them back at the house, and Thomas had muttered a gruff 'Welcome home, laddie.' Beth suspected that he was just as pleased and relieved as she was to know that Fairlyden had a master again – albeit a painfully thin young master. Logan's skin had begun to lose its deathly pallor but he still had some trouble with his breathing. Beth was thankful just to know he had survived and come home to her and Kirsty.

In the hawthorn hedge a blackbird sang his last song of the evening while his mate darted busily back to the nest with a worm for their young. Beth hummed softly. Logan's own weakness seemed to have given her renewed strength and she was thankful for it. Indeed I've so much tae be thankful for, she thought as she looked around the familiar scene.

'I've finished at last! And I've even managed tae stick one o' the pretty flowery borders round the walls,' she announced with satisfaction as she stretched out her aching limbs. She had been painting the big bedroom at Fairlyden, removing all traces of the garish pink distemper Sadie had used.

'I'm glad,' Logan said warmly. 'I dreamed of you so often, Beth, in that sunny yellow room, in the big bed, with Kirsty in the old crib . . .' He smiled down fondly at his small daughter, who was prattling cheerfully at his feet as she tried to feed her pet lamb.

'D'ye remember how we used tae bring all kinds o' pets tae the house tae feed?'

'Aye . . .' Beth smiled reminiscently.

'Peggotty? D'ye remember Peggotty?'

'As though I could ever forget our favourite pig . . .' Beth's expressive eyes shadowed momentarily.

'What is it, Beth?' Logan was acutely sensitive to her every mood.

'I remember thinking it was an ill omen because Peggotty died when ye went away – and it was! Though I try not tae be superstitious anymore,' she added hastily.

'Och, Beth, I love you, and your funny little ways. I hope ye'll never change.' His arm encircled her slim waist and he rested his cheek against the softness of her hair. His eyes moved dreamily over the field; green fields full of fresh spring grass instead of the muddy fields of France where battles still raged, while tanks churned to the sound of guns . . . 'Thank God I'm home,' he murmured softly. His gaze travelled slowly over the familiar view, the silvery glint of the Solway Firth in the distance, the majesty of the hills beyond, shadowy purple shapes against the evening sky as the sun set in glorious splendour. 'It's such a wonderful, incredible world . . . Why do men have tae spoil it . . .'

Beth knew he did not expect an answer. She knew he was grateful, as she was, just to be together at Fairlyden.

'I think I shall come with ye tae the turnip hoeing tomorrow, Beth,' he said suddenly.

'Oh, Logan, ye shouldna work yet . . . Ye ken Doctor Kerr said we had tae be sure tae see the scars frae the gas blisters were properly healed and . . .'

'I'll just work for a wee while . . . There's such a lot tae be done – and I like being with ye, Beth.' He smiled down at her, but his eyes were thoughtful. 'It's a funny thing . . . When I went away nobody cared whether the British farmers produced any food at all, or whether it rotted in the fields and us along with it. Now everybody is desperate for food. I never thought there'd be a day when we could sell all the milk frae as many cows as we could ever want tae keep!'

'I ken . . . Your mama canna quite believe it either. She was just telling me this morning how she and Aunt Agnes used tae return frae the market with half the butter still in their basket and no milk going away tae the cities on trains then! Now we hardly dare keep enough milk tae churn butter for ourselves, or save cream for oor porridge – with all the reports o' folk starving for want o' it.'

'Thomas says he and Anna never dreamed they'd earn sae much money in a term.'

'Aah,' Beth smiled, 'they can afford tae buy plenty now, but there isna much available, even though their mother has the village store! Anyway Anna is saving up tae send Jamie tae school in Dumfries. She's discovered he's related tae the MacFarlanes o' Nithanvale. So she is determined he'll have as good an education as any o' them. She believes his father would have wanted that too.'

'But he's only seven!'

'Old enough tae tell his mama he's never going tae leave Fairlyden. He says he wants tae drive the horses and learn tae plough like his Uncle Thomas,' Beth grinned. 'But Anna is set on giving him what she calls "a chance in life".'

'Mmm, well, we'll forget about Anna's plans . . . I like having ye tae maself . . .' His smile, and the glint in his eyes, brought a blush to Beth's cheeks. She reached up and stroked the hair from his temple with gentle fingers.

'Ye'll have tae mind your ways tomorrow, Logie. Lucy will be back frae visiting her mother . . .'

'Och, I dinna mind Lucy. She's a good wee lassie with Kirsty and she works hard.'

'Aye,' Beth sighed happily. 'We've such a lot tae be thankful for . . .'

'Aye, we have that – or at least I have with you for my wife – and wee Kirsty . . .' His lips brushed Beth's earlobe very gently and she snuggled closer. 'Alex says the government have promised tae guarantee the prices o' all the food British farmers can produce – even when the war is over. I can hardly believe it.'

'Aye, it seems they've learned their lesson; they'll never risk starving the British nation again . . .'

'There's little sign o' an end tae the war yet though, in spite o' all the tanks we've sent tae France . . .' Logan frowned. Sometimes the thought of the men still fighting in the trenches filled him with black depression.

'D'ye think Billy will come back tae Fairlyden when the war is over – if Britain wins?'

'Britain will win! We must win! We must . . .'

'Aye, I'm sure we shall,' Beth agreed quietly. It troubled her when Logan got excited. It aggravated his breathing difficulties and at night he had terrible dreams. 'I was just wondering if Billy will be content tae farm after driving the tanks. Your mama says he aye liked machines better than animals, but Mr Bradshaw thinks we ought tae offer for the tenancy o' the land on the edge o' Muircumwell village. It belongs tae the Guillyman Estate but the family are in America. The lawyers in charge havena been farming it tae the satisfaction o' the new County Agricultural Committee.'

'Could we pay the rent?'

'Well, your mama has been teaching me tae keep account o' things . . . We have money in the bank now – enough tae pay the valuation tae take over anyway, and tae pay the first year's rent.'

'Have we indeed! Fairlyden has really been prospering then!'

'Aye,' Beth grimaced dryly. 'But it's a pity we've tae suffer this cruel war before folks can earn a decent living for their toil. The lack o' men tae work the land is the biggest problem now, especially if we take on more ploughing. Thomas canna manage any more . . .'

Beth felt Logan's arm tighten around her waist and she rested her head against his chest; she heard the rasp of each breath he drew. It would be a long time before he regained his full strength, she thought, although the fresh air of Fairlyden and the milk and eggs were working wonders.

'I think we should forget about taking extra land until ye're completely well again, Logie . . . I couldna bear anything tae worry ye now.'

'I shall soon be well enough tae dae the ploughing myself. I was just thinking what a lucky man I am,' Logan smiled dreamily. 'Did I ever tell ye your new hairstyle suits ye very well, Mistress Fairly?' His lips moved against her temple. She had had her hair cut in a fashionable bob, mainly because so much of it had been cut off after her accident. 'There's nae wonder I survived when I've such a beautiful wife tae come home tae. The poor family who took me in must often have wished I hadn't!'

'Oh, dinna say that, Logan!' Beth shivered.

'They had sae little.' His eyes shadowed and his lean face was grave and troubled as memories flooded back. 'Often they had less tae eat than the Fairlyden pigs. And they lived in fear for months because o' me. Yet they saved my life, and they shared everything they had with me. When the war is over I promised I would take ye o'er the water tae visit them, Beth. They thought you and Kirsty looked like the virgin and child . . .'

'They couldna think that, Logan!'

'You looked so young and innocent and happy in that picture. They kept holding it up for me to see. They knew it was only the thought of you which kept me alive.'

'I shall remember them in my prayers, always.' Beth's voice was husky, but the expression in Logan's dancing eyes brought a flood of colour to her cheeks. 'Well, Logan Fairly,' she summoned a brisk tone, 'if I dinna put your precious daughter into her crib, and make ye some supper, ye'll be accusing me of starving you . . .' Logan's grin widened when he saw her blushes and the sparkle in her blue eyes. His arms encircled her trim figure. 'I think we should take the tenancy o' the extra land at Muircumwell . . .' His eyes glinted wickedly.

'Even if Billy still plans tae go tae America?'

'Oh, I expect he'll go. His heart is set on't, but I'm thinking we shall have at least half a dozen wee farmers tae carry on – probably more if ye blush sae prettily, Mistress Fairly . . .' Logan chuckled, but there was a deep and abiding love in his eyes as he looked at the girl he had adored for as long as either of them could remember.

Kirsty eyed them with childish curiosity, then turned her attention back to the lamb she was feeding. She had an air of contentment which echoed their own.

4	5	6	
14	15	16	1
24	25	26	
34	35	3	
	45		